Logan's Peak

Graeme Ratcliffe

ISBN-13: 978-0-6481065-0-0

Logan's Peak

'Caught in the whirlwind of life,
men commit crimes and perish ineluctably.'

Fyodor Dostoyevsky

There was another German flare. Snow watched it rise. Darcy and Harry saw it too, rocketing high above. They froze, seeking camouflage in stillness. The flare exploded red, not white, and no man's land turned rosy pink.

Prologue

In the rough country of the Northern Rivers hinterland where the Boyd flows into the Nymboida and the Nymboida to the Mann, in the upper reaches of the Clarence and up north to Tabulam and Kyogle, there is a maze of valleys. They spider through the ridges and rise through dark Gondwana rainforest till beaten by the naked granite of the Richmond and Gibraltar Ranges. In hidden places wedged between the tors and crags, these valleys reared a people. They hacked out patches of yellowed green from the rumpled folds of cedar, teak and beech, and made it home; they raised cattle to yield beef and butter, and saw it as a calling; and they often went without, near starved, but reckoned such to be their lot, battling on till better times rolled around.

It was 1921, and though a younger time than now, the men and women of that place were steeped in ways already old, the land they worked yet older. An ancient stock route ran through the district from the tablelands to Grafton and somewhere on its winding course a road traversed its length. Rutted, potholed and neglected, this road journeyed north, snaking through a narrow gorge to an upland valley. Plumb centre of the valley, a dozen miles on from the gorge, sat Berto. Too small to be called a town, but called one anyway, it serviced many properties. By far the largest was the estate of Preston Logan. His mansion squatted at the end of a winding drive, a mile from the road and ten minutes hard riding due north of the Berto Pub. To the west and south of town were many smaller holdings not halfway so impressive. They spread out across the flats and into the valley's branches, the poorer selections nestling in the foothills. Beyond the foothills the pasture gave way to forest, the trees in turn surrendering to the escarpment. These granite cliffs extended proudly to the greater part of the valley's circumference, enclosing everything within like pea soup gone tepid in a cauldron. Above the cauldron's rim, and dominating all below, stood Logan's Peak. Begat in the Dreamtime and older than the Garden of Eden, the mountain was named by Preston Logan's father in honour of the father who had gone before.

It was September and things were busy for all the cockies, big and small, and all those they employed: the farm hands, ringers, jackaroos; sundowners with wives and children in tow; and others besides—swagmen, drifters, remittance men, lads on the run and the like—all astir, drenching the herds before the drives to the Grafton yards.

Chapter One

The cattle bellowed through fonts of dust, dirt collecting in their watery nostrils, mouths and eyes attracting charcoal clouds of thirsty flies. Like a livestock dam reduced by drought to mud, the smell of caking manure was strong enough to taste: dank and rotten on the tongue.

Harried by snapping dogs, this rolling tide of hide and horn was funnelled to the race. There, reduced to single file, the cattle passed a stockman named Mad Mike, the moniker carried like a medal since a distant moment lost in France. Standing on the rails, he walloped each lumbering beast toward the drenching pit, while beneath the noonday sun his war-torn skin burnt red, making more distinct the pallid scar that steamed from ear to mouth. Exhaling hard, he stopped to fan his face with his hat and wipe the sweat from his chin.

At the other end of the race the herd passed a second stockman, Snow Mackay. Tall and wiry, he stood at the anti-bunching gate—one leg him, the other wood—goading each animal into the murky depths of the lousicide. A temperamental bullock baulked at the edge of the pit and refused to budge. The rangy stockman lifted its tail, and with a stock prodder poke up the bunghole, it was soon in the drink.

Charlie Ward was third in line. His job was to walk the

side of the pit and guide the procession as it swam the watercourse. The troublesome bullock approached and he could see the panic in its eyes, legs beating to keep its nose above the surface. The image brought to mind black memories of Passchendaele. Charlie shook his head to erase the thought; this was meat on the hoof, not a man. He tried to prod the animal forward, but it just churned on the spot, frothing the water. The cattle swimming behind began to crowd the course. Snow closed the gate. That part of the herd, still in the race, choked to a halt.

The property's old cocky, Eamon Reilly, waded through the dust and din toward the drenching pit. Snow saw him. 'Nice looking mob!' he yelled.

Reilly stared down, worried by the sight of his cattle thrashing about, but chose to say nothing, leaving Charlie to it, and ambled over. 'How are the ticks?'

'Not bad—a lot better than last time.'

The cocky folded his arms and admired his spring harvest. 'Should do good at the yards this month!'

'What if Preston Logan plays funny buggers?'

Reilly disliked Snow bringing up Logan. He went silent and turned again to the dip. Concern for his stock creased his brow as he watched Charlie struggle to work the drowning bullock. The cocky need not have worried; Charlie knew how to deal with stubborn cattle. Taking careful aim, the stockman shoved a long prodder hard into the creature's back, pushing eye fillet into kidney. Reilly winced as the animal finally moved forward. Those behind, bunched-up and awry, were quick to unravel, soon at the end of the watercourse and rising to the benediction of the drip pen.

Reilly looked back at Snow and re-gathered his thoughts. 'Undercutting the price hurts Logan as much as any other bastard!'

'Yeah, I understand what you're saying to me,' said Snow, opening the gate, slapping more bullocks through, 'but Logan's different, you know that—bloody squatter who gets here first, says it's mine and all youse other bastards can stuff off. Your Poms, they'd say he was landed gentry, us meant to tug the forelock to your duke of this and earl of fly blown that, the viscount kiss-me-arse; but all that means, all that means about him, him and all his greasy mates, is he, he doesn't owe the bank, does he?'

'Yeah, Snow, I know where you're going here.'

'Do you? I mean he'll drive your prices down till the bank calls in the marker and then Logan buys you up for a song.'

'Yeah. I know, Snow.'

'Then when he owns the market, he puts up his flaming price.'

'Yeah, we've been through all this at the pub. Why do you care anyway? You just work here.'

'We're in the same boat,' Snow whined, almost insulted. 'I need you and you need me. We negotiate man to man, but if the Logans of this world can knock the stuffing out of *you*, what the hell are they going to do to *me*?'

Reilly put his hands in his pockets and gazed down at his boots. Snow bunged another reluctant bullock through the gate. The beast jolted forward, terror causing it to leap far into the dip. Grey mud splashed the old cocky's moleskins. He wandered off, muttering soft oaths.

'Hey, Snow,' called Charlie, 'pass us some of that water.'

Snow picked up the canteen and lobbed it over the race. 'The cocky ain't happy,' he hollered, 'I was saying: I hope Logan doesn't stuff things up for you at the yards!'

Charlie joked: 'You always were a little ray of sunshine!' He took a deep drink; it was thirsty work. At thirty-nine, Charlie's back was beginning to play up and each year it took less toil to make him weary. The stockman nudged more cattle through the pit and grimaced; after a quarter century he had never got used to the smell of the drench. If it weren't for the trenches, he would have reckoned it the worst smell of all.

There was a hold-up at the entrance to the race. Charlie was able to stop for a moment. He mopped his face with an open palm and looked around. The valley's grass, grown lush from a wet autumn, was fading to shades of pastel. It would soon be brown, the hot weather come early and the dry season due to linger for months.

Charlie's attention revisited the cattle. Ticks, fat as pecans and dark as prunes, hung from their hide. Enough of the little bloodsuckers and they could bring down a creature as large and powerful as a full-grown bull. However the arsenic in the dip would kill the ticks before the ticks could kill the cattle, long before the abattoir would kill the cattle, and longer still before the arsenic should have killed the stockmen.

Charlie had a bad feeling; the last few years had seen good rains but the Federation Drought was still a painful memory. His stomach growled at the thought of it. Though there had been food on the table since before the war, Charlie's brood had grown with many mouths to feed, the oldest of his kids having just turned twelve. He saw the sun and a little prayer for ten more years of useful rain wafted through his brain.

'Hey, Charlie,' yelled Mad Mike. 'I could do with some of that water!' Then he stammered: 'D-D-Dying of thirst over here.'

Charlie threw the canteen to Mike and glanced back to the gate. 'Snow, what time you got?'

Snow spat on the face of his watch to wipe away the dirt. 'Half an hour since the last time you asked.'

Charlie closed his eyes and smiled; the family heirloom he once owned had broken from its fob and fallen under a cow's hoof. He had sold the scrap for the value of its gold, intending to buy one of those new-fangled wristwatches, but there'd been a sure thing on the fifth at Grafton.

'Cripes, Charlie,' yelled Mad Mike, 'you didn't leave much!'

'Man's got to have a drink,' protested Charlie. 'I'm not a blasted camel!'

Mike turned the canteen upside-down, flicking out the remaining moisture—mostly warm spit. 'Give us a sec to fill her up.'

Charlie nodded as Mike walked to the water tank that collected rain from the roof of the barn. The squeaky tap released a liquid the colour of weak tea; the smell wasn't too good either. Nevertheless, the stockman took a drink and was well pleased; the new water was a bit cooler than body temperature. Mike topped up the canteen, screwed the lid on tight and ambled back to the race, tossing the canteen to Snow.

As with most stockman, Mad Mike could handle just about anything life on the land might throw at a man, but like with Charlie, he hated ticks. There had been an outbreak from up north during the previous wet season and the buggers were proving hard to kill off. This was the third drenching for Reilly's mob, with more treatments still to come. It was the same on all the other properties. So much of the lousicide had spattered Mike he reckoned, if a tick ever bit him, the greedy mongrel would drop dead before it had time to pick its teeth.

However, despite the ticks, the lice and the stench, Mad Mike was fond of cattle. People said cattle were stupid beasts, but people said that about Mike too, so he didn't think it that much of an insult. The stockman was never going to be a Rhodes Scholar and he was dead-set certain his kisser would never end up on a cigarette card, but he was not an ambitious man and he was happy to count his blessings; the war had blown over, he was still breathing, and as for all the scars and shellshock, only a smidge less likely than before to go to Oxford or Imperial Tobacco. With cattle he reckoned, if you got to know them, they had very individual personalities; after a while you could tell their habits and anticipate their mood swings. Ever since the war he had been happy to say: 'They're sort of like German machine-gunners.' Mad Mike never really got to see much of Fritz up close—mostly when the poor prick was dead, or in the seconds before old Fritzy got to meet his maker—but at those times he found it funny how familiar a German looked: not like on the enlistment posters, more like

14

an Aussie. He was surprised to find each Fritz had his own particular face and that had helped to make Mike mad. Stranger still, if a digger took the time to listen close, Germans were likewise particular from a distance. It got so Mike could recognise one German machine-gunner from another; even though he couldn't see their different faces, he got to know their different little ways.

Mike prodded the cattle along the race and recalled how he had told some folks who had the patience to listen: 'When it was gone quiet on the front, Fritz liked to show off a bit—spray out a few rounds, keep us on our toes. Sometimes he'd get bored and fire: Dum-de-da-da-dum, and a gunner in the Aussie trenches would answer by spraying: Dum-dum.' When relating this observation, Mike would always have a chew on his top lip, frown pensively and conclude: 'Took skill to do that.' And he was certain the gunners who got bored were the smart ones—like the heifers, cows and bullocks that wouldn't jump into the dip.

Mike noticed Snow bung another arsehole and was struck by a sudden understanding. Without stammering—Mike never stammered when talking to himself—he said: 'That there last bullock wasn't trusting; he was cautious, cautious as a cat. Now that's a smart animal. Get treated like royalty and give back sweet stuff all. But, I ask you, how trusting is a cat?' Then he saw the dogs working the mob and said softly, in admiration: 'Come to think of it, dogs are pretty watchful too: always circle around a spot of ground before they sit—least the smart ones do. Cattle dogs do. Cattle dogs are smart, but not as smart as cats; a smart animal would never get caught having to work as hard as a cattle dog.' After a bit, Mike affirmed: 'Yeah, a dog's always on the alert: always has a good sniff around before it takes a seat. Not like most people. Most people don't check out their seat before they sit. Stick their arse in anywhere, sight unseen.' Mad Mike liked cattle. He liked steak too.

Not three miles away, the sun that baked the cocky's forcing yard beat down on sleepy Berto. Though soon the cicadas would emerge and trumpet deafeningly, the solitary sound to wake the town this day was the dismal caw of a crow.

Berto stood beside the road that ran the length of the valley, from the bottom gorge to Bluey Corbet's place, and on to other valleys further north. This track was referred to as the Berto Road, but nobody was sure if anyone had chanced to register the name with the Lands Department. Though ungraded and unkempt, for the dozen lazy paces it ran through Berto, the locals called the road a street. They named it Main Street because it couldn't be anything else.

This time of year, after the desiccating August winds, ochre dust would rise up from the street at the slightest provocation. Even a sneeze could coat the town pub's veranda in its tawny dressing.

A ramshackle folly to a more ambitious time, the pub boasted a second storey, public bar, saloon bar—for the ladies—and out the back, stables blanketed in bougainvillea. A peeling sign on its wooden awning told everybody it was the Berto Hotel, but everybody knew that already.

Opposite the pub could be found the general store that

housed the local postal agency and telegraph office. The store had a false front and bullnose awning. Above the awning was a window that winked between painted signs advertising 'Bushells, the tea of flavour,' and 'Vincent's APC'.

To the left of the store stood the remaining buildings of the town—a blacksmith's shop and a sagging livery stable. Behind these was a pen with a couple of ragged mules. Out front a Golden Fleece petrol bowser had recently been installed. Its brightness made the old shop's corrugated iron look all the rustier.

Within the smithy's dark interior, humid, black and sooty, worked Pop O'Shaughnessy. Sheathed in a battered leather apron, he worked and shaped a horseshoe, his vascular hands hammering its iron against the anvil till satisfied with its contour. While it was still red hot, Pop picked up the shoe with his horseshoe holder, walked to a waiting mare, held between his legs one of the horse's feet and hot-shoed the hoof, searing the keratin and smoking the air. The hoary plumes added another coating of soot to the rafters and everything else, including Pop.

Outside, Pop's wife, Ma, swept the wooden walkway of her store. Noticing the petrol bowser, she walked over, pulled a feather duster from her apron string and gave its yellow cylinder a quick tidy up.

About the same time Ma was dusting the bowser Tom Bramble rode into town. Still in his teens, the lad was perched on a Waler, name of Copenhagen. He carried a fishing rod, wore a tattered, wide-brimmed hat and around his neck, a red bandanna. His hazel eyes were clear and beneath a sprinkling of small freckles, his skin was tanned and smooth. Revealing somewhat crooked teeth that nevertheless beamed white, he smiled as he waved to Ma and she waved back. Berto born, Tom was clean and alert and wise to the ways of the valley and the ranges. He could live in comfort on the abundance of a forest seen as barren by those who might easily die through ill-acquaintance with its ways. Resourceful and reliable, he was all a country boy could be, but for lads like Tom that could never be enough.

He dismounted in front of the pub and grabbed a double-sided canvas bag from Copenhagen's withers. His horse departed for the stables out the back while Tom crossed under the veranda awning and through the open doors to the public barroom.

Lucky Bramble stood behind the bar, ruby-skinned and blood shot. No patrons yet to serve, he vigorously polished the previous night's glasses. Every morning he performed this task, not because it was expected, but because providing crystal clarity kept his hands busy enough to stay away from his ever-present rum bottle. As his son entered he took a quick nip all the same.

Tom lifted up his canvas bag. 'Hey, Dad, fish for tea.'

Lucky grunted.

Tom walked through a columned archway that opened to the lobby, swung left, continued down the hall, passed the entrance to the saloon and entered the kitchen. There he took two cod fish from his bag and lay them on a plate. Stepping out to the back veranda, he lifted the hessian cover of the Coolgardie safe, opened its wire mesh door and put in the fish.

As he went to draw down the cover he noticed the hessian had dried out. It would need a seeing-to.

Tom returned to the kitchen and filled up a bucket of water in the sink. Back outside, he poured the water into a tray fixed to the roof of the safe and immersed the top edge of the hessian into its depths. The cover would soak up the moisture, and through evaporation in the breeze, ensure the innards of the safe stayed colder than outside.

Though set to meditate a little longer on this minor miracle of nature, Tom received a sudden jolt from Copenhagen's nose; his horse growing impatient as it waited at the veranda's edge. 'Sorry, Cope,' said Tom, 'was dreaming on the job.'

Tom reopened the safe and grabbed a fresh and crispy carrot. It made a snap when he broke it in half. Copenhagen shook his mane in anticipation. Tom put the pieces in the palm of his hand and held them under the horse's mouth. Copenhagen's lips drew in the carrot and chewed it with a satisfied crunch.

The fish, now safely stowed away, Tom walked down to the stables. Copenhagen followed. Once his horse was watered, fed and curry combed, Tom could attend to the most exciting business of the day.

Up the valley from Berto, the road kinked east to lazily avoid construction of a causeway across the creek, and then meandered through a portion of the timber that skirted the pastures and shoed the feet of the escarpment. Here, a troop of stockmen, horses ambling at the walk, made their way to town. In the lead rode Snow, Charlie and Mad Mike.

Snow squinted at the sun. 'Been a hot day today. This summer could be a real stinker.'

Charlie brushed away a fly. 'Yeah, been wondering the same thing meself—means me kids'll get head lice again.'

'You reckon lice are like ticks and come from up n-n-north in Queensland?'

'Mike,' said Charlie, using his expansive voice, 'I reckon from Sydney.'

'S-S-Sydney?'

'Yeah, all that sort of stuff, anything as such, comes from Sydney.'

'What about c-c-crabs? They lice?'

'Sure are,' Charlie confirmed, warming to the subject.

'Then how come Snow got crabs in Calais?'

Charlie seemed stumped by that one. 'Good question. Hey, Snow, how did you get crabs in Calais?'

Snow pulled down his battered Akubra. 'Brigitte was a nice girl. 'Sides, that was crotch lice.'

'Yeah, so what's the difference?' Charlie asked.

Snow breathed in slow, and with a sigh of world-weary wisdom he explained, 'Some lice go for the crotch. They're your crabs. Other lice, given a choice, go for the head.'

'But why?' asked Mike.

Snow scratched his nose. 'Better view.'

Charlie chuckled, leaned across and punched Mike in the arm.

The stockmen wandered into town and clustered outside the pub. After the horses had been hitched to the rails,

Snow sheared away and limped up to the general store, his wooden leg clunking and jangling. Crudely but laboriously carved with an axe, this post had no hinged parts. It was inflexible and caused an awkward thump each time it met the ground, the loose rowel of the screwed on spur rattling loudly. The other stockmen climbed the steps to the pub's veranda as Pop appeared from the blacksmith's shop. Charlie stopped to watch him shuffle toward them. 'Hey, Pop, you thirsty?'

'I was born thirsty.'

Charlie smiled. 'Born old too.'

They followed Pop into the public bar and Mad Mike asked: 'Hey, Pop, you ever young?'

'Don't know,' the old smithy rasped, keeping his nose ahead of all the others. 'So long ago I can't recollect.'

Lucky pulled the beers in solemn silence as the first of the day's patrons fronted the bar.

'Line 'em up, Lucky,' ordered Charlie, 'me throat's as dry as a bookkeeper's ledger.'

Pop gave the others an optimistic look. 'Whose shout is it?

'Yours,' they answered, their boots clanking down on the slops tray, staking claims to lengths of the bar. Beyond his father's view, Tom crept down the stairs and out the lobby door.

Snow sidled up to the counter and tipped his hat. 'G'day, Ma, me leg arrived yet?

'Sorry, Snow,' said Ma in her lilting Irish accent, 'maybe tomorrow.'

'Bloody government,' he muttered. Clumping from the store, he bumped into Tom.

'G'day, Snow,' said the lad, bright as newly minted penny.

'S'pose,' Snow grunted back, dull and blue as an older penny too long in a wishing well. He limped away sullenly, straight for the pub.

Tom approached the counter. 'Still no leg?'

'No, and a scandal it is too. But I got something for you, young Tom.'

Ma toddled along behind the counter, past tins of Swallows biscuits, packets of Bournville cocoa, Eau de Suez vaccine for beautiful teeth, Huggins Ozone Papers for the relief of asthma and bottles of patent medicine, efficacious in the treatment of lumbago, neuralgia, constipation and catarrh. She entered the post office booth and pushed a small parcel under the bank teller screen.

A minute later Tom was in the lobby of the pub.

'Hey, Tom, where'd you get to?' Lucky yelled from behind the bar.

Tom raced up the stairs with his parcel.

'Hey, I need you down here!' his father persisted, but he was ignored.

Tom burst into Room Two, his bedroom. He dived onto the bed and tore open the precious parcel to find a book: 'The Red Badge of Courage'. He hurriedly whispered the blurb: 'An American classic and an intimate account of a young man's experience of war.' He saw his bookcase. It was filled with the boy's adventure stories he loved, but this novel by a man named Stephen Crane was something entirely different and would affect him in ways he never could have dreamt.

'Tom, get down here and get to work!' Lucky yelled from the bottom of the staircase. Tom rested the new book in pride of place on his bedside table and left for his life's reality of bottles, kegs and taps, tobacco smoke and urine.

The sun had just gone down behind the mountains and a nasal whine, like mosquitoes after blood, issued from the busy pub. The working men from all around were there, falling into formation for the six o'clock swill. Lucky served by touch, his eyes fixed on the lobby's grandfather clock, willing its hands to move faster to last drinks. That would be ten minutes to the hour, allowing time to herd the patrons out before the sounding of the mournful chime.

Charlie, Mad Mike and Snow were drinking at the far end of the bar where Tom was serving. Annoyed about his leg, Snow had drunk more than his usual. 'Hey, Charlie, you know your breath's been stinking lately.'

'Yeah,' said Charlie in sincere agreement, hawking into the slops tray, 'wife told me all about it. It's me gums.' His teeth glistened red as he smiled bashfully. 'They're bleeding a bit.'

Snow threw back his umpteenth whisky. 'Looks like the Barcoo rot.'

Charlie was left nonplussed. 'The Barcoo Rot?'

'Limes,' said Snow, signalling Tom for another drink, 'only cure for the Barcoo Rot.'

'I've read about that,' Tom interjected, grabbing the whisky bottle.

'It's a recognised medical thingy,' Snow confirmed sagely.

Charlie drained his schooner and belched. The gust unbalanced Tom, causing him to slop the whisky he was pouring. 'Sorry, kid,' the stockman said. 'Better an empty boarding house than a bad tenant. Pour us another schooner before your old man strangles the cow.'

Snow grabbed his replenished shot glass. 'You need to get some limes, Charlie.'

'Where am I gunna find limes?'

'Stuffed if I can tell you—I'm not a bloody doctor—but you've got the Rot.'

Charlie felt his teeth. 'Things are getting a bit wobbly. Limes, you say?'

Snow was emphatic: 'Yep.'

Charlie wiped the blood off his fingers.

Tom passed Charlie his fresh schooner. 'No other cure?'

Snow lifted his whisky glass and stared deeply into its dusky contents. 'You might try castor oil.'

'Jeez,' said Charlie, 'strike me pink and call me lady's underwear, but I'll be buggered if I'm drinking castor oil. Sooner lose me teeth.'

Snow blew a mocking 'Pff!' out the corner of his mouth. 'Can't say I didn't warn you, Charles.' He sipped his whisky and took in Charlie's worried face. 'Nasty thing, that Barcoo Rot.'

'Hey, Snow, that what sailors get?' Mike asked, poking

his own teeth.

'In the navy,' Snow replied, his words a bit slurred, but measured as a slow march drill, 'for the old Jack Tars, the Rot was banned. So they had to eat limes. Was compulsory. Was the limes or the lash.'

'Cripes,' said Charlie, 'I don't even like oranges.'

Handing over Charlie's change, Tom suggested: 'I suppose any fruit would do, hey? You know, apples, pears, kumquats?'

'Kumquats?' asked Snow. 'What the hell's a kumquat?'

'Sounds like something your foreign types would eat,' Charlie guessed, equally in the dark.

Mad Mike had a chuckle. 'Hey, Charlie, remember when you lost that bet in Paris and had to d-d-dine out on snails?'

'Oh, yeah, I was farting garlic for a month.'

All the stockmen laughed. So did Tom. 'Talk about poison gas!' He giggled.

The moment froze. The stockmen lost their pulse. Focused inward, all three raced to stick a finger in the dyke, a sea of memories gushing through. Tom blanched; he had crossed a line, assumed knowledge he could not have, bonhomie beyond his ken, and made a hash of it. He put the whisky bottle back on the shelf and rushed to serve a quickly forming wall of waving glasses.

Charlie was the first to break the silence. 'Big drive to the yards next week: always eager to see Grafton.'

'Pretty girls in G-Grafton.'

'Mike,' said Snow, slapping his mate on the shoulder, his thoughts returned to the present, 'you're not as mad as you look.'

Charlie gave Snow an envious leer. 'You after getting any?'

'Germans might have shot off half me shin,' Snow allowed, 'but not me old fella.'

The clock's pendulum swung the big hand onto ten. Lucky had an eye in ambush. 'Time, gentlemen, please!'

Tom served one last beer, put the money in the till, and turned away all further requests.

Snow leaned into the bar. 'Pst! Hey, Tom, be a sport: sneak us another shot. Your old man won't notice—favour for an old digger.'

Tom glanced around to make sure his father wasn't watching. He could not refuse the stockman; Snow was the stuff of legend, the heroes of his books made mortal. He reached back to the shelf and got a hand on the whisky bottle.

'Tom!' snapped Lucky, 'gone ten to six. No exceptions.' When it came to rules and regulations, the publican never missed a trick—even when half pissed.

Tom started clearing away the dirty glasses. 'Sorry, mate,' he said to Snow, 'it's the law. Time's up.'

Snow flipped his empty shot glass upside down. 'Bloody government.'

Lucky yelled out to the crowd: 'Hurry up and finish your drinks! Then youse can all bugger off!'

Metal-capped heels clattered on the veranda planks as patrons drifted from the pub. Snow fell down the steps, losing his hat. Charlie and Mad Mike picked him up.

'Bedtime for you, son,' Mike advised.

Charlie showed the paternal instincts his age demanded and France's trenches had honed keen. 'You right there, Snow?'

'A course I'm alright: never been better.'

Snow tried to stand unaided but fell on his backside. His wooden leg popped out of his stump. He struggled to strap it back on. 'Flaming Fritz! Be glad when I've seen the last of you.'

Mad Mike crouched to help. 'Don't blame Fritz,' he said, placidly defending the leg, admiring its surface, one side oiled to a coal-grey sheen by daily applications of dirt and horse sweat. 'Weren't Fritz's fault—was his owner what done it.'

Snow growled at his wooden shank: 'I hate you, Fritz. And you know what? First thing I'm gunna do—once I get me new prophylactic—first thing I'm gunna do is incinerate you. How do you like that? Cremated, you bastard!'

Mad Mike continued to speak humbly for the defence. 'Fritz has done the right thing by you, but.'

Charlie laughed. 'None of your other mates would be willing to spend every day under those steaming knackers.'

'Piss off, Charlie.' Snow grumbled, finally getting his leg on. He spiralled upright, using Mike for ballast, the sea shifting.

Charlie laughed some more. 'Long John Silver's got himself a bit of youse mal de mer.'

'Stuff youse mal de mer up your aft!' Snow slurred, his words slopping out like curdled milk. 'Wait a sec, not finished yet.' He picked up his hat, smacked it against his thigh and put it on back-to-front.

Mike unhitched Snow's horse and walked it over to him. 'Here you go, cobber.'

Snow could not open his eyes wide enough to see his horse's reins.

Charlie stared at Mike. 'Let's get him onboard.' They lifted Snow onto his horse. He slid off the other side.

It was but a moment later Snow, Charlie and Mad Mike were riding out of town and singing: 'Daisy, Daisy, give me your answer do. I'm half crazy, all for the love of you…'

The stockmen passed Pop outside the general store. 'Night, Pop.'

'Top of the morning to you.'

'Where were we?' Charlie asked his mates. 'Oh yeah,' and he returned to song.

'It won't be a stylish marriage…'

The other stockmen joined in again. 'I can't afford a carriage…'

Pop stumbled through his front doorway and landed on the painted floorboards. He wasn't seeing too good, but he could hear voices. 'But you'll look sweet upon the seat of a bicycle built for two…'

The voices faded into the distance as a round, pink face came into focus. It wasn't happy.

'Now it's a fine disarray you've made of yourself again, Pop O'Shaughnessy.'

Pop watched two wives shut and bolt the front door as a thin strand of drool escaped his slackened mouth.

Ma checked the little sign that dangled from within the front door's window, making doubly sure it still read 'Closed'.

'Come on then, Pop,' she fussed, helping him up, too inured to her husband's habits to invoke the Lord's intervention or demand a penance, 'lets get a bite of tea into you.'

Chapter Two

The Berto Road slithered into gunmetal hills, its talcum surface illuminated white beneath the twinkling dome of the stars. Charlie, Mad Mike and Snow dawdled on flagging horses, leaden hooves kicking up tufts of pearly dust, the closing air and stillness of the night amplifying their dull impact on the road.

'Back in France,' Charlie reminisced, looking at the trees, 'you know what I missed most 'bout home?'

Mad Mike peered up to the overhanging branches, leaning into Charlie's view. 'What?'

'The sounds of the birds,' Charlie crooned rhapsodically, 'bell birds, whip birds, kookaburras—even crows.'

Snow's eyes drooped but his ears were still listening. He responded to Charlie's wistfulness by imitating the call of a crow. 'Ark-ark-ark-ark-ark-ahhh.'

'I think your crow's got piles,' said Mike.

Charlie continued unperturbed: 'But the sound that really gets to me.' His hand rested on his heart. 'I really love magpies—something about them. Like when you're out mustering and you wake up—sunrise, everything fresh—and you hear them, the magpies.' Charlie sighed: 'Sound of home.'

'Hey, Banjo Paterson,' Snow interrupted, pointing and

slurring, 'you were talking about home?'

The three stockmen passed a rustic ironbark cottage, the hint of amber light within, a dilapidated shed out back.

Snow and Mad Mike continued up the road. 'Night, Charlie.'

Charlie waved. 'See youse tomorrow, sparrow's fart.'

'I'll bring the caviar,' said Snow.

Charlie rode down beside his house. He dismounted and walked his horse into the shed. Salt of the earth, Peggy stood on the porch. 'Hurry up before your tea gets cold.'

Charlie saluted to his wife as she turned to see the older seven of their eight children sitting at the table, tin plates and pannikins set for their meal: a steaming pot of beef stew, fresh baked bread and a jug of milk.

Tom had washed the glasses, scrubbed out the slops trays, mopped the floors, peeled and boiled the spuds, set the table and cleaned and fried the fish. Lucky had locked the doors, counted the money, left the float under the till, hidden the night's takings in a cache beneath a floorboard in his bedroom and polished off a quarter pint of rum.

Tom served Lucky his dinner. Behind his father, on the kitchen sideboard, were two framed photos. Each was a portrait of a young man in his brand new army tunic and slouch hat.

Lucky jammed his napkin into his collar. 'Don't go running off when I need you behind the bar.' He reached for his rum bottle and saw the photos. 'Behave like Harry and Darce would have done, like your mother brought you up to be.' He crossed himself. 'May they rest in peace.'

The images of both young soldiers gazed proudly and confidently into the future as their father said to their kid brother—as he had said so many times before: 'This place'll all be yours one day.'

Lucky poured himself a drink and plonked the bottle on the table. He smelt his fish and nodded his approval. 'Good to see your half-caste mate's good for something.'

Tom spooned spuds onto Lucky's plate. 'Neddy knows the best spots for the cod; fishing's part of his culture.'

'Don't give me all that Abo Dreamtime shit; Neddy gets his fishing from his dad.' Lucky crossed himself again and sighed: 'May he rest in peace.' He then got down to shovelling food into his mouth. 'Frank Murphy was a good man, good with his mates, even better with fish.' He paused, becoming thoughtful, before declaring: 'Yeah, his son needs a proper white man's education.'

Tom joined his father at the table.

From within a chorus of crickets and croaking frogs a different noise edged through. It was a racket of combusting gas and tortured steel: a motorcar. Tearing up the road, it ground to a halt on Main Street. With a shudder the din cut out, replaced by a slight and irregular ticking that soon disappeared, the sounds of the bush recapturing the night as the dust settled. Weary from the road and powdered to a grey that absorbed like felt the moonlight, a Model T Ford Tourer, the first to ever visit Berto, had pulled up at the petrol bowser.

Behind the wheel sat Ernest Thorn, a handsome

American with a pencil moustache, symmetrical features and Macassar-oiled hair. He was smartly dressed and obviously a city slicker—though he looked like he could handle himself well enough in a brawl. However, despite an obvious attention to his every well-groomed detail, his manner betrayed a lack of ease about these fairer qualities, fending off enclosing boredom at having crammed too much into thirty-five years of unrelenting life.

Beside Thorn sat Grace. She was a Sydney girl and barely eighteen. Auburn-haired, with eyes as green as crème de menthe, her skin reflected the shreds of night like bone china. Thorn honked the horn. A cricket creaked.

The American got out of the car and banged on the doors of the blacksmith's shop. There was no response. A light flickered from the upstairs window of the general store and he made his way toward it. Under the bullnose awning, the front door rattled as Thorn's knuckles rapped upon the pane.

Grace glanced around the empty street and saw the sign above the pub's veranda. It proclaimed The Berto Hotel with some uncertainty, written as it was in decomposing copperplate.

Thorn paced up and down the wooden walkway and knocked again. He heard footsteps, the gait irregular. Pop, woken by Ma and instructed to see who it was, opened the door. Head throbbing, the old farrier was not feeling well, but having been struck unconscious, exhausted by the effort of digesting dinner, the resulting snooze had sobered him somewhat. Glasses off, he strained to see the impatient face of his evening caller.

Thorn pointed to the bowser and stooped down to address Pop, eye to eye. 'That your gasoline pump?'

Ma's voice squawked from a distant light, way back of the building. 'Who's that at this hour?'

Pop pretended not to hear her. 'Need to fill up?'

'Yeah,' said Thorn, 'running low.'

'That's a shame.'

'What do you mean?'

'The bowser, she's empty.'

Thorn stood straight, and annoyed, braced his fists against his hips.

Ma appeared behind Pop, her hair in curlers.

Like Pop, Thorn tried to ignore her. 'How far till the next town?'

Pop sniffed and wiped his nose on the knuckle of his thumb. 'Won't find another pump for close on sixty mile, up north of the range.'

Frustrated, Thorn spat onto the street.

'Hey!' said Ma, flying out the door. 'Enough of that.'

Thorn backed off and almost lost his balance on the walkway's edge.

Ma moved forward, a rampaging armadillo. 'Let's be seeing a bit more of the patience the almighty might have blessed you with!'

Pop tried to calm the situation. 'Tanker should be coming through soon.'

Thorn looked at his wristwatch. 'How soon?'

Pop wiped his shiny nose again. 'In a day or two,' he suggested, 'perhaps three.'

Thorn took off his hat and scratched his neck. 'Three days?'

'Or four,' Pop added, trying to be helpful.

Ma saw a hint of Grace in the Model-T. 'You and your missus can bed down in the pub.'

Thorn glared at the Berto Hotel, unimpressed. 'Oh, God, tell me this isn't so.'

Ma gave Thorn a dirty look. 'Come on, Pop, it's time decent folks was abed.' She went inside, shutting the door a little too hard for politeness. The 'Closed' sign swayed behind the glass.

Tom stood by the kitchen sink and dried the dishes while his father sat at the table, reading the newspaper. There was a knock on the lobby door.

'Oh, fuck, who's that?' grunted Lucky, displeased by the intrusion.

Tom also wondered who it could be. As was normally the case, there were no guests staying at the pub and nobody ever came calling after tea. He headed for the lobby and unbolted the front door.

'Any vacancies?' asked Thorn.

'Got one room available,' Tom replied distractedly, his sights fast glued to the all-consuming vision of the dust-covered Ford, so transfixed by its contours he barely noticed the shadowy figure of Grace beneath the convertible's canvas roof. 'That your Tourer?'

'Yeah,' grunted Thorn, 'she's more appealing when she's clean. Give me a second, will you?' The American returned to his car and leaned under the canopy to consult with Grace. After a moment's hushed discussion Thorn looked back and asked aloud: 'Could you collect our luggage?'

'Of course,' Tom answered, rolling down his shirtsleeves as he stepped outside. On crossing the street he at last got an eyeful of Grace. He shuddered to a stop, having only ever seen such beauty in the form of engraver's ink to paper, never once as flesh.

'Okay, Romeo,' sighed Thorn, 'you want to grab the bags?'

Tom snapped back to life like a half-drowned boy on a beach, coughing and gasping his return. 'Oh, yeah,' he said, forgetting to inhale and wheezing, 'sorry.'

Tom took two suitcases from the rear seat of the Tourer and snuck a peek over to the front, but the wonder he'd just beheld was turned away from him. All he could see beyond a sun hat and a scarf was an elegant hand extended as Thorn reached in to help his passenger from her seat.

For a cruelly extended time, Tom was denied a second chance to see her face. Like a train conductor lodged in the caboose, he hauled the luggage as he directed his travellers through the tunnel of the lobby and up the stairs. It was only when they'd stopped outside Room One, and he had shunted forward to the door, that he snatched another glimpse of her. Grace's head was tilted down somewhat, and to his mounting frustration, all he could see beneath her sun hat's rim was a pair of painted lips. They were lushly moist and rosebud fresh.

Tom unlocked the door and dragged the suitcases into the room. Thorn and Grace followed, their progress observed by a pair of furtive eyes, for lurking in the stairwell, Lucky peeped, covertly ascertaining proof of marriage. Satisfied by the wedding band on Grace's finger, he submerged crocodilian from view.

Tom dropped the suitcases by the wardrobe as his guests regarded their accommodation: a brass bed, lace curtains, a chipped willowware bowl and pitcher on the dresser. In the corner stood a freestanding, tilted mirror with a crack. As their eyes took in the room, Tom took the opportunity to take in Grace. Her hair was short, her neck was long, her cheekbones high, but all yielded to her eyes. Emerald pools, they seemed deeper than the sea, ethereal as morning mist, eternal as the heavens that lay beyond that final breath.

'When do you serve breakfast?'

Caught out, mullet-stunned, by Thorn again, Tom hastened to the breach. 'Breakfast is at seven, dunny's out the back.' He ducked under the bed and produced a chamber pot. 'But you've got this: gets a bit nippy outside late of a night.' Tom put away the pot and stood up. 'Yeah, so, ah, soon as you've made yourselves comfortable… Ah, nice and comfy, you can like, you know, wander down to the bar. I'll get you signed into the book and you can, you know, sleep tight and we'll see you in the morning.'

Thorn and Grace watched as Tom went for the door. Stumbling on the rug, he bent over and patted it down like the fur on a mangy mutt. 'Sorry, I'd be careful with the carpet; curls up a bit.' Tom cleared his throat and made again for the door.

'Hey,' said Thorn, his voice commanding.

Tom froze, except for his eyes; they swivelled, as if in quest of means by which to make a quick escape should circumstances turn darkly for the worse. Seeing none was clear save diving through the window, he slowly turned, anticipating the American had surely read and would expose to ridicule or even castigation his intractable and daring thoughts. Thorn handed him a tip.

Tom looked at the coins, bowled over by the gratuity. 'Oh, thank you, Mr—Sorry, I forgot to ask your——'

'Thorn… Ernest Thorn.'

'Yeah, thank you very much, Mr Thorn.' Tom bolted for the safety of the hall.

'Hey,' said Thorn again.

Tom, already at the top of the stairs and thinking himself clear, was forced to halt as if Thorn's words were a bridle bit against his mouth. Yet again, he reluctantly turned back, feeling certain nothing was for nothing: no such thing as a free tip. 'Yes?'

'The key.'

'The key?'

'Yes, the key.'

'Oh, the key,' Tom gushed, relieved, 'I'm sorry, yes, of course.' He thrust his hands into his pockets, fingers squirming for his key ring, and finding it, fumbling as he strove to extricate from the ring the necessary key. After some fiddling it was placed in Thorn's awaiting hand, warm as the pocket from which it came, and then the lad was gone.

Now alone, Thorn and Grace were free to contemplate their well-furrowed bed.

Under a waxing moon, the faded walls of the Berto Hotel defied the dark. Out the back, a possum raided the garbage cans, lids clattering onto the flagstones and knocking over bottles. Upstairs and around the corner of the building, in the window of Room Two, a lamp burned low. By its light, snug in bed, Tom gorged on the opening pages of 'The Red Badge of Courage', but his concentration was broken by the muffled voices of Thorn and Grace. Just next door, he could hear them arguing through the vertical joins of the wooden walls.

'I don't like this, Ernie. What are we doing? I want to go back to Sydney.'

'Do what you're told, Gracie. There'll be other auditions, other Tivolis and better Adelphis. We can't go back. Accept it!'

Tom was torn, annoyed by the interruption to his reading, yet curious, yearning to hear more about these exotic lives that had chanced to linger in his valley. He had never heard of a Tivoli or an Adelphi, and the words were not in his dog-eared dictionary, but audition was. He wondered why Grace had to give a hearing or perform and suspected with her beauty, she must be an actress or a singer.

While Tom alternately pondered words passed through walls or pressed to paper, down the hall, within Room Four, atop a quilt stained brown by sweat, his father lay, still dressed and reeking of the grog. On a nightstand a kerosene lamp relinquished its sallow glow, illuminating a photograph, faded sepia: an image of his younger self, his wife, his two schoolboy sons and a baby gathered in his wife's arms—beloved Rachel's arms. The portrait was a memorial to a broken hope, the future lost, a misplaced lock of baby's hair. Lucky could recapture the day the photo had been taken, but not the world the image seized.

Alongside the photo's tarnished frame, a spilt glass dripped, a tear of rum falling to the floor. At that moment, if he'd been sober enough to dream, Lucky would have dreamt a nightmare. It would still come, waiting patiently till later, a demon, dormant in his waking hours but soon to surface, punctual as the swarms of bats that roosted in the bottom gorge. It would drag him from his blessed coma, weaving a purgatory between life and death. The nightmare, though he lied and called it just a dream, was of those once loved, still loved, but out of reach. They would arrive on gusts of scorching air, already writhing, an evil inner heat distorting and soon torching lines, once sweet, now bitter to behold. Then, quickly reduced to ash, they'd fall away, and to the sound of banshee wails, a lancing pain would race from Lucky's fingertips and toes, fill his chest like heartworms, and erupt into another dead, new day.

A python prowled along the corrugated iron, crawled beneath the eaves and slithered into the roof space. Below the snake, brass bedposts knocked against an ironbark wall. They rattled rhythmically to the sound of squeaking bedsprings until, with a shudder and a soft grown, they stopped.

Charlie heaved himself away and fell back like a collapsing spinnaker, settling to the sea. Wife Peggy was of a different mind; she felt the need to sail a little longer before drifting off to sleep. By the light of the moon she turned to appreciate the face of her man. He had a good, strong profile: firm chin, forthright nose and kindly mouth. Peggy liked what she saw and was, for that moment, satisfied. She turned dreamily to the calico ceiling and observed the rippling progress of their reptile lodger. 'Cedric's out and about tonight,' she sighed. 'Hope he catches that rat. Go get 'em, Cedric.' Enjoying the sweet moment, Peggy stretched. 'Hmm, seems unfair.'

Charlie was now talking in his sleep. 'What?' he murmured as he rolled over onto his side, his back to Peggy.

'Thousands of spinsters and widows nowadays,' she replied, looking at the cradle by their bed, 'and I get so much more than my fair share.' Her baby began to cry. 'Maybe too much more.'

Peggy got up and rocked the cradle. 'There, there, my little one,' she whispered, and within seconds her daughter settled, not having cried long enough to make contentment's recollection difficult. She tickled the baby's chin and the little girl inhaled excitedly to release the breath as dimpled cooing. Peggy whispered close: 'Has anyone told you that you have the prettiest eyes? Don't mention to a living soul I ever said this, but I reckon you've got the prettiest eyes of all.'

Charlie started snoring.

'No offence, my darling, but I do hope you'll be the last. I don't think my old bones are up for too much more of this.'

Peggy continued chatting, enjoying a small moment in the day she could call her own, and confided to her youngest: 'My little Helen, I will admit to you now, for you never will remember, and it would be a hurtful thing to say to one that could, but though the war was a heartache for me, and all the women in these parts, it was still a welcome break; my over-laboured nether regions took those war years in their stride.'

Baby Helen gurgled her agreement and Peggy laughed. For thirteen years she and Charlie had been wed. She wondered how many more children she might have borne, and how much more varicose her veins and weak her bladder, if her husband had not enlisted in the late summer of 1916?

She thought back on those distant years, so long ago, and yet as if were yesterday. The dreadful toll of Gallipoli had got folks talking and Billy Hughes was making speeches, pushing to create a third division. One evening, over a few quiet beers, a group of Berto fellows had decided it. They were no ways Empire men, and for Frank Murphy it rankled that the Australian army called itself an 'imperial' force, but there was patriotism afire for the new nation and a belief the fallen could not be left to die in vain. Within days, the baker's dozen had ridden or been transported on Pop's old wagon to the Armidale showground. There, they had signed on for the duration. Some had spoken of joining the Light Horse because they were, to a man, all well acquainted with life atop a horse, some even bringing their own mounts, but the sergeant at the showground told them France was where the real action was, so they had ended up on shank's pony in D company of the 33rd battalion, 9th Brigade. They were bound for Passchendaele, Villers-Bretonneux, Amiens, and God alone might know what hells between, for the ones who made it back would never speak of them. But Charlie did write from there, and often, and Peggy could tell he'd skirted around the worst parts. In one letter, smudged by rain, he'd written the battalion had christened themselves 'New England's Own'.

Chapter Three

Every time Mad Mike moved, the stones rattled in the cans. Every time the cans rattled, the Germans opened up with small arms' fire; their trench was little more than spitting distance from Mike's lips. He knew the enemy to be that close; they were that close when he fell onto the wire. That's what he could conjure from the time when men were charging and shouting all around him: the cracking of bullets and of bones, the ear-splitting pandemonium, and men rending the air with their curses.

There were different voices now. The earlier voices stopped when the advance pulled back. Mad Mike couldn't recall how long ago that was. He couldn't see his watch because his left hand was wedged beneath his ribs. His left hand was numb. He wasn't even sure if his left hand was there at all. He definitely couldn't feel it.

There was now a different sound afield; it was quieter—some yelling still, but mostly moaning—a low-pitched moaning. It was all around him, upon the mounds and in the gullies of the mud: was like the lowing of the cattle in a massive mob, a sound that took effort, a sound that disliked being made. Mad Mike heard a scream. It was piercing, then guttural. It gurgled before it drowned. Any other time Mike would have felt sorry for the bugger, but now he was just something to reflect upon. Mike tried to picture the faces of the clustered men: some begging for their mothers, lost and far from home; some cursing their torture-chamber god; some wailing incomprehensible descriptions of their wounds to nonexistent doctors who proffered imagined medications; and the others who lay beyond such foolish talk, mute within the mercy of death's embrace.

Mike tried to move. A can rattled. He waited for his bullet. One second, two seconds… No, he thought, must have been at least five. They hadn't spotted him. He would be dead if not for the bomb crater. He was on the lee side, a yard behind its rim, sheltered from Cyclone Fritz. Mike should have made more of an effort to disentangle himself when things were noisier, but he wasn't thinking straight then. All he wanted then was to press down on the wires, uproot the bomb-blasted posts with his weight and get as low and small as the barbs would give him leave. Things were different now. He was thinking now. He was going to set himself free.

The rain had stopped and the sun had been shining for a while. Mike thought there should have been the song of birds to accompany such lovely weather, but the warbles and the chirps were brought to mind only through their absence. And the light, now unfettered by cloud, was getting warmer, coaxing steaming vapours from the field. The smell was as nothing Mike had ever smelt before. He thought he'd got used to the stench of the front, but anything, no matter how bad, can always be made worse. This smell of so much death made perfume of the putrid trench, and the trench was worse than an overflowing dunny, which was worse than a cattle train at noon, which was pretty bad for starters. The smell was so crook Mike had to dwell on something else. The other something was no better; it was the burning of the barbs against his chest. As the initial shock and excitement passed, the pain of their tiny bites grew worse. They were a torment, as bull-ant bites could be, only now the bites were legion and not inflicted now and then as were his boyhood stings. He called to mind being bucked from his horse when just a lad and ploughing into a hill of bullies, so he knew what he was talking about. He wasn't talking though; he was silent as a fox beneath a circling pack of hounds.

But the young soldier could not tarry; sooner die in a bullet's instant than suffer crucifixion on the barbs. A reconnoitre by his free right hand told him he must strip and abandon to the field his woolen tunic and his greyback, knitted as they were amid the wires. Remade by circumstances as a snake, he must shed this outer skin to slither free.

Reaching beneath his chest Mike gradually undid his brass buttons. He had never realised before how many held him snug. If he survived this day he'd rip off just a couple and stuff inspection; three could serve as good as five.

Upon the release of the second button the fabric of his tunic slipped away an inch, the wire wobbled and a stone rattled in its can. One stone in one can. Mike could see the can. It was round and rusty and probably was once filled with pickled cabbage. Mike hated cabbage. Then he heard the Germans talking behind their sand bags. Though he couldn't understand their words, he was certain Fritz was surveying the wounded for signs of life. He wondered if perhaps he should wait till sundown; he might crawl away under cover of night, but the Germans too could play at night: slit his throat beneath its shroud. Night wagered with unloaded dice.

Then, as if by the drawing of a blind, the sun disappeared behind a bank of heavy clouds and the earth grew dark beneath their burden, the gloom borne low in threatening shades of filthy green. No sooner than arrived these clouds disgorged their rain, and the droplets fell fat and heavy, eager to be mud. Aural camouflage was what it was. Mike though didn't call it that; he called it noise, but a man could hide in noise no matter what its name. The torrent buffeted the cans and their stones at once were trembling down the line. Mike had to strip while the downpour whipped itself to climax. He undid the remaining buttons, and to his immense relief, he found his absent hand. Peeling away his tunic and his shirt, both spongy and well sodden, he could find no contortion by which to pull the garments past his shoulder. In the midst of this struggle another barb released. The canned pebbles now quaked as good as any siren. Fritz took his cue and opened up. Bullets tore through the crater's rim, the air perforated by red-hot lead. Mud splattered and the rim wore lower. Mad Mike soon would be exposed for all to see, head shattered like a soft-boiled egg for breakfast. He had to get away. He pulled at his sleeve, but the barbs would not give over. He was stuck like a dingo in a dingo trap, the iron barbs a vice, the cruel teeth working deeper, and the more he dragged the more his strength was sapped. The air trembled as he trembled and the Germans were out of their trench. They were on top of him.

In a split second there would be the jab from the bayonet, the turn of the blade in his gut. Mike didn't wait. His hands lunged up, miraculously both free, resolved to do their duty around the German's throat. He was throttling Fritz, squeezing the life from his Godforsaken enemy!

Snow slapped him hard across the chops; a little tap would never do.

Mike's eyes opened, terrified. He released his grip and gasped: 'Snow?'

'Yeah, it's me.'

'Fritz! He's... he's…'

'He's not here, Mike. You're safe. You're back in Berto, remember?'

Mad Mike looked around, panting, sopping wet with sweat and trying to find focus in the bunkhouse dark.

Snow was getting grumpy. 'Mike, for Christ's sake!'

'Where is everybody?'

'Not here!'

'What about Frank?'

'We left him at Hangard Wood.'

'And Big George Philpot—Corp?'

'Passchendaele.'

'Mrs Philpot?'

'She's over in the house.'

'And Charlie's corporal now?'

'Yeah, he made it back too.'

Mike blinked and his breathing slowed, his chest stopped heaving; the nightmare faded and sanity returned. 'Sorry, Snow, I forgot.'

'It's alright.' Snow shifted his weight from Mike's bunk. 'You made it back is all what counts. I'd be dangerous if I ever got a decent night's sleep.'

'Sorry, mate.'

'Don't have to make a song and dance about it.' Snow eased himself into his bottom bunk. 'We're home is all that matters for us three—us and Charlie. We're home.' Snow was already drifting off. 'It's home.'

The sun's rays fell in lazy shafts between the branches of the hoop pine and lapped a creek that tinkled over river stones to form a narrow pond. In a splash of light, diamond bright in this emerald bower, Tom and Neddy fished. They sat upon a hardwood log, burnished smooth by years of use, and though concentrating on their task, dawdled through the languid hours, as if this life were infinite, and waited for the cod that thrived in mountain waters, upstream of the ancient Clarence.

'She pretty?' asked Neddy.

'Oh, yeah, pretty as a sheila in the Horderns' catalogue.'

'They drawings of real sheilas?'

'Yeah!.. I s'pose.'

'Jeez,' said Neddy in awe.

Tom trailed his line across the creek and dreamily agreed, imagining himself as an artist sketching pretty girls. 'Hmm,' he sighed.

'Humph,' snorted Neddy in response, assigning doubt to such a crazy notion and suppressing erotic thoughts with the cudgel of common sense.

'Husband's a bit of a worry, but,' Tom continued,

choosing to ignore Neddy's scepticism. 'Seems old enough to be her dad.'

'Yeah?'

'Yeah, must have a lot of dough.'

'Guess that's how come they've got a motorcar?'

'Yeah.'

'Nice motorcar?'

'Nice for around here,' said Tom.

'Anything's nice for around here,' said Neddy.

Tom laughed. Neddy didn't. Neddy hardly ever laughed, which Tom considered strange because Neddy said some funny things. He observed what others missed; he saw the oddity in what was seen as normal and the normality in that thought odd. Tom considered it peculiar Neddy didn't laugh because he made Tom laugh near most the time; but Neddy, he would simply sniff or scratch or take to other things while others took to laughing; the fact that Neddy never laughed made Tom laugh more.

Tom was four years older than Neddy. The younger lad should have looked up to the other, like some kind of big brother or hero or something, but he didn't. The two were just mates. They were good mates. They didn't know it then, but in almost any other time or place that would have been impossible. From the very start they would have been pushed apart until recognition of the other disappeared into the shadows of ignorance and fear. Such was the outside world, but that could never be in Berto; there weren't people enough for that in Berto. In their valley, nothing prevented the lads from being mates.

'I read something about motorcars in the Examiner,' said Tom. 'There's a bloke selling them in Grafton.'

Neddy whistled softly and said: 'Cripes.'

Tom mused, 'I reckon we'll see more motorcars. Maybe one day there'll be as many motorcars as there are houses.'

A small but telltale current shifted along the water's surface. It captured Neddy's eye and he felt a twitch on the line. 'I got a nibble,' he whispered.

Tom glanced across the creek. 'Yeah, you sure?' he asked, distractedly.

'Yes,' Neddy insisted. 'There's a cod down there. You see him?'

'Nope, but it's the march of time. We're living in a period of great change. Who can tell? One day might be you, might be me, might both of us be driving motorcars easily as ride a horse. Might even buy a motorcar one day. Sounds like bull, but could happen, anything's possible. Love to drive a car.'

'There!' said Neddy, reeling in a juicy cod. 'I got him.'

The Ford still sat beside the empty petrol bowser. It baked under the sun in an otherwise empty street. The pub was quiet. Grace stood alone in her room and stared at herself in the tilting mirror with the crack. Her eyes began to water. She turned away and noticed something outside. She pulled back the lace curtain and looked down to see a police officer riding into town. It was the local trooper, Constable Grimes.

Downstairs, Lucky stood behind the bar. It had been a stressful night, what with guests staying over in the pub and the tribulations of preparing them a breakfast, but the daylight had found him steadfast, welded to delusions of capability, a sure sign he was still drunk. Full of piss and wind, he had dispatched Tom to find more fish for that evening's tea, assuring the lad all would go smooth as lacquered dog shit. This assertion proved correct, but only through good fortune. The gods had smiled, and it was by their blessing his guests wanted only toast and a cup of tea for breakfast.

Several hours had passed since then. Lucky could feel a dawning sobriety and the distant rumblings of a hangover. Though it had been decades since the last time Lucky had been forced to have a chuck, the drink brought retribution by way of other side effects against which he had not been immunised. The evidence of these was plain to see as Lucky held fast to his post behind the bar: his nose was grown to vivid hues, the spider veins raised high, and his eyes were mapped by all the warmer colours of the rainbow. Lucky rarely bathed, but he shaved each morning—face, and head—short back and sides, wielding his straight razor with a confidence not endorsed by the results. Those parts not shaved were rarely trimmed, leaving his crown a turnip top of greasy sprouts, his moustache grown past lower lip and his cheekbones capped with little tufts—not shaving these for fear it might encourage his whiskers to advance into his eyes.

Once more Lucky polished the barroom's glasses with undemanded thoroughness; and save for himself, his own best customer, there were no other drinkers in the public bar. His only company was Thorn, who imbibed from nothing more than his silver box of snuff. Sitting at a table in the opposite corner of the room, the gambler was playing solitaire when he heard the clip-clop of a horse's hooves. Glimpsing through the open double doors, he caught the unwelcome sight of the local copper dismounting and hitching his horse. The American was quick to exit, pocketing his cards and up the stairs in seconds, uncertain of how long Harry Newman's arm could reach— Harry's gang could lunge as far as Melbourne if it had to. Thorn wasn't taking any chances; the bush telegraph transmitted mighty fast—would earn the government a fortune if they could find the means to tax it—and a hayseed cop might easily wave an oily palm as the current buzzed across the land.

Sweating and puffy, chins corseted and bulging from under his high collared tunic, Constable Grimes strode in and walked across to Lucky.

Lucky threw his dishtowel over his shoulder and clasped a beer tap. 'Constable, cold one on the house?'

'Not today, thanks.'

Lucky was quick to release his grip on the tap. 'Busy on your circuit?'

The trooper scratched his balls. 'Nah, she's quiet, the way I like it; no Grafton sergeant breathing down me neck.'

'Sergeant Maguire?'

'Yeah, the prick.'

'So I've heard told; purely talk and speculation, you understand.'

'Yeah, no worries, Lucky, understood.' Grimes squinted as he looked out to the street. 'Whose car?'

'Guests.'

The trooper grunted and turned back to the bar. 'Tom in?'

'Gone fishing.'

'Seen his little cobber, Neddy, around lately?'

'Doesn't come into town much these days.'

'Boy's grown a few years older since Frank Murphy snuck inside Saint Peter's gates. Needs looking after, an education; can't have him living up at the black's camp.'

'No arguing that.'

'Reckon you could get him to wander in…' Grimes checked his fob watch against the lobby's grandfather clock, his toad-egg eyes hopping between the two. 'Hmm, get him to wander in around noon tomorrow?'

Lucky rubbed the early trace of stubble on his cheeks.

Thorn leaned against the wall, peeked beyond the curtains and saw the constable ride out of town. 'Good,' he murmured low, as if someone outside might hear. 'That's excellent. You go home to supper, Mr Lawman.' Thorn returned to the mirror with its crack and continued trimming his mascara-wand moustache. 'Might make some money tonight.'

Grace lay on top of the bed, still in her slip, and leafed through an old issue of Smith's Weekly—unearthed yellowing in a drawer of the wardrobe. The news was old, but she liked the illustrations. Licking the tip of her middle finger, she casually turned a page and moaned; she was bored by Thorn's obsessive interest in their work.

'No,' he said, eyes bright, disregarding Grace's apathy, 'this place smells ripe for the picking.' Thorn snapped his nail scissors into his goatskin grooming case. 'We could do alright if that fat-ass cop stays away.' The gambler flicked the severed whiskers from the front of his shirt. 'I'll call you in when the moment is right. Don't want to waste your talents on the small fry.'

'What am I supposed to do till then.'

Thorn vigorously rubbed Bay Rum between his hands and slapped it onto his cheeks. 'Why don't you see the local sights?'

'I've already looked out the window.'

'Okay, snookums, if that's the way you want to be, but I, for one, will go back down and relax in the bar, see if the fish are biting.' Thorn put on his jacket and brushed his shoulders.

Grace licked her finger again and turned another page. 'Card games in pubs have a limit on the stakes. You know that.'

'I'll slip the landlord a slice of the action.' Thorn adjusted his tie. 'That old rummy would sell his mother for a drink.'

'Perhaps there won't be any takers; it's not the Wild West. You're not in Dodge City now.'

Thorn frowned at Grace and declared: 'You've got to be putting me on! My little darling, your average Aussie would gamble on anything—horses, dogs, football, who'll be the next prime minister or who can piss the highest up a tree.'

Grace reached for her cigarettes.

Neddy sat in back of Tom, twixt saddle and Copenhagen's rump. They rode to where the creek fell sharply off the granite, pooling beneath a stand of brown beech. It was the remotest part of the valley; any farther out and you were up against the shorn-off boulders of the escarpment. An hour's ride from town, this was the site of the blackfellas' camp.

They were a clan of the Gumbaynggirr people, or maybe they were Bundjalung. Few whitefellas thought to ask or seemed to care. Although the whites had journeyed far and from many different lands—England, Scotland, Ireland, Wales—with many different attributes ascribed by each to the others, they were blind to the differences between the black nations in their midst. Despite a deep awareness of their own heritage, the white folks usually failed to bother distinguishing one black man from his neighbour, seeing the exercise as pointless, even petty. For the Aboriginal people it was much the same; they were all whitefellas. However, the circumstances between the colours, new and old, were not so petty. Though impossible to ignore when standing in the light, it was an easy task to brush the black man's plight into the dark. Berto's valley, like all its neighbours, had been the blackfellas' land for almost as long as the human species had trod the earth, and when, like elsewhere, the white man spread his condor wings, swooping with axe and fence, beast and plough, the former custodians of the valley were exiled to the remotest part. Crown land, the whitefellas called it.

A little ways away from the blacks' camp stood a tiny wooden church. Built on stumps and roofed with corrugated iron, it lacked solid walls except behind the altar. The other three sides were canvas that could be pulled aside when the weather was too hot. Attended by a Catholic priest on his circuit every month or so, it was the aboriginal people's umbilical cord to the white man's world and the small change they received in compensation for their loss.

Tom ambled down the track toward the camp, the reins loose in his hand, for Copenhagen had long since learnt the way. On passing the chapel, Tom caught the smell of its humble canvas walls, imbued with a lingering hint of frankincense—as alien to the forest as a waft of lavender from an old lady's handbag.

Neddy's hut lay on the camp's periphery, some distance from the rest. Lowanna, Neddy's mother, sat outside their hut and buried yams in the hot ashes of a smouldering fire. Neddy and Lowanna's hut, like all the others in the camp, was a loose assemblage of bark and wood harvested from the bush, and cast-off timber and corrugated iron harvested from the whitefella middens. In the distance, huddles of elders whispered and chirping children ran about.

Neddy dismounted, his dilly bag swinging from his shoulder. Tom tipped his hat to Lowanna. She nodded back in silence.

'Hey, Tom,' asked Neddy, 'you wouldn't be able to get us one of them Horderns' catalogues?'

Lowanna glared sternly at her son.

Neddy looked guilty. 'Crikey, Mum, thought you'd like to have a look at all the pictures and stuff they got in 'em.'

Lowanna, silent as ever, returned to her yams.

'Alright, don't worry about it then,' Neddy grumbled, handing his mother his catch of fish.

Noticing her downcast eyes, Tom wondered why Lowanna always appeared so glum—rarely speaking. It seemed life had ripped away her tongue, the giggling girl she had been now afraid to use her voice lest she might wake a demon. Tom lifted his hand to Neddy in a single wave, said he'd be back tomorrow then headed Copenhagen home.

As he rode out Tom noticed the approach of Burnum, the local black-tracker. Though often seen in camp, it was not Burnum's home. His home was everywhere and not a soul, black or white, knew where he slept. As far back as he could travel, Tom had heard talk about Burnum. The locals said he was more reliable than a bloodhound, could follow anyone or anything through valley or over ridge. Frank Murphy, before being blown to Flanders dirt, had skited on Burnum's behalf, the way folks do, that Burnum could track an ant across a swollen river, he was that good. Even Preston Logan was a bit respectful, and Logan respected nobody and nothing except money and power, and only then enough to bring all else to book. Everyone agreed, Burnum was different, no doubt about it. Dressed the old way, and never near the church, he might have been carved from teak or cedar or any of the timbers of the northern rivers, or mountain granite, raw and rude, the essence of the earth itself.

As they passed each other, Tom saw the dead kangaroo Burnum carried on his shoulder, and in his other hand, his spear and woomera. Tom inclined his head in greeting, but no inclination reflected back. Burnum just stared at Tom, or through him, like he wasn't there, was nothing, without substance, and the world beyond more worthy of his gaze.

The Widow MacTavish brought her crate of peas into Ma's

store. Agnes MacTavish was a plainspoken young woman with a heart-shaped face and determined eyes. She grew and sold vegetables to supplement her war widow's pension—though never potatoes, for they were The Widow O'Connor's department. She put the peas onto Ma's produce stand. 'Fresh picked this morning, Ma.'

'Oh, that's lovely, Agnes. Here's your crate from last week. Sold out as usual.'

'I'll put it into Kathleen's cart before I forget.'

The Widow MacTavish walked out of Ma's store as The Widow O'Connor lumbered in. She was wielding a hessian sack of potatoes; Kathleen O'Connor was somewhat older and quite a bit heftier than Agnes MacTavish. 'Ma, I have to tell you these King Edwards are a joy. I'm tempted to say they grow like weeds but that would be showing ingratitude, wouldn't it?'

'Now, now, you're being too harsh on yourself,' said Ma as she took the potatoes and tipped them into a large basket that stood next to the sack of chook feed. 'I say it's a smart woman who can find ways to reduce her toil without cost.'

Kathleen looked concerned. 'The wholesale price is still a pennorth a pound, isn't it?'

'Indeed, and that's as it should be. What progress would we have without the desire to get more for less, I ask you?'

'You're not just a pretty face, Ma.'

'I understand the saying, Kathleen, heard it more times than I care to remember, and I'll tell you this, as I've said afore to all and sundry—a pretty face is like the hare; it can get you a long ways fast, but it soon fades, while a brain is like a tortoise; it keeps plodding along, getting wiser every year. And we all been taught who won the race, haven't we?'

The Widow MacTavish carried in a crate of onions. 'Usual place?'

'Yes, on me produce stand between your carrots and your peas. I'll move the old crate.'

Agnes peered at the last week's produce boxes. 'Ma, you didn't sell all my carrots.'

'Never mind, I'll feed those few to Pop's old mules. They like a good carrot and won't complain if it's floppy.'

The Widow MacTavish choked on a hiccough of laughter.

The Widow O'Connor was not amused. 'What are you smirking at, girl?'

'Oh, I'm sorry, Kathleen.' The younger widow winked at Ma. 'It might be a touch of hay fever.'

'Yes,' Ma agreed with a smile of her own, 'it being spring and all. Oh, and by the way, your pension cheques have arrived with the morning mail.'

'Aye,' said the older widow, 'and a pittance for a husband's life it is too.'

'Better than a poke in the eye with a burnt stick,' said the younger widow. 'I'll bring in the eggs. The girls have been very productive this week: must be the new rooster.'

The Widow MacTavish walked back to The Widow O'Connor's cart to collect the eggs. The older widow watched her step out. 'New rooster indeed,' she muttered.

'Oh, go on with you, Kathleen,' said Ma. 'Agnes is only young, much too young to be a widow.'

'And what of me then, Ma?'

'You're much too young too, Kathleen.'

'Damn right! Oh, sorry, please excuse me French.'

'You have to appreciate, Kathleen, that Patrick left you well set up, what with that there horse and spring cart outside.'

'Got no seat like your fine buggy.'

'But that cart's a sight better than pushing your spuds into town in a wheelbarrow, isn't it now, Kathleen?' Ma took off her spectacles. 'My word, yes,' she nodded, and busily polishing the lenses on her apron, continued. 'Plus you got some lovely furniture and that fine piano while Agnes and Fred was barely starting out. Hush now, she's back.'

The Widow MacTavish returned with her wicker basket of eggs. 'Ran into young Tom out there; caught a beautiful brace of cod.'

'Did he now?' said Ma as she walked into the post office booth to collect the women's mail from their pigeonholes.

'He's always been a lovely lad. Wish he was a couple of years older.'

'I'm thinking, Agnes, there'll be a queue you might be having to join.' Ma handed each widow a letter. They at once ripped open the envelopes. 'Did you girls notice the motorcar outside Pop's shop?'

'Hmm?' asked The Widow O'Connor, only half-listening, her little, maroon tongue sticking out as she scrutinised the amount she'd been paid.

'I said there's a motorcar in the street!'

'Yes,' said The Widow MacTavish, somewhat startled, 'it's very nice. Who's visiting?'

'Is it the local member then?' asked The Widow O'Connor. 'I'm told he's got a motorcar now. Paid a king's ransom, he is.'

The Widow MacTavish frowned. 'Is there going to be another election?'

'No, Agnes,' Ma assured, exiting the post office booth, 'least I don't imagine so.' Transferring the younger widow's eggs to a wire basket that sat on the counter, she added: 'The motor car belongs to a couple who is staying over.'

'Why?' asked The Widow MacTavish, she perplexed by the news.

'Why?' asked Ma, she confused by the question.

'Yes, why would you need to stay over in Berto?'

'Oh,' Ma got the drift, 'they're out of petrol and so is Pop's bowser.'

'Ah,' The Widow MacTavish concluded, 'so they're stuck here then.'

'It's lovely is that bowser,' said The Widow O'Connor.

'Yes,' Ma agreed with pride, 'Pop and I like it. We consider it gives Berto something of a modern look, would you not say, Kathleen?'

'Oh, aye, it's lovely to have something new in town. And very attractive colours.' The Widow O'Connor slipped her cheque back into its envelope and her tongue into her cheek. 'Although I must confess I've never seen a ram that was yellow!'

The ladies laughed. The Widow O'Connor often made humorous observations and the women of the valley knew she liked it if they laughed.

Joining in the merriment, the older widow wiped a tear of joy from her rubicund cheeks. 'Oh, gosh, where's me hanky?' She dabbed away the moisture. 'So how long till the petrol tanker arrives?'

'Not long,' said Ma.

'A few days then?'

'Yes, Agnes, I expect so. Perhaps longer; hard to tell with these things.'

The Widow O'Connor shook her head. 'I don't like that petrol. It can explode, did you know? Been told you can't use it in a lamp; blow your head off. It's a piece of luck, Ma, you've still got your buggy and Pop's fine mules.'

'Oh, Kathleen, I would never give up me buggy for one of them motorcars. I don't like all the noise they make.'

'And they go so fast too,' said The Widow MacTavish.

'Oh, I know,' Ma nodded, 'and they can be very costly to run.'

'And so dear to buy in the first place,' said The Widow O'Connor. 'More expensive than a house.'

'Yes, very pricey,' Ma concurred, 'too pricey for simple working folk as us.'

'So who are the fancy couple?' asked The Widow MacTavish.

Ma crossed her arms and leaned across her counter. The widows huddled around.

Tom had put the fish into the Coolgardie safe and was walking up the hall to his room. At the lobby he started for the stairs and ran into Grace. Instantly his groin tingled like he was falling. 'Sleep alright last night?' he sputtered.

Grace said nothing, her expression blank.

'How was breakfast then? Dad can brew a nice cup of tea when he's of a mind. Great bread, isn't it? Ma O'Shaughnessy bakes it.' Tom looked sideways as if Ma were there to take a bow. 'Yeah, Ma runs the store other side of Main Street.'

Grace still said nothing but her eyes appraised him for a piercing second. Tom was glad at least she wasn't staring through him. Not like Burnum did. He had endured enough of that for one day. Besides, there was nothing beyond him now except the wallpaper, bubbling and tearing on the VJs, the crinkles accumulating dust. 'That bed's a bit lumpy,' he conceded, judging that might be the reason for Grace's hesitance. 'I've been trying to get my dad to buy a decent mattress for ages.'

Grace squeezed past. Tom backed away.

'The bed and breakfast were fine,' she said and swept into the public barroom.

'Ah, Miss,' said Tom, sounding pushy more than helpful, hating his words as soon as they were in his ears, 'you can't...' It was too late. 'Damn it,' he swore to himself and sat down on a step, waiting patiently for what must happen next.

Grace strolled up to Thorn. He was playing poker with two locals. Lucky saw her from behind the taps. 'Excuse me, Ma'am, no ladies in the public bar.'

Thorn glanced up. 'You can get yourself a drink in the saloon.' He was as easy as you like. Leaning back, he indicated a hole in the wall at the rear of the bar and then resumed his card game.

Grace looked at the little window bar, then to Lucky, then at Thorn, then back to Lucky, her eyelids stretching wider with every turn, the whites expanding like a pouring of pancake batter, but there was no point in arguing the toss. She took comfort in not caring a hoot for the opinions of monkeys, she who had spurned the homage of organ grinders.

Grace swept out, serene as when she'd first swept in. Continuing through the lobby, she noticed Tom still there at the stairs and couldn't believe he got her feeling embarrassed. Her manner changed, her easy gait shifting to a march as she entered the hallway. Shoulders forward, she headed to the curtain of magenta beads that indicated, with a feminine touch, the entrance to the ladies' bar.

If Grace had thought the saloon might be a little special, a modicum of effort made to appeal to the fairer sex, she was mistaken. The parting beads revealed a sad and forlorn room: bare floorboards, two tables, a scattering of chairs and wallpaper worse than in the hall—this lot bubbling faded cherubs. Opposite was a bay window and adjacent to the beaded door, the reverse aspect of the dreaded little window. Grace approached it warily and saw the back of the front room bar, noticing all the mess housed on its shelves.

Lucky wandered up. 'What can I get you, love?'

Lucky's informal address, dripping with delight at her subjugation to his will, left Grace squirming. She smiled the modest smile she utilized for curtain calls and ordered a seven of shandy.

Tom snuck down the hall and peeked between the

beads. His father passed Grace her drink. She handed him three pennies and settled at a table. Tom ducked back behind the curtain.

Grace gazed out through the bay window and scanned the view. She thought it easily the best thing about the room, the best thing about everything at that moment. Extended before her she could see rolling pastures dotted with cattle, the hazy bluish green of the rising forest, the crumbling ramparts of the escarpment, and way off, up around to the east, a massive peak of gleaming rock, a watchtower to the valley's stockade.

'What's your name?' she asked.

There was no reply. Grace sipped her shandy and waited.

Tom knew the jig was up. 'Whose name?'

Grace took another sip of her drink. 'No use standing out there.'

Tom slinked in.

She looked at him. 'Take a seat.'

He sat opposite.

'I'm Grace,' she stated matter-of-factly, leaning forward with her hand extended.

Tom catapulted to his feet, fumbling for Grace's unsuspecting fingers and puckering his lips. She pulled back from the brink and offered him her hand again, but this time angled vertically in a manner even he could not get wrong. Clamping firmly his palm to hers, she asked: 'And?'

Tom inhaled audibly. 'Ah, Tom Bramble.'

Grace let go her grip, settled into her seat and crossed

her legs. 'Publican your dad?'

Tom nodded as he sat down. Staring at the table, he discovered a hint of Grace's beauty reflected in its scratched but polished surface.

She took a silver case from her purse and enquired further: 'Been here all your life?' He nodded again. There appeared the hint of a smile on her lips as she took a cigarette from the case.

He watched her light up. 'What's Sydney like?'

Grace exhaled a plume of unfiltered Craven A. 'How do you know I'm from Sydney?'

'You're not a country girl.'

Grace shook out the match. 'You can say that again.'

'So, what's it like—Sydney?'

'Dirty.'

'Still, I reckon it'd be bonza.'

'You'd be skinned alive.'

'You've done alright.'

Grace threw the dead match into the ashtray. 'Where's your mum?'

'Passed away.'

'Life on the land's hard for a woman.'

'Was a broken heart did it. Brothers never came back from France—only a couple of telegrams. They're going brown in a box at the bottom of Dad's trunk.'

'You've got a way with words,' Grace noted, 'for a country boy.'

'I've read 'Kim',' Tom suddenly enthused, 'and all the Jungle Books: Rudyard Kipling. Learnt one of his poems—

was printed in the 'Clarence Valley Examiner'. "The tumult and the shouting dies, the Captains and the Kings depart. Still stands Thine ancient sacrifice, an humble and a contrite heart. Lord God of Hosts, be with us yet, lest we forget, lest we forget.'"

Grace stared at Tom for a moment, intrigued by what she had heard, and then switched away to behold the wallpaper's flocking cherubs. 'Maybe you should go to Sydney,' she decided. 'The city's coloured lights and garbage may not kill you, but this place definitely will.'

'Hey, Tom!'

Lucky appeared through the little window. 'Get out here and get cracking!'

Tom stood up. 'Nice talking to you,' he said with absolute honesty before backing out through the beads. Grace took another sip of her shandy.

Chapter Four

A few more drinkers had drifted into town. Tom quickly set to work, grazing around the public bar, picking up empty glasses.

Thorn now played poker with three ringers from up Warwick way: the first was pretty old, the other two were young, remnants from the war, one wearing a patch to hide a hole once plugged by an eye, the other brandishing a hook for a hand.

Thorn laid down a flush. 'Struth!' said the ringer with the hook.

'I'm getting a beer while I can still afford it,' said the eye-patch ringer.

'Won't argue with that,' said the old ringer, turning out his pockets, searching for loose change. Thorn grimaced in disgust as handfuls of the ringer's lint, soiled hankies and old butts stained with tar and saved for later enjoyment were heaped upon the table. As the three men left, the oldest returned his belongings to his pockets. Irritated with himself, Thorn tidied up his winnings and blew away the remains of lint. He had moved too hastily to fleece his three opponents, swooping before they'd made an emotional commitment to the game and spoiling his chance to win yet more. From the corner of his eyes, he saw Charlie, Mad Mike and Snow ride up to the hitching rail.

Tom approached Thorn's table. He picked up the empty glasses and watched the gambler pocket a brown ten-bob note.

Thorn noticed Tom staring at him. 'Wearing something of yours, kid?'

A response was not expected and not given. Tom set a course for shelter behind the bar. The three stockmen entered, observing the American as they shuffled to the taps. Charlie took the first shout, turned to Tom and asked how life was treating him.

'Pretty good, as it happens,' Tom answered, an image of Grace projecting across his memory's retina. He pulled three schooners of Tooheys Hunter Old Black Ale.

Charlie squinted at him. 'You look like the canary that swallowed the cat.'

'Nah,' said Tom, like he was spitting out a water melon pip, 'just a beautiful day.'

'More days like this and we'll be in another bloody drought,' said Snow, hard-boiled as a bookie.

Tom passed the beers to Charlie who handed them on. Snow checked out Thorn. 'Who's the flash bastard?'

'Tom,' called Grace.

Tom swung around toward the saloon. Snow, Charlie and Mike did the same, moving in unison, mouths as open as sideshow plaster clowns rotating to gobble up a ball. Grace stood before them, framed by the little window. For Tom she brought to mind a picture he had seen of the Mona Lisa. Like her, Grace's face was scrutinising yet inscrutable, regal yet flirtatious, cool yet warm, but Tom thought Grace to be more beautiful: as bewitching as Rowena in his edition of Ivanhoe or his treasured engraving of Fiammetta found in an old issue of the Graphic. Grace brought to mind images of Heloise and Juliet, artists' fantasies of Guinevere and Isolde, the Lady of Shalott and Dante Rossetti's Proserpine requesting: 'Another shandy, thanks. I'll have a middy this time.'

Tom shook himself to earth and pulled a tap. He two-thirds filled a half-pint glass with beer and topped it up with Blue Bow Lemonade, gently placing it on the little window's bar.

'Put it on Ernie's slate,' said Grace as she disappeared again.

'No worries,' Tom replied. 'Let me know if you need anything else, Grace.' Turning back, he saw the stockmen grinning.

Mad Mike imitated Tom. 'Let me know if you need anything else, Grace.'

Charlie leaned across the bar. 'Now you behave yourself there, young lad; don't want to be upsetting the town's guests.'

Tom peered in Thorn's direction and observed. 'Word travels fast.' Brimming with newly-acquired confidence, he asked, 'You lot want a word of advice?'

'Yeah, I'm listening,' said Snow, intrigued. 'What you got?'

'That flash slicker over there.'

Charlie, Snow and Mike all peeked over their shoulders at Thorn.

'Cripes,' Tom whispered, 'haven't you blokes ever heard

of subtlety?' All three men swayed back around. Tom had the diggers in his thrall and it was thrilling. 'The dude's name is Ernie Thorn. He's from Sydney.'

Snow raised an eyebrow.

Charlie snorted. 'Never would have guessed.'

'Yeah,' said Tom, 'he's Grace's husband, a cardsharp: empty your wallet soon as look at you.'

'Tom!' It was Lucky speaking this time. 'Need to tap a fresh keg of stout.' His son scowled, annoyed by his father's interruption. He reluctantly lifted up the trap door and ducked down into the cellar.

The gambler left his table and strutted up to Lucky. The three stockmen eyed his reflection in the mirror behind the bar. 'Scotch, three fingers,' he ordered. The publican poured him a triple. 'On my account,' instructed the gambler as he sipped his drink. He went to leave, but before returning to his table, asked Lucky if he had a minute. The publican was dubious but the gambler assured him: 'It's a matter you'll find of interest and perhaps of mutual profit—you and me.'

Lucky scrunched one eye and squinted at Thorn with the other. 'Profit, you say?'

The gambler worked his gums as if chewing on a plug of tobacco. 'Somewhere private we can talk?'

Lucky cleared his throat and spoke softly. 'We can have a quiet word in the lobby.'

Snow watched the two men shift away, their shoulders hunched. He savoured his ale and hinted to his mates of deeds most cunning: 'That dude seems like the sort of mongrel who should meet Preston Logan.'

Charlie sucked in his paunch and pulled up his pants like he was preparing to lift something heavy. 'You thinking of paying a call on the Widow Campbell—quick cup of tea and a catch-up?'

Snow shrugged. 'She's been at me to drop in—take a look at the axle on her buggy——" He didn't like it when Charlie giggled. 'No, seriously, might be an opportune moment for a spot of gossip. How long you think it'd take for the news to cross her boss's desk?'

"I don't know,' Charlie admitted. 'How long would it take him to open the lock on his war chest?' He allowed himself a sly grin and winked at Snow. 'Preston Logan: stroke of genius.'

Mad Mike agreed. 'P-pretty smart.'

Was night now and fruit bats screeched, flying before a moon that ached to be full. The pub had already been an hour closed. Out back, in the kitchen, Tom and Lucky sat at the table, eating their dinner.

Lucky wasn't pleased. 'Sick of fucking fish!'

'But you told me this morning you wanted fish for tea.'

'Did I?' asked Lucky, pouring himself more rum.

'If I can have your rifle,' Tom suggested, the glint of hope in his eye, 'I'll go out tomorrow and bag us a couple of rabbits.'

'Nah, only peasants eat rabbit. And I'm sick of you borrowing me gun, you'll wear it out. In the morning, I'll go out to old Butterworth's place and get us half a sheep. Toss the prick a pint of gin for his trouble.' Lucky glanced surreptitiously at Tom, looking for a reaction, but the lad had returned to his meal, not bothered by his father's whinging. The older Bramble swabbed dribble from his chin and mashed his serving of boiled potatoes with the back of his fork. 'Why don't you invite Neddy over for lunch tomorrow? You could fry up some chops.'

'Thought you had it in for Neddy?'

'Nah, he's not a bad little bloke. After all, half white.'

'You talk about Neddy as if you don't know him anymore.'

'Stop talking shit; strike me pink, I'm his godfather.'

'You've turned different though.'

'Since when?'

'Cripes Dad, been ages.'

'When?'

'Since Lowanna got her telegram.'

'Been that obvious?'

'Like dog's balls.'

'Bloody hell.'

'S'pose.'

Lucky put down his knife and fork. 'Alright, you always were a sticky beak, so I'm going to tell you something—tell you man to man; you're old enough and ugly enough for me to tell you man to man. Frank Murphy—hard to say it, don't like reminding myself—but he was my best mate. Mightn't have told you that before—knew him for years, so it's hard to look at Neddy sometimes; he's a dead ringer for his old man. I can see Frank in his walk, the way he knows the fish and have you ever noticed—I mean really—have you ever noticed the way he wipes his hand down his face after he yawns?' Lucky pretended to yawn and demonstrated the wipe. 'See, that sort of thing? I'll do it again.' Lucky repeated the gesture and blinked as if startled. Indicating the relevant parts, he explained, 'Frank used to always do that—fingers locked on the sides of the head, then drag the palm down the nose, over the chin and all the way to the bottom of the neck, and he'd sniff while he was doing it. The yawn; the wipe; sniff: then give himself a bit of a scratch, like yawning made him itchy.'

'Yeah, you're right,' said Tom. 'It's like Neddy—when he's bored—gets all yawny and then itchy. Wipes his face too, just like you say. Funny that.'

'Yeah, it is funny,' Lucky agreed, slurping his rum. 'You wouldn't remember how Frank did that. Was what, maybe six years ago?' Lucky tilted his head. 'Yeah, I'd reckon five years ago the lads all left. You'd be too young to recollect, but Frank did that—yawn, wipe, sniff and scratch. Yeah, he's a chip off the old block is Neddy. That's why it's hard to look at him, because there's so much of Frank in him. And I'll tell you something else—I've always got that little bloke's best interests at heart. That's why I made a promise to Frank last time I saw him, the day he went, him and all the others— Charlie, Snow, Mad Mike, Big George... your brothers.' Moisture polished Lucky's eyes. He sucked in a breath and exhaled it slowly, as though his last. 'Yeah, like I said, when the lads——' Lucky paused to take a drink. 'The day they all pissed off to France and such. That was the day I made a promise to Frank. I tell you what the promise was?'

Tom shook his head, even though he knew. His father

always told the same story after a few drinks, forgetting he'd told it before. But this time it was different; this time Lucky mentioned Tom's lost brothers. He'd never included them in the story before. Tom wanted to touch his father's arm, connect, but that would have been impossible for them both: the father because his pain was too great to release, the son because it would be too painful to receive. Lucky had to suffer; Tom had to dream of other things.

Lucky swallowed a mouthful of fish. 'I, your old man,' he elucidated, tongue slithering out as it sucked away some food caught between his teeth, 'I promised Frank I'd keep an eye on Neddy, and a promise between mates is a sacred promise. I'm always thinking of Neddy's best interest. In here!' Lucky slapped his chest. 'Don't ever forget that, Tom, don't you ever forget.'

'Jeez, Dad, stop going on about it; just didn't realise is all.'

Lucky grunted, forced by his son's embarrassment to scurry back into his burrow. He set to mashing more of his spuds before adding: 'So, like I said, invite Neddy over for lunch. Be good to see the little bastard again.'

Some time later, Tom lay beneath the covers, chewing on slabs of Stephen Crane's book, imagining himself in the cut and thrust of battle, seeing Private Tom Bramble rise above the tumult and the smoke to wave the regimental colours, bullets whizzing past his ears, mounting the palisades, inspiring his comrades toward the enemy lines. Again, his fantasies were interrupted by an argument behind the slender walls.

'Shut up, Grace!' he heard Thorn growl.

'I should start working this town for myself,' he heard her reply.

Intrigued, Tom pressed his ear to the wall.

'You can take a girl out of the gutter,' said Thorn, 'but you can't take the gutter out of the girl.'

'Least I'm not a thief, Ernest! You won't be happy until you've robbed the whole valley. And stop hogging all the bed.'

There was silence for a moment. Tom pressed his ear harder against the vertically jointed boards as Grace added: 'I hate this place.' With that, the conversation ceased.

Tom was confused by Grace's use of the word 'work'. He looked it up in his dictionary but the exercise proved less than revelatory. Realising Grace was clearly upset about being stuck in Berto, he tapped his fingers lightly on his lips and wondered what he could do to make her stay more of a pleasure and less of a chore. It came to him fast. Like any smart idea, it seemed obvious in retrospect. He decided to do something special come the morning, something better than his dad would ever do.

Chapter Five

Though still beyond the ridgeline of the mountains the new day was heralded by the call of currawongs, red wattlebirds and a flock of noisy galahs. As if at their invitation, the morning sun appeared and filled the valley, revealing tiny Berto.

Emerging from a gossamer mist, dappled by beams that shot the trees, the mail wagon clattered into town, all rattling bones as it pulled up outside the general store. The old roan Clydesdale pumped clouds of steam as white-whiskered Jock, the district postman, winched his chalky frame from down the box and pulled the mailbag from beneath the canvas. He was about to trudge into the store when a thought, nearly forgotten, sparked across the wrinkles of his brain. He circled back to his wagon and collected a large parcel.

Tom had reset his alarm clock and was up before the sun. He had rummaged through the bottom of the sideboard and procured the best linen, put hot embers from the stove into the iron and pressed out all the ancient creases; he had cut a vase full of bougainvillea from the cascades draped from the stables' roof; he had collected fresh eggs from the coop and he had polished the best silver—not seen the light of day since before his mother died. The breakfast table looked just the ticket and the crimson flowers in the centrepiece went well with all the saloon's paper cherubs. Perfect.

A glowing horseshoe sizzled and turned grey as it was plunged deep into a tub of water. Pop was already leaching sweat, when Ma rushed into his sooty shop. 'Hey, Pop,' she said, breathless with excitement, 'I got something you'll be wanting to see.'

Pop dropped his tongs and followed Ma out into the street. 'What's all the fuss about,' he asked.

Ma's backside jiggled every which way as she scurried along the wooden footpath. 'You'll not believe what's finally arrived.

As soon as they had entered the store Pop saw the parcel on the counter. He approached it slowly and respectfully, his mind entertaining thoughts of a reliquary sat high on a lofty altar. He ran his bony fingers lightly on the brown paper and up the knotted string, and he felt the big blue stamp that read: 'War Department'. Pop inhaled and sighed. 'The leg's finally arrived.' Then he slapped his hands together. 'Oh,' he announced loudly, 'this will call for a celebration.'

The smile fell from Ma's lips as if her jowls were all at once tethered to the weight of Pop's anvil. 'Never you mind the celebration,' she ordered, putting the parcel in the post office booth. 'Just you be getting to your forge, Pop O'Shaughnessy.'

Pop stole the moment to reach across the counter. He opened a glass jar and stuck his smelted hand into a treasury of candy swirls. He purloined a fistful behind Ma's back and managed a quick escape.

Thorn and Grace were down for breakfast. China cups, saucers and a pot of tea sat on a white linen tablecloth with matching napkins.

Tom entered, carrying plates of bacon, beans and eggs. Thorn put aside the newly arrived copy of the Examiner. 'You got any coffee in this place?'

'Coffee?' Tom hadn't anticipated that. 'I might have a bottle of chicory essence. Chicory is very good with boiled milk.'

Thorn picked up his knife and fork. 'I'll stick with black tea.'

As Tom poured the gambler a fresh cup, footsteps clomped down the staircase, and then a hacking cough. It was Lucky. He stumbled out the lobby door, leaned on an awning post and hawked, jettisoning phlegm into the street.

Tom remained by the table, muscles rigid while his innards wormed; he had not reckoned on his father's rising. 'So,' he squeaked falsetto, before dragging his voice back down to tenor, 'would you like another pot of tea?'

Thorn ignored him, slicing his bacon into bite-sized chunks.

'Yes, please,' Grace answered quickly, covering for any perceived impoliteness.

Tom turned to go. Pulling aside the magenta curtain of beads, he found himself confronted by Lucky, a brimming chamber pot in his father's hand. The lad pushed past and escaped to the kitchen. Through the swaying beads, Lucky sighted the elegant table setting. He quickly chased his son down the hall and cornered him against the kitchen stove. Dark brown wastewater splashed to the floor. 'Why are you using the good, fucking silver? That's your mother's silver!' He crossed himself, now panting, more urine splashing. 'Reserved for special occasions.'

'What special occasions?' Tom hissed, desperate that Grace not hear them arguing. 'There hasn't been a special occasion here since Mum died.'

As if struck by the hand of God, Lucky stumbled backwards and dropped his chamber pot.

The smashing porcelain was clearly audible in the saloon. Thorn snorted and looked across at Grace. 'Sounds like the chef's not happy.' He scooped up a forkful of beans. 'Hope that wasn't the tea.'

Lucky traipsed around the shattered Willow Ware and pee, stuck his head into the sink and washed water through his greasy hair. Emerging dripping, but somehow renewed, he announced, 'Okay, you're right, no pockets in a shroud. We'll make today's lunch with Neddy a special occasion too. We'll use the good fucking silver all over again. How about that, hey? Twice in one fucking day!'

Tom was immediately suspicious of his father's generosity, but spurned the thought and stepped outside to collect the garbage can, the bucket and the mop. He felt dejected, but his efforts were not in vain. As he had hurried from the saloon, a smile had danced across the lips of Grace.

Mad Mike and Snow sat in The Widow Philpot's dining room and wiped their mouths clean of lamb chop grease with The

Widow's needle lace napkins. Big George Philpot gazed across from a glass cabinet. He was hand-coloured and standing in front of a painted backdrop in the studio of the Armidale Galleries and Picture Framers. Snow stared at the photograph and recognized Big George had never been that big in stature, not tall or broad; in fact, he was a smallish fellow, but he was big in heart and baptised big by those who knew him well. Snow folded his napkin and remembered that was the reason they nominated him corporal of their Section—the Berto Section, D Company, New England's Own. That and the fact Big George had already seen service as Private Philpot in the Second Anglo-Boer War, with medals from Bloemfontein to prove it.

'Thank you for the bonza brekky, Mrs Philpot,' Mike enthused.

'Yeah, thanks,' said Snow.

'Please,' The Widow Philpot protested, 'no need for such formality around here. Like I've said so many times before, fine to call me Gladys.'

'Nobody can fry an egg as you can, Gladys,' said Mike as the stockmen got up to go.

'It's a pleasure to have such lads to attend to. Busy day ahead?'

'Yep,' said Snow, 'thankful it's Saturday.'

'B-B-Better still was Sunday.'

'Yes, Mike, I expect so,' Gladys agreed. 'Going out to the pub, are you, tonight?'

'Yep,' said Snow again, putting on his hat.

'Alright, take care of yourselves, and I'll wash your bed

sheets in the copper if you like.'

'Oh, thank you, Mrs Phil———' Mike corrected himself. 'I mean Gladys.'

'Yeah, thanks,' said Snow.

'It's a pleasure. Now off you go and don't fall off your horses and break your silly necks.'

Mad Mike and Snow rode off, leaving The Widow Philpot at her front door waving goodbye. She liked to have the lads to look after. She and Big George were never blessed with little ones, and life could be lonely on the land, and hard on a war widow's pension, but Gladys still ran a few head of cattle, and she had the boy's room and board payments, plus a little put aside from what she received from selling off the west paddock to her neighbour, Preston Logan.

The Widow Philpot walked back inside her cottage and daydreamed more about her bunkhouse lodgers. Snow is a bit of a dark horse, she thought, but that Mad Mike, why, he isn't mad at all; he's always been a sweet boy and the shrapnel scar from ear to mouth takes nothing from the sweetness. I do like Mike. Clearing the dirty dishes from the table, she whispered: 'What the dickens! So few men to go around these days, a girl cannot afford to be fussy.'

Peggy splashed the porridge pot into the sink and scrubbed away the sticky leftover oatmeal. Charlie kissed her on the cheek. 'See you, love.'

Peggy pulled behind her ear a wayward strand of greying hair. 'Try not to get too pissed tonight. I've got a list of chores as long as my arm for you to do tomorrow and it'll be an unpleasant job if you've got a sickness in your guts.'

'Thought Sunday was a day of rest,' said Charlie, circling the table, kissing daughters and tussling towhead sons.

'That rule's for those who take such matters without your grain of salt, Charles Ward. Ride down to Grafton, attend the midnight mass, and you can put your boots up all Sunday long.'

No way was Charlie doing that. He went to work haunted by the thought, come Sunday, he'd have barely time for his weekly tub.

Tom was set to flee the town as fast as physics would allow. He fastened the buckle on Copenhagen's bridle, dropped the cloth onto his horse's back and went to collect the saddle. Grace was standing at the stables' entrance. 'Nice looking gelding,' she smiled.

Startled, Tom protested: 'He's not a gelding.'

Grace played absent-mindedly with an overhanging branch of the bougainvillea but her eyes were fixed on Tom. He darted to the saddle rail, and lifting his saddle over his forearm, fought against a suddenly oppressive silence. 'Copenhagen's a stallion,' he declared, marching back to his horse. 'He's named after a famous stallion, Wellington's horse at the Battle of Waterloo.'

'The Duke of Wellington?' Grace asked.

'Yep, the hero of Waterloo.'

Grace walked in and sat on the rail. 'Like the pub?'

'What do you mean by that?' asked Tom defensively, his discomfort made worse by Grace's uninvited entry, acting like she owned the place.

Grace folded her arms and rephrased her description. 'What I mean is The Hero of Waterloo is a famous Sydney watering hole.'

This also drew a blank. Tom had no idea what she was talking about. She pushed forward with more explanation. 'It's a famous alehouse, hostelry, ye old rubbity-dub that's down in The Rocks.'

Tom frowned as he gently swung the saddle onto Copenhagen's back. 'I'm not talking about a pub.'

Grace laid her hands on her cheeks, fearing he might think she was making fun of him. 'But there really is a pub called The Hero of Waterloo.'

'Never heard of it.' Tom insisted as he slipped down the offside stirrup. 'Anyway, like I said, not talking about a pub; talking about a famous general.'

'Who had a horse?'

'Of course he had a horse,' Tom snapped, his shame erupting hot. 'All generals have horses!'

Grace stopped speaking and became downcast. Tom bent over and reached under Copenhagen to grab the girth. As he stood up he noticed her change of mood. He had hurt her feelings. His embarrassment over the fiasco of breakfast was achieving a result at odds with his best intentions. 'Sorry,' he said. 'I didn't mean to be abrupt. You weren't to know Wellington had a horse.'

Grace looked up and smiled again. 'You weren't abrupt, just passionate.'

'Oh, alright, that's good then,' Tom mumbled. He

clasped the saddle's Bates Buckle onto the lip of the girth buckle.

Grace leaned against a rafter post and laid her hands on her thighs as though she thought a breeze would shortly bloom beneath her skirt. 'So,' she continued, 'Wellington's horse was named Copenhagen?'

'Yes,' said Tom, patting his horse's shoulder as he cinched. 'The stallion was transported over to him when he was fighting in Spain during the French attack on Lisbon. You may have read of Wellington's defensive perimeter—the Lines of Torres Vedras. Was the first instance of the large-scale use of telegraph by a military unit, sending information from his frontline outposts back to GHQ. Think it was around 1809.' Tom warmed to the subject, enjoying the opportunity to give voice to an obsession few appreciated. 'The General at that time was still Arthur Wellesley, Viscount Wellington. He hadn't yet won the string of victories that led to his being created the first Duke of Wellington. Hope I'm not boring you, am I?'

'No,' said Grace, 'not at all,' and she meant it. Tom could talk about postage stamps or bird watching or anything else that might take his fancy; it was the teller, not the tale that interested her.

Tom rested his arm on the saddle and settled into his story. 'Copenhagen was the Duke's favourite mount. He rode that warhorse for the whole day, the whole of the Battle of Waterloo—imagine that, never took a break—while Napoleon was switching horses all the time. The opposing commanders were different that way. During the charge of d'Erlon's corps,

Napoleon's mount was Marengo—he was a stallion too—but the rest of the day he was on mares. Napoleon preferred mares.'

'Well, he was French.'

Tom's wave of enthusiasm was now cresting, and though he heard Grace's bawdy observation, he listened to no voice save his own. 'Actually, Napoleon was Corsican,' he explained. 'Being Corsican is like you're a cross between an Italian and a Frenchy.' Tom threaded the Bates Buckle through the keepers on the girth and doubled back the tongue. 'And Napoleon's mares were all white Arabs. There was Marie, Desiree… can't remember the others, but the Iron Duke rode the one horse all day—the noble Irish steed, Copenhagen. Horse and man survived the battle without a scratch, even though they were always where the fighting was worst. When Lord Uxbridge's leg got blown off—I mean it, God's truth— blown to bits by a lump of shrapnel, and not inches away from the Duke, his Copenhagen didn't shift an inch, didn't bat an eyelid, and nor would my Copenhagen here.' Tom ran his hand over the horse's hindquarters. 'No way known would he do that.'

'Student of history?' asked Grace, her dainty eyebrows raised.

Tom walked back to the rail. 'Pretty informed about horses—Robert E Lee's horse was named Traveller; Alexander the Great's horse was named Bucephalus.

'Bu-ce-phallus?'

'No, Bucephalus.'

'Obviously another stallion.'

Tom rolled his eyes. She thought he didn't know what phallus meant, but he did; it was in his dictionary. He grabbed his saddlebag and leather-cased quart-pot kit and cursed himself again for going to so much trouble to serve Grace a nice breakfast; it had all gone up the creek. Grace was never going to see him as anything but a country clod.

As he tied the kit to his saddle, he imagined the places Grace must know, the people she had met. He couldn't compete with all those types who went to balls and banquets and palaces too. Then he wondered if there were palaces in Sydney. No, he decided, probably not, but some fair-sized houses.

Tom led Copenhagen out of the stables. Grace hopped up and followed him. She stepped lightly, her hands behind her back. 'Could you take me for a ride sometime?'

Tom was astonished by her request, and though his heart leapt, it was quickly held in check by a sharpened wariness. 'Yeah, could do that, but what about Mr Thorn?'

'My Mr Thorn wouldn't notice, or give a damn even if he did.'

'Jeez, I don't know,' Tom muttered, assessing city people very odd.

'Alright,' said Grace, returning to the pub, 'if that's the way you feel——'

'Tomorrow's Sunday,' Tom interrupted, 'pub's closed. How about then?'

Grace twirled toward him, lips parting, lusciously moist, as if to speak. Tom swooned, a dandelion before a breeze, but then a depressing seed of doubt took root. 'Of course,' he warned, 'provided the tanker hasn't arrived by then.'

Grace coiled away to stroke Copenhagen and admire his velvet face. 'Don't horses have beautiful eyes?'

'Yes,' said Tom, looking straight at Grace, 'they do.'

Minutes later, she stood under the pub's old awning and watched both horse and rider depart from town.

Ma was there, sweeping her store's front walkway. Grace listened to Ma say: 'Hey, Tom, Snow's leg arrived. Come with the morning mail.'

And Tom said: 'About time.'

'Yeah,' said Ma, 'bloody government.'

Tom gave Copenhagen a gentle squeeze and cantered out of town, a fishing rod held in his hand like it was a lance. As soon as he was gone, Ma turned to Grace, the old woman staring like the city girl was something exotic and dangerous: a tigress left behind by a circus.

Grace scurried into the pub. She could sense the cold finger of Ma's stare running down her spine. It made her cringe as though naked and ashamed, like the day she walked out of a powder room with her summer dress tucked up into her panties.

As she climbed the staircase to her room, Grace brooded on the nuisance old women like Ma could be. They were everywhere, ever-vigilant custodians of the public's morality. Flies, always on call, ready to ruin the best-laid picnic. She could count on one hand the number of old biddies who had not hated her on sight. Grace wished they were like men: easy to charm. Women like Ma were nothing but hard work. In all her life no woman had ever chosen to protect Grace.

Tom and Neddy sat on the log, fishing for cod, as light from a sky unblemished by cloud filtered through the trees and once more dappled the rocks and ferns.

'What's her name again?'

'Grace.'

'Yeah, nice name.'

'Yeah,' said Tom. Then he sighed and said more slowly: 'Yeah.'

Neddy glanced at his mate's reflective eyes. 'Seems like you've got a soft spot for Grace.'

Tom frowned. 'Strike me lucky, Neddy, what good would that do me? She's a city girl. 'Sides, she'll be gone soon as the tanker arrives. Never see her again.'

Tom hooked something on his line. 'Cripes, what's this?' He gripped the handle, spinning the reel like billyo, the rod bending such as it might break if pushed a fraction more. Neddy saw something olive green.

'Bloody hell,' said Tom, his catch bursting from the creek and swinging on the line, 'not another bloody turtle.'

Neddy clicked his cheek. 'Shouldn't use yabbies. Make yourself a couple of decent spinnerbaits.'

Tom tried to remove the hook from the turtle's mouth.

Neddy pushed him aside. 'Give it here.'

'It's alright.' Tom pulled away. 'I've got it.'

'No, you haven't. Come on, hand him over.'

Tom ignored the request.

'Crikey,' Neddy persisted, 'you'll hurt the little bugger.'

Reluctantly, Tom stopped. 'Yeah, sorry,' he grumbled.

'Here you go.' He handed over the turtle.

In a flash, the hook was out. Neddy offered back the catch. 'See, easy.'

Tom wasn't interested. 'Nah, you keep it. Give it to your mum for tea.'

Neddy put the live turtle in his dilly bag.

'Oh, yeah, that's right,' said Tom, sticking fresh bait onto his hook, 'Nearly forgot—you want to come into town for lunch?'

'Why?'

'Dad wants to see you. Says you haven't been around for a spell. You could check out Grace's car.'

'Ah, I don't know.'

'I'm cooking lamb chops like your dad used to do.'

'You reckon?'

Tom recast his line. 'Yeah, blood oath.'

Neddy was unconvinced. 'Blackfellas can't go into the pub.'

'Your dad pretty much lived there.'

'He was Irish.'

Tom could see his friend was pretty riled. 'So what are you all sore about?'

'In town I'm a blackfella, in the camp I'm a whitefella. Reckon I'd like to go to Sydney. There, I'd just be a fella.'

A kookaburra perched in the hoop pine. It cackled loud and long, and whooped it up, outstaying its welcome.

Constable Grimes trotted into town, followed by Reverend Goddard and Nurse Cradock, both from Grafton. Goddard, amongst other things, was the padre at the Grafton Gaol. Cradock was involved with something similar. They bounced along on the seat of an uncovered wagon. It jangled and clanged when its wheels crossed ruts in the road. Goddard steered the horse to the front of the pub and parked beside the hitching rail. The three visitors entered the Berto Hotel through the lobby entrance, making a show of avoiding the double doors to the public bar. Grace listened to them pass by her door as they bustled down the hall to Lucky's room.

One hundred yards away due north, Tom rode into town with Neddy, both on the sturdy spine of Copenhagen. Neddy didn't like to visit Berto; the town called to mind his dad. Though his memories of Frank were blurred and soft behind the gauze of infancy, the colours endured, bright as when he first witnessed them. He also retained the memory of his father's smell; it was like smouldering gum leaves: or old and soggy boots, gamey and manure-ish. Neddy had loved his dad and because of that, he missed him—visiting Berto reminded him of just how much. He recalled Lowanna holding him, trying to staunch his tears, when Frank's life tore away from his. Last thing he remembered was his dad's feet dangling from the back of the cart as he and the other men—men same as his dad, or at least appearing the same as his dad—faded from his view. Was over five years ago now, and since that time the blackfella camp had been his home, but it was not his world. That lay somewhere between the camp and Berto. It was a special place where he could be anonymous and free, and nothing cared, not animal nor plant, whether he was black or brown or brindle, white or sunburned pink. In the black's camp he was brown, grown self-conscious of his paler skin, but in Berto too he felt himself to be an alien. He was embarrassed he felt that way because Pop and Ma were always friendly; she gave him lollies and it was fun to watch Pop shoe a horse. On the other hand, Lucky sometimes scared him, but he found it strangely nice how Lucky's smell rekindled memories of his dad. Like the land, Neddy was a place two cultures had to find a way to share. Pop would have said he had two schooners on the bar, but for Neddy both glasses were half empty.

Snow galloped past Copenhagen like the boys were closing on a winning post. Tom and Neddy ate his dust as the stockman dismounted and rushed into the general store.

'Yee-ha!' he hollered from within. 'Me new leg!'

From the front door of the store, old and rustic Fritz flew out and clattered on the road.

'Finally got here,' said Neddy.

'Yep,' Tom confirmed, 'arrived with this morning's mail.'

Neddy noticed the wagon outside the pub. 'Who owns that?'

Tom blinked. 'Haven't got a clue.'

Beyond her hotel room, Grace saw Tom and wondered who the brown boy was. They rode up to the pub and disappeared beneath the awning. Standing on tiptoe, Grace could discern Tom was tying Copenhagen's reins up to the hitching rail.

Inside the general store, Snow sat on a barrel, admiring his newly delivered prosthesis. It looked so real; under boots and moleskins nobody would ever guess he was short one leg.

Ma walked in from back of her general store with a brand new right boot. 'Here you go. I kept it nice and safe for the big day, just the way you asked.'

'Thanks, Ma,' said Snow, slipping his artificial foot into the fresh and glossy leather. 'Now, the moment I've been waiting for.'

'We've all of us been waiting for,' Ma corrected, peering over the rims of her reading glasses.

Snow smiled boyishly and stood up. Right boot squeaking, he limped proudly around the haberdashery section and past the tinned biscuits to lean an elbow against the counter of the postal booth.

'That's real fine, Snow.'

'Bit uneven.'

'Got to break in the new boot. Get Pop to wear it down a bit on his lathe.'

Snow regarded himself in an advertising mirror. 'Wait till all the girls see me down in Grafton.'

'Snow, every widow and spinster from miles about will be flocking in, every homestead parlour empty.'

'And every bench in the dance hall full. It'll be standing-room-only, but I'll be sittin' pretty with a sheila in both arms and one on each leg.'

'Specially the new one.'

'Did you know I can tango?'

Ma put her hands on her ample hips. 'No, I don't believe it.'

'It's true enough, Ma.'

'Oh, they'll be printing wanted posters of you, Snowy McKay.' Ma came over all maternal; though naught that passed her birth canal had lived long enough to walk, Ma was a mother to all the men in those remoter parts, and while she was loath to play favourites, Snow was special: deep tanned, strong jaw but boyish eyes, hands and teeth not gnarled at all; and that thatch of hair, streaked blond by healthy, outdoor living. 'My goodness, yes,' she felt compelled to mutter, 'what a treat. Best looking man I've seen since leaving Dublin.'

Chapter Six

The doors to the public bar were locked. A sign in the window read: 'Gone to Lunch.' Tom stood at the stove, frying lamb chops, making sure they were nicely browned all over. At the kitchen table Lucky and Neddy sat in silence. Centre of the table, beside a pot of mashed potatoes and a tub of butter, was a golden loaf of bread. Freshly baked by Ma that morning, the gentle fragrance of the bread enlaced the rich aroma of the lamb in an intoxicating brew. Tom loved Ma's bread. She had been baking a loaf for the Brambles almost every day since Tom's mum, Rachel, passed to the better place. Neddy, too, adored Ma's bread; it was so crispy on the outside, but sweet and feather-light within. When he crunched the crust between his teeth, he would revel in the creamy sugars the bread released, melting across his tongue, each taste bud blossoming.

All was fine, except this rare act of hospitality made Neddy wary; he couldn't help but feel something was amiss. An upstairs floorboard creaked. He looked at the ceiling. 'What's that noise?'

'It's one of the guests,' grunted Lucky, breaking in before Tom could answer, responding as if to gavel an end to the matter.

Neddy nodded slowly. 'Oh, yeah, right. I remember

now. Not used to hearing people upstairs. Tom was talking 'bout all that stuff when we was gone fishing.'

'What stuff?' Lucky snarled.

Tom stepped across to the table and started slicing the bread. 'Just stuff; you know, ordinary stuff like saying as how we've got guests and all.'

Though the old publican's hostility was unnerving, it sharpened Neddy's curiosity. As with the deceased cat, he needed to know more. Pretending rustic innocence he agreed with Tom, parroting: 'Yeah, how you've got guests and all.' More assertively, he said to Lucky: 'Never seen you with guests before.'

'Sure—we get guests,' Tom interrupted, 'only not that often.'

Lucky turned disdainful. 'You know, Neddy, this is a hotel.'

'But I've never seen a guest here before.'

'Well, mate,' Lucky growled, his voice rumbling louder with each word, 'we've got guests now.'

Neddy shrank back, his silence filling him completely as a foot inside a sock. He yearned to escape to the logic of the bush.

Tom handed Neddy a slice of bread. 'Hey, she's right,' he reassured, hoping his mate hadn't forgotten Lucky's way of railing at things. 'Dad, why don't you ask Neddy how his mum's going?'

'What's that you're saying?' mumbled Lucky.

'Ask about Neddy's mum. You know, Lowanna. You haven't seen her for a while. You might want to ask how she's going.'

Lucky straightened his cutlery. 'How's your mum?'

'She's fine, just fine,' Neddy murmured cautiously.

'Good,' said Lucky. 'Nice to hear.'

Neddy stared down at his plate, longing to speak the truth about his mum, revealing how each day she withered more, but he bit his lip and simply whispered: 'Thanks, nice of you to think of her. She asks after you too… from time to time."

With that exchange of pleasantries the corroded visor of Lucky's face opened to reveal a man whose eyes saw more than his mind could reconcile. 'No worries,' he said softly, and for several seconds, his thoughts trawled a catacomb of memories. Then, as though startled, he switched to Tom. 'When we gunna fucking eat?'

Tom shifted to the stove. 'Getting the chops right now.'

Neddy looked around the kitchen. He couldn't see any sign of pudding. If such were offered, he'd decline and be gone. He'd rather leave on foot than wait a moment longer for a ride back home on Copenhagen.

'Two?' asked Tom, holding a chop with a pair of tongs.

Neddy said thanks as Tom served him from a big iron frying pan.

'I want three,' said Lucky.

'Here you go then.' Tom put three sizzling chops onto his father's plate.

Lucky noted there was only one chop remaining in the pan. 'Glad you made enough for seconds.'

Neddy offered up his plate. 'You want one of mine,

Uncle Lucky?'

'No,' said Tom, returning the pan to the stove, 'If Dad wants more, I can always fry up another chop or two.' Tapping out a dollop of mash for his mate, he continued, 'You enjoy what you've got here.'

Disgruntled, Lucky's hands shook as he tried to pour more rum. Neddy put down his plate and assessed the old soak's grip on life to be no better than that upon his bottle.

As if reading Neddy's mind, Lucky's rheumy eyes shot up at him, lower lids hanging loose, the insides as yellow as pee on a steamy day and filled with lumpy veins. 'What you staring at?' he demanded.

Neddy looked away. 'Sorry, it was nothing.' He noticed a blowfly land on his spuds. The insect inspired him to turn back. 'I thought I saw a midge crawling into your' —he had to look away again— 'think it was your left eye, but I reckon was just a bit of dust or something.'

Lucky ground a knuckle into his right socket and analysed what he'd unearthed, finding nothing from the probe save some granules of sleepy seed.

'No,' said Neddy, waving away the blowie, 'was the other eye, but it's gone now.'

Lucky came over surlier. 'If there was something crawling near me eye, don't you reckon I'd bloody well know?'

Tom sat down and grabbed his knife and fork. 'He didn't mean anything by it, Dad. Don't stand on ceremony, Neddy, tuck in before your food gets cold.'

Neddy didn't move. Lucky sliced into the larger of his chops, cutting off a thick wedge. Caramelised on the surface, moist and pink inside, it was poised at the end of his fork, its succulence beckoning, when Neddy asked, 'Aren't we gunna give thanks?'

Tom bowed his head. Lucky hesitated, and for a second time he felt the downy-feathered brush of compassion. Lowering his fork, he too bowed his head. Without protest, both Brambles had abided by the call to prayer, the way folks do.

There was a long silence.

'Neddy?' whispered Tom, 'We're waiting.'

'For what?' asked Neddy. 'Your table.'

'Your idea.'

Neddy accepted Tom had a point.

Lucky took the moment to slurp more rum.

Neddy rattled off the words he had so often heard from his mother, and which both mother and son had learnt from the mouth of the circuit priest up at their little wooden church with canvas walls: 'For what we are about to receive, may the Lord make us truly thankful.'

'Amen to that,' said Lucky.

Goddard and Craddock entered from the hall.

Tom looked up. 'What's this?'

Neddy knew what it was. His perception of the world began to flash as he jumped up from his seat. Though he had never said a word to Tom, a part of him had feared a day like this would come the copper-coloured morning his father left for war. His saying grace was a plea to get back to the bush unharmed, not praise in gratitude for chops.

Neddy moved as a cheetah, cornering tightly and

throwing his weight toward the open kitchen door and the veranda just beyond. A blizzard of questions filled his head with every loping step. Was freedom only for the dead, and if his priest was right, not even then? He wondered why God had given him this life, only to make it torture, threatening worse in the next if not grateful for the pain. Whitefellas said it was the Lord in heaven's will, but when taken up by men, was quickly called extortion. He got to the door. 'Neddy, where are you going?' cried Goddard, he and the nurse in lumbering pursuit.

On the veranda Grimes lay in wait. As Neddy exploded from within, the trooper grabbed him. Neddy kicked and screamed. Grimes and Goddard took one arm apiece and dragged him back into the kitchen. Tom was now up from the table, pressed against the sideboard by shock and all the scuffling. He lacked the wit to do all else but gaze at Lucky for an answer. None came, his father seeming only half awake, as if the room were silent as a grotto.

Neddy was hauled out through the hotel's lobby entrance. With every drawn out pace he screeched and twisted, his calloused heels striking his captors' shins, but it made not a skerrick of difference. The wagon appeared as he had seen it not an hour before, but now his focus sluiced away the earlier mud and panned its purpose. He bawled, 'I'm not going. I'm not going!'

'Come on now, Neddy Murphy,' Goddard pleaded through gritted teeth, 'this is all for the best.'

Tom followed through the lobby door, still not fully comprehending. Nurse Craddock brushed on past, and with her whiff of starch and bleach, the pressgang's mission became clear. Tom had read about this sort of thing in the Examiner, but Neddy was no orphan, no Moses set adrift among the bulrushes; he had a mum, a loving mum—Lowanna.

On catching sight of Tom, Neddy sang out to his mate. Tom dashed toward him, but was held in check by Lucky. The son was finished with the fifth commandment. Pushing his father from his path, he leapt from the pub veranda and pounced on Grimes. The trooper thrust back with his wooden truncheon. Tom's belly heaved as his lungs compressed, devoid of air, and his legs gave way beneath him, his body balled up like a fetus.

Responding to the din, Grace sneaked downstairs and peeked out from the lobby door. Snow and Ma strode from the general store to see what the fuss was all about. Pop wandered out of his blacksmith's shop, a stockman customer in tow. The whole town was drawn out to the street, all of them inquisitive, then horrified and utterly confused.

Face ropey, twisted, Lucky rushed to his son and tried to give a helping hand. Tom kicked him away as Neddy kept on howling.

Nurse Craddock watched as her charge was thrown into the rear of the wagon. Crashing upon the hardwood planks, Neddy snatched a glimpse of her. The nurse's image summoned memories of the miniature pieta in his little wooden church. 'Please, don't do this,' he beseeched, appealing to the maternal instinct, kindness and mercy, the Blessed Virgin. 'I'll do anything you want—just don't take me away. Please, oh, God, please, no.'

Grimes shackled Neddy's legs in chains, and in that instant, the boy's face froze: the genesis of an ancient anger he would carry, cold as a slab, for years before it thawed. 'You gunna pay,' he murmured, and then, seeming to read words branded on the trooper's cheeks, he added, 'Whitefella bastard!'

The nurse tried to cover his mouth. 'Enough of that,' she spat.

Neddy jerked his head from side to side and his lips escaped. 'Bloody bitch!'

Craddock, horrified, upbraided him. 'Such language! Neddy, you must learn to behave in a civilised fashion.' She tried again to cover his mouth. He bit her.

The nurse yelped. Itching to slap him, she raised her hand and seethed: 'You little heathen devil!'

Reverend Goddard took her arm. 'It's alright, Sister, we'll get him straightened out at the mission. The Lord is patient and bestows in his great wisdom the ways to calm a savage aspect and strip bare to the burning light the beast within.'

Above the street, upstairs within his room, Thorn lay low, shuffling cards, but the sermon rising to his window spun a silken thread, ensnaring memories of Old Kentucky homes. Peeping from behind the curtain's lace, he spotted Grimes and ducked away.

The Reverend helped the nurse up to her seat. Neddy's chains clawed the planks and thrashed the wagon bed behind her settling rump, but his cries for aid went unacknowledged, simmering to whimpers, his tears splashed down on stone.

Tom climbed to his hands and knees, wild-eyed and struggling for breath, but found himself in shadow. Staring skyward he saw Grimes mount his horse and throw a nod old Lucky's way. 'Thanks for that. I owe you one,' he grunted as he eased back in the saddle.

Tom gulped enough new air to swing around. With mouth still bloodhound loose and panting, he glared at his dad, but Lucky's thoughts were gone again, having drifted to some other place.

Goddard sighed as he took up the driver's seat. Seizing the reins, he swung the wagon south and trotted out of town. As the flatbed rumbled by, Neddy and Tom passed into each other's view. Neddy's eyes flashed accusingly, desolated by his friend's betrayal. Tom stared back, his lips mouthing elusive words. Rising to his feet he staggered after the wagon, but Grimes was there to block the way, his horse pushing him aside. Once more Tom hit the dirt, but quick to raise his head, he caught a glimpse of toad-egg eyes, the trooper's chin held high, his jaw outstretched in triumph of a job well done. Grimes turned his horse and departed, trotting behind his little posse. Tom collapsed onto the veranda step and clung onto his stomach. He was a mess, in turmoil, all consternation and despair.

Grace dropped into a well of fellow-feeling. Tom was immediately much older and nobler in her eyes. She sat down by his side and tried to ease his pain. Whatever it was she had encountered, it was an education on the ways of the bush, and the city she'd abandoned arose more worthy in her estimation. 'Tom,' she spoke tenderly, 'what's going on?'

Tom fought to hold in check a weeping rage. 'I led Neddy to a trap.'

Grace looked up at Lucky, assuming he would take the blame and give his son much needed solace, but all he did was scamper back inside his pub.

Pop sighed and returned to his forge, his customer following. Snow watched them leave then noticed Grace. Seeing the softness of her touch upon Tom's arm, seeing her hold the young lad close, the stockman's weathered heart began to splinter, his short-lived happiness a ruin. He untethered his horse from the rail, and in the dust, he saw his discarded friend, old Fritz. He gathered up the clattering parts, sweat-polished wood held tenderly, as if a broken child.

Neddy's tumbrel faded away to black and silver lines, dancing in a mirage of shiny air. 'Poor little mite,' said Ma as she set off toward her store, resigning herself again to God's mysterious ways. 'I'll light a candle.'

'Bloody government,' Snow muttered as he climbed into the saddle, trying to adjust himself; his new limb seemed odd against the stirrup.

At her front door, Ma turned to Snow, a rare frown pinching her mottled brow, betraying her struggle to reclaim normality from a pickpocket who had vanished into destiny's dark alley. 'How's the new leg on the horse?' she enquired, labouring to be mundane.

Snow tucked Fritz under his arm. 'It's fine,' he lied, adjusting the reins. 'Thanks for asking, Ma. I'll see you round.'

Squeezing his surviving leg against his horse's flank, the stockman angled north. Ma waved goodbye like he was on a trek to somewhere distant, Grafton or Glen Innes. Snow thumbed the brim of his hat and trotted back to work.

Tom heard the hooves' report and saw the stockman leaving. He pushed Grace away and ran after him, she left to her own devices, alone on the pub veranda, with only Ma still there for company. Tom's dismissal hurt. She found it hard to accept how much.

Snow was moving fast. Tom fought to catch up. 'Snow!' he yelled, panting, 'Snow, slow down! Snow, I'm begging you, slow down!'

The stockman asked his horse to walk, but his gaze stayed fixed ahead.

Tom ran up beside him, puffing. 'Snow, you saw what happened, didn't you?'

'Yeah,' he admitted, 'I saw.'

'Why didn't you help?'

Snow remained silent, ignoring the question.

Tom wasn't about to give up. 'I can't believe you didn't do anything to help Neddy. Not you, not Pop, nobody.'

'Was nothing to be done.'

'You think Frank Murphy would have said that?'

'You leave Frank out of this.'

'You were in the same platoon, the same section. You were mates. You saw Frank die.'

Snow closed his eyes, trying to shut out the memory.

'I'm sorry,' Tom wheezed, 'but you did. No secret that. So don't you owe something to Frank?'

Snow pulled up his horse and looked down. 'I like you, Tom. You're a good kid, but what did you expect me to do? I take on Grimes and me new leg—' He tapped it. 'Waited years for this bugger of thing—its first night out on the town, it won't be spent someplace nice, the Grafton dance hall, the ladies and such. No, it'll be spent at the bloody Grafton courthouse, in the bloody lock-up.'

Snow asked his horse to trot. Tom stood and watched him get away. 'How was it in France?' he shouted. 'What was it really like in the trenches? How many Huns did you kill? Weren't worried about your leg then!'

Snow stopped, loosely swung his reins around and walked his horse on back to Tom. The lad was getting nervous, but remained pugnacious. He squinted up into a silhouette, the stockman's features lost in shadows, haloed by a sun that blanched the blue from the noon hour sky.

'Tom——'

'Yeah.'

'Don't talk 'bout stuff you'll never understand.'

'When you and Charlie and Mad Mike get on the grog at the pub, you're always yapping on about all the mademoiselles from Armentieres you parlez-voused!'

'Sport, we did a lot of parlez-vousing. Might have been the last vous we'd ever parl.'

'But what about the battles, the glory, the code of honour?'

Snow again turned his horse due north and in that moment quietly sighed: 'You don't want to know.'

'Then why did you fight?'

'So you'd never need to know.'

The stockman pressed his seat into the saddle and

galloped off, soon far away.

Chapter Seven

Lucky sat in the kitchen and looked at the uneaten lamb chops. The word had got out and a swarm of flies had invaded the room. Thrumming, they blanketed the plates and stove. Lucky waved away the annoying pests as best he could and was bitten several times by stable flies. In a flurry he scraped the meals into the frying pan and carried the scraps outside. Sidestepping a whip snake, he lurched to the top of the yard and dumped the chops in front of the lantana that choked the forest's edge. Soon the magpies and the crows would muscle out the insects.

Lucky re-entered the kitchen and discovered his unwanted guests still covering the dirty plates. He grabbed the Mortein from the cupboard and sprinkled the powder over all the crockery, the table and the frying pan. Within minutes there would be a broom shovel full of the dead: dull grey house flies, bronze and green-bottle blowflies, brown stable flies and even some dark purple bushies.

The killing done, Lucky went off to open the bar. As he walked along the hall he saw Grace sitting on the staircase. Hearing his approach, she leapt up, thinking it might be Tom. On seeing the crumpled publican all expectancy vanished from her face. She turned away and retreated upstairs to her room.

Lucky took no notice. Removing the latchkey from his

pocket, he meandered into the public bar and went to open the double doors. Through the greasy windowpanes he saw his son returning. Lucky braced himself for conflict but Tom advanced no further than the hitching rail. Mounting Copenhagen, he trotted up the road without so much as looking his father's way.

From her window Grace had also noticed Tom's return. She immediately wheeled to the mirror to wipe away her smudged mascara. Thorn still lay on the bed, unmoved by all the commotion. With a yawn he announced: 'Might mosey on down to the bar.' He put on his coat and shifted Grace aside to share her mirror, making sure his hair passed muster. 'You should get out too,' he added. 'Take an afternoon stroll or something—instead of standing at the window like goddamned Rapunzel.'

Snow galloped up the road for almost a mile before he slowed his horse to a walk. Tom had called him out and he knew the lad was right; the stockman had grown too old to be fearless: reckless enough to build a wall of confidence so high actions couldn't see their consequences. At twenty-four he'd seen enough of that, but things were different back in the day. Then the younger Snow could get a bit rowdy, especially on the grog. Once he made the mistake of getting into a blue in a pub down at Grafton. He ended up being nabbed by the coppers and thrown in the lockup. That was all right at first, but as dawn's early light shone through the bars, he found himself laid low before the dunny can. Was then Snow decided to take his mind off his depressing and embarrassing predicament by counting the number of tiles in his cell, both cream and green. He had reached about two thirds through when he came across a tile that had a communiqué scratched into its surface. He read it out aloud: 'There are one thousand four hundred and sixty-two bloody tiles in this cell!'

Snow was eventually hauled up before the magistrate, and for his efforts copped a ten bob fine and was ordered to pay for a broken chair. Since then he had studiously avoided the Grafton lockup. He always made sure his blues were in Berto, and out on Main Street too, if time and etiquette allowed. Nah, Snow thought, never want to see the inside of a cell again. Never want to see a war again neither. Someone else can do it next time.

Snow then brought to mind Big George Philpot. The Corp had seen war before—seen it up close in South Africa—but he still volunteered with the rest of the Berto section. He was up for a second shot, and when he got to be in amongst it, was always unruffled. Even when he was swearing at some poor bastard in the section, yelling above the guns, it was just a job that had to be done. Big George knew what he was up against and did it anyway. Big George had guts.

Snow never judged himself brave, just stupid enough to slide in at the top of the meat grinder and lucky enough to slide out at the bottom in one piece—least most of him. The stockman took the wooden leg from under his arm and rested it on the horse's withers, his thoughts drifting. Tom had seen the horror of his best mate taken, but Snow was not much older when he saw his best mate gone for good. Snow was born the same day as Tom's brother, Darcy. All the folks in the valley nicknamed them the Berto twins. They even looked a bit alike, but their characters were different. Snow was the better horseman, better athlete all round, while Darcy was more like Tom; he liked the books. Not like Harry. He was the oldest of the Bramble boys, and a strapping lad he sure was too; nobody at the little one-room school would ever get one over Harry. Darcy was more of a thinker. He should have been a staff officer; he would have been good with all the maps and such. Snow pulled up his horse and observed: 'May not have got himself killed neither.' He slipped out his tobacco pouch, and rubbing the leaf between his palms, recalled the pink glow of the flare, the German guns. He never saw the Bramble boys again. Snow lit his cigarette and noticed Lowanna walking down the road toward him.

The shadow of Logan's Peak advanced across the valley and deep into the afternoon. Tom stood high on a granite ledge and viewed his town, the only place he'd ever known. The cluster of weatherboard and corrugated iron appeared tiny. Turning to Copenhagen, the horse munching on the thin offerings between the rocks, he sighed: 'Ah, Cope, it's been a bugger of a day. No doubt about it.'

There came a wail, weary as a windswept mountain. Tom looked up to see a wedge-tailed eagle crossing overhead, soaring on the thermals, and though impressed as ever by the sight, his thinking at once flowed back into the day's events as water through a siphon. Though he had witnessed fights in the pub or on the street outside the pub, the sudden tornados of flying fists weren't half so bad as what was done to Neddy. His sorrow was not a stranger either. It was a feared acquaintance in the shadow years of war.

For a while Tom paced the ledge, old losses bleeding into view: Harry and Darce killed by the war, his mum killed by their sacrifice. He hawked and spat, as if to tell the mountains and the sky he wouldn't cop it sweet. Thrusting his hands into his pockets, he refused to accept Snow's few and slender words, feeling he'd been told to turn his heart into a pump that beat though dead—as happened to the Widow Adams when she lost her husband and her son, her one and only child, in the spring of 1918. He recalled how the telegrams had arrived the exact same time, both late and following the armistice, their reaping set against the streamers and the joy. The woman kept on going. She went on for two years after that until, mercifully, one Thursday afternoon the flesh let go the dregs of her.

Tom heard again the squeal of the eagle, but this time it was not so far away. He swung around and there, standing behind him, was Burnum. Thin as bone and dark as the hour before dawn, the black tracker carved out the light where he stood, giving back nothing save the flame in his eyes. His spear flashed in the sun. The glint at its point was an inch from Tom's eyes before its rent of the air hit his ears. All else was silent; no part of the tracker, or the ground he touched, made a sound as he circled his foe.

'Burnum,' said Tom, 'I know why you're here—it's a life for a life. I won't lie to you, Burnum, it was my fault Neddy was taken. There's nothing I can say to defend myself. Neddy's my mate and I let him down… I'm sorry.'

Burnum pulled back his spear, ready to throw. Copenhagen plodded between them. Oblivious to any threat, he nickered and sought out pastures greener, further down the ledge. In the stallion's wake, Tom found Burnum gone, vanished as quickly and surely as he had arrived.

Chapter Eight

The Widow Philpot and the Widow O'Connor sipped their tea. Gladys Philpot would pop in and visit Kathleen O'Connor of a Saturday afternoon. Gladys would always bring scones and her quince jam, and Kathleen would play the piano. Gladys liked to sing with Kathleen's accompaniment. Kathleen would play and listen to Gladys sing because Gladys Philpot made the best scones at the Glenn Innes and Grafton shows, and her quince jam wasn't bad either. The arrangement was informal but had grown to be precise: Song for a scone Saturdays. Kathleen O'Connor would accompany Gladys Philpot's singing, playing a song for every scone she ate. Kathleen was a woman possessed of a healthy appetite, as her ears could well attest, and she would pound the ivory and the ebony, her arms flapping heroically as much as Gladys's chins.

The ladies had sung the last tune for the day, the seventh song for the seventh scone. The Widow Philpot loved this final song the most. She adored the words and liked to think of them as written by Ivor Novello because he was such a handsome man. 'Keep the home fires burning while your hearts are yearning,' she'd belt out, Britannic. 'Though your lads are far away they dream of home.' A tear would moisten an eye. 'There's a silver lining through the dark clouds glistening, Turn the dark clouds inside out till the boys come home.'

The Widow Philpot put down her cup and saucer. 'Oh, I do love the music of Ivor Novello. So invigorating.'

'You've lost none of your touch, Gladys.' said The Widow O'Connor. 'I might partake of another of your lovely scones.' She snapped up the second to last and spread a thick layer of jam on it. 'Aren't you having a scone too?'

'No, I've had quite enough,' said Gladys. 'If you like, you can have my last one.'

'Are you sure?' asked Kathleen, already spreading jam on the other scone.

'Yes, I'm sure. I must save my appetite for supper with the fellows when they come home from the hotel. They'll be famished. They always are. Eat like growing boys, they do.'

'And what are you cooking then?' asked The Widow O'Connor, her mouth opening for a shark's nibble of scone.

'I thought I'd boil up a nice tripe and onions; it's Mr Doyle's favourite.'

The Widow O'Connor swallowed hard. 'Does Snow Mackay like the tripe too?'

'No, but I'll make lamb's fry next week. Mr Mackay is partial to lamb's fry.'

'They'd reckon it all to be an improvement on the bully beef.'

'Oh, but I do cook up a nice silverside as well,' said The Widow Philpot, admitting nothing to be beyond her skill. 'May boil up some for the boys if the Widow MacTavish has any cabbages on the way.'

'I think it's only peas at the moment—and the carrots and onions of course—the cabbages being a problem with keeping away the moth.'

'Cabbage moth? In Berto?'

'Yes. Lord knows where they come from. Nobody else in the valley grows cabbages.'

'That is a shame.'

'Yes, it is a shame, but I'm having great success with my new variety of spuds. Now are you sure you don't want this last scone?' Kathleen asked, holding the scone a thumbnail's length from her mouth.

'No, you have it. I must be on my bike.' The Widow Philpot folded the sheet music for The Widow O'Connor.

'Oh, never mind all that, Gladys,' said The Widow O'Connor, licking jam from her fingertips. 'I'll tidy it all up presently. Now, would you like some spuds afore you go?'

'No, I'm good for spuds.'

'Are you happy with me new King Edwards?'

'Yes, I know nothing stays the same forever.'

'Oh, aye, we're living in a time of change: seems nothing stays the same for even a week these days.'

The two widows closed their eyes and sighed.

After some reflection The Widow O'Connor took a bite of scone and The Widow Philpot asked: 'Have you heard about the pub?'

'What's that you say,' mumbled The Widow O'Connor, her mouth still full.

'I was just saying, as The Widow MacTavish was telling me when I was picking up some of her excellent onions, there are guests staying at the pub.'

'Go on with you!' said The Widow O'Connor, as familiar with the facts as The Widow MacTavish, but lying with gay abandon. The Widow O'Connor not only loved gossip, but was also intrigued by its anatomy. She saw gossip as a tennis match and was therefore eager to hear if the return of yesterday's serve would be the same ball, or if it would miraculously lob back as a shuttlecock, a brick or a bomb.

The Widow Philpot was concerned by The Widow O'Connor's reaction. 'Oh, I know Kathleen, I know it's hard to imagine, but The Widow MacTavish, our young Agnes, would never breathe a word of a lie.'

'Oh, no, I would never suggest such a thing. I was merely surprised by the news.' The Widow O'Connor rubbed her hands together. 'Please, do go on.'

'Anyway, Agnes told me, and it's a fact.' The Widow Philpot ran her tongue over her teeth. 'She told me a very la-de-da couple from down south are staying at the hotel. I believe they're city people from Sydney, and the fellow, well…' The Widow Philpot knitted her fingers together and leaned forward. 'Apparently, the fellow, he's a bit of your cardsharp.'

The Widow O'Connor looked at the crucifix on her wall; The Widow MacTavish didn't have to mention that part of the story. The Widow O'Connor's late husband, Patrick, was also one for the cards. Always playing, always losing. Hard earned money frittered away, right up until Villers-Bretonneux.

The Widow Philpot felt her pain. 'Oh, Kathleen, I do hope they don't cause strife. Do you remember when that travelling salesman arrived with a load of those new brassieres?'

'Please, Gladys, I don't want to even so much as think about that particular affair.' The Widow O'Connor wiped her mouth with her napkin.

'Yes, you're right, Kathleen, it's best forgotten. I'm glad you still like my scones. Oh, mustn't leave anything behind.' The Widow Philpot folded her white linen cloth, so as not to spill crumbs, and put it in her basket. 'As I was saying, before I take my leave, the guests at the hotel—he's a dandy, all as fancy as you like, and she seems to be something of a painted lady.'

'No, go on, in Berto?' The Widow O'Connor was enjoying the retelling of the story now.

The Widow Philpot was enjoying herself too, revelling in having such an appreciative audience. 'Of course, Agnes hasn't seen the young lady yet——'

'No, of course not.'

'But she heard as much from Ma when she was delivering a load of peas and carrots to her store.' The Widow Philpot frowned. 'Wait a second. Don't you give Agnes a lift into town of a Friday?'

'Hmm?'

'Weren't you in Ma's store to hear all this too?'

'No, I missed all of it, Gladys: missed the lot. The whole business is news to me; Agnes neglected to repeat a single solitary thing. Not a jot. That lass isn't as forthcoming with information as she could be. Young people—you know what they're like—everything a secret.'

'Where were you then?'

'Oh, I had to see Pop about my horse. The old mare needs a new set of slippers.'

'Oh, I see,' said The Widow Philpot, a little confused. She could have sworn Kathleen's mare had been shod not a month earlier.

'So, why are you stopping then?' said The Widow O'Connor impatiently.

'Oh, sorry, Kathleen. As I was saying—Agnes was saying Ma was saying the lass staying over with her husband at the hotel is very pretty. Very pretty indeed, and young Tom Bramble has taken a bit of a shine to her.'

The Widow O'Connor's bustline convulsed in genuine surprise. 'Go on with you.'

'It's true,' the Widow Philpot nodded, eyes wide, 'and you can understand why—Tom's not used to that sort of thing. Yes, very beautiful she is, and with a city girl's complexion.'

'Not enough healthy sunlight is what it is. Too much shenanigans indoors, I say.'

'You've got a good point there, Kathleen. Plenty of good wholesome girls here in the valley for a young fellow like Tom to give a second glance to, and not some flirtatious floozy from the city who's married besides.'

'Oh, poor Tom, he'll be putty in her hands.'

'I know, and of course her husband's an American.'

'Go on!'

'An international adventurer, and you know what that can mean, don't you, Kathleen?'

'Holy Mary, I've not the faintest idea.'

'The French ailment.'

'Oh, poor Tom.'

'It's most fortunate my lads, Snow and Mike, are too sensible to have their heads turned by that sort, especially my Mike.'

'Your Mike, is it now?'

'No, please, wait till I make myself clear. I wouldn't want you to think me presuming, but I mean, I might feel something for him, for Mr Mike Doyle—more than just a respectful, passing regard for our acquaintance. Please don't disclose a word of this but——'

'My lips are sealed.'

'I appreciate your sense of decorum, Kathleen.'

'As you well know, Gladys, I am nothing if not discreet.'

'I'm aware of that, Kathleen, and that is why I feel I can confide in you.' The Widow Philpot rested one hand upon the other and confessed: 'A man like Mike wants a woman to look after him as he deserves. He's quite missed out to date, and now, with the poor man well into his fourth decade——'

'It's a bit of a scar on his face.'

'None of us is getting any younger, Kathleen.'

'Aye, that's true, Gladys, and I'm told that under that rough exterior there lies a sweet soul. A good Catholic too, so the priest was telling me. Though, like most men, Mike doesn't make a show of it—though it wouldn't hurt if he attended mass from time to time.'

'Do you think he'd mind my being a Presbyterian?'

'Might do,' said The Widow O'Connor, stacking the tea

cups and saucers, 'but you could always convert.'

'Yes,' said The Widow Philpot and cleared her throat. 'Well, I really must be getting along.'

'Then I'll be seeing you next Saturday afternoon then, for the songs and scones?'

'Yes, I dare say,' said The Widow Philpot, making haste for the door.

'Oh, by the way,' said The Widow O'Connor, 'I was wondering about inviting over The Widow Campbell to join us. She has such a beautiful mezzosoprano and she serves a lovely lemon butter tart. Shall I drop her a note?'

'Yes, of course, what a nice idea, I'll be off then.'

The Widow Philpot made a dash for her bicycle. 'Don't want to be late with the tripe and onions.'

'I'll be seeing you then, Gladys.'

'Yes, toodle-loo,' said The Widow Philpot as her bicycle clattered down the drive.

The Widow O'Connor smiled as she closed her front door.

Charlie, Snow and Mad Mike perched on a fence rail. The forcing yard behind them was now emptied, nothing left save drying cowpats.

Snow rolled a smoke. 'Tom's pretty cut up 'bout it all.'

'Tom and Neddy,' Charlie sniffed, 'they were pretty thick. Good mates.'

Snow spat out a loose strand of tobacco. 'It's Neddy's mum I feel sorry for.'

Charlie sucked on his bleeding gums. 'Why'd you tell

her?'

'What else was I supposed to do? You reckon I should be able to see around corners? Struth, can't know everything. Didn't have time to work out some bullshit story. Wasn't to be expecting she'd come wandering down the road looking for him. Bloody hell!'

'Hold your horses, Snow,' Charlie soothed. 'No need to get yourself all wound up like a python swallowing a porcupine. I mean to say, I know what you're on about, but someone had to tell her. May as well be you as anyone else. Just happened, and you were the poor bugger who drew the short straw is all I'm saying. I mean Lowanna wouldn't be the first mum in the valley to lose her son.'

Mike stammered. 'B-B-Bloody Gu-Gu-Guv———'

'Fair comment, Mike,' said Charlie

'You got that right,' said Snow, swatting a cattle fly. He wiped away the insect on his moleskins and fidgeted with his new prosthesis. It still didn't feel right. 'Heap of shit,' he whinged as he swivelled it around, getting his stump to fit properly. 'Kill for a drink.'

She sat in the middle of Main Street, rocked from side to side and stared at the track marks. Ground out where the heavy wagon wheels had turned, they disappeared down the road. Wherever they led, Neddy lay in chains. Lowanna dug her fingers into the earth, her nails splintering and bleeding. Neddy had not come home for lunch. Neddy often didn't, but mother earth had always told Lowanna all was well. Today was different. Crows had settled on her hut, smelling death and cawing, though no trace of meat was thereabouts. Alarmed, she had gone walking down the road in the direction of Berto. On nearing town she ran into Snow.

Ma approached with a consoling cuppa. 'Lowanna, have some hot tea. It'll do you a world of good.' Lowanna pushed the cup away. The china broke, the tea inhaled by the parched earth.

Lucky walked out of the pub. 'Hey, Lowanna, I got Neddy's rod. Wouldn't want you to lose it.'

Lowanna looked up at the rod and wailed.

Ma gathered the broken shards of teacup and traipsed back to her store.

Lucky tried to show Lowanna the bright side. 'Neddy won't be away forever. He'll visit after he's been taught an education. Needs to know how to read and write.'

Lowanna leaped up and snatched away the rod by its butt. 'Whitefella lie!' She shook the rod at Lucky's nose. 'This all he need to know.'

Lowanna gazed up the road. 'Now my son all gone.' Exhausted by her pain, she dropped the rod and turned for home. 'Like boys who go walkabout to war, all gone—all gone.' Lowanna's words drifted into a lament, the baleful chords fading as she grew small inside the distance.

Between the echoes of the afternoon and the reclaimed quiet of the empty street, Lucky's thoughts harked back to his own lost sons. He and Rachel had raised their boys with loving care, only to see both sacrificed to make a richer dish for the appetites of famous men. He wiped his brow and whispered, repeating Lowanna's words: 'All gone, all gone.'

Lucky shuffled over to the pub and sat on the veranda's edge, his memories setting to putrefy. Harry, he recalled, was only twenty when he left; Darcy younger still—just eighteen years, born same time as Snow. Snow got back, but the Bramble boys would not return. Lucky would never even get to see their graves, if graves they had. 'Shit,' he whispered, 'could be grown men now, instead of nothing.'

Lucky knew all twelve in the Berto section, plus their corporal, Big George Philpot. When Big George fell, Charlie Ward became the corporal. 'Bloody Charlie,' Lucky muttered, 'you wouldn't read about it.' Then he snorted: 'Yeah, New England's Own. Who was the colonel of the battalion? Morshead? That's right. Came back, he did.'

The publican kicked his heel into the beginning of a thistle, uprooting the weed. Berto's valley had lost eight of the thirteen sons, the remaining five all wounded in some way, all except for Charlie. 'Bloody Charlie,' Lucky said again before he whistled softly, 'way he's going, he'll replace the valley's losses with the fruit of his own loins.' Lucky took to wondering if Charlie was doing it on purpose, in repayment for his good fortune, returning home without so much as a nosebleed—the digger had won a lottery of sorts. 'If reparation is what Charlie's up to,' Lucky thought aloud, 'it's a big burden he's taken on. Tough job for old Peg too, but no worse than France.'

The old widower stood up and it occurred to him Preston Logan had promised to build a cenotaph. He hadn't got around to doing it yet. Lucky considered what words could be engraved on the monument's melancholy slab. "'If I should die,"' he recited, "'think only this of me; that there's some corner of a foreign field that is for ever England." No, fuck that, forever Australia. Better still, forever Berto!' Lucky reckoned Logan could erect the cenotaph in Berto, France or Timbuctoo; he really didn't give a stuff.

From the shimmering distance down the road, from the haze that swallowed Neddy, there emerged a phantom figure. Lucky squinted and saw a woman. She was drifting along beneath the shade of her parasol, taking in the sights like they were something special, walking and studying the forest and the fields, the cows and tawny trees. 'Rachel?' Lucky whispered; and stumbling forward, went to call aloud his lost wife's name, but it was not Rachel; it was the city girl. Tears of disappointment, then of rage, welled up in Lucky's eyes. He stepped backwards as though in fear and quickly repaired to the safety of the pub.

Thorn was playing poker with the only other patrons in the barroom. Not bothering to take his eyes from his hand, the gambler yelled across to Lucky: 'Hope mammy doesn't come calling by again—goddamned, obnoxious caterwauling.' The other players laughed. Thorn threw a couple of coins onto the pot. 'But I guess you wouldn't be giving the slightest itty-bitty thought to that, now would you?' Lucky shrugged. 'No,' Thorn continued, 'you'd never worry about the ambience?'

'Why should I?' Lucky asked morosely. 'She doesn't have to be driven to the hospital.' He wandered behind the bar and reached for his bottle of rum. It wasn't there.

Chapter Nine

Logan's Peak glowed in the sunset as a rider approached, emerging from the northern road, down from the upper pastures where the land was smooth and rich. The horse was a thoroughbred, gleaming in a coat of polished jet, and the rider every bit as raven: black tie and black Akubra, and a frock coat suit of deep slate worsted. The horseman saw the land around as his domain; much of it was his personal estate. His grandfather was a remittance man who squatted in the valley gone sixty years before. He raised cattle, built a fortune greater than the source of his remittance and died soon after. His sole surviving child, a son, died from snakebite inflicted by a death adder that waited in the forest mulch. He, in turn, also left one child, a greedy, ruthless and stubborn boy. Now the boy was fifty-five, a widower with a son of his own. This fourth generation lived far away, a barrister in Philip Street who cared little for the family farm, save for its monetary worth. There was a lot of that; Preston Logan was easily the richest bastard in the valley, perhaps the richest man in all the Northern Rivers.

As Logan rode into the town, his eyes stalked every corner, slinking and watchful, rapacious as a panther. He approached the store as Ma was closing up. 'Still open?' he asked, looking down from his horse, the question purely a formality.

'Of course, Mr Logan,' said Ma as she scurried back inside.

Logan entered. In the light his features presented flinty and raw-boned. Ma was already behind the counter. 'What can I get you, Mr Logan?'

The cattleman smoothed his thick moustache. 'Deck of playing cards.'

Ma opened the sliding door to the glass-top counter.

'And a receipt,' he added as an afterthought.

Ma snatched a quizzical glance at the catlike, razor eyes.

Grace stood before her mirror. It framed a tart, and even though her beauty shone through the powder and rouge, she didn't like herself any more for that.

She smoothed her hands down her short red dress, tilted her ostrich feather hat and arranged her strands of pearls, the loops falling all the way to her naked knees. It was Saturday, Ernie Thorn's best night. With a few sly bob passed Lucky's way, the doors could be locked, but the bar left open and the punters free to gamble themselves poor. Grace thought men such silly creatures; they'd put at risk a pot emerging like Vesuvius to gawk at her, lose concentration for a fleeting moment, and leave the table poorer—often much poorer. She felt sorry for the bewildered sods, and guilty too, the pangs getting worse each time. If the curtain must come down for the last time on even the biggest musical, then how much longer for Ernie's and her tawdry show. Her contract must eventually ring its knell, though how or when she couldn't say. In consequence, this night she would make her entrance as if it were the first, and do her bit—the magician's assistant. Ernie was a robber, sure enough, and in her mirror Grace beheld the robber's dog.

Grace descended the stairs in T-strap heels and darted past the public barroom. After glancing at the backs of the melee of thirsty stockmen, she made for the pink-beaded entrance to the saloon. At that same moment, Tom appeared from the rear door. Caught out and surprised by her attire, he found himself giving her the once over before he realised he was looking. The timing could not have been worse. All afternoon Grace had hoped to talk to him, talk to him about so many things, and now here he was, here in time to see her at her worst, here out of time for explanation, only time for her to run.

Grace vanished into billowing beads. Tom left too, no less stunned than she, exiting the way he had entered, straight out the back door, all like a man patting down his pockets, feeling for a misplaced wallet.

Walking to the centre of the empty saloon Grace stared out the bay window. It was almost dark in the shadow of the mountains, dark enough to see in the glass the ghost of herself, the ceiling lamp leaving her eyes in shadow. That afternoon Grace had been left wondering what happened to Neddy, trusting that, come the evening, Tom would tell her the wherefores and the why. The urge to talk to him had so consumed her thoughts she had found it impossible to remain in her hotel room. Taking the initiative, she chose to try to seek him out. Following Ernie's blithe advice to go for an afternoon walk, she was out the door by one o'clock, embarked upon her life's first ramble in the country. Unfortunately, a city girl, she had underestimated the length of a bushie mile, naively hoping somewhere in the valley she might accidentally bump into Tom—like it was George Street or something. The valley proved bigger than that.

Grace had gone north—the same way Tom had taken—and wandered up the road to where it cut through the wooded foothills. Beyond this rise, the road wound down again to skirt the valley's southward flowing creek. Ten minutes later she had come upon a bullock track. It split off from the road and led to a causeway that crossed the creek. It was at this juncture Grace had seen a person approaching from up the road. The figure was not on horseback, and definitely not Tom, but a woman. She was black and shuffling through the ochre dust, making rapid progress despite her awkward gait. Something in the woman's manner had caused Grace to veer away, turning left, rushing down the track and across the creek. She had not known why, but the woman scared her. Once on the other side, she peeped back and was much relieved to find the woman had not followed her. Instead she had maintained her steady progress along the road toward the town and was quickly out of sight.

Glancing about, Grace had seen that the bullock track headed south. It was lined with she-oaks and followed the western bank of the creek. Grace decided to take this route, hoping the tree's shade would make the going cooler than the Berto Road. Unfortunately, her deviation led her on a much

more winding course, the creek shifting well to the west and across the valley's entire width before doubling back to continue south. Through these parts she had seen more people than expected: chancing by gangly old selectors and having little chats; being invited in to meet the wife and have a cup of tea, but saying: 'No, but thanks for the kind offer and give my greetings to your missus.' Then, before leaving, turning to ask: 'You haven't by any chance seen a young man riding through on a dark chestnut stallion, one white sock?' After witnessing a second or two of head scratching, all she usually got was something like, 'Why, that sounds to be young Tom Bramble. No, not seen him in these parts of late.' She also had to circumvent a widow's anecdote. 'Do you know young Tom? Well, I could tell you some stories 'bout young Tom.' It had been a temptation to find out what the nut-brown, wrinkled woman had to say, but to Grace that would have been out of order, like spying, and it would not do if the woman chanced to mention the matter to Tom at some future date.

Still following the creek's gentle course, Grace travelled far enough to see the town pass by beyond the opposite bank. At first she was glad to have this bearing, but later became worried for it took more than a little time to find a place to turn back home. The spot she eventually found was where the waters ran from out a deeper, dammed back reach, all scurrying upon a wide flat rock and flowing thin. Though the going had been a slippery affair, the water was shallow enough for her to get quickly to the eastern side, and within minutes, walking up the road on a straight run north to town.

In the end it had proved to be quite a hike. Grace was

relieved she had her dancer's legs, and glad she'd thought to take her parasol and put on a pair of walking shoes. However, in all of her grand tour, she had failed to see Tom anywhere. Now, with her evening's work about to start, the chance for talking all used up, she'd bumped into him in the corridor, the lad standing there like Little John blocking the narrow bridge.

The valley had grown dark and the ghost Grace saw was presently opaque in the window's gathered night. She fine-tuned her hat and walked to the little hole in the wall. Despite the arrival of evening, the lamps—hurriedly lit by Lucky well before the rush—were plenty strong enough for Grace to see again the hidden clutter beneath the public bar and glimpse once more the short back and sides that stubbled to the thatch on top of the publican's greasy head.

Shocked by the appearance of Grace, Tom had not only retreated from the pub, he had determined to withdraw even further by spending the night in the vastness of the mountains. Slapping on Copenhagen's saddle, he looked around the stables at the bales of hay, the walls of dust-laden tack, the red-back infested racks of junk—all part of his home—and wondered if his healing lay not outside in the cool of the mountains but within the crucible of the pub. Should he reject his father for the wilderness and be seen a coward, or do his duty as a son and employee and risk being judged a cur? The latter meant he would be seen by Grace, there to watch him serving the patrons and cravenly serving his father. He was so wound up he had been thoughtless enough to put the prospect of seeing her out of his thoughts, but there she had been in the

hall.

Tom gave Copenhagen a pat. 'What's your opinion, Cope? Hey, boy? Do you suppose everyone expects me to show up and help my old man after how he treated Neddy? Would they show up?' Tom thought about the answer and discovered aloud: 'Maybe that's what you have to do. Maybe that's what Snow was getting at... Nah, they'd reckon I was a piss-weak bastard if I threw in the towel after what Dad did— Dad, Grimes, Reverend Goddard and that nurse—jeez, Cope, you wouldn't credit her. Poor Neddy, I wonder where he is right now. Have to be worse than this.' Tom kicked a wooden pail, water splashing everywhere. His horse harrumphed. 'Sorry, Cope,' he said, embarrassed by his tantrum, 'that was uncalled for. Things have got to me such as I can't think straight.' Tom looked at the upturned bucket. 'If I don't show up, I'll never live it down.' He began untying the leather thongs that hitched the saddlebags. 'Won't be going out, Cope. You've got the night off; I'll be the one working.' Copenhagen snorted and Tom agreed. 'I know, you're right; I'll be starting late, but better late than never.'

Chapter Ten

Stockman, swagmen, selectors, they came from east to west, from the bottom gorge to way up in the northern gullies where ancient men eked out lives in caves or under bark, existing rough and calling it the 'old way'. It was a busy Saturday night and the pub was packed, the air smoked to a milky haze under a wagon wheel of hurricane lamps, their dirty light, reflected in pumpkin hues against burnt umber shadows. Lucky, frenzied, worked the bar alone.

A windup gramophone, bought years before by Lucky for his Rachel, crackled the waxen voices of Violet Lorraine and George Robey: 'Sometimes when I feel low and things look blue, I wish a gal I had, say one like you…'

A remittance man sat by the spinning disk, drinking and crying for old England, distant and longed-for. 'Someone within my heart to build a throne…'

Nobody else was listening; it was merely part of the noise, much of it emanating from Bluey 'One Thumb' Corbett. He had journeyed to Grafton on business, and having chanced by the racetrack, had come home bounteous, pockets full enough to buy his mates a few schooners. 'Someone who'd never part, to call my own…'

Thorn played poker, speculating on when Grace would

appear so he could liven up the stakes. 'If you were the only girl in the world and I were the only boy…'

Pop, Charlie and Mad Mike drank among a throng of ringers. 'Nothing else would matter in the world today. We could go on loving in the same old way…'

Snow stood alone at the end of the bar, pensive and despondent. Charlie approached and gave him a reassuring slap on the back. 'Wasn't your fault, Snow, you just happened to be in the wrong place at the wrong time.'

'I should have kept me trap shut.'

'Nah, you did the only thing you could do. You did the right thing.'

'Was a bad thing and now it's worse, no ladling treacle on that.'

'Ah, piss off, Snow; stop feeling sorry for yourself.'

Snow replied to the dressing down with a wry smile.

The disc kept wobbling along. 'A garden of Eden just made for two with nothing to mar our joy…'

Charlie leaned against the bar conspiratorially. 'I hear tell there might be a surprise guest tonight.'

Snow looked across at Thorn. 'Have little birds been telling tales?'

'Oh, could have been a cheeky bit fly by.'

'That'll raise some feathers. Regular cockfight, I'd hazard.'

'Like the good old days,' said Charlie. 'Just like before the war.'

Snow smiled a bit more broadly and Charlie laughed good and hearty.

George Robey sang across the room: 'I would say such wonderful things to you.'

Violet Lorraine trilled in reply: 'There would be such wonderful things to do…'

Charlie saw the publican, going ten to the dozen. Lucky's face wasn't red anymore; it was violet. 'Hey, Lucky,' Charlie yelled, 'where's the lad?'

'He's taken ill!'

'Tom?' Charlie gazed at Snow. 'You ever hear of Tom chucking a sickie?'

'No,' said Snow, 'but there's always a first time—wouldn't surprise me if he's buggered off.'

Charlie folded his arms. 'I know Tom as well as any man. He'll turn up.'

Snow sipped his old black ale. 'Why would he bother; it's almost last drinks.'

'Shit, you're right,' said Charlie, downing the rest of his beer. 'Hey, Lucky,' he yelled again, 'couple of schooners for me and Snow.'

And the music played on: 'If you were the only girl in the world and I were the only——'

The gramophone needle jumped. With a *rurp* its steel scraped the record's shellac. The bar went silent. All eyes flicked to the double doors. It was Preston Logan. You could have heard a pin drop if not for the needle dragging. Logan crossed the room, the crowd parting before him. Someone picked up the scratching stylus as the cattleman fronted the bar.

Lucky's face drained from violet to mauve. 'Evening, Mr

Logan, you got here just in time.' He looked at the grandfather clock. 'Was just about to call it a night.'

Logan swung around and addressed the crowd. 'Way I hear it, Constable Grimes,' his eyes shifted lazily back toward Lucky, 'he owes you a favour.'

Pop spat into the slops tray. 'Sure does.'

Logan cocked his thumbs in his waistcoat pockets. 'Keep the doors open, Lucky. Next shout's on me!' The crowd surged to the bar.

The cattleman noticed Thorn sitting alone at his corner table. The only person not interested in a free drink, the American did naught else but calmly shuffle his deck of cards. A fawning stockman handed Logan a scotch. He took the drink, strolled up to Thorn and spoke low. 'Grapevine says you're a deft hand.'

Thorn was modest. 'I'm enjoying a purple patch.'

The cattleman took a seat and slapped his wallet on the table: 'Head-to-head, aces high, no limit.'

Thorn shrugged and riffle shuffled the playing cards. He placed the deck in front of Logan, but the cattleman didn't move.

'Gonna cut?' asked Thorn.

Charlie and Snow, Mad Mike and Pop, the whole mob, soon as they got a drink, turned to take in the show. Logan pushed away Thorn's cards and put his newly purchased pack on the table. 'I like to play with a fresh deck.'

Thorn looked askance at the deck, still wrapped in cellophane.

Logan felt insulted. 'You got a problem with that?'

Thorn took the deck and inspected the pack for tampering. The crowd pressed in. Logan handed over the receipt. Thorn noted it was marked with that night's date. He put down the fresh deck and leaned back in his chair.

Logan was even more insulted. 'Are you calling me a cheat?'

The crowd retreated.

Thorn searched around to see Grace standing in the saloon bar window. The timing couldn't be more perfect. He signalled for her to join him.

The lobby's grandfather clock chimed Big Ben's phrase: 'Through this hour, Lord be my guide; and by thy hour, no foot shall slide.' Then, with a stroke of its deepest chime, the clock began to toll.

Grace stepped out onto her stage. Logan straightened up, swept away by the blaze of light she seemed to radiate. The second stroke rang and a hush settled upon the room. The third and all eyes were upon her. The fourth and Lucky dared not complain about a woman in the public bar. The fifth and Grace was at the corner table. The sixth and the cavalcade came to an end, the final stroke's reverberation allowed to fade into silence. Grace put the old deck of cards into her purse as Thorn tore the cellophane from the new. He dealt and the crowd closed in.

Tom walked to the kitchen with the empty bucket. As he approached the sink he could hear the whole hotel had turned eerily quiet. Leaving the bucket, he walked up the hall to ascertain what had happened but stopped abruptly at the edge of the saloon door, mistakenly believing Grace to still be on the other side of the magenta curtain. His first thought was to go back and approach the bar the long way around—sneak by the side of the pub and enter through the lobby—but such a solution would be short-lived; through her little window Grace would be quick to see him once he commenced serving. Knowing there was nothing else for it, Tom continued up the hall, but he could not help but sneak a peek through the beads. He found the saloon empty.

When Tom entered the public bar, all the patrons were at the other end of the room, clustered around Thorn's table. Only Lucky was still at the taps. On catching sight of his son his face lit up. Tom ignored him and moved to the rear of the crowd. Through the gaps he saw Grace. She was standing at Thorn's side. Across the table he saw Preston Logan. He and Thorn were playing a high stakes game, the pot burgeoning and the drinkers watching intently.

Logan held his cards close to his chest, fanned them open and checked again his full house. Grace observed the tiny twitch of satisfaction in his moustache and knew he was ripe for the harvesting. She leaned toward him to realign her garter. With her chin to one side and shoulders back, her bosom strained, at the very brink of bursting forth in a magnificent display. Logan looked up and found himself mesmerized by the silken mounds. 'I'll see you,' the cattleman said, putting a blue fiver on the pot, seeming to end things there. However, on finding Grace's swanlike posture enduring yet, she making little progress with her stubborn garter, cleavage all aquiver with unspoken promise, he felt inspired to show off. 'And I'll raise you ten—no, make that tasty—I mean twenty pounds.' Logan took from his wallet a pair of ten pound notes. The crowd caught its collective breath; they didn't see a lot of tenners in the valley and here were two at once. Her task complete, Grace stood up. She noticed Tom in the crowd and blushed. His embarrassment was no less; no need to consult his books to fathom what he'd seen. He backed away to the bar, found his retreat blocked by his father's lingering stare, and trapped, was forced to do the first thing come to mind: he made himself busy, picking up empty glasses.

At the playing table Thorn appraised the pot, clicked his tongue on the roof of his mouth and weighed up the odds, deciding whether he should bide his time, take a profit, play a few more hands and, perhaps, work his mark up to the maximum payout; or get it over and done with, play the present round for all it was worth, and as a result, blow any chance for glittering prizes yet to come. The night was young and he could see the mark had deep pockets. If Thorn was patient, he stood to make a fortune.

Logan was getting restless. 'If you're all bunged up, I recommend a dose of salts.' The cattleman mugged to his audience, received the laughter his expression commanded, and preened for Grace.

'Yeah, yeah, okay,' said Thorn, pretending irritation at being the butt of Logan's joke; it was a ruse to disguise his decision to play the first option and do the cattleman slow. He threw in twenty-five pounds worth of fivers. 'Call it.'

Logan turned over his cards. 'Full house,' he announced

smugly.

Thorn let a bit of tension build. He waited for a second and then showed his hand: four of a kind.

Logan glared out to the street, instantly aware it was a set-up. He'd been had, and far worse, made to look the fool in front of his fiefdom.

Thorn tucked away the pot. The crowd broke up. Tom cautiously joined Lucky behind the bar and started serving, but his father threw him by being something different, something Lucky had never been to his son before: apologetic. 'Tom,' he said, his face contrite, twisted as a knot in a plank of weathered wood, 'you got to understand———'

'Don't talk to me,' Tom interrupted, cutting him off, being something he had never been to his father before: dismissive. He wanted to vomit, but instead he took an order. On collecting payment he watched his father pulling the taps and loathed what he saw, but at the same time loathed himself for such loathing. Thereupon a thought emerged: My dad's absolving himself of his sins. The lad had read enough of his King James Bible to know it was as God had done to Adam: the father, who'd conceived the plan, was transferring to his son the guilt for the plan going sour. Now filled with resentment as well as shame, Tom muttered: 'What gives you the right?'

'You talking to me?' asked the next customer, a muscled-browed ringer.

'No, sorry, it was nothing,' Tom said distractedly. 'What can I get you?'

'Old Black,' grumbled the ringer, his wariness

unappeased.

Tom shifted a few inches further down the bar, putting some space between himself and Lucky. Feeling the sins of the father being visited upon the son, he mumbled: 'Don't go thinking I'll let you off the hook.'

'Look, mate, is there something wrong with the beer?'

'No, of course not,' Tom replied as he collected the ringer's pennies. 'Just talking to myself.'

The ringer gibed: 'It's dirty pipes, isn't it, mate?' Not waiting for an answer, he walked away. 'Up in Queensland our publicans keep their pipes clean.'

'Don't worry, pipes are clean here too,' Tom avowed. 'Do it myself,' he added softly, annoyed at being chipped. Lucky picked up on what was said and registered his boy's continued commitment to the pub's reputation.

Charlie and Snow were standing at the end of the bar. Tom steeled himself and walked straight up to them. 'Usual?' he asked.

'Yep,' Charlie nodded with a grin. 'See, Snow, I told you he'd turn up.'

Tom's sights swung onto Snow. 'What else would I do?'

Snow shrugged. 'Thought you'd never…' He stopped himself, assayed Tom and thought it best to avoid the chance for further confrontation; one heart to heart in twenty-four hours was plenty enough. 'Get me the usual,' he said and reached for his tobacco pouch. Tom poured their beers.

Charlie laughed. 'Hey, Tom, it's a good thing you did arrive. It's a bloody big night. Your old man hasn't worked this hard since the armistice. Preston Logan's told him to keep the doors open.'

'Calling in Grimes's favour,' Snow noted disdainfully, a cigarette paper flapping on his lower lip.

The irony of his father's reward being paid out as unwelcome toil was not lost on Tom, but he made no comment, and instead was all for wondering why Snow had stopped himself mid-sentence, pondering upon what the stockman was going to say. The beer overflowed. Tom quickly let go of the tap and wiped the bottom of the glass on the counter mat. Charlie laughed some more. 'Jeez, Snow, staff's getting sloppy, wasting good beer.'

Tom gave no response. Charlie's mirth settled to a sigh.

The two stockmen were handed their drinks. Tom collected the money and walked to the till. As the drawer rang open, he again noticed Lucky's fevered working and decided he must drive away his father as surely as his father exiled Neddy. Tom dropped a shilling on the floor. Bending down to retrieve the coin, he was overcome by a disquieting question: how far had the apple fallen from the tree?

Across the room and back at the table, Thorn finished neatly arranging by value his pound notes, and asked Grace: 'Would you like me to get you a shandy, sweetheart?'

Grace saw Tom tending the bar. 'No,' she said, taking out a cigarette, 'I'm not thirsty.'

Thorn agreed. 'I'm not thirsty either.' He lit her smoke before proceeding to arrange in columns the different denominations of his many coins: his ha'pences and big bronze pennies, little silver threepences and sixpences, his shillings and his florins. Logan took a small sip from his drink and glared at Thorn's satisfied tidiness.

'My deal,' Logan growled. All the patrons were back ringside.

Grace was alarmed. Though his reaction had been planned, there was something deadly lurking in the shadows of this mark. It was Logan's eyes. It occurred to her she had never seen their like before; his irises were too big. All people, unless squinting, seemed to have a bit of white in their eyes, but Logan's yellow orbs crowded out the whites completely. In the dim lamplight of the pub his pupils were enormous, his eyelids curtaining empty rooms, pitch-black cavities that rendered him hollow as a mask.

Grace smoked nervously as she located Tom, still serving at the bar. The young man felt the urgency of her fleeting glimpse. He looked straight up at her, his focus homing in on hers. For a split second they were locked, her fear transmitted in a heartbeat.

Logan grabbed the deck, and as he shuffled, looked brazenly at Grace's chest. 'How many of those pearls do you have there round your neck?'

All eyes upon her, Grace shrugged, pretending indifference.

'More than most men could afford,' Thorn butted in, leaning across to finger the necklace.

'A woman should wear just one string of pearls,' Logan grunted, 'two looks ostentatious.' The cattleman pushed the deck across the table.

Ignoring any insult, Thorn cut and pushed back the deck. Logan dealt. The cards flicked back and forth. The players perused their hands. The girdle of onlookers tightened.

Thorn's hand was lousy, but it did include a jack, a ten and eight of clubs. He decided on a long shot: a very unlikely straight flush, and failing that, at least a pair or two, or perhaps even three of a kind. He discarded the remaining cards and picked up the first of the new pair. It was only through long years of careful practice his heart didn't skip a beat; he held the nine of clubs. Thorn made sure it looked useless, leaving it on top and declining the opportunity to place it between the eight and ten. Then he picked up his second card and struck oil, a gusher: the queen of clubs. His face betrayed nothing; it was too soon to get excited. If Logan folded, his great hand would be wasted.

The cattleman gave Thorn a long and searching stare, such to be in any other circumstances an invitation to a fight, but Thorn was used to all the party tricks. He met Logan's gaze until it became obvious there was nothing in the gambler's face worth having. Logan threw out three cards, replacing each with studied solemnity. Thorn's right eyebrow rose ever so slightly; the best his opponent was likely to have was four of a kind. Both men placed their cards face down on the table.

Thorn went in soft with sixpence. Logan raised it to a shilling, Thorn with two bob, Logan four. The gambler tossed in a brown ten bob note. The cattleman tossed in a green pound note. Without hesitation, Thorn doubled it.

Logan paused to weigh up the situation; Thorn seemed awfully confident. Logan thought that could be bad. Logan thought that could be good. The black-suited, black-tied, black-hatted cattleman, colourful as an open grave and joyful as its occupant, double-checked his hand. Keeping the cards low and pressed against his stomach, he barked at the crowd, 'You lot, keep your distance.'

There was a bit of confusion as everybody moved back: everybody except Grace. She remained at Thorn's side, the couple giving each other a bolstering look, but her eyes were worried while his were cool as morning dew.

The room settled and Logan began again. 'I'll see your two and raise you three.' A fiver hit the pot.

Thorn upped the ante. 'Raise you five.' He put down two fivers.

Logan also dropped in two fivers and said: 'See you…' Thorn went to show his hand. Logan stopped him, shaking his index finger teasingly. '…And raise you ten.' Logan emptied his wallet and from its contents threw down another two fat fivers. Then, appraising Grace's comely features, he announced, 'Let's call it twenty.' He added yet more fivers. 'Actually, I'll make it interesting—I'll raise you forty quid.' Logan tossed into the pot another pair of his impressive tenners.

A flurry of disjointed whispering issued from the crowd: 'Fifty quid!' and 'Oh, how's that!'

Apart from rats and mice, Thorn had nothing but his two newly won ten pound notes and a small pile of blue fivers. He counted the fivers and found he had four.

Standing in the front of the crowd, Pop turned to Mike, merrily whispering: 'A tenner short of a look.'

Thorn touched softly the back of his cards, as if uncertain of their worth, but secretly delighted his brilliant hand was being put to such good use, and even more delighted Logan was trying to force him to fold, meaning the cattleman was almost certainly bluffing and holding bugger all. Now was the time to shift gears. Thorn glanced at Grace the way he always did when crossing the point of no return. She opened her purse and handed him a hidden reserve of cash: a wad of fresh tenners. A tremor rumbled through the audience.

Logan glowered.

Thorn patiently counted out ten of the notes. 'See your fifty and double it—one hundred quid.'

Logan raised his eyebrows, reached into his coat pocket and produced his own stash of tenners.

The crowd defied the cattle baron's orders, eagerness for blood pushing them closer to the fray.

Thorn cleared his throat and again exchanged a glance with Grace, but this time with less certainty; they were entering uncharted waters.

Though at the other end of the room, Tom sensed Grace's concern. He swung out from behind the empty bar and joined the throng.

Logan counted out his notes with the efficiency of a bank teller and slung in one hundred pounds. 'See your hundred and raise you...' Logan hesitated and counted out the remainder of his money. All he had was an extra hundred quid.

Thorn's eyes said nothing but he smiled on the inside; things were going to be fine and dandy after all. Mr Cattleman, you've miscalculated, he thought to himself, you know it, and you know I know it too. If I raise the stakes, you won't have enough to make a call, you'll have to see me now, and in a matter of seconds I'll be richer to the tune of more than one hundred and fifty quid. The gambler wanted to roar with laughter; tin-pot Berto was fast becoming a pot of gold. He would soon be folding into his wallet enough money to purchase two ocean liner tickets to the States. Thorn's fingers drifted toward his cards.

'Wait,' Logan croaked, 'let's not be impatient.' The cattleman frowned and combed his moustache with his nails. 'What the hell,' he announced with a flourish, 'I'll raise you the lot.'

Thorn longed to bask in the indulgence of a grin; Logan was effectively giving him another hundred pounds.

But Logan surprised everybody; he reached into another pocket and produced a second secret stash of tenners. He quickly counted them out and added the notes to his existing pile, making twice as many tenners.

Thorn's shoulders slumped. He hadn't anticipated playing with a magic act. He was being beaten at his own game.

'Alright,' Logan grunted with satisfaction, 'I'll see your hundred and raise you this two hundred.' He slid the entire stack of notes onto the mountainous pot.

The crowd murmured. Charlie flicked around to Snow, straining to corral his voice in a whisper. 'Yank'll need three hundred quid for a look!'

Snow was blown away when he thought of it in context, murmuring: 'More than a year's wages.'

Thorn's hands remained steady, his manner unflustered. He counted out two flats of tenners from his fast diminishing stocks.

Pop whispered: 'That's two hundred quid.'

Thorn then slowly added his remaining tenners. He had one, two, three, four, five, six, and… that was it. Thorn recounted what he knew to be the total value of his fivers. As expected, he still had merely twenty pounds worth. There was no point in counting his coins or bothering with the ten bob note; all told, they wouldn't come to anywhere near covering the shortfall. He whispered to Grace: 'You wouldn't happen to have a lazy twenty quid?'

Grace whispered back: 'Where would I get that kind of money.'

Thorn could feel the sharp stab of the bones of his arse, and mumbled to himself: 'Son of a bitch!'

Logan pressed his tongue against his cheek.

Thorn tapped his fingers on the edge of the table, the drum roll longer than the build-up to the explosion of a firing squad. Finally he did it: Thorn flung his pile of tenners and his stack of fivers down onto the pot. Then he looked up at Grace, grabbed her by the waist and pulled her hard against his ribs. 'Two hundred and eighty pounds in cash,' he declared, 'and twenty pounds for the dame. I call it.'

The whole room gasped.

Appalled, Tom tried to twist his way closer to Grace, but the crowd was bunched up tighter than a rugby scrum.

Logan considered the proposition. 'How long do I get with her?'

Thorn's face dropped, amazed by the cattleman's confidence. Grace tried to pull away, but he held her firmly. Desperate, she searched the crowd for Tom. She sighted him.

His eyes were on hers: a beacon from a distant shore.

Thorn wriggled his pinkie in his ear; he had to check he'd heard correctly. 'Sorry,' he inquired, 'but did you just ask how long you'd get with her?'

'Such deals are usually priced by the hour,' Logan smirked, 'or by the day.'

Thorn darkened. 'Don't push your luck.'

Logan was not to be intimidated. 'How long do I get with her?'

'Man, oh man,' Thorn countered, 'you don't just count your chickens before they hatch—you pluck 'em.'

'If they don't hatch, I'll scramble 'em.' Logan pulled out a bank-strapped bundle of one hundred tenners and ran it under his nose as though savouring the aroma of a fine cigar.

Thorn's eyes widened. 'How many pockets you got in that jacket?'

'More pockets than a pool hall. Your girl: how long?'

Thorn rested his chin on his knuckles and looked at the wad of cash in his opponent's hand.

Logan let the bundle drop down teasingly. A thousand quid landed on the table with a confident smack.

Whatever his opponent might have thought, Thorn was unimpressed by the big-cock show. 'You saying you like high stakes?'

'I say nothing; my money talks.'

Thorn surprised the room with his next move. 'Okay, let me tell you a little story, Logan… That is your name, isn't it? Logan?'

Logan's eyes grew limp, hooding with annoyance and

disbelief.

Thorn released a boyish grin; he had drawn a little of the cattle baron's blood. 'You know why there's an American state named New Jersey?'

Logan stared out onto the street. 'Can't say that I do.'

Thorn continued unperturbed. 'Okay, let me tell you. Once upon a time there was this guy, King James the Second of England. We'll call him——'

'Jim,' said Logan helpfully.

'Sure, we can call him Jim if you want, but I don't want to come across as disrespectful, you understand?'

Logan sniffed. 'Spare me the diplomacy.'

'Yeah, okay,' Thorn agreed, 'we'll call him Jim. Now before he got his ass on the throne, Jim was—along with a whole lot of other crap—he was the Duke of York. And it came to pass he played a game of poker with the governor of an island known as Jersey. And guess what? Jim lost his shirt, but he covered his bet. And you know how?'

'His underwear?' suggested Logan.

Thorn waited for the chuckling to subside and then went on. 'Oh no, young Jim, he could do better than that; he happened to own a piece of real estate. It had been, I don't know, commandeered from the Dutch. They'd called it New Amsterdam, but Jim, exercising due modesty, renamed it in honour of himself and called it New York. So, to make a long story short, to cover his debt, our Jim offered the governor of Jersey a slice of that pie—everything west of the Hudson. And the governor, he took it! And now what have you got? You got New Jersey… That's high stakes!'

Logan pulled down on his earlobe. 'I've seen New Jersey. I don't agree.' He was getting impatient for the kill. 'For the fourth time, how long?'

Thorn gave Grace a cocky little smile. She glared back at him; Ernie had played fast and loose before, but this really was the limit. She wished he would hurry up and put Logan out of his misery. The cattleman's vulgar flaunting of his wealth meant he could certainly afford to lose a bit of it.

Thorn had frustrated Logan long enough—it was academic anyway—but he gave Logan one more pinch of ginger, using the moment to thrust home a salient point. 'You're asking me how long?

'Yes,' fumed Logan. 'For the last bloody time, how long?'

'How long? How long? How long?' Thorn repeated softly. 'Hmm, let's see now. I'd say she's yours until…' Thorn looked at Pop, 'until the goddamned gas tanker gets here.'

Pop's raisin head shrivelled to the seeds.

Logan stated the obvious: 'That could be days yet.'

Thorn gazed at Grace with a hint of pride. 'Then maybe she's worth more.'

Logan sensed the need for urgency. He showed his hand, pronouncing: 'Royal Flush, Spades.'

The crowd muttered in shock: 'Jeez. Crikey. Bloody hell!'

Charlie mumbled to Snow: 'That's why I prefer two-up.'

'This isn't going to end well,' Snow prophesied.

The taste in the gambler's mouth dissolved from candy cane to bitter pill. He slumped over the table, and rubbed his eyes. 'I don't believe it.'

Logan smiled at Grace, lecherously accommodating.

Grace wrenched herself from Thorn's grasp and swore at him: 'You bastard!'

'Gracie,' Thorn protested, 'how long were the odds?'

'Don't Gracie me! What did you hold?'

'Does it matter anymore?' Thorn pointed to the Royal Flush, Spades. 'I had a good hand, a very good hand. Excellent, in fact, but I could never top that. It's unbeatable. It's the hand of a lifetime!'

No way was Grace to be pacified. She did what anyone would do, what the crowd was quietly hoping she would do. She flipped Thorn's cards. 'Queen-high Straight Flush!' she announced to all and sundry, managing to do so resentfully, holding at bay an urge to agree with Thorn's assessment of his chances.

The American was a professional. He had no difficulty reading her. 'I figured it was a sure thing.' he explained, turning his palms skyward, innocence itself.

Charlie nudged Snow's arm like the two were at the sale yards. 'Was worth a shot.'

'Not worth enough,' Snow confided, his expression grim as he looked again at Thorn's hand, the cards forlorn as the dead after a suicide charge.

Logan stacked his money and rammed it into his wallet. Grace backed off from the table in dismay.

'What?' asked Thorn, as if the situation had nothing to do with him.

In a silent scream, Grace threw her fists against her

temples.

Thorn mopped up his silver from the table. 'I was down to loose change and a ten bob note. I made the only call I could.'

Tom could stand it all no longer. He barged through the crowd and confronted Thorn. 'Grace is your wife!'

Thorn slipped his coins into his different pockets. 'Congratulations, kid, very observant. You should take up poker.'

Grace ripped off her wedding ring and threw it at the gambler. He snapped it from midair. 'I'm sorry, Grace,' he said, popping the highly pawnable asset into the breast pocket of his jacket. 'I did what I had to do.'

'Of course,' she snarled, 'and, Ernie, you would never go back on a bet, would you?'

'He'd better not,' warned Logan.

Grace pointed at the cattleman, but stared at Thorn. 'Why don't you tell this local rajah why you had to leave Sydney?'

Thorn said nothing. He slid his ten bob note into his wallet and got up to go. Grace drew away, wary, but glared at him defiantly.

Thorn had to shift the goalposts; the crowd was not on his side. 'Grace, I know I'm calling in a big favour here,' he said gently, 'but you owe me and you know it. Now I'd be the very first to admit things have been rough lately, but I'll make it up to you, I promise.'

Tom led the counter attack. 'Ring or no ring, Grace is still your wife.'

Thorn looked at Tom with tired eyes. 'Son, never judge a book by its cover.' The gambler walked toward the lobby archway.

Tom's eyes followed him. 'You are no gentleman.'

Very slowly, Thorn turned back into the room. 'Grace, tell your little boyfriend here he should learn to control his tongue. If he was a grown man, he'd be a dead man now.'

'You'd have to get past me first,' growled Snow, handing Charlie his beer.

'Stop it!' Grace yelled. Then, quietly: 'Stop it, all of you.'

Thorn snorted and walked away. Every patron watched him leave. He climbed the staircase, stopped halfway, and for a moment seemed he might have second thoughts, but no; he continued to his room.

Logan shoved the playing table aside, grating its legs against the bare floorboards. He moved on Grace. Tom blocked his path.

'Son, you're out of your depth,' the cattleman drawled, his tone deep as distant thunder.

'No, I'm not,' Tom answered, voice brave but breaking, squeaking to a higher pitch.

Logan sneered. 'Step aside, son.'

Tom seemed to withdraw from the showdown, pulling his left leg back, but it was a trick to throw his weight behind his right hook. He swung at Logan with all he had. The cattleman deflected the blow and used the force of the thrust to twist Tom's arm around, pushing it up between the lad's shoulders.

Snow tried to help but Charlie stopped him. 'This is a

show for the crowd,' Charlie whispered. 'He won't hurt Tom. Logan's just marking his turf.'

The cattleman spoke in Tom's ear. 'Take it easy, squirt, it's none of your business.' He threw Tom down onto the floor and stood over him. 'Get where you belong—with your old, drunk daddy behind the bar.'

Lucky said nothing and did nothing.

Undeterred, Tom got up for a second go. Snow grabbed him. 'It's no good, Tom, a bet's a bet.'

Mad Mike had been quiet for a long time but his nerves could stand no more. Swaying, stiff as a skittle, he dropped his beer. Pop swept through the shattering glass and caught the stockman before he toppled over. 'It's alright,' he said calmly as he nursed him to a chair, 'the shelling's finished.'

Logan decided it was time to claim his prize. He lunged out and clenched his hand round Grace's arm.

'No!' Tom screeched as he broke away from Snow and charged. Charlie jumped forward and tackled him. Snow regrouped and joined the ruck; the boy was possessed by a lunatic rage. The defensive line of grasping hands fought hard to hold him. 'This is wrong!' he screeched, still heaving toward Logan. 'It's wrong, can't anyone see?'

'We can all see,' Snow groaned as he and Charlie shouldered him down. Tom's body buckled beneath their weight. Snow turned to scowl at Logan. 'We can all see right enough.'

Logan admired his polished nails, waiting till Tom was broken in. Grace shed a tear as the lad fell limp. She was once more stung by fellow-feeling, but this time also shame, knowing she and Tom to be the same age but thinking him much younger, or rather, she a lifetime older.

Logan sensed her compliance and loosened his grip, leaving a chevron of bruises where his fingers had been. 'Pop,' he demanded, 'I want a mule.'

The old man looked up from Mike in disbelief. Nobody in the room moved, just eyes held wide and jaws hung loose. Logan had to stamp his authority upon the situation. His tongue acted as a cracking whip. 'Lucky, another shout, my slate!'

The mob stampeded toward Lucky at the taps, but not everybody was as fast to jump: Pop stayed put with Mike, Snow and Charlie still cleaved to Tom.

Logan regarded the crowd around the bar, all the men at his command. His power to move others was so thrilling he felt the rise of goose bumps on his neck.

The cattleman's arousal did not go unnoticed. Mad Mike was shell-shocked, sure enough, and though his power to speak without stammering was an ability lost in the deafening maul of blasting shells and gaping mouths of battlefield dead, one thing he had managed to keep intact and bring home safe from France was a pair of eagle eyes. He alone saw Logan's neck and its wave of prickling hide. Tom was still down on his knees, his head hung low. Mike got up and crouched by his side. 'Don't fight it, Tom,' he advised. 'If life were fair, be no need for heaven.'

Tom showed no sign he'd listened.

Logan retook Grace's arm and walked his winnings through the double doors. Tom heard the clack of T-strapped heels and glanced up. Grace was staring down at him, her eyes still shining, green as crème de menthe, persisting so until she disappeared into the inky blackness of the street.

Pop peered at the bustle of drinkers at the bar and turned to his mates. 'Guess I'd better go and get the bastard a bloody mule.'

Logan rode out of town, holding a rope. It was hitched to a mule that carried Grace. Feeling elegant as a sack of potatoes, she gazed on Berto and wistfully observed, 'It's like I'm wandering down from Darlinghurst Road.'

'Deary,' Logan smiled, 'you're a long way from Kings Cross now.'

'Am I?'

Lowanna walked to the creek and crossed lightly stepping-stones to a rock that formed an island in its flow. She sat and looked downstream to where the water pooled, fed by tiny channels from which moonlight wriggled white. The pool's surface barely moved from the creek's flow and the stars the pool reflected, they were listless, swelling and subsiding in lazy folds below Lowanna's island. Upstream, behind the rock, the water didn't move at all, dammed back and silent, and the moon lay fat in the water's depths, gleaming bright, unhurried and patient as the ages.

Lowanna stared into this pool, stared until she saw a window to another sky and dreamed she could dive into its depths and not hit water or the bed that lurked below, but instead arrive in another world where the hardness of earthly things turned kind. Neddy would not be in that other place—

not for many years, she prayed—so she chose to linger at the pool till it became her holy place: the gateway. She would always have something in this world if she could sit at the cusp of the other.

In the forest, deep between the ghostly trees, in the shadows, breathing lightly as a moth, Burnum watched Lowanna and took nourishment. He fed and he grew strong on her pain, drawing out its poison, an angel invested with a task to right the wrong. The mother earth had her terms, unheard by most, and high on her writ she ordained balance.

Chapter Eleven

Pop O'Shaughnessy staggered into the pub. It was proving to be a rough old night. Always a drinking man, Pop usually stuck to beer, moderating his inebriation through bulk, but what with all the night's excitement and seeing as how there had been free shouts in the offing, he had switched to Irish whiskey. The liquor had not made him as happy as it might have done and now his feelings were all of badness, worthlessness and self-reproach, such as might occasion the morning after an all too high-spirited wake.

To provide one of his mules for Logan was an act abhorrent to Pop, but the cattleman could ruin the smithy if he was of a mind, and poor old Ma into the contract. Also, as he would later relate: 'Without a mule, that lass from Sydney would have been forced to travel for over half an hour on the rump of Logan's horse, pushed up close, with her sweet, young legs all apart, either side of Logan's hips. By God, Joseph and Mary, and by all the saints, that would have to be far worse.'

Pop was for thinking the decision to abide by the wager was a matter for the city couple alone to make. Peculiar as he thought such people were, and immoral as he knew the stakes to be, he felt it was none of his business to lecture folk on their behaviour. However, this opinion had not protected

Pop from a shivering guilt over his part in the scheme of things. Combined with a fumbling carelessness brought on by the drink, this guilt had caused Pop to take longer than usual to saddle a mule. Logan and Grace, standing only a few feet away, had watched him struggle with the tack; and though forced to wait, neither had uttered a word of complaint, and of concern, Grace had not displayed the slightest emotion. As he was to admit under interrogation the following morning: 'I don't know, Ma, I would have expected a girl like that there Grace to maybe shed a few tears. You'd have to say, was a pretty sad and humiliating predicament: but no, there was nothing. Perhaps I'm getting old and losing me mind, but surely it was passing strange for a girl to be so stoic. She is either the most heroic lass I ever saw or last night was a situation with which she's well acquainted.'

In any case, the job of saddling done, Grace and Logan gone, Pop was soon hastening back to the pub. Unfortunately Lucky had closed the bar the instant Logan's second shout had been served and the old smithy returned to find the night's boozing already done. But Pop was a sly old dog and he wasted no time in establishing his right to a free drink, demanding of Lucky: 'I'll be wanting four fingers of Ireland's finest.'

'You've got to be joking,' said Lucky, which was to be expected, but old Pop used recourse to authority.

'Lucky, me request comes straight from the mouth of Mr Logan. He has instructed I inform you of his desire that I be getting four fingers of a spirit of me choice, as recompense for bestowing the favour of a saddled mule for the transportation of the young lady.'

'Bullshit,' said Lucky, which was to be expected, but Pop was not to be so easily put off.

'Are you saying to me, Lucky Bramble, that I, your neighbour, fellow businessman of this fair town—and, might I add, your best and most loyal client, apart from your good self of course—are you saying that I'm a lying scoundrel then?'

'Fuck off,' replied Lucky, which was to be expected, but to use the lingo of Thorn and Logan, Pop had an ace up his sleeve.

'Now listen here, Lucky, Mr Logan warned me you might say that so he told me to tell you, if you weren't forthcoming with me drink, I was to tell him as much when I come up to his property to collect me mule; and then he says, that being the case, he will have a quiet word to the brewery regarding your account. He seems to have a notion there may be some irregularities, if you know what I mean.' Pop iced the cake of his threat with a wink.

It was a risky ploy, but a man such as Lucky was bound to have the odd mercantile skeleton shuffling about in his closet. It was a lie, but though a chance to fail, a white lie, whichever way you dressed it. Plus Pop knew Lucky would never dare bring up such matters with Logan. Drunk as he was, the smithy had surmised correctly and Lucky didn't miss a beat: 'Jamesons or Tullamore Dew?' he asked, which was to be expected.

'I'll be having some of that sixteen-year-old Bushmills you've had up there gathering dust for fair on twenty years.'

Lucky became suspicious and Pop realised he had pushed his luck too far. 'No, I've changed me mind: only joking with you, Lucky. I'll be having a drop of Jameson's. 'Twill do fine.'

Pop savoured his four fingers till the very end.

'Come on, Pop, let's go; this ain't a doss house.'

'You're a rotten piece of work, Lucky Bramble.'

'Piss off.'

'I'll be on me way. No need for impure language.'

'You're drunk.'

'A fine one to talk,'

Lucky hustled Pop out, locking the door behind him. The smithy glared through the windowpane, his spittle strafing the glass as he observed: 'Least people can tell when I'm drunk. I never knew you drank till I seen you sober, and that was the first and the last time I seen you sober!'

All the drinkers were riding home, the men and their mounts looking more like long-stemmed mushrooms the further out they drifted. The only ones left lingering at the rail were Charlie, Mad Mike and Snow, all slouched on their horses, each rolling a smoke.

Pop waved to the three stockmen as he meandered to his blacksmith's shop, sonorously supposing: 'I'll be for catching up with you boys, some future date, or of its morrow as yet unknown to us: we who are but nothing, the almighty's benighted children.'

'Yeah,' Charlie snorted, riding out, 'you have a good night, Pop.'

Mike followed Charlie, adding: 'Sleep tight.'

Snow followed Mike, subtracting: 'Not much doubt of that,' his humour, dry as the drought of eighty-eight.

'Shh!' Pop whispered, pointing to the general store. 'Don't wake me bride.' Adjusting his hat he strutted on, suddenly all business-like and proper. 'It's best I rest beside me forge tonight.'

The stockmen were soon gone. Pop bumbled into his blacksmith's shop and was swallowed up by its shadows. There was a clang of metal. 'Oh, Holy Mother of… Sorry, Lord, I think I broke me head… No, I think I'll live.' There was another nasty bang, a clatter and a clunk.

In a hidden gully, far from view, flames leapt into the sky, illuminating the granite and the trees in an auburn glow. Around the fire's base Burnum danced, red and white ochre on his skin, becoming the creature he had painted, the rest of him left merging with the night. He clapped together sacred sticks and moved to their hypnotic rhythm, submerging thought into a trance. His body ached, but its pleas for mercy went ignored, shut out, his focus free to summon to his grasp a knowledge beyond his comprehension for, as with gravity, there was a consequence, but not a reason. The knowledge respected only instinct; no amount of figuring bridged the gap, no torch of science shone the way. Like life and death, the truth was merely there, and though many felt it, not recognising what it meant, few could see it. Fewer still could touch it, bend or mould it: shape one construction to the other. The knowledge and the self were, as different sides of a river, wide and deep, but Burnum found the bridge, a link to where all things became their opposite, and in that moment he was the colour and the chord, the power and the glory, and he shook as the bolt of everything passed through him. The purloined rum was Lucky and Burnum cast him to the flames. The liquor showered down, vaporised and flashed in dazzling blue.

The pyre fell to ashes and to air, to build new life, its task complete, and Burnum, exhausted by his work, walked away and took with him the emptied bottle.

Lucky extinguished the last of the barroom lamps but light from the lobby still sparkled in the glasses on the draining racks. A dishcloth over his shoulder, he stacked chairs on tables and contemplated the mop and bucket in the corner. Deciding he couldn't be bothered cleaning the floor, he ignored them and wandered across to the bar. Taking a fresh bottle of rum, and lost in thoughts of how to square himself with his wretchedness, he fell into a stupor.

Upstairs, in Room Two, Tom sat on his bed and gazed at his books, desperately trying to translate the day's events into a language he could read, sifting for the logic always revealed to his heroes at such an hour. He doubted they would sit in their rooms and let fortune, good or ill, pass by. They would seize the moment, seeing not the fearsome peril, but fair prospect. He recalled how often he had cursed the youth that denied him prizes chance had brought his brothers' way. Though he missed Harry and Darcy, he felt them ever near, and this night their presence had grown to be a burden. Having paid their price, made their sacrifice, proved their worth, he sensed them orbiting, probing, urging him to find his own indelible link to the courage they had found. He ran his hands through his hair, knowing this moment was his for the taking, a chance to make his mark, and yet here he was, just dithering.

Out of nowhere Tom remembered a poem by Andrew Lang and he saw two choices: one, a road that travelled low, alluring in its freshly-graded smoothness, but leading to the desolation embodied by his father; to the other side, a more challenging way, a high road that snaked toward dark hills and tangled woods of misery and pain, but which offered a chance for love uncompromised, for valour, and most desirable of all, excitement either way his course might turn. Between these roads he beheld a weathered marker. It indicated no direction, but it read: 'A man lives only once.'

In the barroom's semi-darkness Lucky sat, still staring at his bottle. A thud of boots came down the stairs, Tom materialising in the lobby entrance. Standing tall in his hat and boots, silhouetted by the lobby lamp, his shadow pointed to his father. In its length Lucky could see his boy had grown to be a man, the shadow's tip a gauntlet at his feet. Lucky looked away; he could not face the challenge. Tom left, footfalls banging on the tired timbers, and headed for whatever lay in store. His father waited, and after a time, there was the sound of hooves. They cantered onto Main Street and galloped into silence.

Thorn sat upstairs in his room, counting his diminished battalions of coin. They were marshaled in columns of silver and bronze on his bedside table. The sorry sight of their diminished ranks caused him to suck down on his lower lip; he wouldn't have enough to settle up his hotel bill, let alone pay for the gasoline to get to Brisbane. The gambler slipped off one of his shoes and removed an emergency fiver from under the insole. Limp and frayed, it was gently unfolded, its days as a chrysalis ended. Thorn grunted with satisfaction; he was always prepared for such contingencies.

The American too had heard the departing beat of horse's hooves. Not knowing it was Tom, but disdainful of such loutish behavior, the disturbance had forced him to restart his coin count. Downstairs, Lucky poured himself a glass of rum.

Two hundred yards up from the stables, the bunkhouses and the sheds, the mansion lurked. Embedded in the night, Logan's home was a long cortege of columns and dormer windows, ivy and old money. A wraith of light issued from within. It floated upstairs, tapered off and then expanded in an upstairs room.

Logan led Grace to the side of his four-poster canopy bed. He pressed lightly on her shoulders and she sat down, offering a slight resistance but still sinking easily into the soft depths of the quilt. He stepped back and considered her qualities, inhaling her perfume as he caressed, at leisure, his lavish moustache. She again dared glimpse his pale, predacious eyes, the irises reflecting feline citron, shimmering as they struggled against his gaping pupils. Repelled, she turned aside and noticed the polished bedposts and the silken sashes holding back the royal blue drapes. The décor's grim formality invited haunted visions of Logan's ancestors laid out on this bed. Grace shivered, rubbing her arms to keep warm.

'Cold?' asked Logan, and then continued without

waiting for reply. 'I've got something that'll heat you up.'

Logan struck a match to ignite a second lamp and opened a dainty French cabinet. He poured a couple of cognacs from a Waterford decanter. 'Hope you like Hennessy.'

Charlie took off his hat and sat at an empty table, his meal before him on a tin plate. He looked down despondently at the meat and buttered damper. 'How are the kids?' he asked.

'Worrying 'bout what happened to their father,' said Peggy, standing by the wood burning stove, her arms folded and expression stern.

'Logan kept the bar open past closing.'

'All you blokes must have had one hell of a good time.'

'Not exactly.'

Charlie pushed away his dinner.

Peggy sat down beside him. 'Not like you to go off your food, what happened?'

'You don't want to know.'

'Don't give me that, Charlie Ward. I've given birth to eight strong and healthy children, and they'll stay that way so long as you and I have got the heart to do what's right by them. So don't tell me, your wife and mother of that brood in there,' Peggy pointed to the single bedroom where, except for baby Helen, all the children slept, 'don't tell me I don't want to know something when it's plain as day I do.'

'God, woman, don't you ever let up?'

'With eight children, I could ask the same of you. Now, Charlie, tell me what has happened.'

Snow and Mad Mike lay in their bunks. Snow was falling fast asleep, breaking wind with each descending layer. Above him, in the upper bunk, Mike gazed at the cobwebs in the bunkhouse rafters, wondering if he might see a scurrying gecko hunting bugs. There could be a lot of the little critters, especially when the weather was warm, and he reckoned them an entertainment when slumber proved elusive. 'How good,' he whispered to himself, 'to be a gecko, to get everything you need.'

Mike longed for the days before the war when life was more straightforward, fulfilling its part of the bargain with those who lived. After the armistice, with the killing and the dying done, folks were just so happy and relieved, but it all proved fleeting. Everybody was trying to be doing the right thing, but the shadow of the fallen was so dark, seemed plainly stupid to pretend it wasn't there. Like walking naked in a frost and saying what a lovely morning. Was hard all round.

The Widow Philpot had waited up for Mad Mike and Snow to get home from the pub, feeding them big servings of tripe and onions for their tea. Mike thought Gladys to be a good woman and a credit to Big George's memory, but he would always note it was a shame children passed her by, husband lost, with none to host and carry on the blood, and precious little else to show for the many years gone by. All the same, was a safe bet, there'd be some happy memories to fill her lonely days and that would have to be a comfort.

As for Mike, he was a bachelor who had never thought seriously of wedding vows. Besides, when he was young and in his rampant, courting years there were too many men for the scattering of women. Though many were plain—an awesome truth to admit—all seemed to get a man, but when the music stopped, bloodnut Mike, with blotchy freckles, florid blush and sideways pointing nose, was left without a chair. That was his lot and he never again much considered the prospect of marrying.

Mike spotted a gecko, watched it poke its nose from out behind a beam, look around and disappear again. 'Doesn't trust me,' said the stockman. 'Good on you, I wouldn't trust me neither.' He clasped his hands behind his head and his thoughts began to wander—haphazard as they sometimes were: a mind having a mind of its own, he would say. He thought about his boyhood years and how poorly suited his consumptive mother and melancholic father were to life upon the land. They were both gone by the time Mike set out on his working life, a jackaroo, and he saw it as a blessing for his mum and dad that they had flown this fickle life so near in time. 'Me folks were a couple always set to quarrelling,' he'd observe, 'but pining for each other when pushed apart too long.' Mike believed them to be mad, so what chance lay in store for him but turn out mad as well. Then his thoughts returned to Gladys Philpot, him talking to himself, or to the hiding gecko, like he was madder than reported. 'Yeah, The Widow wanted to know all about the goings-on at the pub, was tearful when we said what happened to young Neddy. I'll tell you this much, that Gladys—childless as she is—she took it hard. She said, far as I can recollect: "It's a sin to steal a babe from out of its mother's arms, unless the mother is an evil witch, and few are that, and definitely not poor Lowanna." I'll tell youse, here and now, truer words were never been spoke. If Gladys was that sort, she would have swore blind with all the fury such as her could muster, but she kept her self-respect and told us: "As sure as the sweet Lord made a dog quick-witted and a rooster smart enough for nothing save breeding and a tasty Sunday lunch—sure as that—I know life would have been prickly as a bed of nails for both Lowanna and her son in the blackfellas' camp. What with Neddy being half-white and his father dead and all, each day must have been a trial—but family is family! It sure as heck should never be the business of some busybody government and definitely not the business of the holy church. If those that rule can steal a gift as precious as a child, then what was the Great War all about—all that sacrifice in the name of freedom? Where's the freedom for Lowanna and Neddy, I ask you?"' Mike noticed the gecko reappear. 'Yeah, I agree with her—agree with every bloody word she said. What do you reckon, me little mate?' The gecko scampered away across the underside of the corrugated iron roof. 'Yeah, I know, you couldn't give a stuff,' Mike chuckled, 'and fair enough—no concern of yours—but what Gladys asked was as good a set of questions as a human's likely to hear, and I'll tell you what—was well put.' Mike rolled over onto his side, thoroughly convinced Gladys was a clever and warm-hearted woman.

Mad Mike's speculations were far from mad that night, despite it being a full moon. Perhaps, he considered as he drifted off to sleep, I should chat more to Gladys with a mind to turning the Widow Philpot into Mrs Michael Xavier Doyle: would be a shame for us both to reach old age lying in our beds all lonely and alone.

Grace remained perched on the edge of Logan's bed, an untouched glass of brandy on the bedside table. There was a gramophone in the corner. Thorn had put on a record, Stephen Foster's music tripping through the horn: 'I dream of Jeanie with the light brown hair, Borne, like a vapour, on the summer air.'

Logan reclined in his rocking chair, swirling and warming the liquor in his brandy snifter, savouring its bouquet. 'I see her tripping where the bright streams play, happy as the daisies that dance on her way.'

Grace kept her arms crossed over her purse, shielding her breasts from view. 'Many were the wild notes her merry voice would pour, many were the blithe birds that warbled them o'er.'

Logan puffed on his Cuban cigar and blew a perfect smoke ring.

'Oh! I sigh for Jeanie with the light brown hair, Floating like a vapour, on the soft summer air.'

The record finished and the crackling of the wax sounded as warm to Logan as his cognac. He prowled across the room, lifted the needle off the disc and, with his left thumb hooked into the arm-hole of his waistcoat, he swung around as if to pose for Grace. She missed nothing, seeing his fob chain gleaming, his Masonic ring radiating darkly, and the studs of his collar pin—to her, hyena's eyes—glowing in the night. She looked away. Logan inhaled through tightened nostrils, aroused by her modesty.

The cattleman crossed the room and shed his jacket, hanging it neatly on his rocking chair. Grace arched her back as a familiar pain returned. It sometimes came to her on stage or after other moments of dire fear. It was the cramp. It wrenched her muscles with cold, sharp claws, each talon sinking deep under her ribs. The spasm flexed and twisted from her kidneys, contractions pulling and ripping. The cramp was as baffling as it was severe and it betrayed a fear every other part of her could hide. Fright could make some people stammer or grow faint, the hands of others might shake, their bodies sweat or their throats turn dry as cork, but for Grace, the cramp was her Achilles' heel.

Logan noted her slight, thrusting movements, her pelvis bowing in and out. The movement was almost imperceptible but he could see it. His discerning eye could also detect the suppressed heaving of her breasts; they were rolling, one against the other: soft as clouds.

Despite the wracking pain, Grace feared Logan would perceive her movements as nervous shaking. Much as she dreaded what was yet to come, she didn't want to seem afraid of him. She had grasped when she was very young how that could serve to make the situation worse.

Finally the cramp subsided. Grace could again think clearly, but only to be confronted by her greatest fear. Though contrary, it was that Logan's manhood should fail him. She had heard whispered how such shame, such loss of control, could make men violent, especially those men who were used to exercising power over others, men who loved power for its own sake, men like wealthy squatters.

Grace watched Logan remove his waistcoat and his tie, placing them over his jacket. She could see how he was relishing each moment, dragging out each phase of the ritual, a cat tormenting before it ate the mouse; the thrill was in the hunt and not the kill. Killing would only leave a need for something new to kill.

Grace had seen some close calls and nasty scrapes in her short journey with Ernest Thorn, but he had done for her some mighty favours. One favour was so great it seemed to her impossible to repay, until tonight. She owed him, but never before had he been forced to call in his biggest marker. She was his last redoubt, his survival due to her. A few minutes more and he would be in her debt, but she didn't want the credit. That night she had discovered more about Ernest than she cared to know. Yet she loved him still. It was a kind of love that might endure more than any other. Nevertheless, this latest chapter of her life would not last forever. All she had to do was get through the grim hours—hopefully not days—till the petrol tanker finally arrived.

Logan took one last puff of his cigar and walked to the side of the bed, a tramp steamer's trail of smoke billowing in his backwash. He leaned on the firm mahogany of a bedpost, traced his fingers down the drapery and played with a royal blue satin sash. Grace stared straight at the wall, losing herself in the grain of the wood-panelling. Logan tossed aside the sash and like the creak of an old leather armchair, his throat rumbled as he settled down beside her. His weight formed a quilted gully into which Grace tipped. She tried to maneuver away but he enveloped her. 'No, Darling,' Logan whispered in her ear. 'Right now you're mine, fair and square.'

Grace froze as Logan gently took away her purse. He unclipped her dress and let it slide down her arms, exposing her slip. A connoisseur, the cattleman ran the tips of his fingers whisper soft across her naked back and kissed her bare shoulder. 'You should have had some brandy. It would have made you more relaxed, more playful.'

Grace caught a wave of stale cigar and cognac.

'I like a girl who likes to play.' Logan's hand thrust up her dress. The abrupt movement broke Grace's strings of pearls. They clattered on the polished floor. She clenched her teeth. Her lungs ached for air but her chest refused to release its grip.

Logan smiled ecclesiastically. 'Now, now, there are worse things in life.'

Grace saw a shadow move and heard the crack of hickory. From the corner of her eyes she glimpsed Tom as he withdrew his rifle butt from Logan's skull. The cattleman's face descended to her lap before his body rolled onto the floor, landing with a crump.

For a moment, nobody moved. Then Grace shifted her feet away from Logan and turned again to Tom, the whites of her eyes disrobed by her astonishment. 'What are you doing here?'

'I've come to… come to…' Tom stumbled, finding it hard to explain something that seemed so obvious.

'Come to what? What are you doing here?'

'Come to help you escape from him,' said Tom, pointing to the mound on the floor.

Grace saw Logan wasn't moving. She had emotionally geared herself like a boxer before the bell and now the fight was cancelled, her debt to Ernest still unpaid. 'You've made things worse.'

Tom looked around the room. 'How can things be worse than this?'

'Believe me, they can. How did you get in here?'

'I slipped in the window of Logan's office, took one of his rifles.' Tom lifted up the gun and ran his hand over the ornate carvings and engravings. 'It's a Winchester. Beautiful, isn't it?'

Grace shook her head in despair and fell to her knees beside Logan. 'I'll check if he has a pulse.' She reached for his wrist.

'Don't worry,' said Tom, 'he's not dead. He's got concussion. I know 'cause people get knocked out at the pub all the time.'

Grace immediately turned away. She fanned apart her fingers to shield herself from the ugly sight of the cattleman's body and noticed all the fallen pearls.

Tom was bemused. 'Don't you want to be rescued?'

Grace picked up the pearls from the floor. 'You can't rescue me.'

'I just did,' said Tom, putting aside the Winchester and hunkering down to help with the retrieval of her broken jewellery.

Grace ducked under the bed, collecting more pearls. 'Where did you think we'd go?'

Tom dived in after her. 'Where do you want to go?'

'Back to town,' Grace sighed, caving through the darkness. 'Nothing else for it now.'

Tom followed. 'You want to go back to Thorn?'

'That's right, who else?'

'He sold you for twenty quid!' Tom squeaked, appalled, and bumped into something hidden in the shadows. He moved aside a chamber pot. 'Haven't you ever heard of William Wilberforce? Slavery isn't legal anymore.'

'You've never danced for a living,' Grace replied. Evaluating her handful of pearls she wondered aloud: 'What am I doing under here?' Emerging from the subterranean darkness, she decreed: 'This is madness.' Then, discarding the pearls, she walked to the centre of the room and asked: 'Could you please do me up?'

'What about all these precious stones?'

'They're fake.'

Tom's head popped out from beneath the bed. 'Fake?'

'Yes, they're glass, fabricated, fraudulent—they're not real pearls.'

Tom looked at the worthless baubles in his hand and poured them into the chamber pot.

'Fake,' Grace said again, though now more softly, and whispering: 'Like my life.' She fidgeted, trying to fasten her dress. 'That's why I need Ernest.'

Tom stepped behind her and helped with the clip.

Grace began to laugh derisively. 'I need him. Of all the men in the world, I need him.' She stopped laughing and concluded: 'Too bad, it's my lot in life—right now, I need Ernie Thorn.'

Tom struggled to fasten Grace's clip. 'But do you want him?'

Grace threw her arms in the air, exasperated. 'I know what I want!'

'Could you not move so much?'

'Sorry. Is that better?'

'Yes.' Tom fastened the clip. 'After everything he's done, you still want your husband?'

Grace turned to face the lad. 'Ernie's not my husband.'

'He isn't?'

'He isn't.' Grace grabbed her purse, seeking to flee.

'What is he then?'

Grace stopped at the door. 'Oh, God, if you must know, he's my——'

'Don't tell me,' Tom interrupted. 'I'm sorry; I've changed my mind. I don't want to hear it. I'm just glad you're not married is all.' Tom grabbed the rifle. 'In fact, that's really good.'

'It is?' Grace asked, frowning.

'Yes, it means you don't have to love, honour or obey him. You've got choices, we both have.'

'No, we haven't.' Grace instinctively held her ring finger. 'Don't you understand? There's nowhere we can——'

'Don't worry, Logan won't catch——'

'No, I mean Ernie; he won't let me out of his——'

'He can't follow you home, can he?'

Grace chewed on her finger nails.

'No,' Tom continued, 'and that's what you really want, isn't it? Return to Sydney, to the theatre?' Tom drew closer.

'You dance, right?'

Grace's eyes moistened.

Tom drew closer still. 'Can you sing?'

Grace stared, lost in the speckles of gold dusting Tom's hazel eyes.

'Yes,' he answered for her, 'you can sing.'

'I love to sing,' said Grace, the words emerging unaffected.

The hazel eyes smiled. 'I hear the song of a nightingale.'

Grace's lips floated to Tom's mouth.

Logan groaned.

Copenhagen reared up to the sky as Tom leaned forward in the saddle, his right arm swinging outstretched, the Winchester flashing white in his hand, the silver-plated gunmetal gleaming against the infinite black of the night. Waving to the applauding stars and the royal box of the sober moon, he dug his heels into his horse's flanks and charged down the drive, whooping: 'Yee haw!'

Grace held on to him, the wind in her hair, the horrid calculations of Logan's mansion renounced as the haggles of the past. In the womb of one night, the heart of her magnum opus took its first beat and dreams never dreamed before burst forth, impatient to be lived.

Copenhagen's hooves drummed as a hailstorm battering Tom's ears, his eyes watering in the blasting air. Nothing would stop him now. Like David Balfour on the Highlands of Scotland, Harvey Cheyne rising on the swirling white caps of the Grand Banks or David as the stone loosed from his sling,

Tom's life opened up, vast and epic, his destiny sweeping all before it.

The tanker ground into Berto. Thorn looked out his hotel window and sighed with relief. The driver climbed out of his truck. Leaving the engine running, he walked up to the general store and knocked. A window slid open upstairs. 'He's not here.'

The tanker driver backed out from under the awning. 'What's that you say?'

'Try next door,' Ma's voice answered.

The driver gave an acknowledging wave and walked down to the blacksmith shop. He tapped on the barn-door entrance and waited a moment. There was no response. He knocked harder and waited longer, listening for sounds within, but nothing stirred. He rapped on the doors till they shook. There was still nothing. The driver glanced around the corner, down the side of the building to the mules' pen, not sure what he was expecting to see. Whatever it was, it wasn't there—only a mule. He climbed into the tanker's cab and engaged first gear.

'Wait!' called Thorn, rushing from the pub across the street. 'Where are you going?'

'Dorrigo. Can't be wasting time. Plenty more stops till the depot.'

'But you can't go yet.'

'Oh, yes, I can; nobody home.'

'The hell there's nobody home,' said Thorn, walking up to the blacksmith shop and kicking open the doors. 'Hold on a minute. I'll be right back.' Thorn ducked inside and reappeared, dragging Pop.

'What are you doing here at this bloody hour?' asked the old smithy, his head swollen and pounding.

The tanker driver peered out his cabin window. 'You want your bowser filled or not?

Pop extricated himself from Thorn's grasp. 'Of course I do,' he griped.

The tanker driver climbed out of his truck.

Minutes later the Ford raced up the road. Thorn sat at the wheel. He reached into his jacket pocket and checked his twin-barrel Derringer.

Tom and Grace road south toward Berto but pulled up half a mile north of town, where the Berto Road skirted the eastern foothills, the creek and all the cleared land lying to the west. Turning east they trotted up a narrow horse trail that tunnelled into the forest and led to the massive boulders at the base of the escarpment.

'Where are we going?' Grace asked.

'Away,' Tom answered.

Fifteen minutes later they had climbed the escarpment and were riding across a granite ledge. Tom looked over the treetops, down into the valley. Twin beams of light travelled along the road, raking the fields. He pulled up and indicated. 'That's a model T Ford—your car.'

Grace peered over the ledge. 'Didn't take long.'

Tom felt a sudden tightness in his chest. 'What do you want to do?'

'He treats me like a dog,' she said, 'but not all dogs return to their vomit.'

Relieved, Tom gazed into the night and proclaimed: 'Proverbs twenty-six eleven—sort of.'

Grace was surprised. 'You do read a lot, don't you?'

Tom changed the subject. 'Things get a bit dicey now.' He swung his leg over Copenhagen's withers and dismounted. 'Have to walk the horse'.

Grace winced at her high-heeled, T-strap shoes.

Five minutes later the Ford stopped at a gateway. It was the entrance to Logan's property, the long drive wending its way into gently rolling paddocks. Through the windscreen Thorn saw wrought-iron letters on an arch above the gate. They read: 'Logan Downs'.

A fox with a fresh-killed possum in its jaws slinked past the stockmen's bunkhouse. Crumbling, the building lay on from the stables and barn, a short distance from The Widow Philpot's cottage and 200 yards from the road. Inside the bat-cavern black of this bunkhouse, a single window shed a thin ray. Uncluttered by curtains, screens or even glass, the moonlight pooled on Mad Mike's cot and was reflected in beads of sweat trickling from the stockman's face, his haunted dreams lost far away in France.

On the lower range the moonlight broke through a forest canopy, falling upon granite boulders. Tom led Copenhagen over the mossy rocks, weaving through columns of the pale light. Grace struggled to keep up. Tom noticed her predicament and asked if she was alright.

Grace pulled off one of her shoes. 'Lost a heel.'

Tom was terse in reply. 'Town shoes—all show and no go.' He extended his hand. 'Climb back on; you can't walk now. Have to ride.'

'What about you?'

'I'm wearing boots.'

Grace mounted up, somewhat put out. 'If I'd known how the night was going to turn out——'

'You'd have worn boots,' Tom interrupted.

'Oh, please, with this frock?'

Tom again took Copenhagen's reins and they resumed their climb.

Chapter Twelve

The Ford stopped at the side of the drive. Thorn bent sideways across the front seat, and beyond the car's passenger window, he saw it: Logan's home dominating the next hill. Dark and brooding, a single lamp flickered from the edifice, its anaemic glow escaping from an upstairs window. Hours had passed since Thorn had last seen Grace. It would take a miracle for him to rescue her before dreadful deeds were done. Even so, the sooner he arrived the better, and if he was too late, then that would have to be. He turned back to the drive and put his foot down. The tyres growled against the dirt as he sped off.

Thorn's eyes were fixed upon his purpose, glaring ahead as a chain of elms flew by, the boughs passing like a flock of albatross. If Logan gave him any trouble, he had a double-barrelled answer in the pocket of his coat. Its bullets might move slowly, but across a card table or a rumpled bed of sullied sheets his Derringer would do its job quite well enough. Over the previous hours he had pieced together a strategy: once in Brisbane he would find the highest table and clean up big, then spend up big atoning, buying Grace new clothes, hats and shoes, jewellery and other finery. Preston Logan had whipped him good and proper but Thorn had yet to meet his nemesis. Like all gamblers he walked a tightrope between triumph and despair, but that danger was not the essence of the thrill, nor was it the money. Though he loved the money for the good life it bought, blowing his winnings as quickly as he made them, the essence of his joy lay elsewhere. To earn a living from a deck of cards was not mere luck. To win he must, each time, locate the key, unlock the door and behold a universe mere mortals never saw. Look carefully, perceive the signs and the face was a window to the inner man, and like the window's pane, it could mirror the other's hidden hand. To read another's mind was to own a slice of their soul, but to carve it to a purpose, the mark must be rendered blind as Thorn was sighted. In that zero sum game, winning was not just luck, it was Delphic.

But all things have their price. Thorn's penance: to deny his soul. If it were there, it could be read as easily as the mark, it could not be hidden, a veil of such opacity not woven. The only way to hide a soul was kill it, leaving nothing but the machinery of life. The ultimate gift of the game was not a gamble, it was a precise knowledge, but to house the knowledge, the soul must vacate. Thorn pushed his foot down hard on the accelerator. He might still arrive in time to save the day.

Thorn believed it would be a good while yet before he met another Preston Logan. Men like Logan existed all over the globe, but they were few and far between: a handful of people who had sold their souls to the game, who had nothing in their eyes but the game—no windows to the heart, nothing but holes projecting light into a shell. Thorn hoped, with a little luck, there would never be another Preston Logan in his life.

Next time he would recognise the signs and not get greedy.

And then there was Grace, but she was just a kid; she'd roll with the punches—kids were resilient. He would look after her again, and in time she'd forgive the wrong he'd done. Grace: his muse, his lucky charm, his darling inspiration, showered in gifts and gratitude, and the promise of still bigger things to come the minute Cinderella ventured Stateside.

Logan's house didn't seem to be getting any closer. Thorn pushed the accelerator all the way down to the floor. The engine over-revved, screeching in protest.

The gambler wondered how many women had forgiven him his sins, each one failing to resist the joyful release of showing mercy. Although it was hard for him to recall a betrayal greater than the one he'd committed against Grace, he'd learnt many women were held captive by the deep and overwhelming need to show forgiveness. The skill lay in coupling their dreams to a promise never kept. Though he should have rewarded such forgiveness, he never did, not in the long run.

Grace was different. He could not live without her absolution. It would come, with time, because it had to; she could never return to the place he had found her. He had spoilt her much too much for that. She would dress him down for sure: crazy not to; pride and dignity demanded it. She'd drive out all her demons, beating upon his chest, or even slapping him across the mouth. She'd expend, exhaust her fury and then he'd charge straight in, loaded with gifts better than a pirate's tribute, more enchanting than the Magi's bounty from the distant east, more deceptively alluring than any horse a Greek could offer up before the gates of Troy.

The drive transformed from dirt to gravel. Thorn entered the gardens surrounding Logan's mansion, the cattle baron's inner sanctum. The river stones crunched beneath the tyres of the Ford. They crunched too loudly. The pebbles flew about, bombarding the inside of the fenders. A bend in the drive was sharper than Thorn had anticipated. He braked, but the wheels lacked traction. The car slid. Its rear swung out and span across the lawn. Thorn's body gave way to forces beyond his control, first pressed against his seat, then forward and from side to side. He almost lost the steering wheel but sunk his nails into its maple rim and accelerated hard. The Ford tore up the manicured grass, came out of the spin, nosed into a hedge, vivisected perfumed lilly-pillies and speared into the base of a sandstone lion, standing guard at the foot of Logan's front stairs. Steam boiled from the radiator. The engine sputtered and then died.

Tom led Copenhagen onto a clearing of level ground. 'We'll stop here for a bit, spell the horse.'

Grace was getting nervous now. The initial excitement of their flight had faded, getting dimmer as the forest gloom grew deeper. A child of the backstreets of Chippendale, Darlington and Redfern, hers was a world of different sights and sounds: noisy railway yards, breaking glass, squeaking night carts, factory whistles and the endless grind of city traffic; it was the colours brown and grey, the hues of mould and soot; it was the sickly smells of tanneries, of rendered fat and waste, and the cloying vapours from the Tooth's and Reschs breweries. She was fearful about being so far away from her natural environment. Better the crowded streets of Sydney's inner neighbourhoods than the lonely mountain ranges. 'There snakes up here?'

Tom went to help her off the horse. 'Oh, you don't have to worry about them.'

Grace surveyed the haunted rocks. 'No, of course not, they're tucked away in bed for the night, aren't they?'

'Maybe: all depends.' Tom rested Grace's feet upon unwelcome ground.

They had stopped under a small cliff, its curved grey wall broken by fissures, deep and cobwebbed. All around them was a carpeting of ferns. To Grace, the undulating fronds of bracken hid a world of creatures—crawling, slithering and slimy. She longed for the certainty cobblestones.

Tom un-cinched the girth and lifted off the saddle, 'Mainly what you'd get up here would be tiger snakes, adders, red-bellies.' He put the saddle on the ground. 'No, come to think of it, too high up for red-bellies.' Tom went to look around.

Grace watched him move away. 'The snakes that are here—they venomous?'

'You cold?' Tom asked, not hearing Grace's question.

'A bit,' she answered. 'Are they venomous?' she asked again, but louder.

'Yeah,' said Tom, starting to collect fallen wood. 'I'll rustle up a fire.'

Grace shivered. 'Enough to be dangerous?'

'No, just enough to keep warm.'

Grace rolled her eyes. 'I mean the snakes. Enough to kill?'

'What'd you say?'

'The snakes—enough to kill?'

'Why would you want to do that?' Tom protested as he disappeared into the forest. 'Why hurt them? They were here a long time before us. This is their home; we're the intruders.'

'Yes, silly me,' Grace whispered. 'Wouldn't want to be rude to our generous hosts.' Now alone, the unease she felt grew more intense and again she yelled to Tom: 'I know we don't belong here. Not arguing that. I love snakes every bit as much as wasps and spiders. In fact I adore scorpions, but could these snakes, the snakes up here, could they kill me?'

'What?'

'Could the snakes kill me?'

'Who, you?'

'Yes!'

'Oh, reckon: dead as a maggot.'

Contrarily, Grace let loose a breath of relief; better to be acquainted with unsettling facts than left in terrifying ignorance. The trees brooded over her, and though it was quiet, the forest was alive with noises. She wanted to know more. 'Which snake is the worst?' she asked.

'Eastern Brown,' Tom answered.

'You never mentioned that one!'

'I didn't want to scare you!'

Copenhagen shivered. Grace jumped.

The only room that wasn't dark was the master bedroom.

When Thorn entered he saw Logan on the floor, wide-eyed and helpless, his hands tied behind his back, feet bound together and leashed to a leg of his canopy bed, every limb trussed up by royal blue satin sashes. Thorn's first thought was for Grace.

The gambler peered under the bed. 'Gracie, you don't have to hide; everything's okay.' He threw open the wardrobe. 'I've got a tank full of gas.' He dragged aside the drapes. 'We can leave now.'

Logan watched as Thorn ran past him and out to the hallway, still pleading: 'Sweetie, we can be in Brisbane by this time tomorrow, Stateside in a matter of weeks—Broadway, bright lights.'

There was no response.

Thorn raced to the stairway landing, high above the oval entrance hall, and leaned across the banister. 'Grace! It's Ernie! Where are you? Come on, honey, let's beat this dump!' Then he begged: 'Snookums?' It was to no avail; she wasn't there. He re-entered the master bedroom and stomped across to Logan. 'Where's she gone?'

Logan mumbled something unintelligible. Thorn removed an Argyle sock from the cattleman's mouth.

'The publican's son,' Logan blurted out, 'he's taken her.'

Thorn felt a prickling numbness rush through his body; manageable discord was degenerating into chaos. He started working at the sash that tied up Logan's hands. 'The young hothead?' he asked.

Logan hesitated and then nodded: 'Must be.'

Thorn leaned closer. 'Are you sure?'

The cattleman looked worried, apprehension germinating.

The gambler didn't like that; he wished he could have read Logan's mind as easily during their poker game. 'Did you see him or didn't you?'

'Not exactly sure.'

'Oh, no, don't do this to me.'

'I'm not doing anything to you,' Logan protested. He squeezed his eyelids shut, trying to see a face in the speckled darkness. 'I was undressing Gray——talking to Grace, and all of a sudden I noticed a shadow on the wall. Yes, a shadow on the panelling, and then I remember everything exploded in this white flash and——that's all I can recollect.' He swung his chin against his shoulder, checking Thorn's progress with the bindings. 'You see? He must have sneaked up on me, sneaked up from behind.'

'Christ's sake,' Thorn moaned, angered by the stubbornness of the firmly knotted sash, annoyed by everything unravelling except the sash. 'Goddamn it!'

'Hey, don't forget who you're talking to,' Logan blustered, bondage failing to mitigate hubris. But, then realising his immediate fate was manifestly in the hands of Thorn, he changed tack. 'Anyway, I'm pretty sure it was the Bramble boy. I can't see how it could possibly be anyone else.'

'Okay,' said Thorn, shaking his finger to underline his point. 'Now, let me get this straight, you're telling me you're not actually sure?'

Logan shook his head, getting yet more irritated. 'No!'

Thorn whistled softly, relieved they'd finally crossed the

first hurdle. 'Good, I'm glad that's settled.' He released the sash. 'Where would he have taken her?'

'No, you've got it all mixed up,' Logan grumbled, rubbing his liberated wrists, alert to the misunderstanding. 'I'm not saying no——'

'You just said no.'

'I know but I should have said, "Yes! Yes, I'm not sure," and not "No," which would have meant "I know."' Then, hope in his eyes. 'You know?'

'Not exactly.' Thorn was becoming as baffled as Logan.

The cattleman tried to smooth the kinks from the satin sash that had so recently restrained him. 'It's only I can't believe that young Bramble would have the bloody audacity to be so disrespectful. Can you believe a young lad like him capable of this outrage?'

'Don't ask me,' Thorn shot back, climbing to his feet. 'You're the one who said it was him a second ago.'

Logan stared skyward. 'I was sure a second ago, but not now!' His voice deepened and took silk. 'I'm not sure now because you are badgering me.' Logan began untying his ankles.

Thorn felt the weight of the Derringer in his pocket. The gambler leaned into Logan's ear. 'Face it, buddy, you haven't got a clue.'

The cattleman blew a gust of wind into the sail of his moustache. 'Now listen here, when I say no, I mean no! Let this be absolutely clear—I don't know because I don't know if I know or not.'

Thorn turned away, even more distressed; Logan didn't

seem to know much of anything.

The cattleman tried to press his thumbnails into the knotted sash. 'Jesus,' he swore, realizing, if word ever got out Tom Bramble had overpowered him, his reputation would be left in tatters. Thorn could never be allowed to breathe a word of it. By fair means or foul the American would have to be hushed, but first he had to be mollified. 'Blast it all, you must forgive me; my mind's all fuzzy,' Logan sniffled, straining to evince contrition. Letting go the stubborn sash, he ran his fingers over his pate. They skated its polished veneer, and through a lyre of hair, reached to the back of his skull. There they touched blood. 'Blood! That's why I can't remember. I must have been hit harder than I thought. He really hit me. The little blighter could have killed me!' With a cool breath of cleansing air, Logan was again lucid. 'That's why I've got a headache.' He rubbed his fingertips together to dry away the spot of blood and recommenced his attempt to unbind his ankles. 'What was I saying?'

Thorn's shoulders slumped and his words leaked out reluctantly. 'You were telling me the publican's son hit you.'

'Oh, yes, certainly enough. Now it's all coming back to me.'

Thorn laughed scornfully. 'Really?' His gaze fixed on Logan's struggle to free himself. 'One minute you say you remember, the next you say you don't. One minute certain, next minute not. You're just a guy who likes to change his mind. Funny,' he added, pushing his hands deep into his trouser pockets, 'wouldn't you say that was a woman's prerogative?'

'Damned knot!'

'Don't cuss me, Logan.'

'I'm not cussing you. It's the bloody knot!'

'You want me to find a knife.'

'Good God, no; this sash is one of a set.'

Thorn's aggravation was at breaking point, the sands of the hourglass falling lower every second they quibbled. He pulled his hanky from his pocket, removed Grace's wedding ring and wiped his sweaty brow. Choosing to take a more measured approach, he said: 'Look, Logan, times are a-wasting. The reason I want you to be sure is because—as I figure it, you'll agree—Grace is a beautiful girl. Now, the pub was full of men. All of them would have been swept off their God-damned feet by Grace's beauty.' Thorn glanced at the gold wedding band and nervously rewrapped it. 'Yeah, she's just such a beauty, nobody else like her. And any one of those cowpokes could have got it into his God-damned… could have…' Thorn's words trailed off as he slid his hanky back into his pocket, his thoughts filled with dreadful images of Grace's plight, or worse still, acquiescence. 'Oh, God Almighty, Logan, time is running out!' Thorn snatched Logan's frittering hands from their toil. 'Give me the sash or we'll be here all week.'

Logan was put out. 'I almost had it untied.'

'Yeah, sure you did, Logan, sure you did.' Thorn ground his teeth as he concentrated on the knot, his deep-set eyes flexing against his finely chiselled skull. 'You see,' he pressed on, 'I have to move fast, but I don't want to go barking up the wrong tree. Can't you see why I have to be sure who to go after?' Thorn felt the cattleman's humiliation and realised how much he needed him. 'Yeah,' he spoke quickly, 'I knew you'd understand.' His tone became supportive. 'Plus, of course, we must be certain of who assaulted you; that cannot go unpunished, by God, no!'

Logan rubbed the palms of his hands into his face, fingers drumming his scalp, exaggerating his anguish to hide his alertness to the American's dispirited concession. 'I wish I could say for sure,' he bleated, 'I really do, but I haven't got eyes in the back of my head.'

Thorn grew bored with his line of inquiry—got bored with the knot too—and shifted away to roam around the room. 'Maybe there's a clue in here somewhere.'

'It has to be Tom,' said Logan, snatching the ends of the sash. 'He's got to be the most likely culprit, don't you reckon?'

Thorn grabbed the brandy decanter, smelling its contents. 'Yeah, it would figure.'

'Yes,' Logan agreed, 'it would figure.' One of his eyebrows elevated, aroused by a newly registered suspicion. 'Unless it wasn't Tom,' he said, 'unless it was you.'

The American slipped the stopper back into the decanter. 'Why would it be me?'

'You expect me to assume,' Logan growled, 'expect me to swallow the line that you've never gone back on a deal?'

Thorn played around with the heavy Waterford crystal. 'Logan, your legs are still tied up. If I cracked you on the head before, let's say I do it again, only this time with added enthusiasm.'

Logan rushed back to his unknotting. 'I'm sure it was

Tom. There, I've said it.'

Thorn put down the decanter. 'But unfortunately you didn't see him.'

'Wait a second,' Logan whispered, fingers once more caressing his head, the tips now favouring his temples, conjuring to the present a vanished memory. 'I didn't see him but I heard his voice. Yes, from when I was being tied up. That's why I've been so certain all along.' His hands shot up to the sky. 'It was his voice!'

Disturbed by Logan's histrionics, Thorn turned away. 'Yeah, right, you heard him while you were still knocked out.' The gambler noticed the pearls on the floor.

'Yes, I'm sure,' Logan readily agreed, failing to discern Thorn's sarcasm. 'Even though, as I've intimated, everything was very muddled then.' Logan became quiet as his reasoning stalked a scattered herd of recollections.

Thorn picked up a pearl. 'It could have been some other young guy. He got any buddies?'

'No, not now,' said Logan, still deep in thought. 'No, it was definitely Tom.'

Thorn played with the fake pearl as if it were real, ignoring Logan's assertion, more interested in how Grace's necklace came to be broken.

'Yes!' the cattleman yelled, unaware of the impending danger. 'It had to be Tom Bramble. I'd stake my life on it. He's the only white man in the valley who doesn't fear me.' Then he attacked his knotted ankles with renewed vigour. 'When I get my hands on him, he'll wish he died in France with his damned brothers.'

Thorn sensed the plausibility of Logan's deduction, but was too distracted by the insistent call to vengeance. 'Why are Grace's pearls all over the floor?'

'No idea,' Logan lied. 'They must have been broken by young Bramble.'

'How?'

'How should I know? I was unconscious!'

Thorn's eyes lit up, recalling the effect Grace had on Tom, realising he should have been more vigilant. The American tossed aside the fake pearl and walked along the side of Logan's bed, searching out further evidence of wrongdoing. 'The horse must have been him.'

Logan was quick to catch the scent. 'What horse?'

'Outside my room at the hotel—it was pretty late by then, some time after the pub closed. I couldn't rightly say when. I thought it was nothing—just one of the pub crowd, a tail-ender galloping home drunk, kicking up his heels—but it must have been the kid. I should have cottoned on to that.'

'Yeah, you should have,' Logan snarled. He tore at the sash and it finally released its grip. 'Little bugger can tie a knot!' Empowered by his recovered freedom, the cattleman reprimanded Thorn. 'It should have dawned on you hours ago that the rider had to be Tom Bramble. You could have prevented this catastrophe: would have saved me having to wrack my brain. See what's happened because of your lack of attention to detail—the lad's had plenty of time to run off with your girl, without so much as a promissory note, and before I got to enjoy my winnings. In future, don't forget; a man should always keep a watch on the details. Everything in life is made out of details—everything!' Logan dragged himself to his feet. 'What are you doing here anyway? The tanker arrive already?' He gripped the bedpost, dizzy from his ascent. 'What was that bloody awful noise out there earlier? You make a mess of my landscaping? What have you hit?' Logan stumbled to the window.

Thorn wasn't listening. He picked up Grace's brandy snifter and saw there were no lipstick traces on the rim.

Logan shaded his eyes and peered outside. 'I hope you haven't damaged my hedge. My grandfather planted that hedge before I was born.'

Thorn turned to the four-poster. The quilt was creased, but the bed was still made. The truth of what had happened was clear to him: Logan wasn't lying; he had been interrupted moments from cashing his cheque. Thorn found dried droplets of blood on the floor and was impressed. 'Kid's got balls, I'll give him that, but he won't have them for long.' The gambler put on his hat and went for the door.

Logan gave up on trying to see outside; the light in his bedroom was too strong. He heard boots marching down the stairs. Thorn was leaving. 'Hey, stop!' Logan shouted, causing a jagged bolt of pain to shoot out from his wound. 'Where are you going?'

'To the pub!' Thorn shouted back.

'Why?' asked Logan, rushing after him.

Thorn halted at the front entrance and saw his smashed-up automobile. In his blind rush to save Grace, he had neglected to check the vehicle for damage. 'Son of a bitch!' he barked.

Lighting his way with one of the bedroom lamps, Logan darted across the entrance hall and pushed past Thorn. He stopped, horrified, as soon as he got outside; the sight in front of him was worse than anything he had imagined. 'Thorn, you madman, what have you done?'

Logan ran down the granite stairs, put aside the lamp and threw his weight against the Ford, trying to dislodge it. The radiator tubes scraped and squeaked, and water poured out of the cooling system. A shattered headlamp snapped off, shards of glass tinkling.

'Wait a second!' Thorn yelled, running after Logan. 'Let me take care of it.' The gambler climbed into the Ford and released the brake. The motorcar rolled off the bottom step, the chassis rattling as the front wheels hit the gravel.

Logan caressed the statue of the lion and checked the monument's base. 'You've chipped the plinth!'

Thorn climbed out of his automobile. 'I'm sorry. I was in a hurry.'

'Oh, God in his heaven!' Logan bayed, wobbling to his garden. 'The ancestral hedge! You've laid waste to my grandfather's lilly-pillies.' Logan bent over for a closer inspection.

'Hey, like I said—I'm sorry,' Thorn protested, but with eyes more concerned for his car, 'that's a pretty tight turn you've got there on your drive.'

'Nobody's ever complained before.'

'Sure, I'm hearing you,' Thorn lied. 'I'll make it up to you.'

The Ford's radiator core was ruined: several of the tubes

were broken and a deep dent had been rammed into the brass upper tank. The gambler feared he would never get out of Berto. He bent over to thoroughly audit the destruction and saw where a stream of rusty water had pooled in the gravel.

For a couple of minutes, the gambler and the cattleman examined the demolition, wandering about, sticking their beaks into everything like a pair of hungry ibis. Finally they both stood up.

Thorn leaned on the front fender of the Model T. 'How am I going to get Grace without an automobile?'

Logan didn't answer but rushed back into his mansion, the damage forgotten. For the want of anything better to do, Thorn followed, chasing the cattleman inside and down the hall. 'Do you have an idea where they might have gone?'

Logan still didn't answer. He kept on toward the rear of the building. Thorn was right behind him. Observing the emptiness of the house, he asked: 'Where's all your staff?'

The cattleman arrived at a large door. As he opened it he divulged: 'Don't like having live-in servants and only hire stockmen on a casual basis; don't pay hands just to sit on their arse.'

'Thought you'd be the type to at least have a butler.'

'Butlers are for poofters!'

Thorn followed Logan into the office. The décor was *belle epoque* plush, all deep green leather and teak. It was like a gentlemen's club or a legislative chamber, the rug and the drapes smelling of stale cigars and well-seasoned profit.

'Damn,' Logan cursed, 'the little prick's taken my Winchester.'

There was but one rifle in the gun rack: a Lee Enfield 303. Logan grabbed it, sat down at his desk and pulled out the magazine. 'Where did I put those cartridges?' he hissed, foraging in his bottom desk drawer. 'I also have a Remington, but it's at the gunsmiths. You got something to shoot with?'

'Yeah,' said Thorn, pulling out of his jacket the pocket-sized Derringer.

'Fat lot of good that'll be,' Logan sniffed as he found his box of ammunition. 'Damned head's killing me.' He produced from his top drawer a packet of headache powders.

Thorn slipped his pistol back into its pocket, embarrassed over the inadequacy of his weapon. 'Where do you think they'd go?'

Logan poured a paper sachet of the powder into his mouth and grimaced. 'Pounds to pig poo,' he wheezed, 'he'll cross the range.' Logan gagged as he tried to swallow the powder.

Mystified, Thorn walked over to a pair of magnificent leadlight windows. They were half open. He pushed them wide. 'There's mountains either side.'

Logan snorted contemptuously at Thorn's trepidation and emptied the box of cartridges onto his blotter.

Thorn gazed upon the grey pastures, black forest, all embracing escarpment and Logan's Peak, lambent white. 'God, like looking for a haystack in a haystack!'

Logan started loading the cartridges into the magazine.

Thorn turned from the window. 'Which way do we go?'

'To the east.'

'Why?'

'Bugger all due west.' The cartridges made a satisfying 'clack' as Logan pressed each of them neatly into place, a snug fit on alternating sides of a double column. 'I hope you recognise one end of a horse from the other.'

'Seventh cavalry,' said Thorn, walking toward the hallway door.

'Fighting Indians?' Logan inquired, momentarily interested in what the American had to say.

'No, we were stationed up in Manila, fighting mosquitoes.'

'Oh, yeah,' Logan nodded, 'bloody mozzies. Hate the evil bastards.'

'Got to say, up there in the tropics the bastards are dirtier than here—full of malaria, dengue fever, yellow fever, almost every pestilence a man could name. Lost a lot of troopers; no place for a white man, but I guess that's the way it is. Halls of Montezuma, as the Marines would say, shores of Tripoli.'

Logan locked the magazine back into the rifle. 'Never got the chance to serve, myself,' he said, somewhat miffed, and grabbed a handful of extra cartridges. 'An army travels on its stomach and the human gut needs beef.' Logan distributed the loose cartridges into his trousers pockets, dropping a few in the process. 'Logan Downs produces the best prime beef you'll get anywhere in this wide, brown land—south of the tick line.'

Logan slammed closed the bolt handle, chambering a round into the breach. He stormed out of his office. Thorn followed.

While gathering wood to start a fire, Tom had taken the time
to reassure Grace the eastern brown snake was diurnal and
rarely active after dark; the nights in the ranges were too
cold—which was not entirely true.

They had turned out the bedroll and Grace now lay
across it, leaning against Copenhagen's saddle while Tom sat
by the campfire. After sharing a can of beans for dinner, Tom
had made them tea in his blackened billy. Grace sipped the
sweet, dark brew from a pannikin and bathed in the welcome
warmth of the little fire. Her red dress was torn and her hat
long gone, but things were comfortable enough; the night was
tranquil and not too cold, even though the Northern Rivers
hinterland could still be frosty that time of year.

'This tea is delicious,' Grace purred. 'I've never had tea
from a billy before.'

'It's the gum-leaf,' Tom confided.

'Really? An ordinary gum-leaf?'

'No, we get them imported from Tasmania.'

'Ah, yes, ask a silly question———'

'Could be the mountain air,' Tom was quick to confide,
lest his teasing seem rude. 'Everything tastes and smells better
up here.' He leaned over to reach for his old canvas bag. 'I've
got a surprise for you.'

Grace sat up straight and focused on the bag. 'A
present?'

'Yes,' Tom whispered, 'but first you have to close your
eyes.'

The knowing smile returned to Grace's face. 'Close

them?'

'That's right, no peeking.'

Grace put down her pannikin of tea. 'Alright, in for a penny, in for a pound; ready when you are.' She shut her eyes.

Tom swung the bag to-and-fro. 'Like I said, no peeking.'

Grace frowned. 'I'm not peeking.' Then her brows rose, stretching her eyelids and exposing a streaked residue of eye shadow. 'Look at me. I can't see a thing; lashes glued shut.'

Tom pulled out a battered hat.

'Wait a moment!' There was rapid eye movement under the lids. 'It's not a snake, is it?'

'No, you've got snakes on the brain; this is a prezzo you'll want.' Tom attempted to massage the crumpled hat into reasonable shape.

Grace frowned again. 'I've noticed that sack thing before—it's always hanging off your saddle. What's it for?'

'It's a snake bag.'

Grace pursed her lips, but chose to say nothing.

Taking the hat by the brim, Tom held it above Grace like a coronation crown. 'Now, you'll have to keep completely still.'

Grace nodded.

'Completely still.'

'Sorry.'

With a sense of ceremony, Tom placed on Grace's head the battered, old Akubra.

'It's a new hat,' she declared, raising her hands to touch it.

Tom shrugged modestly. 'You can open your eyes now.'

Grace took off the hat.

'Why did you do that?'

'How else am I going to see it?' Grace noticed the grime and stains, less than impressed. 'This is a new hat that's been newer.' She investigated under the brim. 'Seen better days, that's for sure.'

'Not necessarily.'

'Alright,' Grace elaborated, 'it's a lived-in hat.'

'Is that a bad thing? Is a home any the worse for being lived in?'

'It gets rundown.'

'Yes, the house, but not the home.'

Grace appraised Tom as if over reading glasses. 'Would I be correct in assuming this is your hat?'

'Was my hat, from a few years ago, but now it's yours.' Tom grew serious. 'Do you want it?'

'Smells a bit like fish.'

'Just needs airing out. So, like I said, you want it?'

'Yes, I do. Thank you,' she whispered, realising the thoughtfulness of the gift. 'I suppose we'll be out in the sun for most of tomorrow?'

'Yeah,' Tom mumbled distractedly, 'long ride ahead of us.' All of a sudden embarrassed, he snatched back his former hat and worked on its shape. 'There are a few creases. Been all scrunched up for a bit.' His effort made little difference to the recalcitrant felt. 'Let's see how it goes with the chinstrap.'

'Wait,' Grace demurred. 'Has it ever been washed?'

'It's been wet.'

'Wet?'

'Rain.'

Grace laughed; she laughed so much she started to cough, and took another sip of tea to clear her throat.

Tom was concerned, 'You'll need it. You don't want to end up with sun stroke.'

'Sunstroke?' asked Grace, her hand against her chest, alarmed.

Tom's eyes grew wide with sincerity. 'Trust me, the sun up here can be pretty crook—hot as a street hawker's watch.' He continued to rub the felt, battling to restore the hat to its former glory. 'She's a little rough around the edges, but should do the job well enough.'

Grace wiped dry her mouth and put aside her pannikin. 'Let's try it again.'

Tom returned the hat to Grace's head and firmly tightened the strap under her chin. 'How's that feel?'

Grace loosened the strap and fine-tuned the hat's position. 'It feels good.'

'Looks good too,' Tom agreed, and retightened the strap. 'Don't want it to blow off.'

Grace glanced around the clearing. 'Wish I had a mirror.'

'No you don't.'

'Why not?'

'Who cares? I'm the only one who's going to see you, and I reckon the hat goes well with your dress.' Tom lay down, using his saddlebag for a pillow and pushing his own hat forward over his eyes. 'We should catch an hour's sleep while we can.'

'Do we really have to rush? How will Logan find us up

here?'

'He will.'

'We're in the middle of nowhere.'

'Oh, pull the other one,' Tom laughed, 'it hangs down lower.'

'Huh?' questioned Grace, not certain of, but imagining what he meant.

'Oh, sorry, excuse my French,' Tom muttered as he sat back up and busied himself, grabbing a stick to tend the fire. 'No, we aren't nowhere. We're on a spur of the Gibraltar Ranges. From here I can get us to Grafton. There's a train to Sydney there—the North Coast Mail. Folks reckon it runs most days.'

Grace squinted at him. 'You have any money?'

Tom sighed at the licking flames. 'Not enough to get to Sydney.'

'What about Copenhagen?'

Tom looked at his horse and his eyes grew glassy. 'I could send a telegram to Snow, ask him to organize for someone to take Cope back to Berto—Bluey Corbett or maybe a drover returning from the yards. Jeez, I don't know.' Tom got up, walked across to his horse and gave the animal a pat. 'Wonder how much a livery stable would cost?'

'More than your train ticket.'

'If I had enough money I'd take him with me.'

'To Sydney.'

'Yeah,' said Tom, somewhat aggrieved as he walked back to the fire. 'How else am I going to get around?'

Grace lifted up her dress, revealing her thighs. Tom

wasn't sure which way to look as she removed a couple of tenners from her garter. 'While you were busy tying up Logan, I borrowed a few quid from his wallet. He won't miss it.'

Tom whistled, impressed by the sight of the red banknotes. 'That's a lot not to miss.'

Grace tucked one of the tenners into Tom's shirt pocket. 'He won't miss the money as much as his rifle.'

'Logan'll know I've only *borrowed* the rifle,' Tom protested.

Grace laughed.

Tom gazed at the fire. 'You're born in Sydney, right?'

Grace sighed her affirmation.

He threw more branches into the blaze. 'Lived there all your life?'

Grace sighed again. 'Born there, survived there, uninvited, unwanted, till Ernie found me.'

'Then what?'

Grace sipped her tea. 'Nothing's for nothing.'

'How many people you seen?'

'Seen?'

'Seen in the flesh?'

Grace tilted her head with a questioning look.

'No,' Tom spluttered, 'I don't mean with no clothes on, but in person, seen in person. Not a photograph is all I meant.'

'Oh, all up?'

'Yeah, even from a distance, a big distance, in crowds and such.'

'God, how many?' Grace asked herself. 'Must be tens of thousands.'

'Cripes,' said Tom, 'if I've seen more than, oh, three hundred people, I'd be amazed. And that's in my whole life, I'd be amazed.'

'What about the pub?'

'Not a lot of passing trade.'

'Not surprised.' Grace finished her tea. 'What about Grafton?'

'Never been there.'

'But you said——'

'I can find the way.'

'Never even been to Grafton?'

'I won't get us lost.'

'Extraordinary.'

'Yeah, I guess.' Tom stoked the fire a little more and put down the stick. 'You wouldn't credit how keen my brothers were to get out of these mountains, see the world. You wouldn't credit it, honestly.' His attention shifted to the edge of the clearing where a cliff fell deep and fast. His view was filled with sky and the air was sharp and clear, the stars so plentiful there was barely space to hold them. Tom spoke softly, his words as simple as a mealtime grace:

'If a symphony could twinkle, the sound of a symphony be seen; Its music would look as the sky that he saw then: One heart, one voice, everything and him, He'd never been that way before, never pass that way again; It was a corner of a place forgot.'

'You pen that?' Grace asked.

'No, my mother.'

Grace frowned. 'It's from a man's point of view.'

Tom fiddled with the fire. 'She wrote it as a gift for me on my last birthday with her—a voice to take for my own, to use as a guide to find my place in the creation of things. Funny, up here, I only meet people known me all my life. Up here, my place might just as well be set in stone.'

'Up here you've got the freedom of the wide open spaces.'

'But no privacy.' Tom looked across at Grace—the first time in ages he had really done so, taking in her face like it was a privilege, now bestowed, and not thought rude. Then he went on talking, telling his story to her eyes. 'Up in this valley everybody's got their nose to the ground, snouting out other people's business, telling everybody other people's business. What kind of freedom is that? I reckon your right to privacy, your right to raise your voice protecting it, I reckon it's the most important freedom you can have. You saw what happened to Neddy. '

Tom turned away as if his illustration of a fact was an accusation he had leveled at himself, thoughts billowing with images of his stolen mate. He spiraled in the moment and confusion flowed from his eyes until staunched by a blink. The ripple effect caused him to again pick up the stick, using it to lift a smouldering branch and lure in fresh air. The fire rekindled and the flames proclaimed themselves in a rally of little pops of crackling moisture. Grace watched as he lifted up a knee, crossed his arms around it, and beheld again the legions of the stars. 'Up here,' he continued, 'you can find solitude— no denying that. Cripes, you can find solitude within yourself wherever you are, but is it freedom? I mean it's a kind of freedom, but it's one you can make for yourself; privacy, on the other hand, is something others give you, let you have. You can't have it if it's not allowed.'

Tom returned to Grace. 'Thing is, in Sydney, I'd just be part of the crowd. Nobody would know me. I'd be surrounded by all these faces, seeing all these gateways into other worlds, but not scared of them looking back, seeing things I don't want seen, knowing things I don't want known, forever painting me from the same old sketch drawn a lifetime ago. In Sydney I'd be born again, free to start over, be who I want to be.'

Grace couldn't help but lean toward him. 'Who's that?'

'I don't know. That's why I have to go to Sydney.'

Grace was not constrained by the neat little circle Tom had closed; she pressed on. 'You must have an inkling?'

'S'pose.'

'Well?'

'Oh, crikey.' Tom went to fiddling some more with the fire.

Grace shuffled nearer. 'I promise I won't tell.'

Tom swung away.

'God,' said Grace, 'this is like pulling tee——'

'I want to be an artist.'

'What kind of artist?'

'Not sure.'

'Not sure?'

'Words, something to do with words.'

Grace stared into Tom. 'Alright, now we're getting somewhere, words?'

Tom did not meet her gaze. Instead, he addressed his

testimony to the fire. 'That's why I have to leave this valley; it's like talking to four walls. What's an artist without an audience? What good's a story without someone to tell the story to?' His eyes returned to Grace. 'When you sing or dance, I don't reckon you're just going through some notes or steps; you're talking to the folks in the audience, talking in the language that feels right for you, and because it's right for you, the folks, they understand, and your song, your dance is not only for them; it is them. Only, you can do it in a way they wish they could, but can't. You are their voice. It's a holy moment. And when one person really touches another through their art, I reckon it's the voice of God. That's how God speaks: through art, more holy than religion could ever be.' Tom sucked on his lips before continuing. 'Religion's use of art, they say, is in praise of God, to serve God, but they're putting the cart in front of the horse—the art isn't there to help us worship God; it is God. Saying art is only there in praise of God means it can be flicked away like a fly, be called vanity, all vanity, all about us, somehow meaningless, but what would religion be if there were no us? The religion is ours to make and the best we can make is art. That's why I hate it when some people like to turn religion into a book of rules, of laws, 'cause that's just housekeeping, not really what we want—least not what I want. You go out in holy quest of an answer, not a law. Shit, laws are easy to find—impossible to get away from the bastard things. Yeah, I reckon we all know what we want to know. It's the unknowable and art's a hint, a clue, great art so close we can almost taste it, but laws can't stick to art, to God, any more than a horseshoe to a waterfall.

God's the thing we search for and art's the thing we grasp, because that's all there is. You know about a bloke named Michelangelo?'

'He's an artist. He painted murals, the ceiling of the——
——'

'Sistine Chapel,' Tom interrupted, nodding the words.

Grace nodded back, happy to mime with her lips that stolen from her voice.

'Yeah,' said Tom, maintaining the rhythm, 'yeah.' The bubble of his exuberance had now burst on the spike of ineffability, leaving him stranded on a sigh, emotionally breathless, so humbly appreciative he had to release the thread of his tale to take stock. Grace was the only person he had ever met—other than his mum—who had heard of Michelangelo. Tom owned a book on the artist. It had been his mother's. He would often wonder at the image of God giving life to Adam; the tension of the almost touching fingers. 'Look at that sky,' he asked. 'Is it greater than the ceiling of the Sistine Chapel? Is it more than that or less?'

'Does it matter?'

'No, no it doesn't,' Tom laughed, intoxicated by their kindred thinking. 'I reckon it doesn't matter either. It doesn't matter what we believe. That's what I've been pondering for so long now. The ceiling and the sky are art if they help us get to something beyond ourselves. It's God, and how it sits with us—that's our private place. God is a private place. A quiet place too… You reckon I'm full of shit?'

Grace was at a loss for words.

'Sorry,' Tom apologised, 'excuse my French.'

'No,' said Grace, 'I like your French.'

Tom shifted close and his eyes were on her. 'Grace, I reckon when you dance or when you sing, you show a little part of you, and that part's holy, but it's also the part that you want known, while all the rest is yours, your citadel, your other place no one else must enter lest you open up the gate. In Sydney I could paint or write or dance or learn to play the tuba. I don't know, but I'd be showing to the world what I want the world to see of me, the part of me that's like a mirror, reflecting something that's like… that isn't in the thing reflected, a little something extra, the strand of hair that tips the scale from nothing to something, and I could do that in a crowd because I'd still be free to keep the part of me that's truly me. I'd still have my engine, my special place that's just for me. But if the world can see that private bit, if it sees the me inside me, sees what people up here have seen of me since I was born and knowing things I wish they didn't know, stripped naked, might just as soon be dead. Some things like privacy you have to fight to get and hold, no matter what the cost. And if that part of life is priced too high and you get burnt, you'd have to ask, what is the point of life? What's the point of living?' Tom sensed he had gone too far and he returned to stabbing at the fire, but he had to know. 'What do you reckon? You reckon artists get burnt?'

Grace's eyes dilated. 'Many a gravestone says it's so.'

Tom reacted like she had dropped a pound into his busker's bowl. 'Grace, don't get me wrong about these things I've said. Don't get put out or anything, but it's the God's own truth when I say I'd never look into your heart and try to own it, but I'd love to see, each day, the little parts you let escape.'

Tom was close enough that Grace could smell the eucalyptus oil that had collected on his skin and the fire's smoky scent that coursed his hair, a fire that was clean, clean burning: mountain fire.

'Do you know what you're letting yourself in for?' Grace asked, feeling as much responsible for Tom as she was inspired. 'The bush is what you know.'

'But the city is what I want. Please take me to Sydney.'

Grace touched Tom's cheek and it was warm from the fire. She kissed him. She kissed him deeply as she had never kissed before, and she could smell the mountain forest in him, taste its freshness in his mouth.

A branch in the fire popped.

Grace pulled back. 'Big day tomorrow, need to get some sleep.'

Tom gaped at her, his mouth and eyes open as a goldfish, and retreated faster than an eel. 'Yeah, long ride,' he allowed, and lay back on his saddlebag, facing away. 'Sorry, Grace, I'm not like you must think. I'm not that sort.'

Grace felt the stars berating her. 'I know that, Tom, I know you're not that sort.'

Chapter Thirteen

Lucky stood in the shrine that was Room Three, gazing upon furnishings untouched since Harry and Darcy's departure; the beds and lowboy, floor and rugs, the Spartan decorations all covered in years of dust, grey and thick as moss. He had stood there many times before, sometimes for hours, but this night merely seconds was all his heart could stand. Stumbling out, he made his way downstairs. Guided by a kerosene lamp dangling from his hand, its insipid light projecting shadows running from his way, he lurched toward the lobby door and checked the bolt latch. Everything thereabouts assessed to be in order, he took himself back up to bed. On reaching the landing he came to a sudden stop, not only seeing, but this time looking at the entrance to Tom's bedroom. He had not crossed the threshold to Room Two for many years: so long ago he could not recall the last time when—it never seemed of any interest—but now Lucky was intrigued. He crossed the hall, and discovering the door unlocked, peeked in. Too dark to make out the interior, Lucky decided to enter, and with that the chamber sprang to life, all topaz from his lamp. Shifting his weight from one foot to the other, the hulks that were his eyes bobbed unsteadily till docking at the bookcase. With mouth agape, he stared at the rows of books and the stacks of books piled either side. 'So many books!' he said aloud. Lucky knew Tom liked to read, but this was a library. Forced to sit, he flopped down hard on Tom's old bed, and the springs were shrill in their complaint. Methodically resting his lamp upon the floor, Lucky set his mind to wondering what his son had read of late and swung around toward the bedside table. He strained to focus on a volume resting there. It was bound in cloth but its spine was leather, a ribbon bookmark at its end. Reverently he took the book and gently thumbed through pages that fanned the scent of newly printed ink. On reaching the end, Lucky, now resolute, returned to the beginning. With conscripted application he ransacked the pages, his agitation mounting, fingers pawing at the paper. Rough treated, often tearing, each leaf rustled by, with Lucky seeing the blocks of type as nothing more than different patterns: none the same, like snowflakes. Annoyed by this, he became more fevered, ravenous for something different, something his eyes could eat, hunting but uncertain of his prey. It might be an engraving, a photo or a map, a chapter heading or a caption, but he hungered for some snippet hidden in the type, a cipher buried in a thicket of words made incomprehensible by drink. Dyslexic, he clawed, desperate to unearth the story's story, its promise of what his son was really all about. He didn't know. He had never thought to ask; he had never cared before.

Lucky closed the book, and like a blind man reading braille, he felt the texture of the title embossed into its cover. Hesitantly, and with effort, he looked and read aloud: 'The Red Badge of Courage.' The publican hiccoughed, clueless as to what the title meant, and tossed the book aside. It tumbled off the bed and fell onto the floor, bumping against a package lying there. Gift-wrapped, it poked out from under the quilt as if to beckon exploration. Lucky grabbed it and found a card attached. He whispered softly: 'Happy birthday, Dad. Something you would never allow yourself. Love, Tom.'

Lucky swelled, elated that his boy had not forgotten, then collapsed, wishing that he had. Sucked out to nothing, he heard the ticking of the bedside clock and saw its hands had shifted past the hour. Sunday had arrived, he making landfall on that distant star called sixty. Lucky felt like Rip van Winkle, while asleep his life had slipped away, and so too, his only living son. He had misplaced both, but only one need go for good. In a fog Lucky couldn't see one remained out there, abandoned, but within his gift to reclaim. He had the wit to know what he had pissed away, but not the guts to save the remnants. That time had passed. He was deaf and blind to that. He could not smell or taste it. All he could do was feel, and all he could feel was pain. All he feared was pain. All he enjoyed was pain. Lucky revelled in it, shovelled it into his mouth and into his ears and up his arse; and this would be his triumphant feast of all-consuming agony. This would be rock bottom.

Lucky turned to the gift. A moment passed and then he lashed out. He ripped the paper and tore at the ribbon, racing against the ticking clock, the seconds plunging to another midnight, his birthday, like his life, gone before he knew that he was living it. Within the wrapping lay a small suede box. Lucky lifted its lid. The glow of his lamp reflected, dazzling from a pair of golden cufflinks. Past melting, Lucky's heart crumbled into dust.

A thunder of hooves shook the earth as Logan and Thorn rode into the aboriginal camp. A burning torch held high in hand, his Lee Enfield slung across his back and daring defiance, Logan cantered from hut to hut, roaring leonine: 'Wake up! Get out of bed, you lazy, good-for-nothing bastards!'

All the clan awoke in terror. Women screamed. Children cried for their mothers. The men emerged with spears.

His audience assembled, Logan bellowed, 'I want Burnum and I want him now!'

Lowanna tore from her hut and charged at Logan, excoriating the night with her shriek. She grasped at his trouser leg. 'What you done with Neddy? What you done with my boy?'

Logan glared down at Neddy's mum. 'No idea what you're talking about,' he grunted and booted her aside, knocking her down to the dirt. Lowanna screamed again. The cattleman's stallion spooked and reared. Logan's arm flew out, stealing balance from thin air. His torch remaining upright as its flame, he leaned forward in the saddle, and seeming to defy gravity, neck-reined his mount. The animal pivoted full circle, but the cattleman stuck to its hide, tenacious as a thirsty tick. Its head twisting behind the bit, wrestling for a freedom long denied, the horse was compelled to accept the folly of its protest. Bowing to the authority of the cattleman's seat, it lowered its forequarters, and snorting in exasperation, its hardened mouth turned soft. With an indignant shiver, the might of the beast submitted to instruction. Triumphant, Logan trotted the still agitated creature from side to side, describing zigzags and figure eights around the smouldering campfires and clusters of wide eyes. With throat still at full throttle he ordered: 'Bring me Burnum! Bring him here and bring him now!' Upon receiving no response, he then insulted: 'Are you blacks damned fucking-well deaf? I said: "bring me Burnum!"' Then he waved his flaming torch. 'Get him here or I'll burn your filthy hovels to the ground!' With waves of equine muscle shimmering onyx, Logan's thoroughbred was made to prance about, the power of its movement swirling the campfire smoke to ghostly wreaths as the boom of the cattleman's voice splintered the surrounding forest. 'Where's the tracker?' he bellowed again, enough to waken with a rustling of leaves and buffeting air all life within the convulsive shadow of his broadcast. 'Get the bastard here and get him now!'

Thorn rode up, leading a third horse. He tapped Logan on the shoulder and pointed to the trees. Burnum emerged.

The room was dark as black. Blinded moans and the creak of the bunk bed's mitred joints scrawled angry strokes of dungeon pitch as Mad Mike tossed and turned, infested again by a blood-gorged war that erupted from his freckled lips and quaked the air with, 'Galloping! Galloping!'

The uproar filled the ironclad bunkhouse like a detonating hand grenade. Snow awoke and was straight up the side of the bunk. Teetering on one leg, he shook his mate. 'Mike,' he yelled, 'for the love of God, wake up!'

'Is that you, Snow?'

'Yeah, it's me, mate.'

Mike's face stretched open, eyes sprung wide, as he aspirated: 'Tom!'

Snow was confused. 'Tom?'

'Galloping was Tom. I saw him. God's honour, I saw it.'

'You were dreaming, mate—same old nightmare.'

Mad Mike sat up, immediately himself again. 'No, was different. Need some light.'

'This better be important,' Snow grumbled as he hopped to the table, felt for the matches and lit the kerosene lamp. Its warmth had barely illuminated the room before Mad Mike jumped down from his bed and started dressing.

Snow eased himself onto the arm of the insect-eaten couch that formed their living room. 'What are you doing?'

Mike pulled on his pants. 'We're going out.'

'Have you gone off your nut?'

Mad Mike stared into space. 'Maybe.'

'No, I mean are you insane?' Snow looked out the window. 'Ah, full moon—you're a bloody lunatic!'

Mad Mike continued dressing. 'Yeah, fair chance.'

'Fair chance? Is that like fair chance the sun'll come up in a couple of hours or fair chance I'll win the flaming Melbourne Cup?'

'How should I know? I'm not a witchdoctor.'

'Neither am I, but here's some free medical advice. You're mad—mad as a cut snake!' Snow got up to return to bed. 'Sorry, mate, didn't mean anything personal about the cut snake bit.' He climbed under his blankets and tried to close his eyes. 'Bugger it. Got to take a piss now.' He reached for his new leg. 'What in hell time is it anyway?'

Mad Mike didn't own any kind of timepiece. Since the war he had made it a rule. All he said was: 'Early.'

'You're not wrong there,' Snow muttered. He leaned over to the side of his bunk and fossicked for his wristwatch.

Mike slipped on his wrinkled flannel shirt. 'I haven't lost the p-p-plot or nothing.'

Giving up on the search for his watch, Snow reached for his new leg and fumbled about, trying to attach it. 'This bloody useless thing's given me a blister the size of a pickled onion. Damn prophylactic doesn't fit me.'

'You got to break it in first.'

'Bloody government!' Snow chucked away his new leg and grabbed the old.

Mad Mike did up every second button on his shirt. 'People call me mad 'cause I'm shell-shocked but I can still think.'

'Nobody ever said you couldn't.'

Mike dragged on his socks, holes where the heels should have been. 'Thanks, mate.'

'It's alright,' Snow purred as he strapped on Fritz, the wooden leg's familiar embrace comforting as the stockman's favourite brand of tobacco. 'No friend like an old friend,' he declared, his throaty rumblings now honey-smooth and blissful. Snapping out of it, he reassured his mate: 'Mike, I know we call you mad—that's a mate's privilege—but if I ever heard some other bastard say you couldn't think, said you was simple, they'd have me fist down their throat faster than a cow can shit on a new pair of boots. Stone the crows, you're the best horseman in the valley. That takes brains; no dill could ever manage it. Don't let any mongrel tell you otherwise.'

'That's right,' Mike agreed, grateful for the endorsement, 'and you're me mate, so act like a mate and b-b-bloody well give me the b-b-benefit of the doubt. If you were Tom, what would you be doing right now?'

'I'd be smarting, pretty grumpy.'

'When we was in the stables, watering the horses last night, you hear anything off in the distance, could have sounded like g-g-galloping?'

Snow observed a gecko race across the underside of the roof. 'Oh, fuck!'

Mike put on his hat. 'Couldn't have said it better meself.'

'Wait,' Snow squawked as he got back up from his bed, 'might've been the horses chewing their hay. Sure it wasn't that? Sure it wasn't grinding you was hearing? A horse chewing close can sound like a horse's hooves a ways away. I mean are you sure?'

'Do I have to be?' Mike asked.

Snow took down their rifles, tossing over to Mike his .22. 'Better get Charlie as well.'

'Yep, was just about to suggest the same.' Mike snatched a box of ammunition and raced out to the stables.

Snow limped after him, trying to dress while carrying his gun. 'Hey, don't forget us peg legs!'

A moment passed till Snow returned. He picked up his watch from the shelf where he always left it.

Tom rode into the black's camp almost every single day, come to pick up or drop off Neddy. Because of these regular visits,

Burnum was used to the sight of Copenhagen's hoof marks. Now, having been summoned by Logan, he used a torch to spot the same distinctive prints on the cattleman's front drive. Fresh from only hours earlier, they were as clear as the Southern Cross on a cloudless night.

On an Appaloosa supplied by Logan, and confidently riding at a canter, Burnum followed the prints. They led him out the cattleman's front gate, and south, down the Berto Road. After journeying some ten minutes, the tracker spotted a narrow path. Revealed by a slit of moonlight that cleaved the shadow of the trees, it led off at right angles toward the eastern range. Without pausing, Burnum turned his horse in the path's direction. Logan and Thorn quickly followed, neither questioning their scout's confidence.

A short time later they found themselves amid a pile of fallen boulders, collected at the base of the escarpment. Burnum dismounted, passed the Appaloosa's reins to Thorn and held high his torch to light the way. Carried on the still night air, all three men heard the rhythm of pounding hooves on the Berto road.

The sun was still somewhere over the Coral Sea but the stars, one by one, had already disappeared into a lavender sky. Below, phosphorous scorched the fringe of the range and heralded the arrival of another troubled day.

Tom awoke and sat up with a start. He checked for Grace. She was still there, yet asleep, curled up snug within the closed side of the bedroll.

Down on the valley floor, Charlie was hard at work, splitting logs for the kitchen stove. Mad Mike and Snow galloped to his gate. From inside the house, Peggy heard the drum of their horses' hooves change to the gait of a trot, then a desolate quiet. She knew what it meant.

The stockmen dismounted and walked up to Charlie. Snow started first. 'Mike's been… umm,' he paused, struggling for the right word.

Mad Mike came to his aid. 'I was dreaming again.'

'Mulling things over in bed,' Snow corrected, and then, with a fresh breath: 'Yeah, Mike's been weighing up the shit that happened in the pub last night, and he got to talking to me 'bout it.'

'I reckon Tom's rode up to Logan's property. Gone up there looking for the g-gambler's wife—that y-y-y———'

'That young Grace Thorn,' Snow added.

'Yeah, he rode up last night while we was watering our horses.'

Charlie leaned on his axe and noted the rifles hung across the stockmen's backs. 'What makes you say that?'

'We heard his horse galloping full pelt up to Logan's place,' said Snow.

'You're a long way from the road. How do you know it was Tom?'

'Who else would it be?' Snow stared north toward Logan's property. 'We need to check things out. See if Tom's alright, hasn't got himself into trouble or nothing.'

'All because Mike had one of his dreams?' Charlie turned to Mike. 'Sorry, mate, but you know what I mean.'

'She's right,' he replied with a genial shrug.

Snow had to clear the air. 'Mike might have been dreaming, but he was mulling in his dreams.'

'Yeah,' Mad Mike agreed, thankful for the lifeline, 'was dreaming and mulling too.'

Charlie waved away a fly. 'Seems to me youse two are going off half-cocked. First of all—you want my two bobs worth—you should be off to the pub. Make sure it really was Tom you heard or find out if old Lucky's got any news. Something like—if young Tom did piss off, where was he headed? Mightn't have been Logan's place. The rider mightn't even been Tom.'

'No,' said Snow, 'don't want to waste time. Was plain as day last night in the pub, Tom isn't speaking to his old man— not after what happened to Neddy.'

Charlie had a scratch. 'Look, Peg's got a list of chores for me to do today longer than a tent-show sermon. You sure it even was a horse?'

If Mike had been that sort of a bloke, he might have been offended. 'Didn't you hear a g-g-galloping horse last night?'

Charlie's face went blank.

'You must have heard something.' Snow couldn't believe it. 'We weren't so pissed you'd be out cold before you ate your tea.'

Charlie frowned, trying to recall.

Snow helped him along. 'Charlie, you're right; Mike and me, we're a long way from the road, but——'

'Yeah,' Mad Mike acknowledged, 'Gladys's—I mean

The Widow Philpot's farm must be what? Two hundred, three hundred yards——'

'Oh, and the rest.' Snow avowed indignantly, gesturing with his hands, spreading them apart to illustrate his estimate. 'A quarter mile from the road at least.'

Mike innocently supported Snow's enthusiasm for an idea that he was the first to put forward, 'Yeah, must be a quarter of a mile… almost.'

Snow recognised his mate's honesty and his own exaggeration. He ventured more soberly: 'Charlie, you're a lot closer to the road than us. If we could hear galloping——'

'We heard it too,' Peggy confirmed, standing on the front veranda, her baby in her arms, a cluster of children close behind.

Charlie rubbed his three-day growth of stubble. 'Youse blokes really reckon was Tom?'

'Charlie, stay here,' Peggy pleaded. 'You've got eight kids who need you.'

Snow turned to Charlie's better half. 'I know you, Peg. I know you well enough to know you've got out of Charlie the whole story—what happened at the pub last night—and I can guess what you'd be guessing at, but young Tom, well, I s'pose he's become a mate.'

Peggy looked at Charlie, watched the husband she loved so dearly, as he slammed his axe into the chopping block, his log splitting done for the day. The baby began to cry. Peggy walked back into the house. Her man had made his decision. She didn't like it, but she saw the strength of it; the bond between Charlie and his two best mates had allowed them to survive the war—it got them home alive. She respected that.

Chapter Fourteen

He could have kicked himself for being so forgetful. It was a shoddy job and Tom was not happy with himself. He poured the remaining contents of his canteen onto the dying embers, stamping and twisting with his boot heel to extinguish the tiny spots of red in the ash that the water had not drowned.

'You alright?' asked Grace.

Tom pointed to their campfire. 'Smoke,' he replied. 'Even just a little bit can be seen for bloody miles up here. We should have been awake before there was any light. Should have remembered, but I didn't—bloody well slept in!' He stalked across to the cliff and crawled to its edge. Grace followed, fearing Tom's remorse might be less to do with smoke and more at revelation of his naked flame, that strangely modest and sometimes evil twin to afterglow. From their eyrie, high above to far below, they saw Burnum. He was on foot, walking through low scrub, followed by Thorn and Logan, both on horseback, leading a third horse.

'Oh, Ernie,' Grace moaned, 'what are you doing here?'

Tom looked at her, not speaking, but filled with fear. She felt his silence and read him like a book. 'Don't worry, Tom, I haven't changed my mind; Ernie's yesterday.'

'And what about me, what will you think about me

tomorrow?'

'Tomorrow, I'll be able to say that yesterday I was with a man I understood.'

'God, am I that easy to understand?'

'No, not at all, but I know you know what you want, and that's more than you think, more than you think worthy, and that's more than I can say for myself.' Grace walked back to their camp.

The beige gravel crunched as Charlie, Mad Mike and Snow cautiously rode up the drive. The Model T Ford still sat in front of the lion.

Snow pulled up his horse. 'This isn't good.'

Charlie stopped beside him. 'Tanker must have finally arrived.'

Snow hopped out of his saddle, eager to investigate, but landed too hard on Fritz and burst his pickled onion. 'Oh, struth,' he groaned.

'You right there?' Charlie asked, more as a criticism than out of concern.

Ignoring the sticky discomfort, Snow nodded: 'Yeah, fine, nothing an extra leg wouldn't fix.' He limped over to the Ford.

Charlie dismounted and followed. 'I mightn't be able to drive one of these buggers, but I'm pretty sure this isn't how you park 'em.'

'No,' said Snow, 'not unless you're in a bloody big hurry.' He handed Charlie his horse's reins and swung around to the radiator. 'Someone's stuffed up the front end: broken her nose.'

Tethering his horse, Mike saw the stain on the steps from the rusty water. 'Didn't realise a motorcar could bleed.'

Charlie strode back and forth through the hole in the hedge. 'Had to be travelling at a fair rate: made a hell of a mess of the garden. Must have gone off the road and skidded over the gravel here.' He returned to the car and kicked a tyre. 'I wouldn't mind getting one of these someday.' He glanced up and had a little chuckle at Logan's mansion with its rows of windows. 'Wonder if any bastard's home?'

Mike walked up the granite stairs, leaned through the open door, knocked and called out: 'Anybody here?'

Snow followed. 'Widow Campbell won't be around: doesn't work Sundays.' Not bothering to announce his entry, he marched across the entrance hall, Fritz clattering on the parquetry. 'I'll have a stickybeak out back. You look up top.'

By the time Charlie had hitched the horses and arrived at the front door, Snow was gone and Mike was half way up the curving staircase. 'Hey, Mike, where you going?'

'Check out the bedrooms.'

Charlie raced after him, behaving like they were a squad again, reconnoitring.

Mike started with the master bedroom. It was empty, the curtains open. He walked to the end of the four-poster and saw that the quilt was rumpled. There was a sash in the middle of the floor. He picked it up and examined its frayed satin.

Charlie entered. 'Had a quick squiz. Nothing in the other rooms.'

Mike handed him the sash.

'Blue for boys,' Charlie noted as he fingered the plaiting.

'The thread's been damaged,' said Mike.

Charlie's russet eyebrows arched. 'Yeah, it's all buckled like it's been torn at, like it's been used to tie up someone nice and tight.'

'And someone didn't take kindly to that?'

'Yeah, like it was knotted and they've pulled at it, trying to escape.'

Mike picked up the other sash. 'This one hasn't been cut or nothing. How's yours?'

'Not cut or nothing neither.'

'So someone untied the knots.'

'Yeah,' Charlie agreed, 'They was tied up and someone turned 'em loose.'

'Who's they?'

'Buggered if I know.'

'Who's them?'

'I'd hazard it was they.'

'Sorry, Charlie, what I m-m-meant was this: who was the someone who tied 'em up? Who set 'em loose?'

The stockman shrugged. 'Maybe Grace was tied up and Tom untied her.'

'Then what about Logan? What was he doing?'

'Jeez, Mike, you tell me; I'm not flaming Houdini.'

Mike walked over to the side of the bed, taking a close look at the crystal snifter and smelling the brandy. He trod on a pearl. As it crumbled under his boot he noticed the pearls scattered all around him and brown stains on the floor that appeared to be blood. He bent over and grabbed the chamber pot. 'Charlie, not asking you to be a magician or a fortune-teller or nothing, no more than a normal b-b-bloke with two eyes in his head, but what do you make of all this?'

'Mike, I reckon somebody was tied up and someone untied them, but I'll be buggered if I can say for certain who done it. We've got two ropes and three bods: Tom, Grace and Logan.'

'And Thorn's car outside.'

'Sorry, four bods.' Charlie wandered over to the gramophone, lifted the record off the turntable and read the label. '"Jeanie with the Light Brown Hair." You like that song, Mike?'

'Yeah, was Mum's favourite, She had it on a piano roll.'

'Youse lot have a pianola?'

'No, just the roll; Mum used to take it to The Widow O'Connor's place when she went calling.'

'Old Kath can play the piano. She wouldn't need your mum's piano roll.'

'Yeah, but Mum was always too embarrassed to ask The Widow O'Connor to play the song, so she'd leave the roll poking out of her handbag, hoping Kathleen would see it and get the hint.'

'Fair enough.' Charlie put back the record. 'What you got there in that piss pot?'

'Pearls.'

'Christ, Mike, must be your lucky day.'

Downstairs, sunrise streaked through the leadlight windows of the office. Their multicoloured rays shed on Logan's blotter and dappled Snow. He stood behind the desk, chewing on his upper lip as he sifted through the contents of the drawers.

Charlie and Mad Mike entered from the hallway door. 'Something's been going on upstairs,' Charlie drawled.

'Yeah, up in the bedroom,' Mike added distractedly, beguiled by the cathedral radiance of Logan's office. He continued without stammering, a sure sign he wasn't listening to what he was saying: 'That young sheila, Grace, her big string of pearls is broken—pearls all over the floor.'

Charlie lifted up the sashes, 'And seems like someone's been tied up with these fancy blue ropes, with these tasselly things on the end.'

'Yeah, they're tassels,' said Mike, still not stammering, his focus roaming over Art Nouveau in glass that blossomed hypnotically. 'All really weird, but.'

'Yeah, really weird,' Charlie confirmed as he walked to the desk and dropped the sashes down in front of Snow. 'You can see where they're all torn up a bit.'

Snow wasn't interested in the blue sashes or broken pearls. He took a fallen round from Logan's desk and pointed to the empty rifle rack. 'You were right, Mike. Tom is in trouble. Pretty big trouble if all these spilt cartridges are anything to go by.'

Mike stepped closer to the mesmerising windows. 'How do we find him?'

Snow noticed his mate was off with the pixies again. 'Hey, Mike?' he spoke roughly and tossed across the cartridge.

Mike saw the metal in flight and pecked it from the air, quick as a hawk. Mike was like that: tongue made slow so everything else moved fast to compensate. He turned the cartridge in his fingers. The brass casing flashed in the morning light.

Lowanna's pupils mirrored flames as she sat and stared into her campfire. From the southern end of the camp, Charlie, Snow and Mad Mike rode up, all steam and rising dust, their horses foaming.

Snow yelled from across the fire. 'Lowanna, you seen Logan?' She did not answer. The stockman climbed down from his horse and limped toward her, doffing his hat. 'Has Logan been here looking for Burnum? Have you seen Logan?' There was still no response. He crouched down. 'Lowanna, it's Snow: remember?' She remained motionless. 'Lowanna, this is important. Tom could be in trouble—big trouble.' He was alert to a twitch in her eye, and though only slight, it was clear she was aware of the shame he felt—his shame over his failure to effect such a frenzied effort to save her Neddy. Snow shut out the gangrenous thought and took a breather. He saw anticipation in his mates and tried again to get through to Lowanna, pronouncing every word as if she were hard of hearing: 'Lowanna… you… seen… Logan?'

Mike could see the futility of the interrogation. 'Snow, it's no use.'

'Mike's right,' said Charlie, 'and Mike should know—after what she's been through: same as shell shock.'

Mike's forehead buckled. 'Jeez, poor woman.'

Snow scrutinised Lowanna's vacant gaze, trying to channel her thoughts, but nothing came of it. He pinched the ridge of his nose as if in prayer.

'You alright?' asked Mike, concerned for his mate and anxious to be out of the place.

Snow's hand arced from his nose in a diving despair, knowing his attempts at communication to be futile. He tramped back to his horse.

'Now, can we go into town?' Charlie barked. 'Like I wanted to do in the first bloody place.'

'Not much choice now,' Snow accepted stoically as he mounted up. The three stockmen pivoted their horses south, hooves drumming the hardened earth.

'Logan take Burnum,' Lowanna declared, her voice raspy, the tone flat.

Snow turned, bending an ear toward her. 'What was that?' he asked, clouds of ochre rising up around him.

Fixed yet brittle as a stalactite, Lowanna's view had not shifted from her fire, her stillness the thinnest tissue to muzzle desolation's wail.

'Lowanna?' Snow persisted, drawing his hand down low on the reins, dragging his horse against its undertow. 'What did you say, Lowanna?'

The stockman wheeled around and dismounted, treading softly as he drew close.

The flames' reflection meandered sharply in Lowanna's now glassy eyes. 'They take him up mountain,' she said, and with a rattle of her bracelet, waved a hand toward the east.

For Mike, a dreadful thought awakened. 'They?'

Snow moved in nearer. 'Was Logan with a man and a woman?'

Lowanna closed her eyes and waved her head from side to side.

Mike asked: 'Only one other, a man, right?' He already knew the answer.

The three stockmen rode off. As the sound of their galloping faded, the crowd that had gathered broke up and peace once more descended on the camp. Lowanna rose to her feet and walked down to the creek. Tiptoeing to the large rock, she sat down and looked into each of the pools. The bottom pool pulsed from the tinkling water, the top, dammed-back, was becalmed as a cave pond. No matter how she concentrated, in neither could be seen another world, merely a creek bottom, its pebbles and its sand.

It was Sunday and neither the pub nor the general store would be open. Ma drove out on her buggy, drawn by the second of the molly mules she and Pop had owned for many years. All primrose and lilac, the old shopkeeper wore her best fabric flower hat, broad-brimmed and set at an angle to keep at bay a quickly warming sun. As Ma turned her mule up Main Street she saw the Ford had not returned. She whispered a little prayer and crossed herself.

Lucky was in the hotel kitchen. As usual, he stuck his face in the sink and twisted on the tap. The cold water poured over him, washing away some grit and seed, but not his pain. He reached for a dishtowel, roughly dried himself and peeked around for Tom, knowing full well he wasn't there; nobody was at the stove, nobody setting the table or bringing in the eggs, these pieces of Lucky's life gone missing. Without his son his house had ceased to be a home.

The three stockmen approached the narrow path that led east from the road and over the mountains.

'Up here?' asked Charlie.

Snow frowned. 'Not sure.'

Charlie frowned too, but put more into it. 'What do you mean by that?'

Snow came over sheepish. 'Thing is it's going to bring back memories.'

'Memories?' asked Charlie.

'Yeah, can't help but dig 'em up.'

Charlie slumped in his saddle. 'Snow, I hate to state the bleeding obvious, but isn't that the plan? You told us you remembered.' Charlie lifted an open palm toward the path. 'Please don't tell us you've forgotten the way you went last time.'

'I haven't forgotten,' said Snow abruptly.

'Then what's the problem?'

Snow said nothing and kept looking up at the gap in the forest undergrowth.

'Bloody hell,' Charlie snapped, his flying spittle capturing dawn's early light. 'That's why we're here. I should have stuck with me flaming chores while you got yourself sorted out.'

The taunt foundered on the reef of Snow's detachment. Charlie dropped his hand. 'Oh, well, if that's the way you want it, but don't forget, Snow, it was your idea. You're the one who talked me into this—you and Mike here. You said you knew the way, swore blind, said you was up through here before the war. I mean you're supposed to be the bloody expert.'

'Yeah, yeah, alright, it's the way,' Snow growled. 'It's the fastest route to Grafton—a lot faster than the damned road.'

'You sure Tom would go this way?' asked Mike.

'Yeah,' Snow confirmed, 'no doubt about it. Neddy would have told him about this track sometime or another. They've probably explored these parts a few times. It's what kids are like—into every nook and cranny.'

'Let's go then,' said Mike.

Snow still wasn't keen. 'Rough country.'

'Strike me lucky,' Charlie sputtered, 'you're like a sheila choosing a dress.' He laughed at his quip and turned to Mike for support. Mike wasn't laughing. Charlie's mirth thinned into his usual sigh, but he kept on talking anyway. 'Jeez, Snow, least it'll give you a chance to break in your new…' Charlie stopped and glanced down. 'Yeah, that's right, been meaning to ask you. What happened to your new leg?'

Snow patted his rustic post. 'Good old Fritz—too soon to lose him yet.'

Mike was of the same opinion. 'He's been a good mate.'

'Yeah,' said Snow, still patting the wooden leg, 'been a faithful friend.'

'Your leg's not some pet pooch,' Charlie protested, 'I could be getting work done right now instead of here with youse two no-hopers. Let's stop buggerising around.'

'I'm not buggerising around,' Snow grumbled, 'I'm thinking.'

'You're a bloody slow thinker.'

'I'm sorry, Charlie, not easy all this. Last time I took this track was with Darce—the thought didn't bother me till now.'

Mike gave Snow a long look. 'What would Darcy want you to do?'

Snow gazed at the mountains. 'Ah, stuff it,' he said and spurred his horse up into the forest path. The others followed.

The Widow O'Connor's plump fingers pounded the keys of her sturdy upright piano. Beside her, the Widow Campbell held forth in a mezzosoprano, her plangent voice filling the parlour, vibrating the windowpanes. Ma O'Shaughnessy, Mrs Reilly and The Widow MacTavish struggled to keep up, the four women of the congregation standing in a makeshift pew, formed from a row of The Widow O'Connor's dining room chairs. Before them, the widow's dining table, moved to the end of the room, was arranged as an altar, a crucifix hanging on the wall behind. Father Lynch presided, a small hinge-frame stepladder performing as his lectern. All sang their hearts out.

'His Kingdom cannot fail; He rules o'er earth and heaven; The keys of death and hell are to our Jesus given. Lift up your heart! Lift up your voice! Rejoice! Again I say, rejoice!'

The Widow Philpot knocked on the bunkhouse door and found her boys weren't there, nor were their horses in the stables. She walked back to the house and sat down to a breakfast set out for three—her silver and best china too. Gladys wondered where Mike and Snow could have gone. It was not like the lads to miss Sunday morning's fry-up; it absorbed Saturday's excess efficaciously.

The Widow Philpot poured herself a cup of tea—white, no sugar—and walked to her shiny glass cabinet. She saw the hand-coloured photo of Big George with his medals, and sobbed.

Burnum felt the campfire ashes, spotted some horse manure and crumbled it loose in his hand. Behind him, Logan and Thorn waited, perched in their saddles, watching.

'How many hours?' asked Logan.

Burnum lifted the first of his fingers and got on with the chase, leaving his horse for the others to lead, preferring to lope fleet of foot.

The trail was still fresh but the ground had changed and now mostly bare granite. The igneous rock was so hard it could resist abrasion by an iron shoe, even when the metal was scraped with the power and weight of a horse. Bare granite, like a swift flowing creek, made it easy to lose a trail, but Burnum was familiar with what he saw to be Tom's course. He was also aware Tom would twig to that: the lad would know the tracker was on his tail; certain Logan would turn to the black man. Tom would use trickery to throw his pursuers from the scent, but the tracker would not be outfoxed; he could chart better the bush than the whitefellas the boundary lines of their paddocks.

Burnum had been tracking for the troopers since the early nineties, and if he had ever cared in the slightest—which he didn't—he would have known the full extent of his enviable reputation for reliability; it was a reputation that extended all

241

the way to the New South Wales state police headquarters in Sydney. Burnum's talents could have been put to great use anywhere in Australia, but the Berto Valley was his home ground and here his ability was nothing short of miraculous. He knew all the gorges and gullies, the springs and streams and ponds of cool water. He knew the flowers and the trees: cypress, blackwoods, brush box and all the different gums. He knew the woods that made the best spears or boomerangs, which saps were sweet, which were bitter, which were poisonous and which were better than any whitefella glue. He knew the fish and the spiders and the bees, the furry creatures and the scaled, the butterflies and birds. He knew his valley as well as he knew himself because he was the valley and the valley was him.

The sky was clear and Burnum felt the breeze on his body. Up on the range the air moved with more urgency. In its currents he could smell the sea when it blew from the east, but the air on the ranges was often dry—especially in winter when the cold, lurking on the slopes, squeezed out the moisture of cotton ball clouds and upland valley mists, leaving the air skin-cracking raw. But this day was warm and the sea air held its softness. It was a moment when mother earth looked kindly on her world.

Burnum padded lightly the receiving earth, feeling its rhythm, feeling its joy; but the tracker would no more show elation with a smile than the igneous mountains shift. He would never grin or wink or hold a hand or slap a back, but his presence could be as reassuring as a rainbow. He would never scowl, but his stare could be as ominous as thunder. He would never yell, though his whisper could be deafening. He would never show surprise, though he could startle like the sticky clasp of a spider's web. He might be the moist air before the coming of the rains, or the sharp sting of a winter morning's frost. Burnum's body was of bone and blood as the mountains were of granite, but his spirit was as enigmatic as the stars.

The tracker followed the shoe prints, spiralling out from any point where they might fade, searching with a raptor's eye till his net enfolded them again, finding a fractured twig or freshly broken leaf to continue on his way. He built up an insight into both horse and rider from Copenhagen's distinctive walk and the different pressures and asymmetries in each of his hooves. For not only could Burnum identify different riders and their mounts, he could distinguish the different farriers, the signs of Pop's work particularly distinctive in the hooves of the horses he shod. The tracker worked out the tricks Tom used to throw him off; they formed subtle patterns he could soon predict, deciphering them at any point where the trail seemed set to peter out, returning to the chase with little pause.

The rocks became warm, holding fast the heat of a sun still waking. It was a perfect day in Berto's valley and on the ranges that made it a valley, a perfect day when everything in and of that place exalted in its balance. Through his labours Burnum too, like all the plants and creatures, huge and microscopic, would aid mother earth in her tireless quest to maintain that precious balance. He would lash his shoulder to the wheel, and with nature's ruthless mercy, help bring order to the whole; the future was as clear to Burnum as the past, the times relentless as the tides.

Father Lynch and his Berto flock of ewes sipped their tea. The Reverend Father celebrated Holy Mass in the Valley once a month, and of all the small communities he served on a circuit extending to the remoter parts of the Northern Rivers, Berto's ladies offered the tastiest refreshments.

Agnes MacTavish looked at the lamingtons and scones and lemon butter tarts, but she had no appetite. She was a thin woman who kept herself busy, burning as much energy as she consumed. She not only grew vegetables and kept chooks, she also sewed quilts, cobbled boots, chopped her own wood and scared the bejesus out of the good Father Lynch. 'Father, today you were talking about the beginning.'

'Yes, that I was, Mrs MacTavish,' said Father Lynch, putting down his cup and saucer and unconsciously clasping his hands together in front of his genitals.

Agnes stepped closer. 'In the beginning God created heaven and earth?'

'Yes, Genesis Chapter One, Verse One,' said the priest, demonstrating his knowledge of the facts as if someone might not have been aware of that fact already.

Agnes nodded naively, as if she hadn't known, hoping to keep the priest off his guard. 'So I need to get this right because it's been bothering me, Father. God exists, does he not?'

The priest spluttered and looked at the other ladies. 'Why, of course.'

'So he lives?'

Father Lynch could see a curly one coming. 'No, Mrs MacTavish, not in the sense that we understand mortal life with all its imperfections; God has no composition and God doesn't change, for he is already perfect, a pure act or being.'

'So what was God doing before the beginning?'

'Agnes, you're forgetting yourself.'

'It's alright, Mrs O'Connor,' the priest counselled, gazing benevolently on Agnes, steepling his hands under his chin. 'Before the beginning there was not time as we conceive it. God is perfect and is, was and forever will be.'

'Ah,' said Agnes MacTavish, shaking her finger, 'is, was and will are measures of time, are they not?'

The priest swallowed. 'I'm not sure that necessarily follows.'

'And if God is perfect then there must be imperfection, for nothing is anything without its opposite.'

'That is so,' said the priest, stuck on a log, racing downstream, Victoria Falls around the next bend.

'And we are in the image of God?'

'Yes,' said the priest, his voice very small.

'Right,' said the young widow, her heart-shaped face angelic, 'God is perfect, and if we are in the image of God, it follows that we are perfect too?'

'No,' said the priest, 'we are filled with sin.'

The Widow MacTavish looked sideways at the priest. 'Why?'

'Because we ate from the tree of knowledge.'

'Why?'

'Because Eve——'

'Ah yes, of course,' The Widow MacTavish confided to the astonished congregation, 'had to be Eve.'

'Eve was tempted by the snake,' the priest continued, determined as a salmon to reach his destination, 'and the serpent was the most subtle of all the animals God had made.'

'Eve wanted knowledge?'

'Yes, Mrs MacTavish, 'she fell victim to temptation.'

'And what was this knowledge?'

'The difference between right and wrong.'

'So,' The Widow MacTavish responded, every bit as determined as her adversary, 'God made us ignorant of the difference between right and wrong, wanting us to act on instinct like any other poor dumb creature, yet gave us the desire to know all about that difference denied us: we are sinners for acting upon an inquisitiveness He created. He even threw in a snake oil selling snake for good measure, to be sure knowledge was even more attractive?'

The priest was becoming agitated. 'We disobeyed the law of God.'

'We rebelled?'

'If you like.'

'But he made us rebellious, did he not?'

The Reverend Father Doyle was well trained to deal with this line of attack for the questions were by no means original. A strand of dry saliva extended as he went to speak, but The Widow MacTavish never gave him the chance.

'So, if God is timeless and perfect, why is there time and why are we imperfect? Seems we're not as much in his image as he would like us to be, which makes God a wee bit imperfect. Unless, of course, God really is perfect—in that case he must have made us imperfect quite deliberately, all according to his plan. He should be working for the bloody government!'

'Agnes,' The Widow O'Connor cautioned, 'you mustn't be forgetting yourself. The Reverend Father has the education of things such as we of his flock cannot possibly comprehend.' She smiled at the priest. 'I'm so sorry, Father, Agnes has been unwell of late.'

'I'm as fit as a fiddle, Kathleen. Don't you start doing my thinking and my talking for me.' Agnes swung her gun turret back upon the priest. 'Now, Father, tell me this—I have a garden where I grow all manner of vegetables, but I would never deliberately plant prickly pear, would I now? I mean that would be just asking for trouble. So why did God create the tree of knowledge?'

'Agnes,' the Widow O'Connor censured, 'I will not have such talk in my home. If you feel the need to ask such things, maybe it's because you've fallen victim to the devil and his clever tricks. Maybe you've become a protestant or a painted and savage heathen!'

'Don't you call me a protestant, Kathleen O'Connor!'

'You're the strangest Catholic I ever met,' said Mrs Reilly, putting in her twopence worth.

Father Lynch stepped aside and tried to make himself invisible.

The young widow was not to be intimidated by the numbers stacked against her. 'Seems we were made smart enough to want the fruit of the tree of knowledge then told we were too dumb to have it? Good God, we were always going to gobble up as much of that apple as we could get!'

The Widow O'Connor's hands were shaking with rage. She was forced to put down her cup and saucer lest spilt tea fall on her good rug, a tea stain being a bugger to get out.

The Widow MacTavish hadn't finished with the priest. 'Father, returning to my vegetable patch, if I plant a seed assuming it's a carrot, but get a dandelion, is that the weed's fault or mine?' She saw the question as purely rhetorical, so the young widow gave no time for any answers other than her own. 'That's right, if we're His garden, you'd have to conclude: God is either a bad gardener, blaming us veggies for his shambles, or he made us, not in his image, but quite deliberately as his imperfect opposite. If he's all that's good, then we are all that's evil. Far as I can see, the devil's out of a job.'

'Get you from this place!' thundered The Widow O'Connor. 'Leave my house this very instant!'

'Girls,' said Ma, ever the peacemaker, 'the Reverend Father is a very busy man and I, for one, have a joint of beef to roast. So perhaps it would be best if we were all on our ways.'

'Yes, I really must be going too,' said The Widow Campbell, her speaking voice almost singing mezzo soprano.

The Widow O'Connor wasn't to be assuaged. 'A fine mess you've created, Agnes. A fine mess of what was a beautiful service, and a beautiful service it was, Father.'

'Thank you,' said the priest, closing his eyes and backing

away like a footman.

'It's a good thing I'm a forgiving woman,' The Widow O'Connor continued. 'Otherwise I would be barring you from any more services, Agnes MacTavish!'

'Barring me? This isn't the pub!'

'No, it isn't,' The Widow O'Connor agreed, 'but the way you go on, it might as well be. This isn't the first time you've been asking blasphemous and disrespectful questions of the Reverend Father. Seems you like to gorge on a bit of the forbidden fruit yourself, hey, Agnes?'

'You should watch your tongue, Kathleen O'Connor, or I'll wash your mouth out with me Solvol soap.'

'What?' wheezed The Widow O'Connor.

'Better still, I'll start growing spuds!'

The Widow O'Connor pumped to bursting, a zeppelin in search of a flame.

'Girls, girls,' Ma appealed, all aflutter, 'we're letting the spring air have its way with us.'

'All very well for you, *Mrs* O'Shaughnessy,' said The Widow O'Connor.

Ma's eyelids and jowls were yet again tethered to the solemn weight of Pop's anvil. 'I'll pretend I didn't hear that, Kathleen.'

The alpha female had spoken, her black-cap judgment handed down. The Widow O'Connor withered in the dock.

Ma grabbed her handbag. 'Now come along, Agnes, I'll give you a lift home in me buggy.' Turning back to the convicted, her mouth smiling, but eyes still at rest, Ma continued: 'I'll see you in me store during the week, Kathleen.'

'Yes, of course, Ma, I'll see you later in the week,' The Widow O'Connor mumbled, her tone contrite, her voice fading wanly as she descended into a dungeon of purgatorial awareness. Having implied desire on the part of her elder and better, she had fueled the inference she must be guilty of much the same. Stripped bare before her peers, she had need of the priest. 'I must sit down, Father Lynch. I feel faint.'

The priest stepped forward from the hallway and led the widow to her sofa. The congregation took their leave.

'You're not really going to start growing spuds, are you, Agnes?' asked Ma as she drove her young friend home.

'No, I won't be doing that: wouldn't dream of it. I'm sorry, but I'm mystified as to what's happening to me lately: haven't been myself at all. I'll make a posy for Kathleen the next time I see her.'

'That would be nice,' Ma agreed.

Agnes started to cry.

'Oh, what's wrong, Agnes, love?' Ma pulled the buggy to the side of the road.

'I'm sorry. I didn't mean to cause a fuss but——'

'It's alright,' Ma soothed, giving Agnes a hug then patting her on the shoulder.

'I meant those questions, you know,' Agnes confessed, weeping softly. 'It was premeditated. A priest should be able to give proper answers to questions, but sometimes I suspect those of the cloth are as confused as the rest of us. I hope to God there is a heaven. Every day I pray there is and that God took my dear Freddy in.'

'I'm sure Fred's in heaven as we speak.'

'But what if he's not, Ma? What if he had evil in his heart when he died? All filled with hatred while killing his fellow man? What greater sin could there be than to take another's life? Germans are God's children too. A lot of them are even Catholics. Fresh after killing each other did all the soldiers rise to heaven in great swarms over the Somme, Germans bumping into Australians or Frenchmen or Poms?'

'I suppose some rose up,' admitted Ma, 'and I suppose a few must have gone the other way.'

Agnes pulled back and looked at Ma. 'Do you think it was a blessing to be free of the war, no matter which way they went?'

'Oh, Agnes, you're still too young to be asking such questions. You've got your whole life ahead of you.'

'What life? I've lost Freddy. What life is there? What's here for me now: one Sunday a month going toe to toe with Kathleen, like a couple of broody hens, and no rooster in the hen house? May as well become a nun.'

Ma's face opened like a budding rose. 'Listen to me now, Agnes, I might have an idea for you to consider.'

Agnes's face opened in response. 'What's that, Ma?'

'I'm going to make a suggestion, but I'm making it because I know you're a woman who would always be after doing the right thing. Ain't that so, Agnes?'

'I was only kidding about the nunnery.'

'Yes, I know that, but this idea is one that any sensible girl, such as yourself, would take up in the blink of an eye. However, if you're lonely for the company of a man, you have to promise you'd be mindful of always doing the right thing by this man.'

Agnes lit up. 'What man?'

'I could arrange for you to bump into Snow Mackay.'

Agnes's jaw dropped.

Ma continued, feeling as magnanimous as Mrs Clause. 'Now he's one fine young bachelor. Only bachelor between twenty and sixty as I know of now, other than Mike, but he might already be spoken for. So, how about Snow?'

Agnes turned away. 'He wouldn't want to pay me a call.'

'Why on earth not?'

'Weren't you saying he's got his new leg?'

'Why? Is that a problem?'

'Now he's got his new leg, he'll want to go out dancing and such down in Grafton. I mean Snow is very popular. I've heard all the girls like him there.'

'He is popular, no doubt about it—young and healthy and handsome too. Oh dear, yes, but you can't simply give up.'

'Oh, Ma, there's all those women to compete with.'

'But look on the bright side; they're all so far away, while you and Snow, why, you're neighbours, The Widow Philpot's bunkhouse not half a mile up the road.'

Agnes pulled out a hanky from her handbag. 'That's true.'

'Of course it's true.' Ma clapped her cheeks. 'Oh, I've an idea—Snow's right boot is too new for the left boot. It wants some adjusting. You'd be the perfect person for the job, what with all your cobbling skills you picked up during the war.'

'If I could fix his boot, I'd be ever so grateful, Ma.'

'I know you would, Agnes. Let me see what I can do.'

'Thank you, Ma.' Agnes's eyes grew wide. 'I could bake him a cake for when he comes to collect his boot.'

'Why wait till then? Bake the man a cake when he drops off the boot!'

Agnes laughed self-consciously and blew her nose. 'Thanks again, Ma, you're a saint. You're a saint, you really are.'

'Oh, get away with you; I'm nothing of the sort.' Ma took up the reins again and they were off down the road.

Agnes slipped her hanky up her sleeve. 'I'll be fine now.'

'But are you sure, Agnes?'

'I'll take your advice: I'll try to see the bright side.'

'Trying isn't buying.'

'Ma, since you put it that way, I *will* look on the bright side.'

'Good, that's the spirit. And make sure it's a sponge cake; Snow doesn't like dried fruit.'

Chapter Fifteen

Lucky stood behind the bar and threw back a shot glass of the hair of the dog. There was a knock on the lobby door. His aspect lightened and for a fleeting moment he imagined it was Tom, but the lad would never knock before entering his own home.

Lucky shuffled across to the lobby and opened the door. He saw Pop waiting there and came over bad, remorseful at how he had acted toward his neighbour the previous night.

Pop, however, was altogether unconcerned about being chucked out of the pub; it had happened many times before. In fact he had once been barred, the ruling enforced for three cruel weeks: until Lucky needed his horse shod. Nevertheless, the smithy was still shocked by the sight that stood before him. 'Morning.' he gasped. 'By all the saints, I gotta say you're looking pretty crook, like death warmed up.'

'Mate,' snorted Lucky, 'you're no oil painting either.'

Pop shrugged.

Lucky peered at the growth on Pop's brow. 'That's one hell of a knock on your noggin.'

'I know,' Pop conceded. 'Did it last night in me shop.' He ran his finger around the bump. 'Such a big egg, be forgiven for thinking 'twas Easter. Been to bed yet?'

Lucky didn't respond. He just glanced up and down the street, as if by some miracle Tom might be lurking around: in the blacksmith's shop, waiting to watch Pop shoe a horse, like he did when he was a tot; or over at the general store to see if his latest mail-order novel had arrived, like he did when he grew big enough to save his pocket money, or older still and drawing a modest wage from his father's parsimonious till. 'You got any idea what today is?' Lucky asked.

Pop cautiously shook his head.

The publican put his hands in his pockets and shivered like a freezing rain was coming. 'It's me birthday,' he said, without a hint of pride.

Pop stared down at his sooty boots, like a schoolboy waiting for six of the best. It took a moment for him to reply: 'That's why Ma sent me over.'

'Sixty years of life,' Lucky mourned, not listening, 'and none the wiser.'

'Aye,' Pop nodded, ''twas ever thus. I pray for all that death provide better instruction.'

The publican's voice became shaky, rattling. 'Tom rode out last night.'

Pop's brow crinkled. 'And still not back?'

Lucky gazed at nothing in particular, his eyes red and wet.

Pop's old heart went out to him. 'Come on. Come over later for some Sunday lunch. Ma's cooking roast beef and spuds. I promised not to tell, but she's even baking a cake, but only one candle, mind.'

'After all that happened yesterday?'

'Ma's a forgiving soul, and don't I know it, but you mustn't fret; Tom will be back, fit as a flea. Logan won't hurt the lad; he's known young Tom since the lad was no more than a lump in his mother's belly.'

'It's not Logan I'm worried about.' Lucky closed the door on Pop.

Copenhagen trudged along a high plateau. Grace looked across the waves of mountains; gum leaf green receding to smoky blue, they extended as far as the tablelands due west. Not a scar by human hand was evident; they could have been Adam and Eve. It was too good to be true. 'You sure this is the right way?'

Tom pointed along the ascending ridge with Logan's Winchester. 'Unless you want to see us get tracked down, that, up there, is the only way.'

Grace saw Logan's Peak rising before them, an arrowhead stabbing the sky, and a ledge angled across its base, scaling and disappearing beyond the shoulder of the summit. Grace found it daunting when viewed close. 'I'm glad I don't get dizzy.'

'What do you mean?'

'Oh, nothing, I was just prattling to myself.'

'It's scary up there. You afraid of heights?'

'Not particularly, I was merely saying—I know how to avoid getting dizzy.'

'How?'

'It's something I learnt when I was at dance school.'

Tom squinted. 'That'd cost money, wouldn't it?'

'Ernie paid for it.'

'Oh,' said Tom.

Uncertain of what that meant, Grace immediately moved the conversation forward. 'You want to know how to stop getting dizzy?'

'Yeah, I'd like to know,' Tom replied, irritated he had been stupid enough to ask a question about money. 'But,' he warned, 'I'm not saying I'll believe you.'

'Nobody pulls the wool over Tom Bramble's eyes, hey?'

Tom appraised the peak and resisted the temptation to bite. 'Alright, how do you stop from getting dizzy?'

'Spotting,' said Grace, happy again. 'It lets you turn like a spinning top, going around and around, again and again, without getting dizzy.'

Tom scoffed. 'I used to make myself dizzy that way when I was a kid—kept turning till I fell over. Can't be avoided.'

'Oh yes it can.'

'How?'

'Like I said, spotting—you fix your eyes onto one static spot as you turn. You trick your body into thinking it's as static as the spot you're looking at.'

'How come you don't screw your head off?'

'Practice.'

Copenhagen froze in his tracks and his ears pricked up.

Grace was puzzled. 'Why have we stopped?'

'We're giving way to a snake.'

Grace poked her nose around Tom's shoulder and saw it. The snake slithered across their path, shiny and dark as a man's ballroom shoes. She pulled up her feet. 'That a red-bellied blacksnake?

The snake wended its way from a stand of scrub and into a crack in the granite, seeming to vanish into thin air.

'No,' Tom answered, 'not a red. It's a blue-bellied blacksnake.'

'Nice to know they come in a variety of colours. Their bite leave you dead as a maggot?'

'I told you, Grace, you only have to worry about browns.' Tom gave Copenhagen a light touch with his calves and they were on their way. 'A brown would have been more alert, might have got grumpy, coiled and reared, holding his ground, but the black didn't really give a stuff. Probably didn't even spot us.'

'Ah, spotting.'

Tom let slip a grin. 'S'pose so,' he said, pulling down his hat. 'When you do that, when you spot, it's like you've got two brains, isn't it? I mean it's as if one brain is fooling the other brain; one tricks the other.'

'Yeah,' Grace agreed as they passed by the dark crack where the snake had disappeared. 'Now that you put it that way, I guess so—two brains. It's a bit like having an angel on your right shoulder and the devil on your left.'

Tom swivelled back to Grace. 'So which of the two is being fooled?'

They reached the final ascent.

Grace was still pondering Tom's question when he swung around and slid off the horse. 'We're at the base of the peak: gets really steep now. From here till the other side, I'll walk Copenhagen.'

'No,' said Grace, 'neither is fooled. The angel and the devil can't be fooled. They can only make a fool of you.'

At first thrown by the leapfrog to his earlier question, Tom was quick to regroup. 'Why would an angel want to make a fool of you? Why would angels hurt you?'

'I don't know,' said Grace, 'but they do.' She dismounted.

'No, Grace.' Tom frowned. 'You're barefoot.'

Grace raised her chin in pride of her upbringing. 'I didn't get my first pair of shoes till I was fourteen.'

'I thought it was only country kids who got around barefoot. You want my boots?'

Grace put her foot beside Tom's. It was almost half the size.

'S'pose not,' he admitted, feeling a bit silly. They set off again, neither riding. Then he reminded Grace: 'You haven't answered my question—give me an example of an angel doing real harm to a person, just one single example.'

'Martyrdom.'

Tom sniffed. 'You really shouldn't be walking barefoot.'

'The ground feels comfortable enough.'

'It'll get worse higher up.'

'Why can't we just walk around Logan's Peak?' Grace asked.

'That's a long story,' Tom answered.

'We're on a long journey.'

'I've chosen the high road.'

'They're all high roads up here.'

'Grace, put it this way—we're taking a track less travelled.'

'That bad, huh?'

The breeze from the sea touched lightly the rocky ground and the sun was getting warmer.

Lucky meditated upon his reflection—the flesh he'd become. He polished off his rum and went to throw the empty bottle at the barroom mirror.

'No,' he confided to his other self, 'seven years bad luck.'

Lucky put down the bottle and noticed his wife in the mirror. 'Hello, Rachel, been some time. Hope you like the place I picked for you. Nice view of the valley, hey?'

Bleached bones glowing through a fog of skin, Rachel failed to answer. Lucky recognised that bloodless stare. It was, from the beginning of their life together, the one aspect that never changed; it tarried after smiles and curiosity, love and lust had long expired. This Rachel was not his bride, but old and beaten up by life, hollowed out as on the day her future ended.

Lucky picked his nose, but not so deep inside he judged it disrespectful: just a little nervous, preening nip. 'I expect you're none too pleased with me,' he said, wiping his finger on his shirt. 'Sorry, but things aren't as they used to be; I've become a good-for-nothing drunkard.'

Rachel still said nothing. Silence meant agreement. Lucky's eyes welled up, his temples twisted; he leaned against the bar and rubbed the heels of his hands into his brow. 'I miss you, Rachel, I really do. And the boys? Oh dear, yes. Oh dear,

dear me, it's hell down here—and I've done a dreadful thing.'

Lucky placed his palms flat on the bar mat. 'I've ignored your dying wish; I've not looked after young Tom as you asked. Been asleep on the job, been dreaming of you coming back, but you haven't, have you? Except like this—to mock me.' He formed his hands into fists and hammered the bar. 'I'm still alone! I'm in the bloody dark, buried in a hole, nailed inside a coffin! I'm wondering—shit, I should be dead. I'm wanting to be dead, but so damned scared 'cause I'm trapped alive inside a fucking coffin!'

Lucky, tears piddling on the bar, wept for close on two, three minutes. Rachel watched and waited like a patient executioner. At last he stopped and asked, as if by the bye: 'How are Harry and Darce?'

'Not pleased with what you've done to Neddy.'

'What's that you say?' asked Lucky, amazed that Rachel had answered him.

'He was Tom's best mate. Now you've driven away both lads, ignoring a sacred promise to both me and Frank Murphy—a fine way to look after two boys who needed you.'

Lucky jutted out his jaw, pride still standing in the earthquake of his shame. 'It was the right thing to do: help Neddy cope with all the shit life can throw at a person.'

'When did you become a liar?'

Lucky's brow contorted. 'I'm not a liar.'

'An honest man would admit he was a liar. When did you start lying to yourself?'

Lucky backed off from the bar, realising Rachel was angrier than he was: up for a fight, and unlike him, already dead.

'Lucky, you were nothing more than jealous, envying every moment Tom spent with Neddy. Tom was all you had and you wanted him all to yourself: a son to be your maid, your nurse, to clean up all your drunken slops, giving nothing in return.'

'You left me, Rachel!'

The reflection grew quiet. 'Yes, I did, my turn to apologise. The loss of Harry and Darcy was more than I could bear, but they understand.' Then she softened in a way not seen since the days before the war. 'Oh, Leonard, I had such dreams for them. Harry was so good with animals. He would have made a fine vet. And Darcy, with his writing, he could have gone a long way too—maybe even have worked for the Bulletin, meeting princes and generals and other such famous people.'

'Yes,' whispered Lucky, 'but God took them away.' Coming over nasty, he snatched the empty rum bottle.

'Don't you dare throw that thing at me, Leonard Bramble!'

The publican wiped his broken face. 'Why, Rachel? Why did God steal our sons? Have you got around to asking him?'

'Ask him for yourself.'

Rachel left the mirror as Lucky walked behind the bar. He put down the empty bottle and opened up a new one.

A wedge-tailed eagle swooped down from the mountains and over the depths of the valley. Its icy shriek cut through the cushion of thermal updrafts as it banked away due north.

Burnum walked to the base of the peak and stopped, Logan and Thorn riding up behind him. He indicated to the summit and wandered back the way he'd come.

'Hey, Logan, what the hell is this?' Thorn demanded. 'He can't just skedaddle.'

'No, you're right.' Logan glanced at the Appaloosa. 'Hey, Burnum, take your horse, feed and water it in my stables. You know where everything is.'

Without breathing a word, Burnum mounted up and trotted down the mountain.

Thorn couldn't comprehend what the cattleman was thinking; he was letting their scout depart. He turned to Logan, shadowed eyes displaying panic to the raw light of day. 'What are you doing? Without him we're blind!' The carefully crafted hoardings Thorn presented to the street were collapsing under the weight of a fearful wind, laying bare the concealed and dreadful excavations of his mundane needs. 'Order him to stay. Order him! I thought you were the big chief of this goddamned stomping ground?'

Logan pulled out a sachet of headache powder.

Thorn sighed, took off his hat and forced himself to calm down. His boiling quickly fell to a simmer and he renewed the argument. 'Logan, we're both of us, one way or another, a long ways from home; we still want a tracker if we're going to catch these kids. Let's get him back. Pay him some money. Make it worth his while. You're a rich man; you can afford to buy and sell men like Burnum. Buy and sell 'em any day of the week. You say the guy is the best tracker you've ever seen, so give him an incentive; I mean, everybody wants something, everybody can do with a little extra cash for those unforeseen expenses. He must need something—couldn't be that expensive. You may not have read about it but Manhattan Island was bought from the Indians for twenty-four bucks. How about that? In any case, we have to have a tracker. Come on, what do you say? We can't let him leave.'

Logan flipped his head back and grimaced. 'Oh yes we can; we're on our own now.' he poured his powder into his mouth and tried to gulp it down.

'Taste pretty bad, huh?'

The bitterness caused Logan's mouth to pucker sphincter tight. 'I've got used to it.' he hacked, lips breaking like the shell of an aged passionfruit. 'Anyway, it's no use arguing the toss with the likes of Burnum. There are some things that can't be bought. Like I said, we're on our own now.'

Thorn emitted a hollow laugh and slapped his hat against his thigh. 'Logan, you don't get it, do you? For you this is plainly about some kid cheating you out of your winnings; it's a matter of—let's call it professional pride. But for me it's much more than that. The kid——what's his name again?'

'Bramble, Tom Bramble.'

'Yeah, okay, that kid has stolen Grace. Now I don't mind telling you I love that girl more than——'

'Anything else you've ever wagered?'

'Hey, I'm a bastard: happy to come clean about that. What do you want me to do? Slash my wrists? Come on, let's talk turkey here, bastard-to-bastard. Let's get the aborigine back. Offer him some beads or an axe or bottle of rum or whatever floats his boat.'

Logan fingered his wound. It still hadn't dried out.

Thorn's eyelids hooded. 'You knew he'd leave before we started, didn't you?'

'Take my word for it,' Logan sidestepped, avoiding Thorn's question, 'there's no use in trying to drag Burnum along against his will. He won't go any further up. Sooner die.'

Thorn returned his hat to his head. 'Why, what's the big problem with this mountain?'

'The problem is…' Logan pinched his cheeks, expediting the flow of saliva. 'The problem is the peak. He won't go near it. He reckons it's cursed.'

Thorn sneered at the ivory pinnacle. 'You've got to be kidding. This is a hill; you should see the Rockies!'

'I have seen the Rockies—bagged myself a grizzly bear: a big nasty boar; got his head stuffed and hanging on my dining room wall—but it's not my opinion that matters.' Some of the analgesic powder had found its way up Logan's nose and he sneezed.

'Gesundheit,' said Thorn.

'Thanks,' said Logan.

'You're welcome,' replied Thorn.

'Oh?' Logan blurted, momentarily confused. But then he recalled from his travels America's routine use of the courtesy. Not withstanding that, he felt compelled to repeat, 'Thanks.'

'You're welcome.'

'Listen, Thorn, I never say thanks more than twice.'

'Not a problem.'

'Thanks.'

'You're welcome.'

Logan coughed and turned away, feeling only a moment's silence could terminate their exchange of civilities. He crumpled up the used sachet and threw it away like his rubbish had a special place to go. 'I'm aware, Thorn, you're upset about Burnum spearing off, and much as I'd love to debate the finer aspects of geography and folklore, I have to emphasise that time—as you would say—is a-wasting.' Logan dismounted. 'Steerage class now; we walk from here.'

Burnum hadn't anticipated being given charge of the horse. He supposed Logan would keep the animal to bring back Grace. Then he realised why Logan wouldn't need it; Burnum wasn't the only one with plans for the day.

The tracker retraced with wasteful ease the trail he had so labouriously sniffed out, and feeling his seat in the saddle, decided he liked the Appaloosa; it reminded him of the horses he rode as a jackaroo. The animal also revived memories of the day he walked away from the whitefella world; a place that valued things he saw as pointless and ignored the things they should have seen. But still, he missed his old horse. He understood his horse and was puzzled as to what might have happened to it. He turned to Logan's Peak and chanted. The mountain would do what the mountain had to do.

Logan and Thorn were already making their way up the foot of the summit.

'Why's it called Logan's Peak?' asked Thorn.

Logan stopped, pushed aside his saddlebag and unhitched his water canteen. 'My grandfather,' his voice croaked, 'good old Granddad, he fancied himself as a bit of an explorer.' Logan took a swig from the canteen and handed it over to Thorn. 'Yeah, so my granddaddy, the old goat, he tried to climb it.'

The American asked: 'What happened?'

It was a high ridge, the spine narrow. Tom slipped and fell. He lost the reins and dropped the Winchester. Spooked by the clatter, Copenhagen stepped backwards. Instinctively, Grace gathered up the reins. 'Hey, easy boy, easy,' she soothed.

Tom gazed in admiration. 'You've got a way with horses.'

Grace stroked Copenhagen's neck. 'No, it was nothing. He was just scared, weren't you, boy?' The horse acknowledged the attention, serene as a man receiving a shave from his barber.

Tom got up and went for the Winchester. It was a few feet down a sharp incline that formed the side of the ridge. At the base of the incline he noticed a thin ledge. Beyond the ledge nothing could be seen save the distant ranges. Tom set off, easing himself gingerly over the incline to collect the rifle. His fingertips were almost on the butt when he trod on a loose rock. His feet slid out from under him and he pitched sideways into a barrel roll. His limbs flailed as dust plumed and small stones flew up, the ledge growing ever nearer. Tom tried to right himself but the ground was dry and loose, the angle too steep. He whipped across the base of the slope, whirled off the precipice and was gone.

Grace screeched his name and heard no reply. She left

Copenhagen and cautiously followed Tom's path down the incline. The rocks drifted under her feet, stable as ball bearings. She collapsed onto her backside and found herself sliding, but not as swiftly as Tom had rolled. She used her hands and heels as brakes and dug in, managing to come to a halt inches shy of the cliff-face.

On the other side of the rim, Tom dangled. In a split second, too little time to think, but long enough to act, his hand had grasped the root of a tree. Tom gaped at the narrow length of ropy wood straining under his weight, and screamed.

Grace saw the root pull against the slope. 'I'm coming. Don't let go!'

'What?' Tom yelled. He heaved himself higher, taking the root in both hands, his boots scraping against the cliff, struggling for a shelf, a tier, a pocket. He looked down. A ravine yawned open, a picturesque mountain stream waiting far below, a straight drop of over three hundred feet to its pure but shallow waters. He looked back up.

Grace leaned over to see Tom's terrified face distorting, the mountain shearing away below him and the chasm funneling down and enticing. She retreated.

'Grace!' Tom cried, thinking she might desert him.

Grace could do no more than ignore his pleas. Small whimpering sounds rose from her throat as she searched for an anchor, knowing she was useless without one. She glimpsed a crack in the upturned lip of the granite ledge. Shadowed black in the bright sunlight and a foot or so up the slope, it awakened undesired memories of another crack, the crevice into which the blue-bellied black snake had secured a home, but Grace didn't hesitate. She reached out with one hand and grappled the ominous split in the rock, wedging her fingers deep into its dark mouth. Matted spider webs brushed against her skin as she took a firm hold. Now, latched to the slope, Grace peered over the rim of the cliff. The ravine opened up again, drawing her in like an expanding pair of bellows. Her stomach heaved. Tom immediately lunged up with his left hand. She caught his wrist as he grabbed hers. For better or worse, for richer or poorer, they were clasped together as one. The blood felt like it would burst from Grace's limbs, but a voice said, 'Stay.' She held her grip on Tom, and Tom his grip on life.

'Pull!' he shouted.

'I am' she shouted back.

Tom's feet, still scrambling, bumped against an outcrop. He grafted a boot to it and prised himself up to chest height with the ledge. Again, he saw Grace and she saw him, each seeing their reflection in the other's eyes.

The root gave way. Rootlets popped in a trill of flying dirt. Tom's arm flew out, but Grace held tight to the other arm and his foot held tight to the outcrop. He let go the once precious root, flung up his loose hand and clawed at the ledge. Nails grinding against the rock, he dragged himself high enough to hook his chin to the rim of the cliff. Grace felt the relief of a weight much reduced. A soft breeze skated across the mountain.

Tom's foot slipped. Skinning his jaw, he dropped as a man on the gallows. Grace groaned as if its wrenching hemp. A scalding blade raced through her arms as the burden tore at her muscles, her fingers reduced to the status of implements. Then she heard hissing.

Grace looked around and there it was: a snake, not black, but armoured in scales that shone brown. Beneath angry brows, its stare allowed no mercy, boring into Grace as its body slid and flexed from the cobwebbed crack in a slowly expanding and slithering loop.

Grace tried not to move, but her body was trembling under Tom's weight. Suddenly her glands were seized by the dreaded cramp. Adrenalin once more embraced her kidneys in its razor claws.

Tom heaved himself higher, dragging down on Grace's arm. Her face went crimson as a needle of pain stabbed into her wrist and her knuckles cracked. The snake recoiled and became rigid, fixed as a welded rivet.

All was quiet again, just the whisper of the breeze. Tom grunted loudly as his foot reclaimed its little outcrop. He reappeared from below the ledge.

The snake didn't move, but Grace could tell it was all of one thing and her focus was such to fill her every thought. She ignored the cramp, impelling its expulsion, and her shaking abated, leaving her motionless, still as the beast.

With his foot firmly wedged in the outcrop, Tom stretched his arm across the ledge, feeling for something to grip. The gravel scraped noisily. The snake turned, the movement quick and precise. It glared at Tom's arm, his fingers wriggling like a spider's legs, scratching like a cockroach.

'Don't move,' said Grace through teeth locked tight.

Tom ignored her, the serpent didn't. Tongue tasting the air, measuring, assessing, ribs embracing the ground, it slinked in quest of its kill.

Grace's heart pounded as the eastern brown prowled nearer. Her hand was in its way. An inner voice implored: 'Let go of the rock, be gone,' but another voice said that meant certain death—not just for Tom, but her as well—his clasp around her wrist, a sinker to her line. Grace tried to think of other things: the first time she went to the ballet, Ernie at her side, watching the dying swan.

The snake stopped beside her hand. She felt the serpent's feather breath. It raised its head and rippled forward. Scales met skin, ranks of delicate muscles working their way across the bones of her hand, caressing the sinews that held her bones in place.

Tom became aware of Grace's stillness and in that suspended moment, he felt a nodule of rock. His fingers dug in around this mooring, but the work of his hand crunched the gravel and gouged the air as a plough to earth. The snake coiled and reared up—a spring-loaded figure S.

Ignorant of this threat, Tom used the nodule to heave himself higher. 'Don't,' Grace murmured under her breath, 'there's a snake.'

The serpent hissed!

Tom finally noticed it. The serpent hissed again, the shining beast looming, primeval, towering and arcing above him, tensioned as a crossbow to strike. Tom let his eyelids fall: he played possum.

Fastened to the serpent's stare, Grace couldn't even

blink. She watched its head crank further back, accumulating yet more energy.

Not a muscle moved in Tom's entire body, or any part of Grace. The snake seemed cast in bronze, its hue a perfect camouflage from the unwary: picnickers and hikers, children playing hide and go seek in tall grass. Grace wondered how many times the beast had killed. As if aware of her thinking, Tom reopened his eyes and his view swirled into the depths of the reptile. Orange light flamed across the black orbits. Close above, an eagle shrieked!

A blurred undulation and the snake had whipped up the incline. It was gone. Tom knew he would never see it again. Grappling against the cliff-face, he pulled his hips to level with the rim, swung up a knee and squirmed to the safety of the ledge.

Grace let go of the crack and collapsed beside him. Slowly they relaxed their grip on the other's wrist, their tautened sinews hesitant to retract.

'Thank you,' said Tom, the words so small, inadequate to speak his gratitude.

Grace let loose a weary smile. 'Yeah?' she said softly, her eyebrows rising with the effort.

'I mean it,' Tom insisted. 'I'll be forever in your debt.'

'You wouldn't be here on this bloody mountain if not for me.'

'Still I'll never forget what you just did. When I die, will be the final thought to cross my mind.'

A short time passed till Tom sat up. He shuffled forward and peeped over the edge. 'Big drop,' he observed, as if he had never seen the precipice before.

'Is it?' asked Grace. She too sat up, rubbing her aching arms. 'I couldn't really see how high you were dangling. Your head was in the way. Want me to check?'

'No, take it as read.'

'I'll do that.'

As Tom shifted back to the incline he accidentally dislodged a rock. It rolled off the cliff. Tom watched, Grace waited, and both listened for the impact. After what seemed like an age, there was a distant crack of granite crashing into granite. The sound echoed against the mountains and through the winding gullies, all the way down to Logan and Thorn.

Tom cleaned the dirt from under his nails. 'Like I said, big drop.'

They rose to their feet and started to climb back up the ridge.

'Struth!' Tom fell, grabbing the bottom of his leg.

Grace knelt beside him. 'What is it?'

'Not sure.'

'Ankle?'

'Yeah, maybe.'

Grace held Tom's calf and gently slipped off his boot. He inhaled sharply. 'Either twisted or broken,' she said, turning his foot slightly. 'How's that?'

'Feels alright.'

'How about this?' Grace slowly rotated his foot in the opposite direction.

'Ouch!'

'Sorry.' Grace pressed different points around Tom's

ankle and foot.

'That all feels fine.' he said.

'Right, with a bit of luck it's only a sprain.'

'How do you come to that conclusion?'

Grace took his hand and helped him to his feet. 'I'm a dancer, remember?'

As Tom stood up, the valley spread out below him. He bent over to grab his boot. His sudden movement unbalanced them. Grace again gripped his hand but the scales dipped in Tom's direction. She was flung around, step by falling step, as a pendulum angling over the precipice. The ravine whooshed beneath her. The distant stream shimmered. She slipped on the gravel and fell to Tom's opposite side. Her momentum brought him down as well. They clung to the ridge like starfish. More rocks tumbled into the abyss. He squeezed out a nervous laugh. 'Whoa, that's it for all our eighteen lives.'

Grace spoke precisely. 'Do not do that again.'

Tom made his excuse as they got up. 'I lost my balance, felt dizzy. Have to practice my spotting: couldn't decide what to look at.'

With a sigh Grace advised: 'Next time, don't be so fussy.' She guided him up the incline. 'Next time, commit. No second chances. He who hesitates is lost.'

As they neared the spine of the ridge Grace retrieved the Winchester and saw Copenhagen waiting patiently as if nothing had happened.

Tom hobbled the remaining few feet to his horse and sat down. Grace again attended to his ankle. 'Starting to swell up. Give me your shirt.'

'What?'

Grace was of no mind to muck around. 'Tom, give me your shirt.'

He removed his shirt. She tore off the sleeves and ripped them into strips.

'Hey, what are you doing?'

Grace grunted as she pulled off the wrist buttons. 'I'm going to bandage your ankle, ease the swelling.'

As she tied the sleeves together and wrapped his sprain, Tom found himself nodding in trusting acceptance, as patients do, and took the opportunity to view the endless miles of forest and mountains. Renewed by the titanic power of altitude, the pain in his ankle receded and he felt sufficiently confident to quip: 'I didn't know they taught survival skills in dance school.'

'You better believe it,' she said, tying off the makeshift bandage. 'There, that should be right.'

Tom eased his foot into his boot's worn leather. A knot in his bandage hit a tight spot. He gritted his teeth and tugged till his heel found the sole.

'All good?' she asked.

'Snug,' he wheezed, and took back the remnants of his shirt.

Grace grabbed Copenhagen's reins. 'Now we have to get you onto the horse.'

Tom pointed to the rising track. 'It's safer to keep walking. Anyway, why should I ride when you're the one with no shoes.'

Grace whispered in his ear: 'You've got no ankle.'

'I can still walk.'

'I can walk faster.'

'No,' he persisted, 'the tracks too steep. Better I keep walking Cope. Like you said, only a sprain.'

'Tom, your ankle's swollen up like a puffer fish!'

'What's a puffer fish?'

'A fish that puffs up.'

Tom put on the remains of his shirt. Grace handed him the Winchester, and pouting he said: 'I still don't like this arrangement; it'll slow us down.'

'Tom, try to be optimistic.'

They continued toward the peak. The wind died down. The temperature rose, obedient to a blossoming sun.

Chapter Sixteen

Pop sat on his kitchen step, peeling potatoes over a bucket of water. He yelled inside the house, 'These are King Edwards again!'

Ma sat at the kitchen table, icing Lucky's birthday cake. 'I told you afore, The Widow O'Connor don't grow the Bambergs no more.'

'Why not?' asked Pop, wielding the vegetable knife imprudently, cutting deep below the skin, 'I don't like these King Edwards. Apart from the unattractive name, they don't have the nutty flavour you get with the Bamberg.'

Ma checked Pop wasn't looking and licked the leftover chocolate icing from the knife. 'The Widow O'Connor is of the opinion your Bamberg is too hard to grow. She told me as much again last week. She said it's much easier to grow the King Edwards.'

Pop washed the dirt off the peeled potatoes and put them on a plate. 'It's a crying shame we must eat an inferior spud. That's what I'm about.'

'Oh, go on with you,' said Ma, putting the cake on the sideboard. 'With all your airs and graces, you fancy yourself as some toff dining at the Ritz or the Savoy Grill.'

Pop checked Ma wasn't looking, carried his bucket over

to the fence where the paspalum grew high and chucked out the water and peel into the neighbouring paddock. 'I don't find it too much for a man to ask for a halfway decent spud.' He picked up the plate of potatoes and walked into the kitchen. 'Here, I peeled your Billy Boys.' He put the plate on the table and noticed the cake. 'Oh, by all the saints, what have you gone and done now, woman?'

'What?' said Ma, opening her cast iron oven and prodding her roast.

'You've written something here in hundreds and thousands.'

'It's a birthday cake.'

'Not sure Lucky would appreciate a big sixty written on his cake. It's not like he's turning twenty-one.'

'Are you after believing he'll come over for his birthday?'

'I'd love to say yes, Ma, but I'm sensing he's not too hungry today.'

'Well, he won't be able to say we didn't at least try to make his misbegotten life a little bit better.' Ma started putting the potatoes in the roasting tray. 'And there was no sign of young Tom, then?'

'No, nothing,' said Pop, settling into his favourite chair and perusing the Examiner.

'So did you hear the galloping last night?'

Pop's face went blank at the question.

'No, of course not; flotsam floating through the Land of Nod was Pop O'Shaughnessy.'

Pop buried himself in his paper.

Ma closed the oven and wiped her hands on her apron.

'Aye, and a bubble on your skull like a walnut. A costly nut I'd wager too.'

'No, Ma, it's like I told you—Logan shouted us all a drink, not just once, but twice.'

'Yes, but how many more servings did you partake of at your own wallet's expense, hey? I ask you that. How a man can drink as you and still wake up with an appetite is beyond all calculation—either a blessing or a curse.'

'It's a blessing.'

'Is it now?'

'Ma, would you prefer I spent me mornings lying in all sorry for meself, or busy at me forge?'

Ma returned to the table and started shelling peas. Pop peeked over his newspaper and frowned. 'Don't worry,' she reassured, 'The Widow MacTavish still grows the same variety of peas.'

'Why would The Widow MacTavish change her peas? Did she not win a blue ribbon for 'em at the Glenn Innes Show?'

'Aye, your memory does not deceive you. That your brain still functions, despite the pains you put it through, can be considered nothing short of a blessing too—a blessing bestowed by a benevolent saint choosing to turn a blind eye to the habits of one of the Almighty's lesser angels.'

'Oh, hush, woman.'

'So, did you not hear the galloping then?'

Again, Pop remained interred in yesterday's news.

'No,' said Ma, 'I can see you did not, so let me tell you there was a galloping last night. It fair woke me up, no sooner

than I was finally asleep after the noisy goings on at the pub.'
She took a break from her shelling. 'Pop, I tell you now the
galloping horse was Copenhagen. I can feel it in me waters, I
can.'

'Aye, Ma, your waters are to be relied upon. I've a bad
feeling meself, even though my waters are less reliable.
Besides, Lucky told me as much when I dropped in.'

'He did?'

'Aye, he did.'

'You might have told me.'

'Why, when you've got your trusty waters.'

'Logan would never hurt Tom, would he?'

Pop put down his newspaper. 'I told Lucky that Tom
would be fine, but may God forgive me for I was lying. That
Preston Logan is a work of evil. You can see Old Nick in his
eyes. When he's angry, they flare up and I swear the pupils
narrow like a wild beast—a snake.'

'You sure that's not the liquor?'

'I'm not hallucinating, if that's what you mean, Ma. I
know my own brain.'

'Do you, Pop? If you were in charge up there in those
draughty cavities, would you drink the way you do? I mean, a
brain should no more wound itself with the drink than a foot
stub its own toe. Your brain is of two minds.'

'And I've admitted as much to you afore, Ma. I've said
it all afore. 'Tis nothing new. Like I said to you the last time
we chanced to speak on this particular subject, there's another
part of me as takes over and I can no more stop it than put me
leg over a railway track to trip up a train. 'Tis the devil in me

and I know it, and I don't want him there, but there he is, and he'll always be there whether I've me nose in a glass or not.'

'And what of Logan?' asked Ma, returning to her husband's observations.

'Why should you care what I'm presuming? You said I was seeing pink elephants.'

'I only said you *might* be. What about Logan?'

'He's not of two minds. The man is different. When you look into his eyes, might as soon be looking at a serpent. The eyes are like glass with nothing behind but levers and gears. There's nothing there to call a soul, to show mercy, nothing there but a reptile's brain, a machine with needs—fuel for procreating, and then more fuel because a little bit of procreating ain't enough, not nearly enough. He'd take the world and more besides if given half a chance, just so he could have it. His needs cannot be met. He's a machine, I say, he's not tempered by a better angel; he would either eat it or have his way with it. He's pure evil.' Pop was out of breath.

'Would you like a cup of tea, love?'

'No, I'm fine thanks, Ma, but I fear for Tom. God forgive me, but I do.'

'You're a wise man, Pop O'Shaughnessy. You see things as others miss. Sometimes I wish you didn't. God forgive me for that.' Ma crossed herself. 'Lucky must be going through a terrible torment of worry about his boy.'

'That he is, Ma. Not like Lucky to be showing his softer side. Keeps that well tucked away, he does, but he's worried about Logan—worried about that Thorn too.'

'Aye, I heard the American yelling at the tanker driver

last night.'

'Aye,' Pop agreed, 'throwing his weight around, he was: eager as a man could be to be going. I should have asked if he'd paid Lucky his tariff. He left in a mighty hurry. Didn't see any trunks on the back of his car, so I suppose he'll have to return once he's located the girl.'

Ma bundled up the emptied pods in newspaper wrapping. 'Was a sinful thing that Logan and Thorn did, treating that Grace like she was nothing but livestock. I can't say as I liked the cut of her jib, but was more than disgusting what them two did to her.'

Pop withdrew into his paper. 'Still, I've seen some card playing in me time, poker and such, and I seen some big pots, but I tell you I never seen nothing like last night: there was hundreds of pounds—no, thousands of pounds worth of tenners on the table. Was a sea of red so large wouldn't even part for Moses.'

Ma greased a tin for the Yorkshire puddings. 'Why would two men gamble so? It seems beyond all reason.'

'You'd think so, but that American had an excellent hand: queen-high flush.'

'And that's good?'

'Oh, aye, not much more to be got than that.'

Ma wiped the butter from her fingers. 'Then what did Preston Logan have that was better?'

'Spades royal flush.'

'And that's good too?'

Pop gazed up from his paper, imagining the fan of spades, and spoke with deep reverence: 'There is nothing better than a spades royal flush. Best hand of all.'

Ma sat at the table and crossed her arms. Pop got nervous as she raised her chin and stared down her nose at him. He anticipated a lecture coming on. 'I wouldn't be lying to you, Ma,' he squeaked defensively, 'and I didn't play any hands. Haven't touched the cards in years. The grog's me curse of choice.'

Ma didn't move. 'Tell me now, were they playing with a brand new deck?'

Pop breathed easier. 'Aye, 'twas still in its wrapping and all.'

Ma still didn't move. 'These new decks, were they Logan's?'

Pop turned away.

Ma leaned toward him. 'Well, were they?'

'Why would you ask that? Logan only had the one new deck.' Pop put down his newspaper. 'I mean to say he showed Thorn the receipt as evidence he'd bought the deck that evening, bought it from here at the store. I seen your receipt, your own particular hand, with me own eyes.'

'Oh, aye, I wrote a receipt for the first deck he bought, but he changed his mind as he was leaving and decided to get a second deck. I don't recall ever writing a receipt for that. He never asked for one.'

Pop's old body drooped, his sinewy head inclined over the table, and he covered his eyes with veined hands. 'I might be for igniting one of your blessed candles, Ma. I have to say a prayer to the Almighty, begging his forgiveness for insulting his creation by comparing his beautiful snakes to Logan; that man must surely be the devil himself.'

'No need for language like that.'

'That's as may be, but was a sinful spectacle to begin with, and is now become all the worse.'

Ma shuddered as she stood up from the table and went back to her cooking, beating again the well-beaten pudding batter, pounding the bowl so hard the wooden spoon was fixing to snap. 'Wasn't just Logan, takes two to tango. I never liked the look of that gambler.' Her voice quavered, her whole body trembling with fear and anger. 'Right from the moment I first laid eyes on him, I felt he was an ill wind that would bring this valley no good. I hope and pray that poor, innocent Tom doesn't become the one to pay for their sins.' Ma became very still and whispered: 'Oh, merciful Father.' She put down the bowl and crossed herself again. 'Should I be telegraphing Constable Grimes?'

'Why?' asked Pop, somewhat bewildered. 'What could he do? Nothing's happened as would be his concern unless he chose to make it so, but no ways besides would he be traipsing all the way up here on a Sunday on account of nothing more than the fears of a couple of old codgers and their sensitive waters.'

Ma crossed herself yet again.

'Oh, stop crossing yourself, woman!'

The early morning's crispness had burnt away and the air thickened, closing in and moist, gathering its strength and oiling for the sun. Snow followed fresh hoof marks left by several horses. It was the same old route he and Darcy had taken, one he suspected Burnum would know well, known to the aboriginal people since the dreaming.

Charlie followed, second in line after Snow. 'This track's seen a lot of traffic of late.'

Snow nodded. 'Has to be Logan's party. If Burnum reckoned this way, so did Tom.'

The going was hard; Snow's horse struggled to get up the mountainside, the effort so great, it farted.

'Was that you?' asked Charlie, looking up at Snow.

'No, it was me britches busting. Shame I don't wear undies. It won't be a pretty sight for youse lot down there.'

Snow's horse farted again. Charlie detected swamp gas. 'I see your mood's improved.'

'Was just the jitters,' said Snow. 'Game's started now.'

'No regrets?'

'Don't believe in regrets.'

'Jeez,' Charlie pronounced, winking back to Mad Mike, 'imagine having no regrets.'

'I didn't say that.' Snow protested. 'I said I don't believe in 'em. Be plenty of time for all that when I'm six foot under.'

Charlie snorted. 'The dead don't give a stuff.'

Snow ducked under a low branch. 'That's right, why should they? Done their time.'

Mad Mike shouted from behind: 'I reckon me mum still gives a stuff. When things go ti-ti-ti-belly up, I can feel her there beside me, wanting things to go good for me—better than they done for her.'

'Yeah, I'm hearing what you're on about,' Charlie conceded. 'Still, I'm praying me kids don't have to put up with all the shit that's landed in our laps. Would never have had them if I thought they'd cop all that shit. Sooner bite off me nuts.'

Mad Mike squinted at the deep blue sky. 'Having a kid is a sign of hope.'

'Yeah, sign of hope.' Charlie groaned. 'I must have plenty of hope; hope's costing me a bloody fortune. With my brood, mealtime's like feeding a flaming army.'

'Oh, come on,' Snow countered, 'you feed your kids better than that.'

Charlie's teeth ached in remembrance of trench mouth and hard tack. 'Snow, you was saying the last time you was on this track was way back when, way back with Darcy?'

'Yeah, not since I was a kid; was a big adventure then— me and Darce running off to Sydney.'

'Oh, yeah, the f-f-famous jailbreak.'

'You got it in one, Mike, a golden duck.' Snow grew strangely sentimental, reminiscing: 'A lot of what I'm seeing today, I can still recollect from then, all those years ago: some of the rocks, the views, bits I remember. Nothing seems to have changed much. Could be yesterday, could easily.'

'Bloody stupid thing to do.'

'Oh, come on, Charlie.' Snow started getting cranky. 'Was that why you brought it up? Have a go?'

Charlie looked aggrieved. 'No, but still a bloody stupid thing to do.'

'Fair enough, but where would we be today—where would we all be if people never did stupid things? I mean who was the first bloke to try an oyster? People probably said:

"Bloody hell, mate, don't be flaming stupid, you can't eat that!" Sometimes the stupid ideas turn out to be smart.' Snow saluted his observation. Then he shook his finger. 'Of course, I mean they *usually* turn out smart: got to expect the occasional casualty. I mean where would we be if we didn't say stuff it and give it a go?'

'Happy,' offered Mad Mike.

'Yeah, alright,' Snow accepted grudgingly, 'but then we'd still be living in trees like monkeys. I wouldn't want to be a monkey no matter how happy it made me. Anyway, you know what Darce was like—a dreamer. I did nothing but catch the bug was all I did, but Darce, he was smart. Everybody knew that—Darce always thinking as well as dreaming.'

Snow's eyes became distant as he reminisced in words unspoken about his fallen mate. Charlie recognised the silence and didn't disturb it, his focus returning to the chase. He bent over his horse's shoulder to keep a close eye on the hoof prints between the boulders, making sure Snow's daydreaming didn't lead to their losing the trail. Charlie was the older of the two by twelve years. Didn't mean much now that they were all grown men, but before the war, Charlie was a bit of a local hero to all the young lads.

Within seconds they were turning a hairpin turn. Charlie glanced sideways up the rocks at his younger mate, ready again to continue the debate. 'Youse should have known better than piss off the way youse did. Youse really should have. You and Darce should have talked to me about it. God, two fourteen-year-old kids from the land reckoning they could get jobs at a big city newspaper.'

Snow patronised for emphasis. 'You still don't understand it. Do you, Charles? A man's got to take chances in this life.'

'Maybe.' Charlie stopped to spit out a comet of bloodstained saliva. Snow winced. Charlie continued regardless. 'But you've got to admit—we've all three of us, taken more chances than a man's got a right to take. I feel guilty about it sometimes, how I've got away with it. Hope for me kids' sake I haven't used up all me good luck on meself. I don't see any reason how a man's got to take chances, at least not big ones; the odds are always stacked against you. That's why a chance is the same as a risk. Just that a chance doesn't sound so risky, but a man having to take a chance… Can't see how you can still think that.'

'Sorry to disappoint you, Charlie, but I do. Darce and me, we could have made pots of money after we'd done our apprenticeships and such. Make a heap by writing stories. Not only at the Examiner, like, but writing big stories.'

'Snow, you couldn't write a grocery list.'

'Jeez, Charlie, you can be a rude bastard.'

'Just telling the truth, Snow.'

'Darce reckoned I could write and he got an article published in the Examiner, so he couldn't have been talking through his arse. Wasn't for the war, who knows what might've happened—might be a war correspondent now.'

'There isn't a w-w-war on right now.'

'No, not here,' Snow grumbled, getting irritated again, 'but Mike, if you perused the paper once in a while you'd have read there's a war going on in Russia.'

'B-B-But you hate cold weather.'

'Yeah, I s'pose, but must be other wars in warm places. I read there's a war on in Mexico too. I'd say it's pretty warm over there.'

Mad Mike nodded in agreement, not sure where Mexico was, but certain Snow would never lie to him.

Charlie knew where Mexico was. It was near America. He'd seen Mexicans in a Tom Mix movie at the flicks down in Grafton. The knowledge gave him the confidence to offer Snow a quick reminder: 'Folks say the Great War was the war to end all wars.'

'Yeah, I reckon they're right there,' Snow relented. 'Was the last of the big ones. Least I hope it was. Strike a light, be a bunch of drongos if it wasn't. But still, you'll always get plenty of little wars. You know: toe in the water. It's the way people are. No more stop it than stop dustups at the pub. I mean to say, we're in a sort of war right now.'

'Us, at war?' asked Charlie. Old habits still not dead, he gripped his reins in his teeth and gave his rifle the once over. After a moment, he mumbled, mouth full of leather. 'Australia isn't at war.'

Snow's grumps returned. 'Not talking about Australia, talking about us.'

'U-us?'

'Jeez, Mike, sometimes you worry me—us, meaning the three of us—me, you and Charlie.'

Charlie snatched the reins from his teeth. 'Bullshit!'

'No, mate, I'm being fair dinkum here; what we're doing now is a kind of war, I reckon.'

'Jeez, Snow,' Charlie insisted, a metaphorical bit in his teeth though he'd spat out his reins, 'aren't we supposed to be riding to prevent a stoush? I mean, we've brung our rifles and such, but that's like, just a, you know, sensible precaution.'

'Yeah, s'pose we don't need guns. Any case,' Snow adjusted his belt, 'I can settle my account with Logan the old-fashioned way.'

'Stone the crows,' Charlie warned, 'do that and you'll never get work in the district again. You'd have to move to Queensland or New Zealand or such. Anyway, it was the Herald, wasn't it?'

'Yeah, Fairfax and Sons. Old Darce, he said we could work our way up to be copy boys, but they wanted letters from our parents and cetra. I mean: that'd be pushing daisies up hill. No way could me old mum write a letter.'

'Why not?' Charlie spat again.

'Cripes, mate, you really gotta get some limes into you.'

'Listen, Snow, stop changing the subject. Why couldn't your mum write you a letter, like a letter of introduction, like?'

Snow looked down, embarrassed. 'She wasn't literal.'

'No fuss, Snow,' Mad Mike sympathised, 'my mum couldn't write neither. Me d-d-dad neither too.'

'Yeah,' Snow muttered, 'not nothing unusual in that, I'd reckon.' Then his mood brightened. 'And Darce, how about him? Never mind letters and cetra, he didn't even bother to let his folks know we was buggering off. No farewells, bye-byes, kiss me arse, nothing!'

'Hey, Snow,' asked Mad Mike, 'your mum ever learn to be literal?'

'Nah, after the old man died, I used to read all her letters to her—the way me dad used to, before the cancer got to him. Me mum used to like that—was proud of me.' Snow pulled out his tobacco pouch and rolled a smoke as he led them all around another hair-pin turn.

Charlie took off his hat and fanned his face. 'Caused a bit of a stir up here while youse two was gone. Darcy's mum, old Rachel, more or less had kittens.'

'Yeah, I know that, mate. You must have told me a hundred bloody times. Was fun, but—especially when we both got jobs at the *Truth*. That John Norton, only seen him now and then, but cripes, you couldn't miss him. Talk about drink! Made old Lucky look like a Methodist.'

Charlie brushed away a fly. 'Big stink when youse two got arrested and brought back by the coppers. Good thing youse weren't dragged off to some gaol for kids, like Neddy.'

'Yeah, like Neddy,' Mike agreed.

'Yeah, like Neddy,' Snow muttered, agreeing too as he lit up his smoke. 'But, Charlie, me old mate, if I've told you once, I've told you a thousand bloody times—I'm starting to sound like a broken record—we didn't get properly pinched or nothing like that. I mean how was we to know the bookie was going to get raided—we was only runners.'

'Copy boys,' said Mike.

'Yeah, copy boys,' said Snow.

Logan and Thorn walked their horses along the spine of the narrow ridge. The squatter stopped and picked up one of Tom's buttons.

'Hey, Thorn, have a gander at this.' Logan handed it over. 'Nice and clean, any money it's theirs. Can't be far ahead now.'

The gambler examined the button. 'Doesn't belong to Grace. Might be the kid's. You think it's his?'

'Who else would be up here? Isn't Pitt Street.'

'Not a popular place for a picnic, then?'

'Not if you're superstitious, but most of the people around here are.'

'All because of your father?'

'No, the local aborigines maintain this mountain's been cursed since the year dot.'

Logan set off again but Thorn didn't follow. 'Wait up a second,' he said, pointing. 'You see that?'

Logan looked down to the edge of the cliff. 'Hmm,' he nodded, 'that's interesting.'

'Yeah,' Thorn agreed. 'The ground's pretty mussed up. Here, hold my horse.' He gave Logan his reins and carefully negotiated the incline, loose pebbles rolling from under his feet and over the precipice.

'Watch yourself, that ground's pretty unstable,' Logan yelled, not wanting to lose the assistance of an extra gun, even though it was a Derringer.

Thorn slithered to the rim of the ledge. 'These marks are recent.'

Logan didn't like being caught in the wings, stuck like a porter with the horses. 'What is it? Someone go over?'

'Hard to say.' Thorn hunkered lower and inspected the hole where the tree root had been. The broken earth was fresh and white while the undisturbed ground was surfaced grey. He put both his hands on the rock ledge and peered over the precipice. His head spun a little as his eyes plumbed the depths of the ravine.

'Anything down there?' Logan asked irritably.

'No, nothing, but it's a long way down. There's a creek at the bottom. It's flowing clean through; no bodies in the water or on the rocks or anywhere else as I can make out.'

Logan hawked and spat. He was annoyed; this was his valley and his show, not the property of some American Johnny-come-lately.

Thorn backed away from the edge. 'Appears like someone's almost gone over: a lot of scrapes and footprints in the dirt. Where did your grandfather take his big plunge?'

'Can't say for sure, but it may have been where you're crouching right now.'

Thorn was up with his horse in seconds. 'Let's get going. Time—as I would say—is a-wasting.'

Logan handed him the reins. 'How long you been playing cards?'

'Almost as long as I can retrace.'

Logan led his horse off and Thorn followed.

'You're hard-to-read,' Logan noted. 'That comes with training. Not easy to make a living from gambling.'

'How'd you know I was professional?'

'I didn't.'

'Touché.'

'Not really, it's not a big deal; you're not concentrating on your game right now. You're away from the table, off your guard. A poker player's got to get warmed up like an athlete, get in the right state of mind. I don't expect you to haul your work home with you.' Logan passed the time amusing himself with the American gambler, delighted at the ease with which his handiwork had relieved Thorn of his money, his adversary suspecting nothing. 'When did you first start living off your poker skills?'

'The Philippines; I was still stationed there when I resigned my commission.'

'Trouble getting promoted?'

'No. I was already a captain but I was told to get out or be drummed out.'

'Gambling?'

'A major's wife.'

'Ah,' Logan nodded. 'One plus one is two. One plus two is too many.' His eyebrows rose. 'Attractive?'

Thorn shrugged. 'I thought she was worth it.'

'Did that mean you had to leave Manila?'

'The major was the son of a general. The wife was the daughter of a congressman.'

'She must have been very attractive.'

'Like I said, was worth it.'

The once whistling branches of the trees were silent now and their fluttering foliage drooped, grown weary in the parched air. Snow rode on a little, staring down and searching for any trace of prints hidden under the carpet of leaves and bark. At every step the ground crackled beneath his horse's hooves, and as he heard the rustle made by tiny living things that scurried off, radiating from his hub on unseen spokes, his mood grew lower, filled with bad omens. 'This weather's playing havoc with my guts.' Snow had become lost. He removed his hat and wiped his face against the crook of his arm, frustrated and worried by the time expended through his forgetfulness.

Charlie scratched his reddened neck. 'Want me to take over?'

Snow didn't answer. He could be like that. It wasn't rudeness; he'd just set his mind to thinking, excluding all else, recalling moments written years before, moments painful in their recollection. Like memories of him and Darcy: he, never again to be as young as then, Darcy, never to be much older.

Charlie gnawed at his fingernails. 'What you say, Snow, want a help? I'm pretty familiar with these ranges meself.'

Snow took a drink from his canteen. 'I don't know. Do anything to summon up which way Darce and I went at this point.'

Above them, a bird sat in a ghost gum and sang a cheerful song. The fluted notes vented the leaden air.

Mad Mike saw the bird. 'You hear that?'

'What?' asked Charlie, spitting out a sliver of his fingernail. 'Hear what?'

Mad Mike persisted. 'Just listen, Charlie.'

'Listen to what? I can't hear noth'n.'

The bird swooped down and dive-bombed Charlie. 'Bloody hell!'

Mad Mike smiled with satisfaction. 'One of your magpies.'

Charlie took off his hat and poked at yet another hole in

the felt's collection. Mad Mike could have wet himself; it was so funny. He didn't, though, because he noticed Snow's consternation. He rode across to him. 'Don't worry, mate, the three of us make a good team. Like you said to me, I'm the best horseman in the di-di-dis—I'm good on a horse. And we've got all of Charlie's experience too, hey, Charlie?'

Charlie closed his eyes and tilted his head, ever the shrewd elder.

'Yeah, that's right. We've got Charlie,' Mad Mike continued, 'and all that's left of the old bugger's brain.' Charlie spat out another nibble of fingernail.

Mad Mike turned back to Snow, his warm, brown eyes irresistibly honest. 'But you're the smart one, mate. We all know that.'

Snow slouched in his saddle, attempting to endure the compliment. 'Not feeling too smart right now.'

Mad Mike was firm in his support. 'No, that's where you're wrong. You're worried you'll let us all down, but jog your memory; you were the bastard that dragged me out of the barbed wire, straight in front of old Fritz's nose, and you'll pull Tom out of all of this shit too.'

Burnum appeared on a ledge above them. Charlie saw him. 'Hey, we've got company.'

How you going, Burnum?' Mad Mike called out, smiling broadly. 'Warm day for a ride, hey? You haven't seen young Tom by any chance?'

Burnum pointed north, and without saying a word, cantered his Appaloosa back into the bushland's embrace.

Chapter Seventeen

High above the shelter of the tree line, the sun was free to blaze unhindered on the weathered rock. Leeward of any hint of ocean breeze and sweating in the oven heat, they climbed the last few dozen steps towards the summit. Grace stumbled and a sharp pain shot up from her left instep, forcing her to relieve the pressure by leaning on a fallen boulder. Tom quickly dismounted and limped to her side. She said nothing as he examined her foot. The thin skin of her arches and the recesses between the pads of her toes were cut in a dozen places, the wound to her instep bleeding steadily. Tom was amazed she hadn't complained sooner. 'You can't go on like this.'

Grace rubbed her forehead. 'Is it bad?'

Tom avoided a direct answer. 'Depends on what you'd reckon to be bad. You wouldn't call it good.' He took her hand. 'You'd better sit a spell.'

Grace slid down, making herself as comfortable as she could against the side of the boulder. Tom untied his red bandana and wrapped it around the latest gash, trying to staunch the flow of blood. 'You might have gone barefoot when you were little, but it's been a few years since these feet were last exposed to the elements. Might be your turn to ride on Cope.'

Grace glanced at Tom's sprain, stubbornly insisting: 'You can't walk on that ankle.'

'You reckon? I'm a fast healer. Check out this.' Tom got up and hobbled in a circle. 'See, no problem.' He pretended to waltz and started humming. 'Da-da-da-da-dee, da-da da-da.' Circling around and holding an imaginary woman, he went through the steps Ma had shown him. 'See, Grace, belle of the ball. You aren't the only one who can dance.'

The air exploded! A bullet crashed into the rocks above. A rifle's report echoed across the range. Terrified, Copenhagen galloped off, retreating over the shoulder of the summit. Tom dived and yelled for Grace to get down too.

A second bullet lanced the blistering air. Its blast followed the first, reverberating through a maze of winding gorges.

Two miles down the track, the three stockmen heard the shots and recognised the all too familiar sound of a Lee Enfield 303. It rolled over them, the pulse seeming like an avalanche. Snow needed no further prompting. He spurred his horse forward, its legs grinding up the mountainside. Charlie and Mad Mike struggled to follow.

Grace darted behind the boulder. Tom crawled up beside her.

'They're trying to shoot you!' she cried.

'What makes you think it's just me?' he asked.

Grace got up. 'Ernie wouldn't hurt his——'

A third bullet rent the air, smashing against the boulder's edge. Grace ducked down, dust drifting over her.

'Told you,' Tom chided, pulling her close.

'Maybe it's not them. Maybe it's somebody else: a deranged old hermit?'

'All the deranged old hermits live up the other side of the valley—reliable creeks over there. No, it's Logan alright.'

One hundred and fifty yards below, the cattleman crouched, hidden among a cluster of rocks, the path of Copenhagen's hoof-prints winding between him and the gambler.

Logan's rifle was trained on his quarry as Thorn hissed: 'Watch what you're doing with that thing.'

The cattleman hissed back: 'Don't worry, I won't hit anybody. Doing nothing more than teaching that randy little bugger a lesson. Lad's getting a bit of the old-fashioned arse-slap, potty training his mummy was too soft to give.'

Up the curving track, Tom hunched, still holding Grace. 'You know,' he admitted bashfully, 'you know how you suspected we were in the middle of nowhere?'

The flush drained from Grace's face. 'Yeah?'

Tom surveyed the terrain. 'I think you suspected right.'

'But you said this was the Rock of Gibraltar… or something.'

Tom didn't answer. Instead, his arm slipped from her shoulders as he shifted to gape at the peak, muttering to himself: 'Copenhagen won't stray far. Probably just on the other side of the summit.' He returned to Grace. 'We can still get away. We can get to Grafton. You still fair dinkum?'

She hesitated for a second before suggesting: 'Maybe, they're not here anymore. Maybe they just wanted to teach us a lesson and now they've gone.' She stood again and looked out, checking down their path. Another round roared up. It barely missed her.

'Don't keep doing that,' Tom squawked, his throat straining to repress the need to shout.

Grace betrayed her confusion, blinking rapidly. 'I don't understand it. Don't understand.'

Tom leaned back and aimlessly drew a little triangle in the sandy soil. 'I have to tell you. Would have told you sooner, but it didn't seem necessary, and I didn't want to… worry you.' His voice faded as he took to chewing on his cheeks.

'What, Tom, what are you saying?'

'Logan's a killer,' he blurted. Then whispered: 'He's killed people before. He doesn't shy away from killing. He's insane; if he weren't so rich, he'd be hanged. Leastwise locked up in a madhouse.'

Grace flared with indignation and the flush returned. 'How dare he!'

Tom crossed his lips. 'Shush!'

Shaking in disbelief, Grace tried her best to shush. 'What gives him the right to go around killing people?' she seethed. 'Stealing people's lives just because he can. Just because he's so rich and powerful he can? How dare he try to kill me!' Her shaking increased. 'I've had enough of all of this. He won't get away with it.'

Tom shrugged. 'He's done stuff like this before—way it is.' He adjusted the boot on his sprained ankle and prepared to move out. 'Situation won't change. Not in this life.'

Grace's anger combusted into searing outrage: 'Oh,

yes——' She lowered her voice. 'Oh, yes it will. If we ever get out of these mountains, I'll make the situation change. That Logan reckons he's tough. Ha! I'd like to see how he'd go against the Harry Newman gang.' Her entire body quaked ferociously, her scowl beading with a new coat of sweat. 'He wouldn't be such a big man then!'

Tom saw Grace anew, impressed. She ran her finger inside the leather strap of her Akubra. 'What about the aborigine? What's he going to do? Throw a spear at us?'

'Burnum? I don't think so.' Tom levered the Winchester, ramming a cartridge into the firing chamber. 'In fact, I'm certain we won't have to worry about him.'

'How do you know that?'

'He would have buggered off by now.'

'Gone walkabout?'

Tom grinned lopsidedly. 'No, not walkabout, Burnum would never come up this far is all. You see, the local aboriginal people, they believe this peak, they believe it's cursed.'

Grace was shocked and then annoyed. 'I wish you'd told me that earlier.' She wanted to yell at Tom, but found she was distracted. For a fleeting moment all she could do was see how much she liked the gap between his two front teeth.

Tom traced her line of sight to its target. Embarrassed, he averted his eyes and commenced to search the ground. 'We've stuffed around up here too long.' He snatched a fallen twig and balanced his hat on the twig's blunter end. 'When I signal, poke this up.'

'P-poke up your hat?' Grace spluttered. 'Logan's a

madman with a gun, thinks he's above the law, and your answer is a hat on a stick?'

'Grace, we haven't got time to argue. Do you want to go back to Ernie?'

'I could never do that.'

'And Logan?'

'Oh, God, of course not!'

'Then listen to me. This is my plan: they see my hat above the rock, then when they shoot at it—and they will shoot at it—you nick off. Get to the other side of the summit as quickly as you can and grab Copenhagen.' Tom gave Grace the stick and hat. 'And remember to keep down.'

'But they'll see me before I get to the other side.'

'Yes, but like I said, they'll both take a shot at the hat. Least I'm hoping they will. They should do. Both so competitive, they'll have to make a contest of it. They'll take a few seconds—if we're lucky, even longer—to chamber a second round, aim and shoot. By then you should be safe. Plus, if they reload faster than I reckon, still won't do them tuppence worth of good 'cause you'll be a moving target—can be pretty hard to hit a moving target.'

Grace gawked up the rise. 'This moving target can't travel that far in two or three seconds.'

'Grace, you reckon I'm going to let them get off that second round?' Tom gripped his shining rifle. 'This is a Winchester.'

'What if you accidentally shoot one of them?'

'Crikey, Grace, they're shooting at us.'

'But if Logan's as powerful as you say——'

'You seen my mug on a wanted poster?' Tom pointed at his head. 'This the face of a killer?'

Grace sat against the boulder. 'God, my foot's giving me curry.' She prodded the bandanna wrapped around her wounded instep and fiddled with the fabric till driven to glance back. 'No, you don't look like a killer,' she acknowledged, seeing again the flecks of gold in Tom's eyes. 'You look beautiful and I don't want to see you hurt.'

'I know what I'm doing. I won't get hurt and they won't either. I'm a good shot.' Tom rubbed his thumb over the engraved frame of the Winchester. 'You ever had rabbit pie?'

'I've had the stew, but not the pie.'

'When we get out of this, get down to Sydney, I'll bake you one of my rabbit pies.'

Grace tried to hold in her frustration. 'This is crazy. It can't be happening.'

'But it is happening. What I'll do is shoot to scare the living daylights out of them, shoot to keep them pinned down. That's all.'

Grace rubbed her temples, her fingers pressing down, describing hard circles. 'I can't make sense of this. It doesn't seem real. It doesn't add up, doesn't add up at all: Logan perhaps, but Ernie? Why would Ernie——'

'Use your body to pay off a bet?'

Grace dropped her hands, boneless as a rag doll. 'I thought he loved me.'

'Might not be in him. Might be he can't love.'

'I thought he could,' she whispered, staring at the blood seeping from her instep. 'I thought he was the first man I'd ever met who was able to love. I really did. I really thought he loved me.' Grace beheld Tom, not doubting his integrity, but silently praying for reassurance. 'Is there such a thing as a man who can love?'

'I can.'

'Can you, Tom? Can you love?'

'I can love you.'

Grace shifted towards Tom and he to her.

Thorn loosened his tie. 'Those two have been up there for a hell of a long time. You want me to see if I can swing around, get behind them.

Logan's view had not strayed from the boulder. 'You notice the drop from this ledge?' He grumbled. 'Must be a good fifty feet, worse every other direction except from the east—up over the other side of the summit. The only way to get to them from there is via Grafton.' The cattleman waved a fly off the barrel of his 303. 'No, we stay put. Sooner or later they'll do something rash. They're just a pair of kids with too much juice—got to gush out soon. Won't be able to help themselves.'

Tom was the first to rise for air. Grace sighed as he released her. She could have stayed forever in that moment, floating as the flitter settled in her snow dome. Tom glanced up the trail that led past the summit. Everything was different now; the prizes that shone beyond the mountain's rampart seemed so much closer. All they need do was get past the peak and he and Grace would be free. He would sooner die than give up on that dream, but his life was no longer all his own. 'Grace,' he said, 'if my plan doesn't work, we'll give up.' He nodded in quest of her agreement. 'Yeah?'

Grace nodded back, at first relieved, then plundered by doubt, panicked by Tom's newfound willingness to surrender, fearing she had given him all he really wanted.

Tom felt her alarm and the whites of his eyes streaked tints of burning vermillion. 'But if they so much as lay one hand on you I'll——'

'Never mind me, what about you?' Grace insisted, touching his cheek, her initial fear replaced by one yet worse. 'God, I mean at least Ernie cares for me.' Her focus wandered and her voice lowered. 'At least a bit, I guess.' Then her words grew strong again. 'But you, I mean what's planned for you? They both must hate you so much it doesn't bear thinking about. I don't want to think about it.'

'You're right. I don't want to think about it either. You fine with the hat thing?'

Grace nervously practiced balancing the hat on the stick. 'God, I can't do it. I work in music halls, not the circus.'

There was a bit of scrub sprouting from between the rocks. Tom reefed off a small branch and jammed the leafy end into his hat. 'Won't wobble now.'

Grace warily accepted the hat. 'What's going to happen to you? How are you going to get away?'

Tom failed to reply. He slid off on his belly, in a flanking maneuver across the ledge, making for the upward side of the cliff face. It lay a few feet to their right.

Down the mountain, Thorn was getting worried. 'Hey, Logan, I figure you've scared them enough. Let's call out for a powwow. I'm sure the kid's learnt his lesson.'

Logan wasn't listening; all his concentration was fixed upon his prey.

Thorn was not to be ignored. 'Could be one of them has been hurt. You've been spraying bullets all over the joint. Could be one of the rounds hit Grace. Could be she's bleeding to death while we just sit here waiting for the eighth day.' Thorn was getting shrill. 'Logan, you're not hearing me——'

'Shut up,' Logan growled as his panther vision detected Tom's progress, the lad's movement betrayed by a small tuft of dust drifting through the broiling air. 'Wait a little longer. Longer we wait, longer they'll have to wait; more they wait, more scared they'll get, more respectful they'll be when they throw in the towel.'

The branch trembled in Grace's hand as she watched Tom draw himself up inside a recess in the cliff. Sitting on one knee, he lifted the Winchester across his chest. 'Now remember to raise my hat really slowly, just a tiny bit at a time. You ready with the hat?'

'Yes,' she answered, though her face displayed the opposite.

'Fine,' said Tom, 'as soon as they fire, you get out, fast as you can… And Grace,' he winked, 'don't forget the old saying.'

'What's that?'

'He who hesitates is lost.'

Her jaw dropped.

Tom grasped his rifle firmly. 'Alright, Grace, push up the hat.'

She didn't respond, instead reflecting on Tom's dig.

'Grace, what was it you said about hesitation?'

'I'm doing it,' she snapped, the dig forgotten. The hat rose up.

Logan saw it and aimed precisely.

Thorn glowered. 'Logan, are you nuts? This is going too far.'

Logan didn't react. His hands rock steady.

Thorn stared up the hill. 'For God's sake, Logan, that's enough.'

Tom's hat rose higher. Logan's finger slid lightly on the trigger. Thorn's concern knifed down to raw fear. 'Stop, goddamn it!'

The air convulsed as Logan's 303 spat out a burst of flame.

'No!' screamed Thorn.

The round ripped a hole through the middle of the hat and it dropped behind the boulder. In that instant Thorn realised Logan was out to do murder.

Tom leapt out from his cover.

The cattleman pulled back the bolt of the 303. The spent casing flew out.

Tom aimed at the rock that sheltered Logan, his sights aligned on a point an inch from the cattleman's left ear.

Derringer in hand, Thorn crossed to Logan, trying to stop him from firing again. He was too late. The cattleman drew a bead on Tom and discharged the 303.

Tom fired his Winchester. At that very moment, he felt a slap to his forward arm.

Logan ducked out of harm's way. A bullet pinged as it

skimmed past him.

Wounded, Tom dropped the Winchester. It slid down the incline.

Logan tore at the bolt of the 303, ejecting another spent casing.

Tom fell back behind the cover of the cliff as his rifle slid further away. It came to a stop on open ground and well out of reach.

Logan chambered the next cartridge and aimed at Tom's new position in the cliff-side.

Thorn found himself standing behind Logan. Eyes wide, he locked his Derringer onto the cattleman. 'Logan, what have you done, you pigheaded bastard?'

The cattleman took his eye off his target, looked across his shoulder and saw the Derringer. 'Why are you pointing that thing at me?'

The gambler's mouth grew slack and it was hard for him to speak. 'I should have shot you last night, killed you in the bar.'

Logan noticed a small hole in the breast of Thorn's jacket. 'You saying I cheated you?'

Thorn didn't answer but his aim was growing unsteady.

Logan sensed the gambler's diminishing strength. 'You got it wrong,' he assured, confident enough to turn away, his thoughts back on the gunfight. 'I don't cheat, merely take a reasonable risk; nobody ever got rich playing by the rules. You want to meet a real cheat, it's the boy up there who stole your wife.'

Thorn put the Derringer back in his jacket pocket, and

trembling, he sat down. 'That's not a boy,' he coughed, arterial blood spreading over his shirt and dribbling out of his sleeve. 'He's not just a boy. He's more than that. More than he knows.' He gazed at Logan, his brow furrowed in supplication, and pleaded: 'Please don't hurt my Gracie. Don't let this be for nothing.'

The cattleman ignored him.

Thorn's chest rattled, his strength faded and he leaned forward, settling slowly, staring at the dirt. Logan withdrew from his pocket another sachet of analgesic and tore it open with his teeth.

Back near the summit, Tom clasped his arm. It was only a flesh wound but it stung like hell. He winced off the pain.

'Tom!' Grace shrieked: 'They shot you!'

Logan looked up; he'd heard her every word.

Tom whispered loudly: 'Grace, I told you to bugger off.'

Smirking, the cattleman poured the headache powder into his mouth and felt again where Tom had struck him. The bleeding had stopped, but the scab was moist and sticky, flies swarming to it. He pushed back his hat, covering the oozing mass to keep the hungry insects at bay.

Tom ripped off his shirt and dabbed his bullet wound. The ruptured skin bloomed, and though the gash had barely penetrated to the muscle, the flow of his blood was such to excite him.

Grace stared at the lad, her fear revealed by succeeding waves of perspiration that glossed her features. Her flimsy dress clung to her breast, the delicate fabric presenting sheer with percolating heat. She watched Tom's blood; it still wept from the ripeness of his wound, beaming scarlet, adhering to gullies in his lean and youthful frame. In those seconds, her lust burnt through her fear, creating the merest sliver of abatement through which the cramp attacked. The adrenalin was in her kidneys, her glands injecting the slice and dice of shards of glass and waves of other things that gouged and ripped. Grace dragged her knees against her chest and stretched to relieve the torture, her body twitching as she waited for the cramp to fade and slink away.

'Are you alright?' Tom asked.

'Don't worry about me,' she gasped. 'You're the one who's shot.' It was only a hopscotch skip and a jump to liberty, but with Tom wounded and their gun lost, the freedom of the east side of the peak might just as well have been another country.

Logan removed his sweat-soaked jacket and slipped up onto his rock. Skink flat, he again trained the muzzle of his rifle on Tom's small recess in the cliff. With Thorn dead, Logan calculated it would be perfectly legitimate for him to kill the publican's son, excusing it as self defence. He could kill Grace too if required. Logan's pupils narrowed in the white-hot light.

As the cattleman watched for a glimpse of his prey, his prey glared at the Winchester: out in the open, the weapon beckoned.

Grace's cramp faded, leaving her free to be gripped by the sight of Tom's blood. She panted: 'Tom, you need help.'

He wiped the sticky redness across his face, like it was Viking war paint, and whispered: 'Stop being so loud… and stay down!'

'This is crazy, Tom. It's madness, complete madness. It's not worth it. I'm not worth it.'

Tom bolted for the Winchester. Logan fired. With a thud and a smack, the round burrowed through the dirt. Tom fell back against the cliff.

Grace gaped in shock. Though Tom was pale with fear, she noted anger and determination in his hardening lines, and something else she didn't like: not the need to survive, not the need to escape, but the need to win.

'Right,' she yelled, 'that's it. Enough!' She angled her voice to the sky and shouted, 'Ernie! Logan! Stop firing, I'm coming down!'

Tom's face ironed smooth. 'Grace, what are you doing? They'll kill you.'

'No, they won't.'

'Yes, they will!'

'Tom, put a sock in it.'

Grace stood erect, her hands in the air. Tom watched in disbelief as she started down the hill.

'Sweetie,' she spoke low through the corner of her mouth, 'now you can get away, get that gash seen to. I'll meet you at Grafton station, I promise. Wait for me there.'

Logan calmly aimed at Grace. Tom jumped out to grab her. The cattleman swivelled his sights onto the lad and pulled the trigger. The bullet slammed into the granite, missing Tom by yards. Grace swerved away, lost her footing and tumbled over.

Logan cursed himself for rushing. He wrenched back

the bolt. His mouth was dry as a sun dried-brick, his saliva gone thick as lard.

Grace kept rolling till her hands could seize the earth. Half-stunned, she crawled to her feet again, but now she was battling to breathe. Her Akubra had flipped over, the strap twisting around her throat. She struggled to loosen the strangling leather. Tom's bandanna, bandaging her instep, grew loose, further impeding her progress. It was sodden, marbling at the edges where her blood had evaporated in the heat, but she kept stumbling on, all the time tugging at her choking hat.

Tom was still out in the open, mesmerised by Grace's blundering progress. Logan fired at him. The slug chiselled the rock of the cliff. Tom hit the deck. Grace fell sideways at the rifle's report. Logan cursed himself and chambered another round. Another empty casing arced away from the breech.

Grace got back up, cast aside her hat and staggered forward, her pains forgotten. Three paces on, she was able to look beyond the rocks and see Thorn. He was bent over in a puddle of blood. The puddle blazed red on the chalky track. She screamed and lurched into a run.

On hearing Grace's cry, Tom peered from the cover of his position. He saw Logan's 303, its muzzle trained on her. He stood to draw the cattleman's fire, waving his arms and yelling. Spoilt for choice, Logan again shifted his sights to the lad; but Grace was moving forward too swiftly, immediately blocking the way. Logan slid off the rock and aimed from a different angle. Tom ducked down. Logan fired and yet again missed, but he had not rushed and his aim was surer. Tom felt the bullet crack above him and smelt the brimstone of singed hair. His mind swimming from the concussive force of the cattleman's round, he scrambled back behind the cliff.

Grace closed in. Logan ascertained she was unarmed. He would use her as bait. 'Where's your boyfriend? Why no holding hands?'

Panting in his granite recess, Tom knew all hope was lost, yet he still felt compelled to screech Grace's name.

Determined though she was to get to Thorn, she slowed—not because she heard Tom's call but because she could see Ernie wasn't moving. Despite the heat her face went grey and her sweat ran cold.

Grace hobbled past Logan, ignoring him like he was no more than another boulder. Moaning faintly, she collapsed beside Ernie and took him in her arms, holding the gambler to her breast and rocking him gently as though he were a settling a child.

Logan couldn't work out what was going on. He began to ponder. Had Tom taken Grace against her will? At some time in the past had Thorn done the same? He tried to reconstruct the previous evening and deduced his brain must be playing tricks on him. After all, he had sustained a big hit to the skull and his recollection of the previous evening was fuzzy. He considered the thought that perchance the lass had actually been starting to fall for his charms. It wouldn't be the first time he had won a lassie despite the odds. But none of that mattered right now. Logan had a fight to win. He jumped out behind Grace, and using her body as a bargaining chip, aimed the 303 between her shoulder blades. 'Tom, you've gone and done it now,' he roared, 'you're up shit creek! Come out or Grace cops it!'

Grace paid no notice. Tom snuck another look. He saw her among the boulders, kneeling away from Logan, the gun pointed at her back. He saw nothing else.

Logan raised the stakes. He lifted the muzzle higher, the rifle aimed at Grace's head. Tom scanned the ground above and behind. He was confused, wondering where Thorn was, wondering if the gambler was somehow sneaking up behind him. 'Logan!'

'What?'

'I'm coming down!'

'Then do it!'

Tom contemplated the nearness of the Winchester.

Sweat trickled down Logan's jaw line and dripped from his chin. 'I'm waiting,' he half sung, menacingly. 'Show yourself!'

Tom steadied his nerves and stepped out from the recess; if he were to be shot it would be then—shot by Thorn who would be lurking somewhere, unseen.

Logan kept his gun on Grace, but glanced at Tom. 'Put your hands in the air and walk down real slow.'

Tom did as he was told and took a couple more steps. He could see the Winchester clearly. It was adjacent to his foot.

Logan's 303 remained rock-solid as he teased. 'Come on, laddie, get a move on.'

Tom reluctantly obeyed. The butt of the Winchester brushed against his boot. It was so temptingly close, but if he went for it, Logan could fire and Grace would be killed. If Logan showed her mercy, the cattleman would instead have plenty of time to shoot Tom. Shoot him long before he could pick up the Winchester, chamber a round, aim and return fire. It was useless. And there was Thorn. Tom had no inkling where the gambler was, but he held no doubt the gambler's gun, wherever it might lie, was aimed on him that minute.

Tom limped away from the fallen Winchester. As he crept down the mountain, the low rocks gradually angled away. They no longer obscured his view of Grace. He could see she was not kneeling before Logan in submission but was cradling Thorn. Tom's expression turned from fear to horror. He stumbled closer, numb to the ache in his ankle, numb to the gunshot wound to his arm, numb to everything.

Tears flowed from Grace, glistening her cheeks as she brushed the hair from Thorn's brow and shut his dead eyes. The nearer Tom got, the more he saw, and the more he saw, the more he felt her pain, a pain he, right away, understood he'd caused. 'Grace?' he beckoned, already pleading for forgiveness.

Logan glared at him. 'She doesn't want to talk to a murderer.'

Tom's mind was everywhere, his thoughts scattered to the four winds. 'Grace, say something!'

Grace wept. 'What? What do you want me to say?'

Tom's pace accelerated. Logan switched his rifle onto him. 'Stop right there,' he warned, but Tom kept coming. 'I don't want to have to shoot you, matie.'

'Stop fighting!' Grace screamed. Then she murmured:

'Please, stop fighting.'

Tom came to a halt. Naked above the waist, Logan saw he carried no weapon worth the name. Once more, the cattleman held all the cards. Largess within his gift, and Grace's favour a possibility, he lowered his rifle and cautiously stepped aside.

Tom walked a little closer. 'You still loved him?'

She kissed the gambler on the forehead. 'Yes, I've loved him since the day we met.'

'But why?' he asked, his heart throbbing enough to crack apart his chest.

Grace rested Thorn gently on the ground. 'He was my brother.'

Tom felt limp, detached, a marionette swinging too loose on its strings. There was a ringing in his ears and beyond the spin of clattering rackets and the din of high whistles, he heard himself ask: 'Thorn?'

'Yes,' Grace nodded slowly, 'Ernie came to Australia searching for his father.' Her words were released through gulps of air. 'Instead… Instead he found an orphan… an orphan sister.' Her voice lowered. 'You *weren't* to know.'

Tom suddenly recalled Snow's telling him: 'You *don't want* to know.'

Grace kissed her brother on the lips.

Tom vomited.

Logan sneered in disgust.

The young man fell to his knees, his mouth caustic, his throat and lungs as parchment, and all he could do was rasp: 'I don't want to know. I don't want to know.'

'Bit late now,' Logan grunted. 'Cat's out of the bag.'

Grace's tears dried to grains of salt. 'And curiosity killed the cat.' She slipped her fingers inside Thorn's jacket.

'What are you hunting for?' Logan asked, and then he called to mind the gambler's Derringer. The cattleman caught a glint of metal in Grace's hand. He pointed his rifle into her face, the muzzle so close she could smell the cordite. Grace was unfazed. She climbed to her feet and stood tall, the pistol held lightly by the barrel as if she were ignorant of its purpose, a foreign thing in her hand. Logan stepped back a little but his aim didn't shift.

Tom remained on his knees, paralysed by his confusion; he could not discern what Grace was doing. A calm seemed to come over her. She stared down the barrel of Logan's 303, stared past the rifle sights, stared into a lemon iris and the slit of a feline pupil, stared into the empty darkness that lay beyond, and not a drop of adrenalin sullied her blood.

Logan had to kill her; she was begging for release and he, full to bursting with desire, was powerless to deny her request. He pulled the trigger. The hammer clicked. Silence. He had forgotten to chamber the next cartridge. Thwarted, he slid back the bolt, his grip grown slimy with excitement. The spent casing flew out. Desperate to recapture the moment, he slammed home the bolt. Metal snapped into metal. The sound was to Tom like the clicking fingers of a hypnotist. He leapt to his feet and pounced. Logan saw him from the corner of his eye. He turned his gun on his attacker and squeezed. The hammer clicked. Again nothing fired; the magazine had been stripped, its cartridges spent.

Tom was upon him. With one hand he yanked down on the barrel of the 303. With the other he pushed up on the stock, ripping the rifle from Logan's grasp. As the butt swung it clipped the cattleman's jaw. He fell backwards, recovered, and crawling sideways to escape, looked straight up the snub nose of Grace's Derringer.

'Okay sweetheart,' he pronounced with a sniff, 'take it easy.' He pulled away from her, settled on his haunches and raised his hands in the air.

'Grace,' Tom asked, 'are you alright?'

She ignored him, her gun riveted on the cattleman. Tom could see her eyes were empty, but he couldn't let her go, saying softly: 'Grace, you've won. You don't have to kill him.' He shifted toward her. 'Grace, it won't prove anything.'

She didn't move.

Tom drew nearer. 'Killing Logan won't bring your brother back.'

'Tom's right,' said Logan.

'Shut up!' Grace shouted, thrusting the Derringer at the cattleman. He fell backwards, spread-eagle before her.

'Grace, it's not worth it,' Tom pleaded. 'Put down the gun.'

Grace's finger touched the trigger, caterpillar light.

Tom took a deep breath. 'Listen to me, Grace, this place, it's got enough ghosts already. You don't have to add another one.' His thinking diffused as he gazed across the broad sweep of the range: the world as he knew it. 'My valley's full of the dead—my brothers, their mates. I'll never see any of them again, but I can hear them, hear them clearly; they're in the

318

granite, they're still around. Oh, God,' he sighed, 'they'll always be around. So many of them.' He bowed his head. 'So many men.'

The breeze returned, blowing from the south and cool.

Grace lowered her arm and whispered: 'Men.'

Tom removed the pistol from her hand.

Two hundred yards down, Charlie, Mad Mike and Snow surged out of the trees. They galloped up the mountainside and stopped in a cloud of billowing white dust.

Snow saw the guns Tom held and turned to Mike, wordlessly acknowledging his mate's nightmare had been on the money. Mike turned away, wishing he'd lost the bet.

Snow dismounted and crouched down in front of Thorn. He observed the pool of blood and felt beneath the gambler's jaw.

Grace kneeled at the stockman's side, unable to speak. Snow read her mind, knowing the question she couldn't word. He touched her arm and shook his head; there would be no miracles this day.

Charlie beheld again life's beauty vandalised by Logan's touch. He watched as the cattleman dropped down his hands, the smugness returning; the boss in charge once more, feeling it as his right by birth. The bile rose in Charlie's gut. He noticed his rifle waiting in its bucket. He itched to use it: shoot Logan without hesitation, like he had learnt to do in the trenches. Easy as lop the top off a chook.

Tom dropped the Derringer and discarded the 303.

Snow got up and approached him, his voice admonishing yet soft: 'Now you know how the apple tastes.'

Tom fell forward and was caught in the stockman's arms.

Grace felt the cooling breeze intensify and she saw Copenhagen. He stood on the shoulder of Logan's Peak, the southerly fluttering his mane.

Tom appeared, doubling Grace and leading a horse that carried Thorn. The others rode in, all silent; enough had been said for one day. Ma and Pop emerged from the general store. Logan pulled up his horse. 'Telegraph Grimes,' he ordered.

Ma saw the corpse draped over one of Logan's white Arabs. 'What's happened?'

Logan sat straight in his saddle and thrust his fist against his hip. Like a master of hounds fresh back from the hunt, he turned with pride to his grandfather's towering namesake. 'Blood's been spilt on the peak,' he declared. 'It was a mortal wound from a bullet. A man killed.'

'In self defence,' Charlie countered as he road up to the hitching rail.

Logan snorted his contempt. He and the three stockmen dismounted and tethered their horses outside the store and its telegraph. Tom rode over to the pub. He and Grace eased themselves off Copenhagen and helped each other hobble up the steps to the front entrance. Tom pushed against the closed lobby door only to find it bolted shut. He limped along to the double doors of the public bar and took his keys from his pocket.

It was dark inside, the blinds still closed. The late afternoon sun elongated their shadows in a rectangle of light and illuminated an upturned chair. Straining rope creaked.

Chapter Eighteen

Constable Grimes pulled back the bed sheet. Lucky lay on a makeshift trestle table, neck jaundiced and purple from the convulsions of his asphyxiation. To the left of Grimes stood Sergeant Maguire, on the other side of the body, Detective Inspector Brunel.

Grimes gave his fellow police officers a quick briefing. 'Leonard Bramble, the publican, known as Lucky, found by his son this afternoon, hanged here in this barroom.' He pointed to a hemp rope. 'He secured the noose up there, around the lamp wheel.' The officers all noted how the bottom of the rope was frayed where it had been roughly cut. 'Suicide,' the trooper explained.

'Apparent suicide,' said Brunel.

Grimes bridled at the correction, then led the inspector and the sergeant to a second table with another body. 'You might be familiar with this one, Sir—Ernest Thorn, gambler from Sydney, on the run from the Harry Newman gang. Shot… apparently.'

Brunel stepped away. 'Grimes, Maguire, strip him to the waist.'

The policemen grimaced as though the gambler's condition might be contagious.

'Hop to it,' the inspector snapped, 'before the riga spreads.'

The sergeant and the constable lifted Thorn to a sitting position. A little air remained in the lungs. He groaned, seeming to be alive. The two officers continued regardless, going about their business, exhibiting a professional disregard for the body's protest. They removed the gambler's jacket, waistcoat, shirt and tie, dropping the garments to the floor.

Brunel pushed open the exit wound with his ungloved hand, his fingers weaving their way into the grisly rosette. That done he pushed the middle finger of his other hand into the bullet hole at the entry point. For a minute or two he gazed out the doors while he probed around. Eventually his opposing finger tips located each other. 'Maguire, take this down…'

The sergeant took out his pencil and notepad.

Brunel continued. 'Fractured clavicle and the… ah… scapula's shattered. Ouch!'

'Anything the matter, Sir?' Maguire enquired.

'No, it's nothing—a bone—damned sharp edges when they break.' Brunel withdrew his fingers. 'Maguire.'

'Yes, Sir.'

The inspector looked at his left index finger. 'So much blood, I can't tell if I've cut myself… Maguire.'

'Yes, Sir.'

'When we go up the mountain, better see if we can find the bullet.'

'Yes, Sir.'

'Nothing in the body?' asked Grimes.

Sergeant Maguire peered at the constable. 'If there was a bullet still in the deceased, we wouldn't have to go up to the peak to find it, now would we, Grimes?'

Grimes ran his finger under his collar. 'No, Sarge.'

Brunel re-entered the wound, sinking his fingers deeper. 'Maguire, there's more—subclavian artery severed. Cause of death would appear to be due to massive haemorrhage.' Brunel removed his fingers. 'Alright. Thank you, Constable.' Grimes lowered the body. Brunel looked again at his bloodied fingers. 'Grimes, if I could borrow your handkerchief?'

Chapter Nineteen

It had been a busy afternoon. As soon as she received the news, Ma had telegraphed Constable Grimes, just as the trooper was sitting down to lunch with his family—his one-man police station was also his home. At first annoyed at having his roast interrupted, Grime's temper quickly changed as he wrote down the message. However, the first thing he did was telegraph back to Berto to be certain each word he had received was absolutely correct, and more importantly, that everything was on the up and up; he had no intention of being made to look a dill by some damned prankster. Within a minute Ma confirmed the first telegram, using an emergency code-word she and the trooper had agreed upon many years before: 'Berto killings STOP One shot STOP One hanged STOP Bodies in pub STOP Sao END.' Only then had Grimes grabbed the phone to the Grafton district police station.

Detective Inspector Brunel, recently transferred from Newcastle, had received the call not five minutes later. He immediately dropped everything, picked up Sergeant Maguire and drove to Berto in the detective branch's black Wolseley sedan. The inspector had gone as fast as he dared, but on the winding, dirt roads it still took them almost an hour to make the journey. Upon arrival, Grimes was waiting to greet them,

325

standing on Main Street, their horses saddled up.

After his preliminary examination of the bodies, Brunel, accompanied by his sergeant and Constable Grimes, had followed Logan and the three stockmen back up the escarpment to Logan's Peak. In addition, Brunel had taken Pop's remaining mule and loaded it with his photographic equipment and forensic kit. They had to move fast lest the sun go down before a thorough examination of the crime-scene could take place. Tom and Grace were told to remain at the pub, left waiting; their dead relatives for company.

With the track up the mountain now well worn, the police investigation party had made good time returning to the summit: trotting, and at times, even cantering much of the way. Once there, Brunel had gone into action, his well-practiced operation running like clockwork: measuring out and sketching on graph paper a map of the crime scene, scouring to find all the spent cartridges, numbering each and noting their position on his hand-drawn map. He then took his photographs.

Though the sky had been clear, the daylight soon died, the detective forced to use flash. Packaged in cardboard tubes containing a volatile mix of magnesium powder and potassium chlorate, flash was tricky to handle. Sergeant Maguire hated the stuff, but had been ordered to hold the flashgun for every exposure, the principal light source needing to be set at an angle to facilitate the shadows that defined the bullet marks. The most important of these was the scrape across Logan's boulder that had come from Tom's ricocheting shot. The detective had also photographed the positions where Tom and

Grace had huddled, as well as the blackened blood where Thorn had fallen.

Brunel felt confident the witness accounts would concur with the evidence. Then, through his scrupulous attention to detail and use of the best available technology, there would be no loose ends about which his superiors might whinge. The file could then be closed, the papers buried in a warehouse, and the detective's excellent record for closing cases neatly maintained.

Lowanna looked beyond her fire and saw Burnum, the flames as molten metal in his eyes. Justice had been done but no seed of joy had been sown. He handed her the bottle. It glimmered in the burning light, reflections of the blaze sluicing the glass. She focused on the bottle's darker depths, knowing, in the convolutions of rum-sullied umber, Lucky's soul lay trapped.

Lowanna looked up again but Burnum was no longer there. Seen and gone: a falling star. She rose and walked to the creek, back to her pool at the cusp of her worlds. The night was clear and the depths of the water plumbed its furthest galaxy: to the end of everything.

The bottle was dipped in the creek, releasing bubbles redolent of Lucky. When it was almost full, Lowanna tossed it to the centre of the pool. The bottle bobbed there a moment, lapping up more water till the weight of the glass swallowed the neck into its reflection. For a while, the waves rippled, searching in and out, feeling for their source till burnished flat. The heavens, again at rest, twinkled, silent, as if nothing had existed there before.

With the two dead bodies laid out on their trestles, the public bar was, in all but name, a morgue. Tom sat at the table, so recently favoured by Thorn for the cards, and stared blankly at the bed-sheet covering his father's corpse. Stunned by all that had happened, he remained oblivious to the pain in his arm and the spots of red appearing on the sleeve of his shirt. It was a fresh, clean shirt found in his wardrobe and furnished by Snow after Charlie had finished his doctoring. The old digger had been nominated to stich up the gash, revisiting skills the exigencies of war had made necessary, but despite his best efforts, blood still seeped through the bandage, and though the opiate in Ma's administrations of Drake's Carramos cough syrup relieved a portion of Tom's anguish, the medicine only soothed his surface wounds; it disabled and postponed any understanding of the shocks inside.

On the opposite side of the table, Brunel and Maguire waited for Tom to respond to their questions. They were making little progress. No matter what they said, he just sat, listless in his chair, gazing mutely at his father's shroud.

Sergeant Maguire grew impatient. 'Grimes!'

The constable stepped forward from his post at the lobby door.

The sergeant flicked his hand in the direction of the pub's kitchen. 'See if one of them can make him a cup of tea or something.'

Grimes helped Tom out of his seat and led him from the public bar. As they walked past the saloon, Tom glanced through the bead curtain and noticed Logan sitting by himself, feet up, reading the Examiner. The pair moved on. All those waiting in the kitchen rose from the table when they entered. The ructions of the day had rendered Grace as silent as Tom, but Ma, Pop and the three stockmen had not been near so quiet. All had whispered speculations that led to frightful consequences, much exaggerated by the lack of anything else to warrant their attention at that hour. Between long silences, and always in hushed tones, they had each attempted to discuss the matter: arguing whether or not charges would be laid against Tom or the shooting seen as justified; wondering, if arrested, would he be granted bail or held on remand at the Grafton gaol; and if so, all agonising over what might be the charge—manslaughter or even murder. All this they had mumbled over, their words punctuated by sips of tea, until mounting awareness of Grace's frail condition drew all conversation to a close. It was during the ensuing silence that Tom returned from his interrogation. Everyone was relieved he seemed nothing worse than drowsy; but still the drowsiness of a man awakening from a stupor, not a sleep. On seeing him, Grace's thoughts, like a bottled message on a beach, washed back to life. Reaching out, her hand warm though the night was cool, she guided him to a chair. Well aware of the debilitating effects of opiates, Grace had refused a dozen offerings of Ma's cough syrup. Fully conscious, but with eyes red from tears and skin stinging, pink from sunburn, she was naked to her physical pain and raw emotions, with tea her only salve. In spite of what they'd both been through, it was clear to all, Grace's loss was worse by far than Tom's, for she had lost a brother, not a grand illusion. She had also lost a blood that ran so thick it changed her life to hope from grim despair, rather than Tom who'd lost a blood so spiralled down to places dark, so thinned by rum it nurtured nothing but the dreams that flourished within the pages of his careworn books. Yet, in spite of this, Grace shone the light and comfort of her smile, and Tom, who had been in the hours before that smile a withered thing, was now made strong again by the power of the heart, the strongest muscle of them all.

Ma looked at Tom the way he recalled his mum would do. 'Have some hot tea, darl'n,' she said softly. 'It's freshly brewed.' She poured a strong and steaming cup.

Tom glanced across to Snow, and for a second their eyes met. There was no necessity for either man to speak.

It was the early hours of the morning, and though still dark, the time of day when country folk must usually rise. Sitting outside the pub, the Wolseley sedan, so shiny the previous morning, was now caked and dulled with ochre. Inside, Ma, Pop and the three stockmen remained at the kitchen table, drinking yet more tea. Logan had been with the police officers for some thirty minutes. Up until then all had been quiet but now there was a great commotion.

In the public bar Logan's face was brick; he was letting Brunel and Maguire have it with both barrels. 'That's bloody well outrageous! I'll have you know my son's a barrister, and not just any barrister—he's taken silk!'

Upstairs in Room One, Grace lay on the quilted double bed. Washed and changed, but body red and aching, she stared at the ceiling, a damp flannel across her forehead.

Tom lay beside her. He was also staring at the ceiling. Both couldn't help but hear Logan's tirade, his voice booming: 'I am also on close speaking terms with the chief justice of the State Supreme Court.'

Tom took Grace's hand as she took his, both set to hold the other till events might tear them apart.

Downstairs, Logan kept giving it to the coppers. 'Forget any notion of a guilty verdict from the local courts,' he declared, and with voice grown low, assured: 'I'd always win on appeal.' The cattleman got up and gave every sign he had listened to enough antics and was leaving. But his wish was not to be; Grimes marched forward from his post, truncheon firm in hand.

Brunel pointed to the cattleman's chair. 'Sit down, Mr Logan.'

Logan slipped from his wallet his business card. 'May I?' he asked, pointing to Brunel's fountain pen. The inspector did not react. Logan took the pen anyway, and while writing on the card, explained: 'These are the contact details for my solicitors; if you wish to speak with me again, you can arrange an appointment through them.'

Brunel was not impressed. He took back his pen. 'We have no intention of phoning Sydney on your behalf, Mr Logan.'

'I'm well aware of that,' he replied. 'No need for the expense of a trunk call, these are my local lawyers: conveyancing and the like. Their offices are in Grafton.'

'Sit down, Mr Logan,' said Maguire firmly. Grimes moved in closer.

Logan turned toward the double doors and scrutinised the street beyond. 'Sit down!' Maguire ordered.

Grimes, mindful of Logan's power, politely offered him his seat. Fuming, the cattleman sat down. The local constable's fawning was not lost on Brunel. The inspector put his fountain pen safely away in his jacket pocket and cleared his throat. 'From five witnesses we have signed statements to say your 303 was fired at least ten times.'

'Yes, so what?' Logan blustered. 'Nobody's disputing that.'

Brunel placed a small evidence jar on the table. It was filled with labelled shell casings. 'In each of their statements the witnesses maintain you fired five times before Tom Bramble's Winchester returned fire.'

'His Winchester?' Logan fulminated. He adjusted his jacket. 'The Winchester belongs to me. The boy stole it.'

Brunel shook the glass jar. 'These ten Lee Enfield 303 shell casings were found at the scene.' Brunel put the jar in front of Logan. 'Ten spent shells, a full magazine, exactly where you admit you stood.'

Logan blasted like a howitzer: 'Young Bramble killed Thorn!'

'Yes,' Brunel replied, impervious as a concrete embrasure, 'that he did, but with only one shot, a shot not aimed at the deceased. Its ricochet mark is clear for all to see on the boulder where you sheltered.' Brunel took back the glass jar and added quietly, 'My photographs indicating such will be processed and printed in the morning.'

Sergeant Maguire put a different jar on the table. 'Mr

Logan, you'll notice this is a single casing.' He tapped the lid of the jar with his finger. 'It's from the single shot fired by the Winchester.'

Brunel put a third jar on the table. 'This is the slug, the only Winchester round we could find. It was located by the sergeant here.'

'Yes,' Logan growled, 'we all know that. I was up there with you.'

The inspector's voice remained calm. 'Then you will recall Maguire finding the spent bullet amongst the rocks, behind where you admit the American had been standing when he was hit. The bullet came to a halt against the rocks and was lying not three yards from his body.'

The misshapen bullet lay in the jar, the lead, dull as its victim's skin. Brunel put it to one side and stated matter-of-factly: 'With a little luck we will find traces of granite embedded in this projectile.'

Logan straightened his tie, preening. 'Then we are agreed—the kid shot Thorn, ricochet or no ricochet.'

The inspector leaned in toward Logan. 'I believe, and I'm sure the Crown Prosecutor's office will concur, Tom Bramble fired in self defence—not just trying to protect his own life, but also that of the girl.'

'He tried to kill me!' Logan bellowed.

'I don't think so,' Brunel countered, his tone still civilised. 'Tom Bramble is known by Constable Grimes to be one of the best shots in the district.'

Logan glared up at Grimes. The constable clasped his hands behind his back, wishing he had not been quoted.

Brunel continued: 'Tom Bramble was only a little over one hundred yards away. If he had wanted to kill you, he would have.'

Maguire took over. 'And if you were at least half as good a shot as the lad, he and the lass would both be dead and you'd have an appointment with the hangman.'

Both police officers were stony-faced, unyielding as black letter law. Logan glanced down at the barroom table and wiped away an imaginary piece of lint. His eyes twitched. He made a run for it. Grimes tackled him. Maguire leapt up and slammed the cattleman's head onto the table, slapping him in handcuffs.

'Bastards!' Logan roared, 'you'll pay for this with your jobs.

'Perhaps,' said Brunel, unruffled by the commotion, 'but, as an officer of the New South Wales State Police, I am sworn to uphold the law without fear or favour.'

Maguire and Grimes pulled Logan back into his seat. The cattleman stared at Brunel. 'There's still English common law; I'm innocent until proved guilty. I've not shot anybody, haven't killed anybody. Not done murder. Not manslaughter either. Not even common assault. What are you charging me with, bad breath?'

'Resisting arrest,' said Brunel.

Logan's panther pupils narrowed to slits, the citric irises expanding with demonic rage. 'But what's the charge?'

'Resisting arrest,' Brunel repeated.

'Arrest for what?'

'Resisting arrest.'

Brunel ordered Grimes to put Logan in the car. After the two were gone and the CIB officers were packing, Sergeant Maguire asked his inspector if it were wise to be taking a man like Logan on such a flimsy charge. Brunel was quick to answer. 'I've met Logan's type before. He thinks he owns everyone and everything in the district. A few hours in the Grafton lock-up will teach him an important lesson. I might be the eleventh son of a broken-down selector but that squatter does not own, nor will he ever own me. I've been up against his type before.'

Maguire wondered if that was why Brunel had been transferred from Newcastle to Woop Woop.

Tom and Grace stood with Brunel, a few yards from the Wolseley. Ma, Pop and the three stockmen watched from the hotel veranda. The car's engine was running, Sergeant Maguire at the wheel, Logan cuffed in the rear seat.

Brunel addressed Tom. 'The undertaker will pick up the deceased tomorrow morning.' Then he turned to Grace. 'Don't leave the district.'

Grace gazed at Tom. 'I'm not going anywhere, Inspector.'

Brunel inquired: 'Cocaine Harry Newman was after Ernest?'

'Yes,' said Grace, admitting the fact freely, 'but Ernie made his living playing cards. He wasn't involved in the drug business. He did nothing illegal—only owed money to the wrong people.'

Brunel signalled Maguire to wait. 'Would they know you

were with him?'

'They may suspect it, but I'm just—was just his little sister. I've been in a show at the Tivoli Theatre for the past twelve weeks. Like I told you, Ernie insisted I go north with him. His plan was to lay low by taking the back roads, and when we got to Brisbane, he'd make some quick money. Then we'd sail Stateside, as he called it.' She held Tom's hand and continued. 'He said I could try my luck on Broadway, but you were never really sure with Ernie.' Grace shuddered and fresh tears formed in her tired eyes. 'Sometimes Ernie meant what he said, sometimes it was nothing but talk.'

'So nobody in Sydney's after you?'

'No,' said Grace, 'not even any lousy producers.'

Brunel put on his hat to go. 'We won't be releasing your brother's identity but you can be assured everyone will hear what's happened once Logan's bailed. If there are people who wanted to hurt Ernest Thorn, they'll be up in Grafton soon enough, even if it's only to make sure there really is a corpse.'

Grace blanched and her weary eyes found yet more tears. Tom held her to his chest.

The inspector turned away, regretting his lack of tact, but he hid this softer part of himself, as always, behind gruffness. 'However,' he continued, 'if what you say is true, you should be safe enough.'

'Will there be a trial?' Tom asked.

Brunel shrugged. 'I don't know. There'll be a coronial inquest, but as to a trial? Perhaps Logan will press charges, do you for breaking and entering, theft of his rifle.'

Grace frowned. 'You mean Logan will get away with all

of this and Tom will be the one dragged up before a judge?'

'Who's to say? Sorry, but I have to get going.'

Grace wasn't to be brushed aside so easily, but mindful of the cattleman's close proximity, she held her voice to a whisper. 'Hasn't Logan committed a major crime?'

Brunel shifted away. Reluctant to be drawn in on matters beyond his control, his tone was measured. 'Logan would likely say he witnessed a crime being committed; that he had the right to make a citizen's arrest; that he was merely helping your brother, and might I say, legal guardian; helping him to rescue his baby sister, an eighteen year old minor; assisting him in a brave attempt to save you from the hands of a kidnapper.'

'Kidnapper?' gasped Tom.

'But what about attempted murder, isn't that a crime?' asked Grace. 'He tried to kill us.'

'Did he?' Brunel asked back, stepping toward his car. 'Remember Tom was armed too. That's why a man's dead.'

Tom blocked his path. 'So the rich bloke walks away scot-free.'

'Look,' said Brunel, silently agreeing with the lad's opinion, but still trying to get to his car, 'I've told you too much already.'

'Way it is,' said Grace, her solemnity eradicating any hint of sarcasm.

The remark was well understood by the detective, and it irked him, but he had learnt through life's hard climb to keep his opinions to himself.

Grace closed in. 'Could Tom be sent to gaol?'

Grace's desperation marred Brunel's better judgement.

'The Crown Prosecutor,' he allowed, 'may seek to charge your boyfriend with manslaughter.'

Grace clutched her arm around Tom.

'Notwithstanding that,' the detective was quick to point out, 'there are mitigating circumstances. But I can't make any promises with respect to the prosecutor's office. You would be better off putting your questions to a solicitor.'

Grace sighed: 'When will we know if Tom's being charged?'

Brunel folded down the brim of his hat, saw the young couple's long faces and took pity. 'Listen, both of you, I don't know how long things will take. I can't say anything for sure, but Logan's a powerful man. If he has to front the courts, his lawyers, in arguing his case, could provide you, Tom, with much of the ammunition you'd need, should you have to argue yours. A smart mouse can always sneak a lick of the cat's cream.'

'What if Tom is the only one charged?' asked Grace.

Brunel was getting very eager to be gone. 'As I said, I can't speak for the crown prosecutor, but I can assure you, I won't be recommending any charges be laid against your boyfriend.'

'What about the theft of the rifle?' Tom asked.

The detective said nothing, but flourished a wry smile as he climbed into his car. Sergeant Maguire drove off.

Grimes mounted up. He looked down from his horse at Tom and Grace, suspicion in his beady eyes, and anger also at the damage done that night to his reputation. He was much diminished in Logan's eyes, but though never one of God's sharpest creatures, he realised the problem was largely of his own making; his error lay in telling his boss too much. The trooper scanned the town, as always, head held high. For a moment it seemed he might speak, but once bitten, twice shy, his lips stayed firmly shut and he left, following the Wolseley's dust.

Ma watched the trooper go then took her husband's arm. 'Come on, Pop, time for bed.' They crossed Main Street, shuffling home.

Charlie, Mad Mike and Snow recognised their cue to leave. Snow conceded to Tom, 'after today, things round here won't be the same'

Tom stared at the police car's headlights as they disappeared into the southern night. 'I guess that's true, I guess they won't be.'

Snow tipped his hat to Grace, Charlie and Mad Mike did likewise, and the three rode home.

Ma and Pop walked to the front door of the general store. As the three stockmen passed, Ma yelled to Snow: 'Don't forget to drop off your boot at Agnes's place. I'll make sure she's expecting you come Wednesday afternoon. You fine with that?'

'She'll be apples, Ma,' said Snow with a wave.

Pop raised an eyebrow. 'What are you up to, woman?'

Ma smiled back at her man, pride in her wrinkly eyes, and happily changed the subject. 'First time the pub's been open on a Sunday since before the war and Mr O'Shaughnessy is sober.'

Pop opened the front door. 'Took two men dying to do

it.'

The husband followed the wife inside and closed the door behind them. The 'Closed' sign swung to and fro against the windowpane.

Charlie, Snow and Mad Mike made their way slowly along the Berto Road, their horse's hooves lightly padding the grey dust, the stars fading, the night sky whitening in the east.

Charlie moved as a sailing boat on the gentle swell of his horse's back and deftly rolled a smoke. 'Hey, Snow,' he drawled, 'what you going to do with the new leg?'

'Save it for special occasions—Grafton and such.'

'Yeah, G-G-Grafton; that'd be right.'

'I don't know, Mike,' said Charlie, licking his cigarette paper, 'the word going around says it might be you who's got a little something bubbling in his billy.'

'Oh yeah,' Snow grinned, 'could be very tasty.'

'You reckon, Snow?' asked Mad Mike, too honest to disguise his enthusiasm. 'You reckon the Widow Philpot might have a soft spot for me? Hey, Snow?'

'Yeah, I reckon so.'

Mad Mike beamed in the glow of the approaching dawn. 'Jeez, I had me suspicions, but I didn't think anyone would notice.' He inhaled the crisp morning air and it smelt good. 'You know what?'

'What?' asked Charlie, holding his reins high as he lit his roll-up between cupped hands.

'You think Gladys——'

'Gladys is it now?' Charlie interrupted, shaking out his

match very thoroughly, the way country people do.

'S-sorry,' said Mad Mike, 'I mean the Widow Philpot. Anyways, you know, like I was saying, it just occurred to me, she's always reminded me of someone, has Gladys. I could never put me finger on it, but I reckon I got it now: Gladys Philpot looks a b-b-bit like that ginger-top in Amiens. What do you think, Snow, the one you was on with? What you reckon?'

'You may have a point there,' Charlie chimed in.

'Amiens? Amiens?' Snow muttered to himself as his memory's vault creaked open. 'Yeah,' he shouted, pointing to Mike, 'that's right! She was a great little sheila—fiery but. Won't ever forget that one—she taught me how to dance the tango. Was a good sport, was Claudette.'

'Collette.'

'What?' Snow grunted, shaken back to the present.

Charlie repeated the correction. 'Was Collette,'

'Bullshit,' said Snow.

'Collette,' said Charlie for the third time.

'Bullshit,' said Snow, 'was Claudette.'

'Colette.'

'Claudette.'

'I thought it was A-A-Annette.'

Tom and Grace stood in the lamplight of the lobby—before them, the still dark public bar, Lucky and Thorn's shrouded bodies lying on their trestle tables.

'Do you have other family?' Tom asked.

'I don't have any family now,' Grace answered, and her

words, unanchored, commenced to drift, each bumping against its neighbor in no particular fashion. 'At least I don't have any family I know about—none I know of. Like I told you in the kitchen, she was only a serving girl before she met my father. There could be people in America. I don't know.'

Tom leaned against one of the columns at the entrance to the bar. 'What was your father like?'

'He wasn't like anything really. I can't remember much. It's all a memory that's faded, gone dim. I remember him as nice, though. He looked a bit like Ernie, but with grey hair. Not a surprise, that. I saw how much Ernie looked like him the first time I met Ernie, but Ernie never really looked like Daddy again. He never reminded me of my father after that. Once I got to know Ernie, he didn't look like my father or anyone else. He was just, you know, just Ernie.'

'How old were you when you first met Ernie?'

'Fourteen.'

'Still with your mother?'

'Oh yes, with my mother and a man.'

'A man?'

'Yes, a man—don't ask me what his name was—just another bloke, passing parade. Some of them stayed for a night, some longer, some even longer than that: most of them too long.' Grace suddenly dropped anchor, addressing Tom directly. 'Do you know, of all those men, all those faces and habits and smells, and all those things that make a person a person, of all those things, all that, there's not a single, not a single good thing I can say about any of them. Not one of them. They were, all of them, horrible—bad in some way. A couple so bad it's hard to describe… I don't want to say how bad.'

'You don't have to tell me how bad,' Tom assured. 'You don't have to tell me that.'

Ironically, Grace persisted. 'It's strange when you meet a person who seems to be without a single redeeming feature. Can a person be completely bad?'

'No,' Tom replied without hesitation, 'that wouldn't make any sense. Nobody can be all bad.'

'Why not?'

'Because nobody can be all good.'

Grace nodded, smiling thinly as she walked into the public bar. 'Live and learn.'

Tom found her words ambiguous but hazarded a guess at what they meant. 'Maybe you were right,' he suggested. 'Right about what you said on Friday—that Sydney would skin me alive.'

'Was that only Friday?'

Tom counted on his fingers. 'Yeah, two days ago.'

'It seems longer.'

'Berto's like that,' he conceded. And then he asked: 'Would it, you know, would it skin me alive?'

Grace tilted her head and sighed. 'No, this valley's all the training you need to cope with Sydney.' She touched Thorn's shroud, thoughts floating this way and that. 'My mother was punishing herself. All those men, she didn't really want them. She just wanted the punishment. She was punishing herself for my father's death—like she'd been wasteful or something, like my father was her inheritance and she'd splurged him on some passing trifle, spent a life she should have banked.'

'Why would she think that?'

Grace became silent, seeming to be searching the past for an answer, but without success. 'It's all guesswork,' she offered in capitulation.

'S'pose it's too late to ask her now,' Tom mused. 'Oh, sorry, that was careless of me.'

'No, it wasn't; it's true. Anyway, she went to a better place. Nowhere could be worse than the place she was.'

'Where you were too.'

'Where I was too.'

'And you had no sisters,' Tom hesitated, 'or other brothers?'

'Nope,' Grace said abruptly and lifted the shroud to view her silent sibling. 'My mother was dying of consumption when Ernie arrived on the scene. Two weeks later she was dead. It was like Ernie was an angel who swooped down just in the nick of time, an angel she'd been praying for.'

Tom remained in the lobby, not sure whether to join Grace or not, and trying to cobble together some words of sympathy for her mother's sad and sorry end.

It was Grace who spoke next. 'My mother had more things wrong with her than she had lovers. Does that offend you?'

'Of course not,' Tom said softly. 'It must have been very difficult for a widow with a small child.'

'My father never married my mother. The reason I have no brothers or sisters is because my mother was very ill. By the time she died she was riddled with disease. Tuberculosis was

the culprit the doctors *chose* to write on her death certificate.'
Grace lowered the shroud, fussing at the edges to make sure
all was neat. When she had finished, she stood very still and
stared as she might into a mirror.

Tom limped across the barroom to guide her away from
her brother and out to the lobby. They sat down on the
staircase. 'Grace,' he said, 'I've lived a pretty sheltered life. I
haven't seen many of the horrible things you've seen, endured
things you've endured, but one thing I do know is what it's like
to lose someone you love, and I know what it is to be alone.
I've been alone… I mean, I've had no family since my mother
died.'

'Isn't Lucky your father? Wasn't he your dad?'

'Yes, he was, but he died when my mother died. The
body in there, in the bar, it just took its time. It needed time to
let go, to give up the ghost. Please don't get me wrong, I'm not
speaking out of anger or resentment; it's just what I believe. In
the end, he merely got around to doing what his body wouldn't
do—let go. I should be sad—crying. I know I'm supposed to
be crying, but I can't. I don't know why but there are no tears
to cry. Do you think I'm cold because I haven't cried?'

'No, I don't think that. I don't think that at all.' Grace
took Tom's arm in hers, as if they were out in a blustery day.
'It seems we've both lost a person dear to us, someone who
was all the family we had, the someone who betrayed us.'

'But have they really? A life's a life. It's not for us to
grade people. It's not for us to give people a mark out of ten.
It's not like you get a blue ribbon for being the best carcass,
like you're a side of beef at the Grafton Show or something.

345

Even if you did get a prize, not like you'd get to enjoy it any more than a dead bullock. I'm sure a bullock would rather be a failure, munching his cud, than a raging success on a meat hook!' Tom flicked his hair out of his eyes, embarrassed for getting carried away. 'That was a bit rough. I shouldn't have said that.'

Grace smiled the pencil rubbing of a smile: more in her eyes than in the other threads that weave a smile. 'It's alright,' she said, 'I know steaks don't grow on trees.'

They both laughed a little at that.

'I'm happy for my father,' Tom confessed. 'He's either in a better place too, or he's asleep. Sleeping soundly, not like he used to sleep—no more nightmares now, all the demons gone.'

'Are you worried what will happen to him? He committed suicide.'

'You saying he may go to hell?'

'No, I don't believe in hell and purgatory and ghosts; don't believe in all that sort of thing, but isn't it thought a sin to take your own life?'

'A sin in whose eyes—God's or people who reckon they know what God thinks?'

'Alright, not a sin, but isn't it a pity?'

'A pity?'

'Yes, a pity; it's so sad—he thought he only had one option. He should have tried to talk to someone.'

Tom's eyes welled with tears, and the tears were not only for his father. 'Stuff it, Dad chose his time and he took charge.' Tom bit down on the knuckle of his thumb, holding back a torrent of emotion. Then he loosened his grip and everything was clear to him. 'His light can't be forgotten like some fly that's just been swatted. His life should be celebrated. I'm his only living child. It's my job to celebrate his life. It's the least I can do.' Tom's eyes grew bright. 'That's it! That's why people dance at wakes!' Tom was at once buoyant. His joy caused his tears to break their levies, rolling down his cheeks. 'We never had that dance.'

'Dance?'

'Up on Logan's Peak, you know—the waltz!' Tom grabbed Grace and led her back through the public bar; both unsteady on their wounded feet, fumbling their way to the opposite side of the room, the side of the public bar where the gramophone stood. He lifted its lid and cranked the mainspring.

'What are you doing?'

'We're going to have a wake,' he answered, as if his plans should have been obvious. He limped to behind the bar and ducked down, rummaging through the cluttered shelves.

Grace couldn't work out what Tom was up to. 'Isn't that showing disrespect for the dead?'

'No, Dad enjoyed a good wake,' he chuckled, 'couldn't get enough of them.' In words punctuated by loud protests from the accumulated junk, he observed. 'My old man loved wakes until people started dying that he never expected to outlive, but I reckon he's gunna enjoy his own wake. I reckon he'll see it as revenge—a mongrel biting back a mongrel world. How about Ernie? We can make it his wake too. Wouldn't he want a wake?'

'Ernie wasn't one for sentiment.'

'Yeah, fair enough.' Tom re-emerged with a record in his hand. 'But he'd want to see his little sister happy, wouldn't he?'

'I don't know. He might. If he were here, he might…' Grace's words began to peter out. 'But he isn't, is he?' She was silent for a moment, envisaging where her brother might be. Then she pulled back her hair and said: 'I'm not sure about this wake thing, Tom. It's all too strange.'

'Give me one example,' he countered. 'One example of a thing in life that isn't strange.'

'Strangeness.'

'Yeah, s'pose,' Tom acknowledged, the wind sucked from his sails but nevertheless impressed.

If Grace was likewise impressed by her observation, she wasn't letting on. 'We should show respect for those who've passed.'

Tom slipped the record out of its brown paper cover. 'You mean respect the past?'

'Yeah,' said Grace, 'I guess.'

'What about the future?'

'You can't respect what hasn't happened yet, but the past is done.'

'So is the future.'

'No, Tom, the future isn't done; we can change the future.'

'Yeah, that's true, we change the future all the time; the changes make the future. The future's as fixed as the past because those changes will always be made.'

Grace squinted at Tom. 'What if the changes are changed back?'

'Then the changes were always going to be changed back.'

'Oh, God, Tom, alright, but at least we know what the present is.'

Tom shrugged as he inserted a fresh steel needle into the reproducer. 'There is no present. By the time we think about the thing we call the present, it's already become the past. We're always stuck between the future and the past—can't be anywhere else. We're the place where the future becomes the past. Only thing you have a choice about is the direction you face.'

Grace scratched the back of her neck, and thinking the flow of their conversation too challenging, at least for the present, returned to an earlier subject. 'So you prefer a knees-up wake? No period of respectful mourning?'

Tom eased the disk onto the turntable. 'There's been too much mourning already.' He released the brake and gently lowered the soundbox. The wax crackled.

Tom took Grace around the waist. She felt the transfer of his energy as the music began. She was no match, but protested one last time: 'What about your sprained ankle?'

'What about your cut feet?'

'And your arm?'

'And your wrists? Thanks for that, again, I'll be forever——'

Grace put her finger to his lips. 'Don't mention it.' She pushed herself up close to Tom. 'So you reckon you can dance?'

A smile was the only answer she received.

At first they limped, but soon the music of the waltz swept up their feet, the strains of Strauss swirling around the room, both imagining themselves at a ball, all aglow beneath huge chandeliers and gliding over shining parquet floors, radiant in the splendour of a Viennese palace. The mundane world became a thing apart, except for when they bumped into the trestles. Though Lucky and Thorn wobbled about, neither seemed to mind.

Epilogue

Tom and Grace were in for a wait while the wheels of the law slowly turned. Ernie's remains were forced to bide their time, shelved on ice in the Grafton morgue, but Lucky Bramble didn't have to wait. His passing being less complex, he soon slept beside his Rachel in the valley's little cemetery.

Meanwhile, Mad Mike borrowed Ma's buggy and took Gladys for a drive. Rising before daybreak, they journeyed all the way to Grafton for lunch and a matinee showing of a Douglas Fairbanks movie at the local flicks, not getting back till midnight. Snow dropped off his boots at Agnes's place and liked very much her orange sponge cake. The Widow O'Connor enjoyed accompanying The Widow Campbell's mezzo-soprano and lustily partook of lemon butter tarts. The old cocky, Eamon Reilly, got a good price at the yards and Mrs Reilly invited Father Lynch to tea. Bluey 'One Thumb' Corbett won again at the track and shouted everybody a beer at the pub. Charlie almost finished his list of chores and Peggy was late.

Some days on, Tom asked Grace if she would like to go fishing. She told him she had never been fishing before but said she would be happy to try it. The next morning they were down by the creek. Tom had a sticky beak and saw everything was as it was in the old days. So much had changed in his life and yet here time had stood still, and he could feel something else: it was Neddy; the little clearing by the creek was imbued with his presence. He was in the tinkle of the rills that tumbled between the rocks, in the light shed through the trees, in the cool and humid air, the fragrance of the moss, the scent of pine, and Tom felt certain Neddy wouldn't mind his offering to his new friend his old friend's place on the log.

Once settled, they cast their lines to harvest what they hoped the creek might bring. As time passed by, all remained as perfect as Grace first saw it and as Tom recalled it would be. The warm rays of the sunlight shifted imperceptibly as the day grew older and soon the kookaburra joined them, perched at its post, vigilant and ready to laugh at the dusk that still lay off at longitudes east.

For Grace the moment lingered, as if eternal, and she thought of him. 'Tom, do you believe you'll get Neddy back?'

'Neddy's my mate—always has been, always will be.'

'You'll be up against it.'

'I'm not going to stuff about. If everything blows over, I'm going to go down to Grafton, finally, and I'm going to do some studying up on things I need to know about. I'll see if anyone's willing to tell me where Neddy was sent.' Tom rubbed his chin as his father would have done and his enthusiasm dampened a bit. 'I know I'll hit a brick wall. Bound to; I just know it.'

'Way things are,' said Grace.

Tom's face hardened. 'No, not the way things are, not

the way things are at all.' And saying that, his happy mood returned and he smiled. 'So, I think we'll be heading off for Sydney. Do you still want us to go to Sydney together?'

Grace smiled back. 'Of course I do.' She touched Tom's cheek. 'But what about the pub?'

'There's someone who could manage the place, even buy the licence.'

'Who?'

'One of the war widows, Agnes MacTavish.'

'Could she manage?'

'Agnes could manage anything.'

'And Neddy?'

'In Sydney there's got to be people I can talk to. Suspect I'll have to talk to lots, and some will be hard to find, but some will listen. S'pose just a few at first, but I'll go after everyone I have to. And I won't shut up. I'll write and yap till my fingers drop off and my tongue falls out of my mouth. Can't be that everyone will turn away. If the world was made like that, who the hell wrote all my books? Who the hell bought all the other copies of those books, and read and felt those books? I'll get Neddy back to Lowanna, back to his mum, back to this valley, his valley, the place where he began. Don't know where he's been locked up, but I'll bust him out. I'll flaming well write to politicians, the police, teachers, doctors, ordinary folks, and the papers too. Yeah, all the bloody papers! My brother Darcy wanted to be a newspaperman. Perhaps I'll end up the journalist, tapping away.'

'Can you type?'

'Nope, but I'll get the hang of it. I've got Darcy's old

typewriter. I'll do so much typing, be like I was born with a typewriter ribbon up my arse.'

Grace started laughing. 'You want to excuse your French?'

'Not if I'm going to be a newspaperman.'

'Have you got any idea how many people you'll have to chase?'

'Not sure, but O'Malley's law says it'll be pretty much everyone.'

'Who's O'Malley?'

'A bloke who reckoned Murphy was an optimist.'

'Want a partner?'

A fish swallowed a hook. Grace had a bite on her line. The cod struggled and fought, sparkling the water, but Grace reeled it in with a skill that belied her lack of experience. She was a fast learner and the fish was a biggen. Grace was a natural, and as with her angling, her charm, wit and focus would net school upon school of a different kind of fish to her basket, she often fishing alone during the years Tom spent in gaol, still fishing after Neddy was set free, long after Tom was released; fishing with Tom, fishing with Neddy, fishing with others, persisting past the day when the melanoma sent Tom into the ground, long after Logan, old as his money, had died in his mahogany bed, and yet longer still, fishing and still fishing more; but today, Grace laughed. She laughed herself breathless as Tom felt the fish's weight, he falling into laughter too, and as he laughed, he glanced downstream, still laughing while he came to wondering, thinking how the mountain waters would flow between the banks of she-oaks and casuarinas, through pastures fat with Herefords and Friesians, down the valley's length and to the gorge, and further down to meet with rivers far beyond. Then the rest of him caught up, and he went quiet. He realised the people didn't flow with the creek, they remained in the valley and the new people would come to respect and nurture the valley as the old people had learnt to do before. One day the new and old would be as one and keep the valley safe. They would live and work and love and toil and die there in the valley because the valley was the thing they shared and could not exist without.

Tom heard Charlie's beloved magpies sing and his thoughts gathered to his ears as he listened to the other birds: the whip birds and the bell birds, the thornbills and the pied currawongs too. They were there, as always, in the cedars and the beeches; and then he felt the sun that dried the road to ochre powder; he saw the escarpment that rose from forest foothills; and all of this he heard and felt and saw, roaming free until he knew he could look at it: He gazed on Logan's Peak, its granite shining, inviting the game, the foolhardy and the unwary to test its will.